Apart from this sequel book to *The Curse of the Cobalt Moon*, Lou Hernández has previously written a host of non-fiction, baseball-themed histories and biographies. He was born in Cuba and resides in South Florida.

# Other Books by the Author

*The Curse of the Cobalt Moon (2019)*

*Bobby Maduro and The Cuban Sugar Kings (2019)*

*Manager of the Giants: The Tactics, Temper and True Record of John McGraw* (2018)

*The 1933 New York Giants: Bill Terry's Unexpected World Champions* (2017)

*Chronology of Latin Americans in Baseball, 1871-2015* (2016)

*Baseball's Great Hispanic Pitchers: Seventeen Aces from the Major, Negro and Latin American Leagues* (2015)

*Memories of Winter Ball: Interviews with Players in the Latin American Winter Leagues* (2013)

*The Rise of the Latin American Baseball Leagues, 1947-1961: Cuba, the Dominican Republic, Mexico, Nicaragua, Panama, Puerto Rico and Venezuela* (2011)

To Gavin. May your life's travails be few and your triumphs many.

Lou Hernández

# THE COBALT MOON'S FURY

AUSTIN MACAULEY PUBLISHERS™

LONDON • CAMBRIDGE • NEW YORK • SHARJAH

**Ordering Information:**
Quantity sales: special discounts are available on quantity purchases by corporations, associations, and others. For details, contact the publisher at the address below.

**Publisher's Cataloging-in-Publication data**
Hernández, Lou
The Cobalt Moon's Fury

ISBN 9781643783659 (Paperback)
ISBN 9781643783666 (Hardback)
ISBN 9781645367581 (ePub e-book)

Library of Congress Control Number: 2020905259

www.austinmacauley.com/us

First Published (2020)
Austin Macauley Publishers LLC
40 Wall Street, 28th Floor
New York, NY 10005
USA

mail-usa@austinmacauley.com
+1(646)5125767

# Chapter One

Joshua Puig opened the afternoon newspaper. The front-page headline from *The Miami News* shouted at him:

SEVEN DEAD BODIES FOUND AT VIZCAYA
Four of the Victims from West Side High School

*Last night, Vizcaya, Miami's Italian Renaissance villa turned museum on the bay, became locale for a bloody homicide scene involving several local teenagers. Four high school students and three other men, one a fishing boat owner, were found dead on the ritzy premises.*

*The police believe the teenagers may have chartered the fishing boat of the murdered man to bring them onto the grounds from Biscayne Bay, where they encountered a maniacal killer, or killers, which led to their ghastly slaughter. Particularly disturbing reports that three of the teenagers were gruesomely disemboweled and one of the men's arms and legs were removed have been confirmed.* Cont. on page 10.

As he read, Joshua absently began to scratch his forearm, which turned into full scraping motions to satisfy a suddenly strong, cropped-up itch. Joshua then folded the five-cent broadsheet in two and stuffed it into the side of his seat. He did not have to turn the newspaper page to seek any more details of the story. He had all too painfully lived it less than eighteen hours ago…

It was not until the boat approached the Rickenbacker Causeway that it throttled back from its relentless pounding over the calm waters of Biscayne Bay. Inside the decelerated craft, Joshua wondered how he and the four other occupants had survived a harrowing variety, on both land and sea, of near-fatal experiences.

No one in the escaping boat had cheated death more often than him. Drawing upon natural survival instincts, some luck, and a great deal of help from his three high school junior friends, especially one of them—Milagros Ricardo—Joshua found himself refreshingly breathing in the sea air whirling all around him. Joshua's most timely self-preservation initiative had involved firing the flare gun his best friend Jerry Porter had locked onto with his alerting eyes, a flare gun inside a fishing tackle box that Joshua's heel inadvertently kicked open on the boat during the evening's most climactic phase.

His target had been Alegría Pérez, exposed vampire demoness of the fatal evening. Alegría Pérez was the most tantalizing and horrifying female imaginable. Alegría Pérez was the mother of Raúl Pérez and the deceased Cira Pérez, high school contemporaries of Joshua. Alegría Pérez was the seeker of wholesale bloody vengeance for the death of her daughter— for which she erroneously blamed Joshua. In the confined space of the isolated boat, Joshua's aim had been true. His fired shot tore into the diabolical woman's abdomen, sending her careening over the side of the boat and permitting their intended escape to successfully continue.

But Alegría knocked one of the other passengers overboard with her—Dawn Landis. Joshua, who had a one-sided amorous interest in the girl, despite her status as the girlfriend of the senior classman Raúl, pondered her unknown fate. Raúl's imposed station as antagonistic tormentor over Joshua complicated the issue of Joshua's unrequited affections for Dawn. It was an issue Joshua had entangled forever by literarily poking Raúl's eye out with a stickpin. It occurred as a last-ditch, life-preserving measure for Joshua, who was being strangled to death by Raúl. He was enraged over his sister's death. That rage and Raúl's inborn dislike of Joshua easily allowed him to misconstrue the fractured event he witnessed of Cira accidentally falling off a second-floor balcony at Vizcaya and to pin the blame unjustly on Joshua for appearing to push her off. In fact, Joshua had been reaching for the toppling girl with outstretched arms.

Joshua most contemplated, however, how he had not only utilized natural but *supernatural* survival instincts as well, manifesting from a latent paranormal power he never knew he possessed. Facing the grim reaper herself, in another of the life-and-death pivotal moments of the heinous crime-filled evening, Joshua had incredibly leaped over a thirty-five-foot divide of water to a stone breakwater with Dawn heroically in his arms. From there, he dashed over and tumbled onto the waiting boat. The boat's owner, Juan Montes, was one of the unfortunate casualties of the evening.

On Juan's boat, now finally heading to safety, Joshua no longer could deny what Milagros had been telling him in the days leading up to this night. What he had refused to believe was that vampires existed. There also existed half-vampires, and that he was one such being. And so was she. Joshua had undeniably felt something come over him during the direst circumstances of his and Dawn's attempted getaway from Alegría, something that enabled him to hurdle to safety when all appeared lost.

Since the expulsion of Alegría from the boat, few words had been spoken, except for a brief, testy exchange between Lacey Hayes, Jerry's heretofore-missing girlfriend, and Joshua. Despite the verbal clash, the unexpected presence of Lacey had pleased Joshua immensely—for Jerry's sake especially.

Steering the boat, Jerry followed the coastline back, most likely the way he had come with Juan and Manolín, passing under the causeway until they reached the mouth of the Miami River. He guided Juan's boat up the river into the marina and the slip that Manolín, the only high-school graduate in the bunch and Milagros' cousin, finished directing him into.

Joshua and Milagros helped Manolín Suárez out of the moored boat. He had been the only one of the crew seriously injured in the battle with Alegría. He had suffered a deep, accidental stab wound under his shoulder blade from a wayward knife thrust from Joshua, which was intended for Alegría. In noticeable pain, Manolín clung to a bloodstained, yellow rain slicker wrapped tightly around his shoulder. Trudging along the dock, they stopped at a bench Manolín pointed them toward. The shadowy marina lay quiet in all directions. A couple of feet away, a payphone stand was opportunely stationed underneath one of the spaced apart lamp posts lining the wooden walkway.

"Call the police," Manolín said.

"You better believe it," coincided an eager Jerry.

"No, listen." Manolín's grimaced response made Jerry tone down his expressiveness.

Milagros sat next to Manolín on the bench. "What is it, cuz?" she asked, putting an arm over him gingerly.

"Call the police and tell them you saw somebody stabbed at the Miami River Marina. To send an ambulance." Manolín brought out a jangling keychain from his pocket.

'Juan's keychain,' Joshua suspected. He had seen him take it out of the boat's fishing tackle box. "Drive them home and then go back to your house with Joshua. Call my mother and father and tell them I'm in the hospital."

Manolín had identified Jerry and Lacey as *them*. Lacey, who had her arm curled around Jerry's, reacted. "My parents," she said, breathing deeply and fluttering her eyelids with a jogged sense of recall, "my poor parents."

"It'll be faster if we take you to the hospital," said Joshua.

"And have to answer questions about what happened to me, and how you happen to be involved."

"We'll drop you off at the emergency-room door and leave you," Milagros offered.

"It's too risky. A car full of kids… Somebody might see you. I'm going to tell the cops I was walking down by the river and was jumped. I didn't see who it was." Manolín slumped back, holding his bleeding shoulder. His sweaty hand grabbed Milagros as she stood up. "I'm sorry, we lost Juan. Tell your mother he died protecting us."

\*\*\*

It was close to midnight when Juan's light green Chevy Impala pulled up to the corner of the street where Lacey lived. Lacey had been briefly indoctrinated to half-vampirism by Cira during her captivity, she told everyone. Milagros filled in the missing blanks for her on the ride from the marina.

"You've got your story?" Milagros confirmed.

Sitting up, Lacey gripped the top of the front seat. "Persons unknown abducted me from my house. They wore masks. Kept me blindfolded during my confinement. I was unable to determine any clues as to my location."

"Hate to make you lie to your parents," said Jerry, seated with her in the back.

"Like Milagros said, a lie is more practical, not to mention much more believable than the truth," answered the previously sequestered girl.

In the driver's seat, Milagros placed her hand on top of Lacey's. In the passenger seat, Joshua put his hand over Milagros', and Jerry covered all of them with his. The warmth of Lacey's face conveyed a heartfelt gratitude to the pair. Only two nights earlier, Lacey had sat in the backseat of a car with Jerry as she sat now. The circumstances were much different, Milagros remembered. It was Lacey's first date with Jerry, being driven as a couple to attend her close friend Cira's seventeenth birthday party as part of a double date with her and Joshua. Little did Lacey know that night would become the prelude to a terrifying two-day ordeal under the appalling authority of Alegría's family.

"I'm sorry about what I said on the boat," said Lacey.

Joshua acknowledged, and Lacey slipped her hand free. She kissed Jerry quickly and hugged him. "My hero."

Having cut the car's headlights, Milagros slowed to a stop across from Lacey's house. Breaking her warm embrace with Jerry, Lacey opened the car door. The interior light disclosed everyone's young, cuffed-marked faces, with Milagros self-consciously thinking her own bruised face as the most afflicted, previously discerning half-ring shadows that had crept under her eyes.

Following the farewell pause, an emotional Lacey hopped out and hurried up to the front stoop of her home. The porch light was on, as were other lights inside. Pressing her thumb to the doorbell button, the noise of the rapidly clanging bell inside infiltrated into the quiet street.

A man—certainly Lacey's father, in an untied robe and pajamas—opened the door. Lacey tumbled into his arms as his weary-eyed face lost the apprehension it originally displayed. Seconds later, a woman ran forward with heavy, barefooted steps. It was surely Lacey's mother. She spread her arms, shouting hosannas to the ceiling, and engulfed her husband and child.

As other extended family members, some younger and some older, appeared, the front door swung close, hiding the joyous reunion inside from the unnoticed car on the street slowly driving away.

\*\*\*

They found her in the room among the saints. Rosa sat in front of the shrine to our Lady of Charity, wearing a chapel veil over her head.

Joshua and Jerry stayed near the door as Milagros walked softly over to her mother and knelt at her side. She let Rosa tenderly touch her face, lightly making contact with the welt over the bridge of her nose where Raúl had coldcocked her.

Rosa gazed at Joshua and Jerry who did not hold the sorrowful greetings in their eyes for long before diverting them.

Taking a grip of her mother's hands, Milagros said, "Manolín is in the hospital. He's going to be alright."

Milagros then answered Rosa's unspoken question, "Juan is drinking rum with Changó."

Milagros let Rosa absorb what she had told her, that her husband was dead. Inhaling deeply through sealed lips, Rosa's eyes quickly welled with tears. Trying her best to maintain her composure, she stared straight ahead at the smallish, blue-cloaked statue with the Baby Jesus in her arms.

"If Juan hadn't come to get us..." Milagros made sure she had her mother's attention before continuing, "Juan and Manolín—and Jerry saved us."

"His body?" asked Rosa.

Milagros shook her head.

Jerry walked over and offered his hand. "I'm sorry, Miss Rosa."

Joshua took Rosa's hand as soon as she released Jerry's. He spoke to her in Spanish, something he could not remember doing in a long time. *Señora, lo siento mucho.*

Joshua became aware that he had not offered Milagros the same type of condolences. He hugged the brave girl, offering kind words for her stepfather. Taking a cue, Jerry did the same.

After the consolation, Milagros addressed her mother again. "I have to call *tía* Clara and *tío* Manolo to tell them about

Manolín. You should come to the kitchen with us. I'll make some *café*."

"Not now, maybe later. I want to stay here among Juan's things and say a few more prayers."

\*\*\*

Joshua did not have a fixed curfew—he had not reached the point of requiring one. Without his own mode of transportation, his time outside his home was limited to mostly daylight hours. But he knew that past midnight, the current hour was too late for someone of his age not to be in his own residence without permission.

Joshua rang Katherine from Milagros' house. Katherine conveyed her unhappiness with the late phone call and out-of-the-blue news that Joshua wanted to spend the night at Jerry's house. She pointedly told Joshua that his absence coupled with watching, for the second time that day, the detailed television account of the boy who had committed suicide at Joshua's school that morning had rendered her sleepless.

"After what happened last night," said Katherine into the telephone receiver. "To dump this on my lap at this hour. Honestly, Joshua. Didn't you tell me Jerry's house was being fumigated?"

Fresh in Joshua's mind was the fabricated story about Jerry's house being treated for bugs that he used after a perturbed Katherine had found the snuck-in Jerry in Joshua's room during the middle of the previous night. That afternoon, Joshua had impotently squared off with his foster father, Thomas, over Jerry, staying overnight at their house without their prior permission. *"Katherine told me about your little sleepover from last night. What's going on in that mind of yours, boy?"*

As so often happens with deceitfulness, Joshua's original fraudulent statement to Katherine from last evening led to more of the same. "Yes. The fumigators said his home was okay to inhabit. It was a one-night tenting."

An impatiently long pause came through the line from Katherine's end. "Well, Thomas won't be happy. My having to stay home alone all night without advanced warning."

"Sorry, Katherine," said Joshua, "and thanks." Joshua hung up the receiver. He felt bad about lying, but what could he do? He could not tell her the truth. Things had spiraled way out of control. He needed time to reevaluate the incredible state of affairs he was presently living through.

As Joshua spoke on the phone, Milagros had opened the kitchen faucet for Jerry to rinse the dried blood from his hand. He had informed all that he had ripped some skin from his palm while swinging his bat-handle weapon at Alegría's mother, in the ravine, during his rescue of Lacey. Milagros helped him clean out the superficial wound and then placed two Band-Aids over the skin break.

Next, Jerry phoned his house and told his concerned mother that he would be staying over Joshua's house again. Esther Porter agreed but reminded Jerry about certain chores she expected to be done tomorrow and recommended that he not 'dilly dally' in arriving in the morning, her strong voice permeating through the receiver end of the phone. She also told Jerry to relay her gratitude to Joshua's parents for their hospitality toward him and directed out a sincere desire to meet Katherine one day soon.

Jerry hung up the phone softly. "My family," he said to Joshua with a concerned look. "What if Alegría comes after them?"

Milagros brought over a tray of coffee from the stove to the kitchen table. "Right now, you and your loved ones are not a priority for her."

"You heard what she said about hunting down everyone in our families and…"

"Alegría doesn't know where you live, Jerry. She doesn't know where any one of us lives. And she can't enter a residence without being invited inside." Milagros poured coffee from the espresso-maker into a metal cream pourer, the bottom coated with white sugar crystals. Thin plumes of steam rose from the pouring, filling everyone's noses with the java's strong, freshly brewed aroma. Milagros stirred the coffee with a teaspoon until the black mixture foamed brown at the top. She poured the ferment out from the pourer into the awaiting, small demitasses on matching saucers. Joshua raised his cup to his lips and blew softly, decomposing much of the dark liquid's hot, frothy traces at the surface. In small sips, he drank the brew. *Sweet nectar of life.* Coffee had never tasted so good to him. As he finished the invigorating drink and softly sighed out a hearty approval, Joshua was overtaken with a deep sense of appreciation for just the simple pleasure of this coffee, for just the company of his two wonderful friends…for just being *alive.*

*** 

"We have to cauterize your eye," Alegría advised Raúl. "We can't risk an infection." She understood from Raúl's leery reaction that he was not completely sure what she meant but suspected it would involve experiencing additional pain.

"My head feels like it's in a vice," he said, touching the tips of his fingers above his eyebrow.

Alegría had brought Raúl into the reception room of the mansion. An eighteenth-century Venetian chandelier dominated the room, hanging down in crystalline brilliance from the molded plaster ceiling. Bright palm tree themes, woven in French silk from the same period as the chandelier, adorned the walls in stylish recognition to the tropical setting of the magnificent home. In the room defined by Louis XV furniture, Raúl was laid out on the period sofa against one wall, his head on Alegría's lap.

Alegría helped Raúl sit up and then rose from the sofa. Her still-wet azalea mod mini dress clung to the dynamic crooks and curves of her body. On her feet, the damp, formed folds of the hiked-up fabric, from her sitting, steadily exposed Alegría's garters and the normally hidden area of her thighs at the top of her sheer black stockings. The tear in one of the stockings, from her roof traversing, had enlarged and added to the aura of combative eroticism that she exuded.

Overturning a small reading table a few steps away, Alegría broke off one of its legs. She walked over to the fireplace where Margot stoked a fire she had helped Alegría start. Neither woman paid attention to the prominent bust adorning the mantel. Alegría twirled the end of the broken furniture leg over the crackling flames. When the tip had blackened to her satisfaction, she nodded to her mother. Alegría turned, tugging down her dress to a less revealing status.

The women trudged back to Raúl, who became unnerved at the sight of his mother holding the furniture stick, a trail of smoke curling from its seared tip. At the opposite side of the room, a wide, mirrored wall panel with a period French clock bracketed to it reflected Raúl's objecting face along with Margot and the fuming wooden stick eerily floating in mid-air.

Just off to the side of the mirror, in a chair sat Dawn in an unusual torpor. Both her arms slumped off the armchair rests. Her clothes were noticeably wet, with her electric-blue bathing suit easily delineated under her thin blouse. All previous bloodstains from Raúl's disfigurement had been washed away from her abducted time in Biscayne Bay with Alegría. She stared directly ahead, breathing easily. When Alegría and Margot crossed into her view, her head meekly followed them without raising her eyes to take in their full presence. Neither bound nor gagged, Dawn had no physical restrictions of any kind to her person. She simply sat deferentially and without exhibited purpose.

Margot tried to restrain Raúl, but it took Alegría to push him back on the sofa.

Alegría placed a firm hand on his chest and leaned in with her face. "My darling," she said, "this has to be done. Please understand." Without warning, Alegría cocked her head and forcefully brought her forehead to bear on Raúl's.

The jarring blow quieted the cowering teenager in an instant. Sitting down, Margot placed her knocked-out grandson's head on her lap and unwound the colorful dressing that was tied around his head, previously fashioned from the torn sleeves of Alegría's azalea dress. She removed the soggy clog of rolled up sleeve strip that had been placed as a makeshift gauze over Raúl's destroyed eye. Margot and Alegría traded looks of pity and sorrow with each other over the eradication. Margot then held Raúl's head tightly within her hands, and Alegría carefully lowered the overheated tip of the wood into the dark red mush of Raúl's eye socket.

The smell of Raúl's singed flesh rose acridly into Alegría's nostrils and made her nauseous. She dropped the smoldering wooden stick to the floor and cradled his head in her arms. From the lower fringe of his eyebrow to the top of his cheekbone, a blackened hollow of burned flesh mutilated Raúl's face. Alegría could not bear to look at him. She had turned her ruggedly handsome boy into a revolting one-eyed monster. She feared he would never forgive her. "I'll find you the best plastic surgeon, darling," Alegría said to her unconscious son. "I swear to you— what you've gone through will all be worth it. You'll see."

Off to the side, Margot had pulled her slip down from under her dress. She handed the white cotton intimate accessory to Alegría, who began tearing the slip into strips to wrap around Raúl's wound.

Milagros leaned over the table and showed Joshua the cleaned stickpin she had picked up from the floor of the loggia balcony. "You dropped this," she said, pinning it back through his shirt. Her hands lightly infringed over Joshua's chest, culminating with a soft pat. His clothes had dried off from the boat ride, she noticed.

Joshua gently touched the modest clothing ornament that had saved his life. "Thanks," he said, capturing her eyes with a transmitted world of meaning.

Jerry put his coffee cup down on the saucer with a noisy clink.

"So, what's the plan, Sam?" he asked, awkwardly interrupting a potential tender interlude between the teens.

Milagros distinctly read Joshua's now-petitioning eyes, seeking not direction but rather assistance. She masked her hurt as she said, "We are going back for Dawn."

"*We?*" responded Jerry. "As in *we* and the *whole* Miami Police Department, I hope?"

Silence from Joshua and Milagros decidedly eliminated from Jerry's proposal the inclusion of any law enforcement agency, the understanding of which slumped Jerry back in his chair. "Jay, I'm down with this one-for-all-and-all-for-one stuff. You know I am. But we had our Three Musketeers' hour. It ain't happening again. And we can't be sure…"

"Dawn is alive," Joshua finished. "But if she is…"

"It means Alegría survived, too," completed Milagros.

Joshua lightly slapped Jerry's wrist, saying, "You're right."

Though it appeared Joshua had conceded, Milagros knew he would head back alone—for *her*—if it came to that. The sheer selfless intention that he tried to hide swelled, at that moment, the chambers of Milagros' heart that were exclusively devoted to Joshua.

"You and I will go back," she said to Joshua. "But *not* until sunrise."

***

Under the moon's reflected pale light, an inanimate Dawn watched the proceedings. Alegría leaned over the corpse of her daughter, her dearest Cira. She had snugly wrapped her young body in the silky bed canopy curtain from the master bedroom. Though her head was completely covered, her facial features were visible through the chiffon transparency of the inner bed curtain. Alegría kissed her offspring sweetly on the lips and drew over her face the mantis green canopy curtain that cocooned the rest of her body. She then slipped Cira through the loosened opening of the sea bag that had been used to hide Lacey, knotting the drawstrings three times, tears running down both of her cheeks.

Alegría picked up her dead daughter in her arms and walked ahead, followed by Margot and trailed by Dawn, seemingly staring at nothing. The three crossed the East Terrace. Only Alegría descended the steps to the Sea Wall Promenade, the sea breeze swirling around her.

Dawn had not turned away when Alegría head-butted Raúl, or during the anxious interval leading up to the bestial sterilizing of Raúl's eye. She had not squeezed shut her eyes when she saw the heated wood make contact with Raúl's face. She concisely heard the tenderhearted groans from Alegría and Margot. As she heard Alegría advise her mother in the reception room that it was 'time to tend to Cira,' while Raúl remained knocked out.

She became aware of Alegría zipping upstairs to bring down the master-bedroom canopy curtains that she used to encase Cira. And from outside the East Loggia doors, Dawn had dually observed Alegría lugging a large pottery storage jar outside and her rummaging the fishing boat moored near the promenade sea

20

wall, all within the last few minutes. Through it all, Dawn maintained an outward malaise, her higher conscience trapped in a subconscious level of her mind that prevented her from speaking or displaying any outward emotion.

On the promenade, holding the cylindrical cadaver in her arms, the grieving mother twisted around long enough to acknowledge her own mother standing at the top of the steps. Margot lowered her pain-stung eyes, her hands clenched into fists she did not know how to manage.

Alegría vaulted onto the Barge and put Cira's body down gently on the cement ground. Using the fishing reel she had taken from the boat, she began encircling the strong spool around Cira's waist. Alegría's eyes began to well with tears again, and her mouth contorted in a quivering frown as she windmilled the reel around Cira. She tied the end of the fishing line around the thick-lipped neck of the large pottery jar she had transported out to the barge from the house.

At the sea steps, facing the bay, Alegría positioned Cira's body toward the water like a human torpedo. She dropped the heavy pottery jar off the barge. It tipped to one side. Within seconds, water filled the sizable rotund interior and it sunk out of sight; two bubbly gulps of vacuumed air rising to the surface of the water yielded the last traces of the engulfed jar. The fishing line around the jar pulled taut and quickly yanked Cira's body, feet first, into the water. Alegría was stroking Cira's canvass-covered head when the body slid out from under fingers. Cira's encased body entered the dark green water at an angle, swiftly guided to its watery tomb by the weighted pull below.

\*\*\*

Alegría stood gazing at the barely ruffled surface of the unforgiving water, a debilitating sadness weighing on her. The flare gun pellets that had ripped into her mid-section two hours

21

ago and the searing physical pain it had generated was nothing in comparison to the present emotional wrenching of her mind and body. She yelled savagely, leapt off the barge onto the Sea Wall Promenade and ran up the steps, past Margot and Dawn.

Alegría stopped at the meat cleaver-pierced corpse. She picked him up by the wrist and ran off with him into the Formal Gardens, dragging him down the steps of the South Terrace, through the Cross Axis of the garden, and along the Center Island. She passed the mutilated bodies she had slaughtered earlier in the evening inside one of the twin grottos, one with a distorted arm protruding from the grotto in its permanently immobile state.

At the top of the water stairway, Alegría encountered the Baroque Casino on the mound and ambled through the middle of three open-air entrance doorways of the loggia. At the back of the airy building, the corresponding doorways overlooked a swampy mangrove. In the breezeless enclave, the air smelled brackish from the mangrove's stagnant runoff from Biscayne Bay.

Behind the low wrought-iron railing of one of the back doorways, Alegría began ripping apart the battered body with her bare hands. After momentarily studying the man's bruised and bloodied face, she planted her foot on his pelvis, grabbing each forearm and pulling. She knew just where to break the bone joint first to facilitate the removal of the extremities. She flipped over the armless torso, driving her shoe into the protruding meat cleaver until it disappeared inside the collapsed ribcage. Twisting off the legs, her brute strength left pink and yellow bone marrow shreds dangling from each flesh-torn end and flung apart the holster he had tied to one of them. Limb by limb, Alegría threw the parts of the dismembered body into the gloomy water beyond the barrier wall. The body had lost a considerable amount of blood from his fatal wound, but there remained enough plasma discharge from his ruptured muscle tissue for his trunk to smear the floor in a red, curling pattern much like that of a sloppy string-mop swabbing. The malevolent entity heaved the remaining stump out of the casino and into the bay's shallow runoff where it slowly sank facedown.

Alegría turned and whisked down over to the broad steps that were on either side of the mound, leading back down to the Formal Gardens. She chose the flight of steps facing east, looking out at the Fountain Garden tucked away in its own circular enclave. Behind the Fountain Garden, more mangrove shoreline buttressed the Tea House and partitioned the bay beyond.

Alegría halted and, under the revealing moonlight, transformed into the four-hoofed, spear-tip-tailed animal of her supernatural alter ego. Her face lost its humanistic features, with widened muddy yellow eyes filled by oversized black irises and ears that mutated with distinctive animal-like points. The reshaped Alegría galloped alongside of the Fountain Garden and, following a sharp turn, entered the East Statuary Walk.

Swiftly and destructively, like some dispassionate force of nature, Alegría sent crashing to the ground every chiseled work of centuries-old art lining the terrace walk. She knocked over large marble urns from their low-lying wall placements and toppled from their pedestaled perches every mythological marble representation on display. Alegría cracked the head off Neptune in one pass and then knocked the god of the sea over with a fierce kick from her hind legs in a coordinated second strike. One of the arms broke off upon impact with the ground and the statue suffered irreparable cracks that spread out over its naked torso. The enraged four-footed beast similarly mistreated Minerva, the Roman goddess of wisdom and invention. Alegría disrespected Apollo, smashing off the lyre that the son of Zeus cradled in one elbow and shattering the opposite arm that showily depicted his motionless playing. She then brought the armless statue crashing down with another demolishing hind thrust.

When Alegría reached the end of the walkway, irreplaceable sculpted works of skill and imagination lay in piles of broken limestone on the ground behind her.

The wicked animal then charged across the center axis of the garden to the West Statuary Walk and, in the opposite direction, repeated the laying-waste tactic upon the matching seventeenth and eighteenth-century statues stationed there. Alegría took great pleasure in her destructive rampage; she roared with contrary delight every time she sent another weighted work of art to its broken end.

At the completion of the aggregate demolition, the beastly Alegría lifted her front hooves to inspect them. They were badly scraped and cut, the fur above the hooves dampened with her blood. Her front hooves hurt and so did those of her hind legs, but Alegría did not care. She welcomed the physical pain which brought a helpful dulling of her own distraught emotional state. Jumping down from the walkway into the garden, she paused at the entrance of the grotto containing the bodies of the dead teenagers. Taking pleasure at her previous grisly handiwork, she roared at the bloody sight before hoofing off in a full gallop along the Center Island back toward the mansion.

As Alegría's outstretched front legs attempted to hurtle the South Terrace steps in one bound, she was lifted by her tail off the ground to her shocking dismay. The deviant beast that was Alegría rose suspended over the sarcophagus-shaped fountain of the South Terrace. Strung up by her aerodynamic appendage, she shook violently in midair like a cruelly captured animal in the wild. She managed to see what was holding her, what could have dared grab her, and she transformed back to full human form.

A much less frightening-looking Alegría fell onto the South Terrace. She was on her feet as the shrieking winged creature swooped in on her. She swung wildly and viscously at it with her badly bruised hands. Its wings were compact, with a surprisingly hard exoskeleton that was both lightweight and flexible. The flapping wings pummeled Alegría, preventing her from landing any blows. The creature had a disproportionately small head compared to the rest of its body which was about six feet in full height. The spiky-eared half-bird-half-beast easily matched Alegría's own supernormal strength and, with its wings, appeared to have the edge. But Alegría's present take-no-prisoners mental state exhorted from her an extra quantity of rage-inspired power.

Avoiding the creature's incessant but short-reach clawing at her neck, she pried its wings apart. Holding onto one wing, Alegría reached her other hand under the creature's jawline. From its small mouth, the winged assailant emitted a squealing, painful cry as Alegría's fingers squeezed the coarse, blue-gray exterior of its scaly neck. Its small mouth enlarged to twice its size in its gaping misery. Its whitish upper teeth were puny, rounded, and spaced apart. The bottom row contrastingly lined up in a sharp, pointy assembly similar to shark's teeth. A dry, black tongue twitched uncontrollably inside its warped mouth. The suffering creature furiously flapped its free wing trying to escape the incensed clutches of Alegría, who had now planted her heel on her opponent's opposite taloned foot.

The free wing started to lose its energy, and just as it seemed Alegría was pressing her advantage to a fatal conclusion, she was struck on the head with the force of a falling brick. Alegría went flying off to the side, rolling twice on the ground from the angled blow from above. A second screeching winged creature had come plummeting down from the sky and smashed its hind legs into Alegría, who remained conscious—although barely so.

The second winged creature, of similar shape and size as the first, interestedly attended to the first. It came over to its companion, walking completely upright but with wings gently flapping, its thick four-claw bird feet barely making contact with the ground. It held out one of its short upper limbs to its companion, making curt communicative noises that sounded like an abridged seal's cry.

The first winged creature rubbed the area of its neck where Alegría's fingers had dug into, a dark bruise rising over its bluish-gray skin. But instantly, as Alegría began stirring more, its face changed from a display of personal injury to a demonstration of deep resentment in her direction. In these descriptive mood shifts, its face exhibited pure human-like qualities. Followed by its companion, the scowling snub-nosed character came over to Alegría. Again, the walking pair seemed to float as they moved, their fluttering wings keeping their taloned feet scraping marginally above the ground.

The two picked up Alegría, grabbing her by the arms with both sets of their three-digited upper limbs. Alegría briefly resisted, until she realized that she would not be able to break free of the incredibly strong double grip to which she was being subjected. She resentfully heard her captors release several undecipherable sounds that gloated over her seizure.

The pair brought Alegría up to the south façade of the mansion, in front of the stone-columned, stained glass archways of the south doors. Then a bright light appeared from outside the doorway, temporarily blinding Alegría and even forcing her captors to look away. The light generated a colorful crystallization of atmospheric particles from which three figures materialized. They were human forms. Two were male and one female. When the three transparent beings solidified several feet from Alegría, the peculiar light that had announced them completely faded.

"What do you want?" Alegría discourteously asked.

The three beings each answered Alegría's query with an easy, flowing, and organized response.

"Perhaps we should…"

"Ask the same…"

"Question of you."

Alegría did not hesitate to respond. "I want you to tell these stinking gargoyles to let go of me!"

# Chapter Two

"How is she holding up?" asked Jerry.

"She wants to be by herself a while longer," answered Milagros. "I think the café helped…a little at least." Milagros raised the empty coffee cup she held in her hand while walking over to the sink. After disposing of the cup and saucer, she sat back down at the kitchen table with Joshua and Jerry.

Following an extended silence, with all parties exchanging flitting glances, Joshua scratched at his temple and asked, "Am I going to grow fangs?"

Jerry expressively raised his eyebrows, awaiting a response from Milagros.

Milagros pulled her chair closer and straightened her posture. She folded her hands and spoke with an even-toned voice. She came across like a professional counselor, experienced from years of the same case study. "I think, Joshua, we should concentrate on what we seek to achieve collectively—and I mean as Docile half-vampires, you and I." Milagros gestured at Jerry as if to beg his pardon from excluding him from the subject theme, and Jerry responded with hand and face mannerisms that assured everyone he took no offense.

Joshua's body language indicated that the term *Docile half-vampire* would take a little more time to grow accustomed to. "Something tells me I'm going to need more coffee," he said, reaching for the metal pourer.

"Tomorrow night—" Glimpsing the clock on the wall, which read ten minutes to one, Milagros corrected herself, "— Tonight is the cobalt moon. The seventh in our lifetimes. The Hostiles will be after us. To drain our blood and, therefore, kill us so that *they* can become full vampires. We're not going to let that happen." Milagros shook her head slightly but with resolve.

Joshua shook his head in the same manner, more from an expressed desire to agree with Milagros' closing statement than from a sense of conviction. "What do we do? Barricade ourselves inside our homes?"

I suppose that would *seem* like a viable option for us here." Milagros waved her hand at her surroundings. "Batten down the hatches and ride things out. But…that, from what I understand, is going to prove difficult."

Joshua squinted, seeking more information.

"Too bad your dad's still in Cuba, Jay," said Jerry. "I mean, I know he skipped out on you when you were a kid, but we sure could use a hand now."

Milagros struck the table with the heel of her palm twice in a manner requesting everyone's attention. "Joshua's father could not help, even if he was here. Just like my father—wherever he is—can't help. No parental interference, remember?"

Jerry's face showed confusion, but he was distinctly hesitant to open his mouth again.

Milagros nodded slightly at Joshua, peering at her with interest. "Vampire parents are forbidden from interfering the destiny of their children on the night of the cobalt moon."

Joshua exchanged a glance with Jerry and, without much of a pause, turned back to Milagros, asking cautiously the question on both their minds.

"Forbidden by whom?"

\*\*\*

The gargoyles released Alegría, obeying the dismissive hand motion of one of the three beings—the one standing in the middle and the tallest of the three. The gargoyle who had been choked by Alegría did not hide its disdain for the captive, letting go of her arm with an intentional push and soured face.

The pair of gargoyles separated from Alegría, their billowing wings lifting them backward into the air. After a few crisscrossing swoops, they perched themselves in tandem on the slanted roof above the breakfast room, the others directly below.

The taller male being took a half step forward, following a satisfied nod at the winged-malformations. He wore a high-collared, double-breasted, shiny, satin lavender-blue jacket with showy epaulets and parallel rows of gold buttons down the front. Its collar and cuffs were trimmed with gold piping. The well-tailored jacket falling past his waist had the appearance of that of a high-school drum major's uniform. The excessive length of his perfectly creased navy-blue slacks untidily covered his feet. He divided his rather longish hair down the center of his head in a prominent part.

The other male, a few inches shorter than his colleague, stayed in place. He sported an elaborate raspberry-red overcoat with brass buttons, epaulets, and wide flapped cuffs. The knee-length overcoat resembled a British Navy captain's formal uniform from the Colonial Period, buttoned at the chest and left open over a red waistcoat fit smartly around his belt. Matching straight leg pants tapered widely at the ankles, touching the ground and hiding his feet. The male's full head of hair was split down the middle of his head in a razor-sharp part.

The female of the clique, of equal stature to the male farthest from her, also did not move. Her attire consisted of a fuchsia velvet frock coat bordered with gold embroidery and unpretentious epaulets. Under the frock coat, a similar-colored body shirt revealed no cleavage. Buttoned to cinch her waist, the coat reached her ankles. Her too-long bell-bottom pants gave no hint of her shoe-wear taste. She wore her hair short, a strawberry-blond color which did not style well with its dead center part over the top of her head. Her makeup was moderately applied.

Alegría straightened her dress and initiated a quick self-inspection. Her body's self-healing mechanism steadily progressed, treating the deep scratches and bruises on her hands. Separated from her high heels, her feet's prior cuts and contusions were also waning. She knew she looked terrible, probably as terrible as she felt. She also knew that her comportment in front of these three should be deferential, if not subservient. Had they appeared to her under different circumstances, or at another time, it likely would have been. But her sweet, innocent daughter—her Cece—had been taken from her a few hours ago, and all she could do to fight the pain of the crushing loss was to breed scorn and anger.

"Well, if it isn't the Sergeant Pepper's Lonely Hearts Club Band," she said sardonically, her appraising eye falling over the three in fast order.

The statement was greeted grimly by the trio. Each of them registered their discontent in some muted manner: pursed lips, narrowed eyes, and impatient exhale of breath. And each rather self-consciously touched some part of their garments in the wake of Alegría's acerbic comment.

The taller one eventually managed a half smile and calmly spoke. As earlier, his opening words were curt and equally added on to by the others, constructing, shaping, and completing one orderly reply.

"Perhaps with an introduction…"

"We can diffuse the…"

"Apparent hostility between us."

"My name is Libor…" said the taller one.

"I am called Equin…" stated the female.

"Umber is my name," said the remaining one.

"Something tells me I don't have to tell you mine," replied Alegría standoffishly.

Libor lifted his chin toward Alegría and breathed in patiently. Equin and Umber exchanged doubtful looks with each other.

"We know who you…"

"Are, and we are…"

"Here to help you." Although Libor had once again opened, Equin this time finished the group response. An unconvincing smile accompanied her closing remark.

Alegría's eyes tilted upward at the scowling gargoyles above her. She returned their look of unkindness. "I've had the most terrible personal tragedy," she said to the three.

"It appears the grounds here…"

"Are littered with personal tragedies…"

"Most caused by your hand."

The three left clear that they were not inclined to offer Alegría sympathy of any kind.

"I have a right to avenge my daughter's death," Alegría said firmly, with a hard blink of the eyes and a toilsome exhale after hearing her own words.

"As long as you…"

"Do not kill two…"

"Birds with one stone."

Equin and Umber stepped even now with Libor. "As we are perfectly balanced…"

"In our thought patterns and…"

"Our speech, we cannot allow…"

"An imbalance to…"

"Upset the supernatural…"

"Order of things."

The 'imbalance,' Alegría clearly understood, meant *her*. Her plan to capture Joshua and Milagros to then serve them up, literally speaking, to Raúl and Cira the next night—the night of the cobalt moon—had spun tragically out of control. The way she had originally thought it through, it involved no intervention on her part—at least none on the night of the cobalt moon. Joshua and Milagros would have voluntarily placed themselves in harm's way on the very eve of the most dangerous night of their lives. What pity would there be over their deaths for being so damn stupid? Who could castigate her children for spotting an opportunity and seizing it?

"I haven't interfered," Alegría blurted out loudly.

Libor and the others remained impassive. Libor then gazed up at the gargoyles and, as if he had given them a telepathic command, they shot off the railing straight up and back beyond the mansion. In a matter of seconds, their blue-gray silhouettes disappeared against the starry purple sky.

Libor took two steps back. Equin and Umber followed suit, together. As Libor had done, each picked up one covered foot and placed it back down behind the other. They seemed to have no trouble stepping with the extended fabrics of their too-long leg garments. The instant the two came even with Libor near the arched stained-glass doors, the bright light appeared at their rear as briefly blinding as earlier, with crystallized atmospheric particles kicking up again in a shimmering kaleidoscope of slow-motion dance around their vanishing figures.

"My son is half blind!" shouted Alegría at the evaporating trio. "How will it be for him tonight? He'll be at who knows what kind of disadvantage. He only gets one chance. He only gets one chance!"

Before they dissolved within the dissipating light, the three answered Alegría.

"For every imbalance, there must…"

"Be a counterbalance. Tread lightly…"

"Daughter of darkness, tread lightly."

\*\*\*

33

"What's an equilibrium?" asked Joshua.

"Not *an* equilibrium," answered Milagros, "*the* Equilibrium."

Joshua turned his palms up, accepting the correction but still wanting more information.

"The Equilibrium is three trans-dimensional beings from a micro-particle domain. They are the gatekeepers of the supernatural underworld."

Jerry let out an exaggerated whistle. "This just gets farther and farther out there, huh, Jay?"

"Their non-metaphysical state permits their existence in two of the three states of matter," continued Milagros. "Excluding solids, they are able to co-exist in both liquid and gas environments."

Joshua's mind was no longer the sealed vault of the past few days; it was now humbly open to all of Milagros' dictums. Joshua asked the first question to come to his mind. "Whose side are they, the Equilibrium, on?"

With her fingertips, Milagros pinched into a small pile the crumbled *turrón* in the small plate in front of her. She lifted into her mouth the tatters of her portion of the nougat candy she had put out on the table for everyone's consumption. Brushing off her fingers in a napkin gave her time to swallow. "The Equilibrium is not on anybody's side. They are impartial. Their purpose is to deter any inclination of interference by parents— usually vampire parents on the night of the cobalt moon."

"They're like the police of the creep world," said Jerry, reaching for more hard honey almonds.

"You might say that," answered Milagros with a slight smile.

"They got ways of kicking a vampire's ass?" inquired Jerry prior to taking a bite of candy.

"They have at their disposal the means to kick a vampire's behind-," confirmed Milagros. "The Equilibrium commands a legion of...gargoyles." Milagros had deliberately hesitated before completing her statement. "The gargoyles are said to be as strong as vampires, if not superior to them, because they can fly."

Joshua, who had not eaten any of the laid out hard confection, leaned back in his chair. "How do you know all this?" he asked. Milagros blinked and then lowered her eyes. Joshua understood. *Juan,* he remembered. "Is that everything?"

Gazing at both Joshua and Jerry, Milagros nodded, exhaling deeply.

***

After several seconds of silence, Jerry posed a question that left the others unable to answer. "How did Alegría get Lacey on the night of Cira's birthday party?"

"Raúl," said Milagros with uncertainty.

"Raúl dropped her off," replied Jerry. "I went to her house after and saw her, remember? You said Alegría can't get into our houses."

"She can't," assured Milagros, "unless she's invited inside."

"Then how did Alegría kidnap Lacey? Her parents didn't let her in. Alegría can't hypnotize people, can she?"

"No. That's a screenwriter's invention."

"Then how?"

Milagros pondered things a bit and then answered. "I don't know, Jerry," she said, sounding a bit frustrated. "Maybe Lacey was lured outside."

Jerry did not think that probable. He thought about that night, the night of Cira's birthday party, his visit to Lacey's house afterward, ringing the Hayes' doorbell at the late hour, and being turned away by Lacey's irked, bath-robed father. Jerry had wanted to see Lacey so badly and filled with honorable intentions. He had fully convinced himself that he would be permitted the opportunity. Lacey's father's denial had driven Jerry to sneak into Lacey's room through her bedroom window.

He remembered a trailing thought of wiping his feet several times on the Hayes' welcome mat before Mr. Hayes opened the door. The welcome mat that had the family name on it stood out to Jerry as a novelty item he had never seen before. Under the porch light's shine, he saw the conjured image of his feet scraping over the mat's coarse texture, its personalized greeting displaying an intended sentiment of warmth.

*Welcome All to our Humble House. The Hayes family.*

Jerry stood up with alarm in his eyes. "Lacey," he said. "We put her right where Alegría can get her again. We've got to go back to her house—now!"

*** 

Sheila Landis wanted to call the police an hour ago. But her husband had stopped her. The couple was expecting their daughter Dawn almost two hours earlier, at 11:00 o'clock. She had been excusably tardy, arriving home past her curfew on previous occasions—ten or fifteen minutes—but never this alarming late.

Sheila was beside herself. She did not know how to contact Dawn's boyfriend or his parents. She did not know where Raúl lived. There was nothing in her daughter's personal effects that indicated her boyfriend's phone number or home address. The boy called their house quite often when the two had begun dating, but not as much recently, Sheila recalled. And Dawn never called him, as Sheila had instructed her not to. *A lady does not solicit the attention of gentlemen.* Sheila, perhaps unfairly, now castigated herself for not knowing more about her daughter's social life. Thinking that she should have known

36

where Dawn's boyfriend lived, she began having larger concerns over where else she had possibly failed as a mother.

"What are the cops going to do at this point?" asked Randall Landis. Dawn's father had moved beyond the point of being angry with his daughter for radically abusing the curfew hour to being incensed at her boyfriend for keeping her out so late, Sheila gathered. He was more or less fully clothed, unlike Sheila who wore a bright kimono-like robe over her nightgown. At 11:45, Randall had put on his work boots, his notorious *clodhoppers*, to which Sheila for the first time paid no mind to him wearing through the house.

While Sheila stayed ever vigilant by the drawn-up shade of the living room window which fronted the street outside their house, Randall sat on the couch. He purposely avoided using the ottoman Sheila had bought to accommodate his habit of elevating his feet while he watched television. He instead placed the heel of one of his clodhoppers on the living-room table and crossed his other work-boot-fit foot over it. "What channel is Johnny Carson on?" he asked in a manner not meant as a direct question to his wife but rather more like a verbal jogging of his own memory. "Oh yeah, I got it," he replied to himself, the TV remote in his hand.

As his wife sent a blank stare in his direction, Randall settled in, unperturbed it seemed, with his eyes glued to the boxy RCA television console in front of him. He calmly sipped from an aluminum beer can he held in one hand. Lowering the can from his lips, his wrist fell over the black metal barrel of the pump-action shotgun he had brought out of the garage after he had put on his boots. The shotgun lay across the couch, its barrel extending over Randall's lap. Sheila knew that he intended on confronting Dawn's boyfriend as soon as he arrived with their daughter and put the fear of God in him that he would not soon forget.

A few minutes past midnight, Sheila had called Dawn's drama-class friend Jessica's home. She apologized to her parents for disturbing them at such a late hour but explained her situation. Jessica's mother, sympathetic to Sheila's plight, roused her daughter as Sheila asked. From Jessica, Sheila obtained a gladdening bit of information, gaining a concrete location on where Dawn might be—or at least where she had been.

"Vizcaya? Yes," said Sheila into the phone's receiver, "I've heard of it. Thank you kindly, Jessica dear. Thank you." She hung up the receiver without awaiting a reply.

Jessica had not been able to offer Sheila the location of Raúl's residence. She explained to the elder that she had not been invited to Cira's birthday.

Just prior to 1:00 a.m., during the final commercial break of the Tonight Show, the man of the house checked his watch and rose from the couch. He let out a burp as he buttoned his gray short-sleeve shirt, hooking over it the straps of his denim bib overalls. He walked over to Sheila, holding by the barrel the shotgun in one hand. "Let me have the address to that place," he said. Grabbing the paper Sheila handed him, he read out loud, "*Vizz-kay-uh*."

At the front door, he turned and gave even-tempered instructions to his wife. "I want you to look up the phone number of the school principal and call him. I want the home address of that Cuban boy ready if I come back and I don't have her. I don't care if he has to get his ass out of bed and go over to the school to get it. Tell him I said so."

Sheila nodded obediently at her husband. She watched him, with restrained approval, leave through the front door, out into the night to search for their daughter, his shotgun slung casually back over his shoulder.

\*\*\*

38

Juan's Chevy Impala stopped around the corner of the street where Lacey lived.

"Let's make this fast, Jerry," said Milagros, dimming the Impala's lights. "Whatever it is you have to do."

Joshua sat in the middle of the two after having sat in the backseat with Jerry during the first stop of their trip—to the hospital, to take Milagros' mother to see Manolín. Milagros had suggested it, and Rosa agreed. Rosa extracted a promise from Milagros that she would head straight home afterwards.

Joshua had stayed quiet during the exchange, knowing about their intended detour to Lacey's house. He watched as Rosa, soothed by Milagros' fibbed response, stroked her daughter's sleeveless arm. Milagros had changed out of the lilac blouse and pleated skirt she had worn on the evening into a two-toned jersey seersucker dress. Rosa then leaned over and kissed her daughter on the cheek, keeping their cheeks pressed together. The mother's head nudged from side to side, staying connected at the temple with Milagros, in a strong display of affection that Joshua could not help but wishfully envy.

Parked on Lacey's street corner now, Jerry nodded agreeably at Milagros' command not to dawdle. He folded into an envelope the lined sheet of paper on which he was scribbling, the devices of stationery he had requested from Milagros prior to leaving her house. The interior light flooded the car as Jerry opened the passenger door. Joshua noticed that Milagros had done a good job softening the welt over the bridge of her nose and covering the rings under eyes with makeup. Her mouth was also shaded with a deeper application of lipstick than he had ever seen.

"It's not broken," Milagros said in an obvious reaction to Joshua's visual lingering. "My nose. It doesn't even hurt...that much."

A shoulder's length away, Joshua snuck one last assessing peek at the girl, at the dark curls framing her round face. "I'm

39

glad you're on our side," he said, squeezing Milagros' hand unexpectedly before sliding out through the passenger door.

Milagros called after him. "Joshua, take the crucifix."

***

The three walked on the sidewalk opposite to Lacey's house, the street quiet and deserted, with cars parked in small driveways, an occasional vehicle spilling out on the swale.

"So, give it to me straight, Milagros," said Jerry in a subdued voice. "What happens to the Hostile half-vamps if they don't, whaddaya call it, change over into badass vamps?"

Jerry, in his affable manner, had the tendency to unintentionally mispronounce Milagros' name. Despite sharing an English class for eight months with her, apparently his foreign ear had been unable to pick up on the name's proper, straightforward enunciation. He stressed the back part of her name, ending with a harsh-sounding consonant of *z* rather than the softer *s*. Milagros instantly recalled how in middle school she had been teased by North American girls who purposely skewered her name. "Mila*gross*...Mila*gross*," they would chant, emphasizing their cruel estimation of her.

Unbothered by Jerry's imperfect pronunciation, she answered his question, speaking to both him and Joshua. "Hostile vampires' minds begin to rapidly deteriorate if they do not achieve their demonic purpose at their appointed age of conversion. They quickly become mentally unstable. They regress so badly. Many have been known to be committed to asylums. Those that survive are plagued with violent and deranged thoughts that run rampant through their deteriorating minds."

"So, there's no get-'em-next-time for Raúl and his kind?"

"No. It's the price you pay for a chance at near-immortality." Passing under a streetlight, Milagros casually hooked onto Joshua's arm, picking up the pace. "On the other hand, Dociles, like us, are practically freed from the effects of any subsequent cobalt moon."

"Practically?" asked Joshua, awkwardly cradling the crucifix under his other arm.

"The point is," answered Milagros, "we continue to nurture our humanity." She noticed Joshua struggling with the religious artifact. Breaking her arm's hold, she relieved him of it. This one was silver-plated, but of equal size to the one left behind at Vizcaya.

"Thanks," offered Joshua, his shoulders leaned to one side as he briefly rubbed his ribcage. "I must have bumped against it coming out of the car."

"All of this is so far, far out," Jerry said. "I mean *way* far out there."

With Jerry in front, they crossed the street. Lacey's house was dark except for the porch light. Sneaking up to the front stoop, Jerry pointed to the floor mat. Milagros and Joshua read the personalized greeting. After trading appraising looks, Milagros sighed with understanding, as Jerry rolled up the floor mat, tucking it under his arm.

"Let's go," Milagros said in a whisper.

"Wait," Jerry replied in an equally low voice, pulling out his folded envelope and a small roll of scotch tape. "I want to stick this to Lacey's bedroom window. It's just a note telling her I'll see her soon."

Milagros' mouth curled in a warm way, giving Jerry her blessing.

Milagros and Joshua backed into the street while Jerry snuck around the corner of the house to deliver his special message to his special girl. Walking in silence, they both saw the moon over a treetop in the distance, white and round and almost impossible to tell it was not yet at its cyclical plenitude.

"What's going to happen to us?" Joshua asked in a hushed tone that carried a mixture of interest and concern.

Milagros hesitated to answer. She knew Joshua's query was time-specific to the next eighteen hours or so, but she allowed herself to interpret it as more open-ended as related to her and Joshua. *What's going to happen to us—as in you and I, us—after today and tonight?* She replied in a firm, honest way meant to reassure Joshua.

"*We* are going to survive—no matter what happens."

\*\*\*

Down the sidewalk, as they both stepped off the curb to cross the street, Joshua and Milagros were knocked off their feet by a powerful rush of air which carried the two of them over the asphalt for a good twenty feet, the crucifix flying out of Milagros' hand and clanking to the ground. As the two scrambled to get up, a sporadic, giggly laughter reigned over them. Three youths, two males and a female, half encircled them, looking quite menacing.

"I smell a pup," said one of the teenage boys, dressed in straight black corduroys and a silver button-down shirt, his dark hair in a pompadour.

"*Two* pups," sniffed out loud the girl. She stood opposite to Joshua. "Have you been sweating? You smell funny." She then placed her hand sassily on her swiveled-out hip. "No matter. You are scrumptious-looking," she opined, eyeing Joshua from top to bottom. A dyed blond with stringy hair, she wore a jacquard-check skater dress. The large round choker beads around her neck did not suit her slim neck and pencil-thin figure.

The third in the intimidating group wore a buttoned leather vest over a plain white T-shirt. His brown hair fell over his forehead but was maintained trimmed along the sides and back. Dissipating some of his menace, he could not resist satisfying an apparent itch and began scratching his wrist, gradually and abrasively extending up to his forearm.

"Would you stop with that scratching, already?" said the pompadour boy. "You're like a dog with fleas."

"I can't help it," replied the leather-vest boy in a frustrated and feeble manner. "You know how much I've been itching all week."

The rather emasculating exchange all at once made Joshua quizzically arch his eyebrows at Milagros. Then, in an inspired moment, he reached for the kitchen knife Milagros had armed him with before leaving her house, which he stuck between his belt. In one coordinated motion, the fingers of one hand wrapped around the knife's wooden handle while the other hand pulled off the flimsy cardboard sheath around the blade. Joshua brandished the knife to his assailants. "Hostiles!" he yelled, along with instructions for Milagros. "Backs together, now!"

"There's no one behind us," Milagros said coolly, squashing the strategy.

"Why haven't you pulled out your knife?" asked Joshua anxiously after a quick, deflating look behind him. Not waiting for her reply, he pivoted toward the aggressors, motioning combatively with his knife-clenched hand. "The center of the chest," he said, instructionally to himself. "Thrust, dead center."

In his edgy state, Joshua had not executed a clean unsheathing of his weapon. Somewhere along the length of the blade's sharp edge, it sliced through the sheath and into Joshua's palm. He was the last to notice his bleeding hand sticking out in its defensive position.

One after the other, the teenage attackers sordidly reacted to the red ooze in Joshua's fingers. Pompadour boy leaned forward and opened his mouth wide. Fangs grew from his canine teeth and strange, short gurgling sounds emanated from his throat.

The dyed blond nearly came out of her black sling back pumps. Her hand slid off her hip and the muscles of her face

43

pulled tightly from her mouth, as if in pain, to reveal upper and bottom rows of straight teeth. Inside her open mouth, two miniature tusks sprouted from the upper row, diametrically apart. She rushed air into her yawning mouth, sounding like the wind passing through a tunnel.

The leather-vested one opened his mouth twice before he could trigger the signature vampire apparatus from his teeth. From his gaping mouth came a sound similar to a suction tube draining a wet shallow. All their three pair of eye whites flared a cobalt blue, following a blackened enlargement of their pupils.

The three took intimidating steps toward Joshua and Milagros. "Where's your knife?" asked Joshua of Milagros, again.

"It's in my skirt pocket," she answered calmly.

Joshua did not understand Milagros' behavior. Had she given up? Was she just going to surrender without a fight?

Suddenly, Jerry made his presence known, yelling and charging out of the darkness like the cavalry into the mix. The pompadour boy turned around quickly. He stuck out his arms and grabbed hold of the picked-up crucifix Jerry carried out in front of him; Jerry skidded to a halt. Losing his balance, he released the crucifix, obviously stunned at the combined sight of the fanged, eye-distorted boy holding firmly on to the tried and true Achilles heel of vampire dom.

Milagros then walked right up to the pompadour boy. Perhaps because she was so calm and unaggressive, the other two no-good collaborators stood by idly. Milagros offered a sprawled-out Jerry a hand up. She eyed the ringleader who held the crucifix up and away from him by the rear cross section. "He doesn't have full power," she said, yanking the crucifix right out of his hands and handing it back to Jerry. "None of them does." Milagros offered incriminating looks at the other two. "We're no good to them, *yet*," she divulged and stared directly into and vanquished the cobalt stare of the pompadoured half-vampire.

Having been defrocked and seeking to regain the advantage of the situation, the teenage half-vampire tried to recapture a level of intimidation. "It doesn't mean you pups can't serve a purpose." The boy sniffed twice at Milagros; his fangs, which had retreated when Milagros had stared him down, resurfaced, as did the distinct shade of blue in his eyes. "Ever heard of practice?"

Before he could move, Milagros stomped on the threatening boy's foot, twisting his wrist behind his back and, with her free hand, pulled out her kitchen knife, whipping off the sheath with a flick of her wrist. In no time, the knife was aimed at the teenage half-vampire's heart. In a beautiful succession of quick, table-turning moves, Milagros had subdued the pressing enemy.

"The center of the chest, like you said, Joshua," Milagros called out, emphasizing the location of her knife, pointing against the straining upper torso of the pack's leader. "Although in his case, we can still afford to miss the heart with our aim. Any thrust to the chest will do."

The other two aggressors stood down, the real threat to their leader dissuading any interference on their part. Their fangs shrunk away and their eyes returned to their conventional state. With the normality returning to his own eyes and teeth, the pompadoured half-vampire cried, "Uncle!" Milagros withdrew the blade and released his wrist.

The teenager, who was bent uncomfortably backward from the pressure Milagros exerted on his crooked arm, straightened in a huff. He gave Milagros a dirty look and took off running up the street. A whoosh of air trailed behind him as he slingshot out of sight into the darkness. His associates stared after him as if they had to confirm his disappearance before they could move.

The dyed blond half-vampire then peered back at the assailed trio. She clamped her hand to her waist, expressing utter disdain for Milagros. When she altered her perspective toward Joshua, a smile crept over her face. She blew a kiss. "Take care of your boo-boo, Scrumptious," she said with a sniggering laugh. She cocked her head at her remaining cohort, which meant as a directive to leave. Lifting one foot in a deliberate manner, the second it touched the ground, she sped off running. The leather-vested half-vampire accelerated right behind her, scratching hard at the back of his neck.

"Just a couple of Hostiles feeling their oats," said Milagros. A dumbstruck Joshua and Jerry watched her, still obviously impressed with the self-defense moves she had put on display.

Lights in two homes across from them blinked on. Apparently, the ruckus in the street had awoken one or more of the occupants.

Jerry then spoke, capturing a sentiment shared by all. "Let's split before their mommas come looking for them."

# Chapter Three

Randall Landis eased his 1965 pine green GMC pickup truck in behind the red Chevy Corvair—Raúl's Corvair—parked behind two other cars on the side street.

Out of his car, Randall noticed only the two small back windows of Raúl's car were raised. He could smell a briny consistency in the night air, expressly when he turned in the direction of the cooling breeze. He knew he was near a large body of salt water. Randall determined that the deserted side street turned into a winding access road to other waterfront homes tucked apart somewhere deeper along the unseen eastern edges of the pine jungle that loomed around him.

Removing the car jack from his pickup truck, he rolled it as close to the sidewall as he could. Wrenching the raising lever of the jack stand, he cranked it to its maximum height. After flinging his shotgun over the wall, he stepped carefully on the flat metal-lifting pad, weary of keeping the jack's wheels from sliding. The foot-and-a-half elevation Randall gained helped him reach over the top of the wall and climb up and over.

Dropping himself down on the other side, Randall fell to both knees but quickly righted himself, picking up his shotgun and releasing the trigger safety. He followed the narrow clearing along the inside of the wall back toward the entrance gate, occasionally peering into the thick brush at his side, unable to distinguish more than a few feet deep.

After a short while, Randall encountered the front gate and followed the vehicle roadway entrance into the grounds, eventually passing through the entrance plaza, a circular area that apparently allowed for the free flow of vehicular traffic. The man in overalls continued ahead, holding his weapon loosely but close to his body, with the shotgun's barrel angled casually downward. He walked through the arrival lane, barely glancing at the bubbling waterway fountains lining its path. He reached the oval forecourt where he was formerly greeted by the great white-walled edifice. The mansion basked in the moonlight, which added a cream-colored radiance to its stucco walls and altered its burned-orange tiled roof to a dark red against the dominant night sky.

Randall persisted on his search for his daughter, trooping along the north corridor of the grand house, with his shotgun now cradled more firmly in his arms, its barrel no longer angled downward. The only sound Randall heard came from his own cautiously moving feet. It was quiet, but not heedfully so. Some tightly shut windows on the side of the mansion filtered light, making it easier to see. He recoiled when he sensed a shadowy figure pass in front of one of the windows above him but calmed himself into thinking he had been mistaken after a black bird flew close overhead. A few feet from the pared back thicket, he spotted something on the ground. He identified the object before he picked it up—a ladies' purse.

Randall did not recognize the purse as Dawn's, as far as he could tell. But he stuck his hand inside to see if he could find a clue as to the owner. He pulled its lined interior inside out in an act of dejected frustration. As he turned to throw the empty purse away, he saw her.

"Hell's bells!" he exclaimed, startled but more annoyed with himself. How hadn't he heard her behind him?

A few feet away, the woman stood calmly with a hand out, mutely asking for the purse.

Randall wanted to ask a series of questions but settled for one. "Who are you?"

The woman again gestured for her purse, this time pointing as well. She spoke one word: *"Mio."*

Giving her the once over, Randall gathered enough from her gesticulating to decipher the spoken meaning. In the shadowy area outside the borderline of trees, the woman appeared more than a little worn to Randall from her hair to her dress. He then caught a glimpse of the bruise on her face and he straightened his shoulders suspiciously. "I'm looking for my daughter. Her name is Dawn Landis. She came here with her boyfriend, Raúl."

The woman blurted out a string of words that passed unintelligibly through Randall's brain—except for one. *"Yo soy la abuela de Raúl. El está aquí."* She pointed again, this time back at the great house. She took a twisting half step back, beckoning Randall. *"Ven conmigo."*

"Rah-ool?" asked Randall, taking interested steps forward. "Where is he? Is my daughter Dawn here?"

Randall inched up closer to the stranger. He had not at all been threatening at any time with his weapon, but he observed the woman anxiously eyeing its close proximity now. He dropped the shotgun to his side in one hand. She held out her hand and Randall slapped the purse into it. She nodded her thanks and agreeably walked away.

After a few steps, Randall was at her side. He wanted to ask her if she was Raúl's mother. If she knew what in blazes hour it was? But he feared if he heard any more of her gibberish language, he would become too frustrated. Besides, he believed that he would soon be encountering his daughter, or at the very least, he expected information as to her present whereabouts.

As their pace quickened, Margot spoke, giving Randall the feeling, she wanted to keep him invisibly tethered to her. *"Raúl está aquí. Raúl está aquí."*

Randall's lips convoluted into a smirk and his hand tightened around the hard, middle casing of the leveled shotgun at his side. "Yeah, yeah. Rah-ool. Rah-ool."

***

"How did those half-vamps find us?" asked Jerry, slamming the door behind him in the backseat of Juan's car.

"The Hostiles smelled us," answered Milagros. She settled in behind the wheel and shut her door a second or two after Joshua sat in the passenger seat. "Me and Joshua. Our scent."

"They can smell you? Don't tell me it's like that. You guys won't stand a chance." Jerry quickly tried to mollify the prickly candor his skeptical amazement had brought out. "I mean, unless you two—we two—uh, we *three* stick together."

Milagros put her hand at the top of the steering wheel. "We'll stick together. Joshua and I, for sure." She handed Joshua her knife and motioned at the glove compartment. "Put yours in there, too."

Joshua obeyed, unable to shake a feeling of inadequacy, his perceived foolish behavior in the face of the just-passed low-level threat, the cause. He rubbed his thumb over the palm cut he had given himself. He was no longer bleeding, and the cut was barely detectable. "I guess I acted pretty silly back there," he said, offering Milagros a sideways glance. "*You* were GI Joe brave."

Milagros' eyes came off Joshua for a scant moment while she slipped the key into the ignition and started the car. "No one's ever going to question your courage. Not after what you did for Dawn tonight. And not after what you tried to do for me before that, luring Alegría away from us to chase up the staircase after you."

50

As Joshua watched Milagros pull down on the shift lever of the steering column, his feelings of inadequacy slowly dissipated.

***

Randall and the woman walked past the lit swimming pool and up the stairs to the East Terrace. Randall permitted himself an extended look at the lit pool's clear blue water and the captivating golden illumination coming from inside the double-arched grotto. He likened it to something out of a Hollywood movie.

Walking across the East Terrace, he briefly took in the stone barge buttressing the saltwater doorstep of the mansion, and he spied a fishing boat moored tranquilly as if awaiting the promise of an early morning excursion. He and the woman stepped up to the shattered East Loggia glass doors with a large cracked-open floor vase conspicuously nearby. Avoiding the varying splotches of what appeared to be dried blood staining the limestone floor, Randall's boots scraped over bits of shattered glass crunching under his feet. "What in Sam Hill went on here?" he said aloud.

The woman maintained a silly smile, guiding Randall onward through the smashed door and the interior of the loggia. The hanging caravel briefly caught his eye as a coastal breeze blew stiffly through the obliterated opening. "Where's Dawn?" he asked firmly and on the verge of agitation.

Randall followed his suddenly silent guide in a more distrustful manner after noting that her smile had turned impish. He came out into the rectangular courtyard and its surrounding lush, tropical vegetation. Gazing up, he saw a section of starry sky through the open-air centerpiece design of the mansion and understood why the unchecked breeze through the East Loggia circulated so strongly around him.

Nearing the end of his rope, Randall turned to confront his disobliging escort. She did not appear where she had been—directly in front of him. His head snapped from right to left in a ninety-degree encompassing swivel. She had vanished. Randall's hands tightened around his shotgun as he warily raised it chest-high. "*Hello*," he called out in two different directions.

As he prepared to do the same into a third area of the courtyard, Randall saw him. He was standing on the North Arcade, near the steps to the courtyard. Randall impatiently approached him. Raúl stepped down and met him.

Randall stopped. Raúl resembled a military casualty off the combat field. He had a white dressing around his temples and plainly damaged eye. His shirt and pants were stained with dried blood. It did not take long for Randall to associate the battery inflicted upon the boy with his daughter's unknown status. "Where's my daughter?" he asked, filled with anxiety. "Where's Dawn?"

Raúl blinked twice with his serviceable eye. He then calmly lifted the angled wrap covering his other eye and leaned toward Randall. The unexpected repulsive sight, together with Raúl's tipping movement, made Randall kick back. Below Raúl's eyebrow, a swollen lump of blackened flesh plugged the eye socket and integrated hideously with the skin of his cheekbone.

Skittishly backpedaling, Randall bumped into the braced fixture of the woman he had first encountered. The reappearing woman smiled at Randall, a smile that grated him now due to its perceived deception. Randall was at wit's end. He raised his shotgun straight up and fired. The loud noise carried out through the open-air space of the courtyard into the still quiet of the late evening outside. The woman scooted away, annoyed. Randall pumped the handgrip of his shotgun to reload the firing chamber and further show he meant business.

The weapon then lowered in his hands slowly as he witnessed another woman—*leaping off* the East Gallery above him. She descended, not dropped. Randall saw clearly her garter bands along her separated fleshy thighs; he glimpsed her black and pink panties as the downdraft of air lifted indecently her short dress and billowed beneath her feet as she softly landed a few feet from him. She looked as if she had been through a difficult ordeal and had not escaped unscathed. One of her stockings was torn; there were rips in her mini dress at the shoulders and an outright fabric gouge at the stomach that revealed a shredded portion of the waist cincher of her garter belt. She exuded a battered sexuality, but without the vulnerability that would have made her desirable to many men in a perverted way, Randall included. Her lewd Mary-Poppins drop from the second floor was something Randall's mind could not mystically or lecherously shake either.

"Jesus Christ on a cracker!" exclaimed Randall as he tried to keep from losing his reason.

\*\*\*

"That's an interesting supposition," said Alegría, pulling down her skirt, sauntering toward Dawn's father. Taking a side-to-side non-aggressive route, her high heels dug lightly into the coral stone floor of the courtyard. "Why doesn't anybody ever reach out in the other direction? Why not, *Oh, Satan!* Or *Lucifer H. Beelzebub!* Or even *Hades on a cracker!* That's got a ring, doesn't it? I don't get it. Everybody would rather stick to pious oaths. They're *insults,* don't you know?"

"I'm here for my daughter," Randall said, trying to assimilate things as best he could. "Tell me where she is, and we'll leave."

Alegría's face grew harsh. "Your *daughter?*" Her heart achingly compressed and her stomach miserably sank at the mention of the word. She decided killing this Purebred would help her feel better—at least temporarily. Then she wondered how many other meddlesome parents would be following the trail of their overdue children—their *dead* overdue children—like this one had. Perhaps she could obtain some information from him first. *Did you come alone? Who else knows you are here? Did you call the police?* Alegría surmised that she would not receive a straight answer from the shotgun-toting man. She then deduced the answers to all her questions herself. *Yes. His wife, more than likely. And no.* He had nothing valuable to offer her. The parent had maintained a defensive posture with the shotgun since he had seen Alegría magically float down in front of him. But with her lightning-fast movement and strength, she easily relieved him of the weapon, flung it way, and snatched him by the throat.

Margot and Raúl watched unflinchingly from the North Gallery. Right behind Raúl, Dawn appeared. Her father made eye contact with her as Alegría's sharp-tipped fingers began slicing through the muscles of his throat, spilling runny red lines of blood from irreparably ruptured vertebral arteries down his neck.

"Kitten," he uttered with his dying breath, his clodhoppers wriggling a foot off the floor and then going limp. Dawn serenely watched her father brutally killed, watched the collar of his gray shirt turn a purplish color as it soaked up the flowing blood around his neck. She did not move a muscle. Her face betrayed no emotion. She simply blinked naturally as one would when one's gaze is fixed on something vaguely interesting. Both Margot and Raúl, within a few steps of her, witnessed the strange inaction.

Alegría grabbed Randall's sagging body by the scruff of the neck. She disdainfully wiped the blood that had stained her butchering hand over the front of his overalls. She then tossed the dead man to the floor with as much regard as a used napkin. She paced over to Raúl and Margot. Right then, as she gazed at the crumpled heap of her father's slain body, Dawn's eyes closed and she fainted—Raúl's arms catching her.

"She's in shock," said Alegría. "Psychogenic shock. Looks like her mind just finished shutting down."

Alegría's reduced family waited eagerly for her next instructions. "I have got to change these clothes," she said with a couture look of self-despair. "Where did you park your car?" she asked Raúl.

"On the street outside the east wall," answered Raúl. "My keys are in my pocket." Occupied with Dawn, Raúl turned his hip for Alegría to reach into his pants and pull out his car keys.

Keys in hand, Alegría gazed out at the open-air courtyard. The leafy perimeter of the entwined green plants and trees were indisputably a pleasing sight. Her eyes swept across the arcades, glimpsing small sections of the East Loggia, the tea room, and Entrance Loggia, all surrounding her. Her vision was then drawn to a strewn booklet on the floor. Folded open, its littered image stood out in the immaculate environs. She reached down and picked it up.

"Things have changed, darling," Alegría said, scanning the walled galleries above her. "We are going to have to improvise now."

\*\*\*

Milagros drove Juan's Impala across the Rickenbacker Causeway, the bridge over Biscayne Bay that connected Miami with two of its barrier islands, Virginia Key and Key Biscayne.

Jerry had been the first to pose to Milagros, "Where are we going?" when she had veered off the path back to her home.

"We're going to find guidance," Milagros had answered.

Unsure of what she meant, both Jerry and Joshua, by now, were content to simply scan each other's faces and await further explanation from her. Riding with the windows down, a ceaseless wind swirled inside their car.

They passed few vehicles on the four-lane aquatic roadway before reaching the first key's outer strip of land. Milagros followed the directional sign on the road and made a left turn through an unoccupied outside booth and into a large parking area. They passed under a boxy theater marquee sign centered on a flat, inverted, triangle-shaped post with big white lettering on top that read: CITY OF MIAMI MARINE STADIUM. The changeable black lettering on the illuminated face of the sign announced a marine concert for Saturday at eight p.m. and a powerboat race on Sunday at one p.m. Milagros navigated around a wide circular center court containing a pair of ring-shaped reflecting pools and headed toward a cluster of parked cars near one side of the stadium.

"What's with all the wheels?" asked Jerry to no one in particular, referring to the parked vehicles.

"Maybe there was a midnight show," replied Joshua with little seriousness.

After she had parked, everyone followed the driver's lead and exited the car. Jerry and Joshua took a moment to take in the setting before meeting Milagros at the rear of the car. They had parked close to the distinctive rectangular-shaped stadium that apparently neither of them had ever visited. The folded plates of the cantilever roof that joined together in a crowning row, forming a pyramid-shape design, held their interest the longest. Of all the parking light poles in the lot, only two were turned on, both closest to the stadium. Away from all artificial city lights, the stars and practically full moon radiated with a gray translucence on everything and everyone around them.

Milagros opened the trunk of the car, revealing an abundance of fishing accessories. She searched around a folded net and snorkeling gear until she found what she was seeking. Wrapped in a small towel near a hand pump, she extracted what resembled a large pickle jar. Three quarters full of a liquid concoction, Milagros shook the jar, disturbing the settled white cloves at the bottom.

Asking Jerry to hold the stirred-up glass jar, Milagros had trouble twisting off the lid until Joshua helped her open it, with Jerry holding it firmly against his breadbasket.

Detecting the strong odor emanating from the jar, Jerry held it out in front of him like something distasteful. He issued an identifying pronouncement proceeded by an amplified whistle sound: *"Garlic."*

"Yeah, garlic paste," Milagros said. "We have to soak ourselves. Out here, our scent will carry who knows how far."

Without thought, Milagros unbuttoned the top buttons of her dress to the boys' mutual surprise. Part of her bra became visible at the center of her chest. She asked Jerry to pour out some of the jar's gruel into her cupped hands. He did so, and she rubbed her meal-covered hands over her arms and neck as if she were frothing up with soap during a shower. Milagros alternately stuck her hands in the jar and brought out some soggy garlic cloves and smeared her chest with them. "Lather up, Joshua. Show's over."

Joshua hesitantly stuck his hands into the jar and came out with a dripping mass of sodden cloves. Milagros rudely pushed his hands into his face. The soggy cloves fell in clumps from his forehead, along the sides of his cheeks and neck like cracked eggshells.

"Get inside your shirt and over your shoulders," instructed Milagros.

Joshua reluctantly obeyed, unbuttoning his shirt and rubbing his fingers inside his shirt. The rancorous odor of the liquid pierced his nostrils with apparent near-sickening effect.

Satisfied, Milagros reached for the jar lid.

"How about me?" Jerry asked, his hand covering the top of the jar.

"You're not a Hostile target."

Jerry jabbed his hand inside the jar. "You can't be too safe." He splashed his face a few times and smeared the back of his ears and neck with the pungent mix. "This stuff is nasty."

Milagros put the depleted jar back into the trunk and closed the hood.

The three walked side by side toward the stadium. "The window seat is all mine on the way back," stated Jerry, purposely separating a bit from the reeking couple. "So, this instruction we're here for, I hope it's got something to do with how to kill vampires—from a distance."

They reached the outside ticket plaza of the concrete structure, passing through a ticket booth station and chain link fence opening along the stadium's ground perimeter. Scaling a five-step walk-up, Jerry glimpsed movement behind one of the three-pronged, cement pylons supporting the slanted grandstand directly above them. He halted and signaled to his companions. Unlike him and Joshua, Milagros did not seem alarmed.

A boy, high-school aged, allowed himself to be seen. Milagros scrutinized him and lifted her hand, with two fingers standing out as in a 'victory sign.' The boy, who had shaggy hair and a pair of light-framed granny glasses riding down his nose, imitated the hand signal. His revealed fingernails were shaded a yellow color similar to Milagros' displayed nails.

Milagros bumped Joshua with her arm. "Give him the sign," she said, emphasizing the two-fingered demonstration of her hand, 'the docile half-vampire sign.'

Joshua lifted his hand above his waist and offered a two primary-finger greeting in the manner he had seen Milagros and the mysterious boy exchange.

The boy similarly acknowledged Joshua's signal. He adjusted the small-framed glasses on his nose, his eyes tarrying on Joshua's unaffected fingernails. The boy then turned suspiciously to the third party in their group.

"Hold up two fingers in one hand, Jerry," stated Milagros. She raised her hand chest-high, sticking out two fingers horizontally.

Jerry instead lifted his hand with two fingers pointing upward, hiding three bent digits to the boy. "Peace, brother," he said mildly.

Milagros yanked Jerry's wrist halfway down. "Like this," she said, repositioning his hand. "The two fingers have to be facing nails out and horizontal."

The boy promptly whistled twice in rapid shrills that sounded like warnings. From out of the shadows and behind another cement pylon, three more teenagers appeared in a perceptible show of solidarity with the shaggy-haired boy. One of them was a sandal-sporting girl dressed in a peasant blouse and bell-bottoms decorated with flower patches. A thin headband kept her long auburn hair mostly in check, and a slim, upturned nose pleasantly balanced her face. The four of them assumed a posture intent on obstructing any further progress by the visitors.

"That one's a Purebred," said the shaggy-haired one, gesturing at Jerry.

One in the group of four stepped forward. He was blond, with longish hair parted down the middle, wearing a bright orange-tie-dyed T-Shirt, and tinted, metal-framed prescription glasses. "Whose bright idea was it to bring *him*?" he inquired of Milagros and Joshua.

"Mine," said Milagros unflinchingly.

"And who are you?"

"Milagros. West Side High. Who are you?"

The blond-haired boy identified himself and his academic affiliation. "Peter. Coral Park High." He then slapped his thigh repugnantly. "This is the stupidity we have to deal with—*from our own kind*—hours from the most momentous night of our lives. A weak Purebred here. To put us all at risk."

The shaggy-haired boy and the other one nodded in loathsome agreement. The third boy's hair was not as long as Peter's, but it was grown out enough and sufficiently unsupervised to give him an unkempt look—especially when combined with the patchy facial hair germinating his face.

"His name is Jerry," said an undaunted Milagros, "and he's challenged the devil's daughter this very night."

Peter took an appraising regard of Jerry. "Is this true, Purebred?"

Jerry could feel the diminishing change in everyone's aggressive body posture.

He stuck out his chin. "Yeah, me and the devil's daughter, we threw down tonight."

Milagros moved closer to Peter. "Jerry's a friend—and he's vampire-tested. We all are. Are any of *you*?"

After a conceding shrug, Peter peered at Joshua. "What's your bag?"

"They told you he's one of us," said Milagros.

"Why haven't his nails turned?" asked the shaggy-haired boy.

"They will," replied Milagros.

The steadfast response seemingly broke down any remaining barriers as the others all came up and introduced themselves.

"I'm Antoinette," said the girl. "But everyone calls me Toni—except Peter. I go to AC High with him." She punctuated her final words with the same two-fingered salute-interchanged moments earlier by the shaggy-haired boy with the new arrivals. Her exposed fingernails were an identical shade of yellow as Milagros'.

Jerry knew what Toni meant by 'AC High.' He remembered reading that Coral Park High School had become the first high school in South Florida to have installed air-conditioning. Their students liked to boast about it, especially during encounters with other-area high schoolers.

"I'm Teddy," said the shaggy-haired boy, raising the two-finger greeting and bobbing his head at the new callers.

"Tommy," informed the scruffy-faced boy, flashing the same two-digit hand signal at everyone. "We're both from Palmetto Senior High."

Milagros, after offering a two-fingered acknowledgment back at Tommy, Toni, and Peter, took it upon herself to the complete the introductions. "I'm Milagros, in case you didn't hear, and he's Jerry, once again. And he's Joshua."

Jerry, in the spirit of things, presented his differentiating salute with an urban-inspired flair that seemed to win over everyone but Peter. Jerry presented and retracted two fingers to each individual as if they were playing *rock-paper-scissors* with him and he was perpetually bound to a sideways *scissors* sign.

Joshua then held up his two longest fingers, distinguishably self-conscious of his fingernail-color difference, causing suppressed giggles and forced throat-clearing from those in the greeting party.

"Let's go in," said Tommy with an uncertain glance at Joshua. "It's getting close to his arrival."

Jerry and Joshua swapped puzzled glances. Before either could ask Milagros, Peter blocked their path. "No weapons past this point."

"We're not carrying any," assured Milagros.

Joshua flipped over the palms of his hands in a gesture meant to exhibit his unarmed state. Jerry smirked and moved around Peter with Joshua.

Toni saddled up beside the pair. "You guys got close to a lady bloodsucker? What did she look like?"

"*Antoinette,*" said Peter testily. "Let them get inside. You and I will stay out here on watch a little longer."

Putting off her interest, Toni grudgingly peeled away from the boys. The symbolism came across clear to all. Toni and Peter were an item. Toni half-waved at everyone and skipped back to join her boyfriend near the pylon.

As they were about to pass through the nearby entrance into the stadium, Jerry tugged on Milagros' arm. "Who's arriving?" he asked.

Milagros faced Jerry and Joshua. "The shepherd is coming. *Our* shepherd."

*** 

The group navigated a curved ramp that brought them out to one end of the open-air stadium and exposure to stronger salt-whipped sea breezes. Lit halogen lamps hanging along the edge of the cantilever roof offered better clarity. Joshua saw long rows of seats crowded with dozens and dozens of teenagers in spaced-apart apparent factions, kids of all types and manner of dress, kids of both sexes. A high frequency buzz emitted all around from their idle chatter.

Joshua touched Milagros' forearm. "Are all these…?"

Milagros nodded. "Dociles. Like us."

"This is the central gathering place for our region of the country—from Key West to West Palm Beach," said Tommy. He seemed to speak for Joshua and Jerry's benefit after detecting their surprise.

"It's a regular half-vamp sit-in," stated Jerry.

At that point, someone called out specifically for one in their party. *"Milagros! Milagros!"* He came running up to her along the concrete lane in front of the first row of seats along the water's edge.

Milagros' face brightened when she saw him. She took a few hurried steps to happily meet him. "Lazarito, baby! What's up?" said a beaming Milagros with a quick but intensive hug.

"Hope I'm not too rancid," she remarked, fanning her arms.

"Looks like you got competition, Jay," Jerry said off to the side, for Joshua's ears only.

Joshua made a face at Jerry and then peered back at the reunited friends, in particular at Milagros' chummy pal. He was a head taller than Milagros, as tall as Joshua, or taller, which Joshua would not concede at that moment. His black hair was pushed up and back from his forehead in a loose but appealing way that suggested he preferred using his fingers more often than a comb to keep his thick locks raked in place.

His short sideburns were exceptionally neat and trim above the smooth skin contouring down along his jawline, indicating to Joshua that he shaved regularly—including today.

"This is Lazarito," Milagros introduced. "My best bud from Jackson High."

"Everyone calls me Laz," said the young man, lifting his hand to his chest with two fingers pointing to one side. "I'm the shepherd's son."

Tommy and Teddy presented their own two-fingered greeting to Laz. "We met outside, remember?" Teddy said.

Laz nodded. "The security detail."

Cued by a nodding gesture from Milagros, Joshua duplicated the lookout boys' greeting with Laz. "Who the heck is this shepherd anyway?" he asked brusquely.

Tommy and Teddy traded side glances and then cast their eyes at Joshua in a lightly piteous way. "We're heading over to see some other kids we know," said Teddy, breaking away.

Before moving off to follow Teddy, Tommy flashed the unifying two-finger sign of their brotherhood. "Keep the faith," he said with a more benevolent look at Joshua this time.

Joshua sensed Milagros' eyes on him; he stubbornly refused to acknowledge her.

Seemingly pleased by the knowledge that he was not alone, Jerry replicated the level-two-digit sign Laz had displayed.

"Jerry's my name. And I'm an earthling, too. Is it just the two of us here?"

Laz grinned. "Quite possibly."

Milagros released her light hold on Laz. "This is my friend Joshua. He's a Docile who's lived with Purebreds his whole life. This whole thing has kind of caught up with him all at once."

Laz smiled warmly. "My father is Lázaro Candela. He's leading this small army. He was like you and Milagros once. Now he's just like Jerry and me."

"We had an encounter with a mother vampire tonight," Milagros stiffly told Laz. "An ugly one. Joshua and Jerry were heroes."

In his own mind, Joshua could not fully accept the commendation and remained silent, but Jerry had no problem receiving the praise. "Oh, yeah, we and the serpent of Satan. We had it out," Jerry said with a projected boastfulness.

"Was there much bloodshed?" asked Laz with a raised level of interest.

"People died," said Joshua. The too-straightforward reply succeeded in making Laz—and Jerry—sound insensitive.

Some stirring cropped up behind them just then, picking up energy as it rippled through the crowd. A two-mast sailboat could be seen veering around the bend of the mangrove forest lying at the far side of the stadium's U-shaped basin. Even to Joshua's untrained eye, he deduced the symmetrical manmade cutout in front of him filled by the waters of Biscayne Bay.

"It's my pop," said Laz, moving away from everyone. "C'mon," he called back to the threesome. As he strode down the concrete lane, Laz lifted his hand, holding up two fingers to the young, anticipating crowd. He made sure to accentuate the initial gesture by leveling the fingers across his chest and keeping them in that position. He raised his other hand into a fist and began yelling, "Shepherd! Shepherd!"

The yell turned into a chant by the young audience and grew louder as the boat with bulging white sails neared the stadium. Many teenagers stood to further exert their rising enthusiasm.

Joshua, Milagros, and Jerry scurried along the walkway in front of the cheering throng to catch up with Laz. They plopped into the empty first-row seats Laz indicated for them. Laz remained standing with his fist pounding high in the air until the sailboat dropped its fore and aft sails and came up along the floating platform anchored about thirty feet from the front-row seats beyond the retaining wall railing.

Two crewmembers, men with white yachting jackets, secured the schooner to the floating platform mooring. A fog light illuminated the rectangular platform which Joshua determined, in its positioning, qualified as a cool stage for musical performances at the venue. From the schooner's below cabin emerged a figure which hushed the excited crowd. Guided over an extended ramp to the floating stage by his crew, the male figure sported a tan Nehru jacket with a yellow cravat.

The sight of the modish man-made Milagros gush. "Look at your dad," she said to Laz. *"Está en la moda."*

"Yeah, he's a regular Sammy Davis, Jr. now with his wardrobe," cracked Laz in return, broadening Milagros' smile.

Joshua, seated on the other side of Milagros, found nothing amusing in the overheard banter.

One of the jacketed men handed Lázaro Candela, Sr. a bullhorn. Lázaro held up two fingers from his free hand and then winched his arm to his waist with a nod at the anticipating crowd. The boys and girls all responded in unison with a cheer of approval; they crooked their arms at ninety degrees, returning the two-fingered aspiring salutation.

Lázaro raised the bullhorn to speak. "My children, my flock. The time has arrived. The hour approaches to meet your destinies. Your virtuous destinies. To hurdle past this malediction none of you asked to be born with…" Lázaro gladly paused to accept the cheers and roars his opening declarations had triggered. He then picked up again. "To hurdle past this malediction…as I did."

More enthusiastic cheering erupted before Lázaro could continue, "I stand here as proof of your imminent success. There are many, many more like me. And there will be many, many more that come after me and all of you. Ours is the true calling. We are on the side of good. I will lead you, my flock, down the path of righteousness."

The few in the crowd not standing rose to their feet and began chanting with the majority. Everyone's eyes sparkled with a powder-blue resonance. Energetically, they waved the two-fingered Purebred salute: "*Shepherd! Shepherd! Shepherd!*"

Visibly succumbing to the combination of the elements engulfing him—the muggy night, his suffocating attire, the bombarding heat from the boat's fog light and the turned-up passion from the audience—a dappling of sweat beads assailed Lázaro's forehead and soused his white-haired temples.

He pulled out a handkerchief to wipe his face and brow as he waited for the chanting to subside. Like an adroit speaker with a good sense of timing, Lázaro then delivered his closing statement which touched off the loudest cheers and wild feet stomping.

"Follow me—all who wish to survive the cobalt moon's fury!"

# Chapter Four

Alegría enjoyed the showerhead's soothing, hot streams of water massaging her neck and back. She had stripped off her tattered clothes as soon as she had arrived home and headed for the bathroom to wash away the smell of slimy seawater all over her. Eyes closed, she tried to push Cira out of her mind, tried to push away the unforgiving pain that encapsulated her and battled her for every breath. After a few moments, through half-opened eyelids and the steady cascade of water over her naked body, she touched the wound near her stomach; it was healing well, now with little trace of where the flare gun pellets had torn into her and the exterior damage caused.

Alegría replayed in her mind the partial disposal of the vehicles from the side street outside of Vizcaya's walled enclave and how she and Raúl had rolled them all down into the tall brush outside of the mansion's grounds. She knew all the vehicles—Pete Singer and Chris Fisher's later model cars, along with the newer pickup truck of Randall Landis, would be discovered eventually, but she hoped not right away.

Alegría emerged from the shower and wrapped a champagne-colored towel around herself. In front of a partially steamed vanity mirror which showed no hint of her reflection, she expertly combed her short hair with a side part much like a man's.

She walked into the hallway and began rummaging through boxes stacked along the wall. Alegría owned only two black dresses in her extensive wardrobe. She wanted to find them to wear, as she was in mourning. She had not packed the dresses in her one fleeing suitcase. She did not care for black very much. She preferred vibrant colors. But now she needed the dresses. They were in one of the boxes packed up by her mother.

Alegría opened the top box and ruffled through the compression of clothes, not finding what she desired. She opened a second cardboard container, the attire inside much more dated. There were clothes Alegría had not seen in ages, clothes she had worn when she first arrived in the United States from Cuba. She wondered why her mother had kept them. She kept digging. Removing a layer or two of blouses, she found an infant's gown stiffly spread out in its own plastic cover. It was instantly familiar to her—Raúl's white and blue trim christening gown. A subdued smile crept over Alegría's face as she held the garment up by the hanger. Her mother had sown an identifying nametag inside baby Raúl's gown.

Alegría admitted the rising memories through her mind, welcoming the temporary relief the unexpected imagery offered to her state of mental anguish.

\*\*\*

Alegría came along, pushing with purpose her stroller. She had been hurrying as quickly as she could without jostling her infant inside the carriage. She had seen Carmen and the young man kissing out in the open in front of everyone, including her nearby father! Her father was infinitely appalled, judging from the irritated look on his face and the wounded bark of his cry: *Carmencita!*

On the disrupting course she enacted, Alegría and her carriage reached Carmen and the young man just ahead of Carmen's father, Benigno. "Señor Sánchez," Alegría said loudly and pleasantly in front of the red-faced man who had broken away from a circle of men his own age, with whom he had been immersed in conversation. "How are you this fine day? May I present my son, Raulito?"

Alegría knew Benigno Sánchez was a man of dignity and civility. That civility, brought out by Alegría's interposed presence, spared his daughter a sure public scathing. He composed himself, so as not to ill-manneredly ignore the young mother. "*Buenos días*, Alegría," he answered, allowing himself a reproachful look at Carmen and her suitor.

Alegría ceremoniously pulled back the stroller's netting to reveal her child. Benigno removed his hat and bent his shoulders to peek inside the baby conveyance. He saw a peacefully sleeping babe, his thin eyelids not fully shuttering his hidden eyes. "A fine-looking infant," said Benigno. "How old is he?"

Alegría beamed. "He was born on February 27—so he is three months old today."

Carmen gladly accepted the shield that Alegría's presence offered. After a pause, she stiffly motioned to the person at her side. "Aly, this is Rodolfo," she said to Alegría…and then timidly to her father.

Removing his hat, Rodolfo smiled at Alegría. He next extended his hand to Benigno. "A great honor to make your acquaintance, sir," he said. Rodolfo did not seem at all embarrassed over the situation. He smiled more broadly than before, his mouth retaining a slick look and his lips a chafed quality from the kissing act he had just broken off.

The more Carmen's father inspected Rodolfo, the more disgust he showed. The striking cleft in Rodolfo's jutting chin Alegría interpreted as appearing to Benigno, in his angered state, like an ugly scar. Benigno exhaled harshly. "I will not shake the hand of someone who…" he hesitated as he focused on Carmen; her lips had the same shiny and chafed attributes as Rodolfo's. "…imposes himself in such a deplorable manner upon my daughter." The repelling words melted the smile from Rodolfo's face.

"*Ay, papi*," Carmen bemoaned.

Benigno's eyes grew cold. "Go and find your mother," he told Carmen sternly.

"I'll walk with you," Alegría said to Carmen, knowing she would not argue with her father's edict.

"And you," Benigno said, turning to Rodolfo, "you are not to come near my daughter again."

Rodolfo nodded at Carmen with a benevolent half smile and cordially at Alegría. His signaled departure evident, he calmly placed his hat on his head and confronted Benigno. "I will not be able to stay away from your daughter any more than I will not be able to take my next breath." Rodolfo inhaled deeply and walked away.

Left tongue-tied, Benigno shot a venomous look at Carmen, which snapped the suddenly moon-eyed girl back to her senses. She spun on her heels and briskly walked away.

"Hey, don't walk so fast," called out Alegría, which prodded Carmen to slow her pace.

"Thanks," Carmen said to her friend and then refocused her attention on the baby carriage. She lifted away the netting, peered inside, and rhapsodized with approval in all aspects of the infant's appearance.

Alegría dabbed her forehead and chin with a hanky. "I've been perspiring so much lately when I go outside. The sun, for some reason, has been murdering me."

Reaching into the carriage, she pulled out a garment, holding it lightly with the tips of her fingers. "Look at the gown my mother sewed for his christening."

Carmen's gloved fingers gently inspected the white gown with blue trim before Alegría folded it back into the carriage. "Oh, it's so adorable," she responded with over-the-top

70

sentimentality. "With its own name tag sewn inside. *Raulito.* The christening is next Sunday, right?"

Alegría carefully slid back the netting to cover the carriage bed. "Yes," she replied, pushing the stroller forward again with Carmen at her side. Her eyes glinted with intrigue and a mischievous smile crept over her face.

"Now, tell me all about Rodolfo…"

\*\*\*

Alegría's magnetized thoughts to the past lost their pull and she found herself back to the task at hand. Ruffling through another box, another garment garnered her attention. It was a bright yellow taffeta dress she had once proudly worn. She held it up, also raising with it a tide of pleasant, bygone memories…

\*\*\*

What Alegría wanted most in her current myopic teenage existence was to go to Tacajó, a not-too-far-away town which had elaborate music halls with weekend dances that attracted couples from far and wide. Antilla may have been a thriving corridor of commerce, but other than the movie theater and the annual *carnaval,* there was not much by way of fun entertainment in the town.

One Saturday evening, Alegría finally persuaded her boyfriend to take her to see the dance haven she had heard so much about from older Antilla residents. "Thank you for permitting me to go unchaperoned," Alegría said as her mother fussed over the daffodil-yellow dress she wore.

"Raúl likes you very much," Margot responded. "He has a good job down on the docks. I spotted him talking to Angel *el joyero* last week." Margot did not try to hide her coyness. "Not many boys his age have business with the town's jeweler."

Alegría stepped back from the wall mirror in her room. Her mother would not meet her intrigued eyes, and she did not push the matter. She had not been forthright with her mother about her intended plans for the evening, knowing Margot would not let her go out of town unescorted.

Once the *abuelas* in the park got wind of their unaccompanied date, however, Margot would be subject to official censure for permitting the outrageous occurrence.

But Alegría knew her mother would not care about that; Margot's name was already sullied as a divorcee. However, letting the impertinence of youth guide her, the teenager did not realize how much she was opening herself up to town's gossip until much later.

Raúl came to pick up Alegría right on time. He was spit-shined and polished from head to toe. Margot greeted him warmly at the door, nodding approvingly of his attire. "*Que elegante*," she said.

Alegría wedged into the doorway before her mother had the chance to ask Raúl inside. The anxious girl led Raúl away from the house an instant after she had dispersed a goodbye kiss and a hurried farewell to her mother. Looking back a final time from the sidewalk, Alegría thought she detected her mother's brow wrinkle with anxiety and an uneasiness deflate her entire body.

\*\*\*

From the time he was fifteen, Raúl Pérez, Sr. lived on the same street as Alegría. Soon after he turned twenty-one, earlier in the year, Raúl began working at Antilla's busy docks, unloading the cargo ships that came from abroad almost daily. He did so with the recent sole intention of buying an engagement ring and asking his four-years-younger girlfriend neighbor to marry him.

The retiring sun maintained the early evening warm with little breeze as Raúl and Alegría walked down their familiar street of familiar homes with familiar tin roofs.

"Thank you for tonight," Alegría said happily, briefly taking hold of Raúl's arm, cranking it like a lever. "Thank you for taking me dancing!" In a flurry, her hands patted her taffeta dress and fluttered the flouncy hem of its skirt.

"I'm glad you're happy," said Raúl as they halted at a street corner. A thin elderly man in a straw hat, driving a horse-drawn cart with sacks of flour and a crate of cackling chickens, passed in front of them. He barely gave them a glance.

Alegría played with the buttons of Raúl's jacket. She tucked his tie inside his lapels with a playful tap. "I feel like an adult woman on this adult date." The delighted girl wrapped herself around Raúl's arm as they crossed the street.

Through the reinforcing composition of her strapless brassiere, Raúl could feel Alegría's perky breasts pressing against his triceps. He crooked his elbow to nestle her marvelous, accommodating bosom deeper into his bent arm. As they walked, the refined fabric of his jacket and the smooth material along the neckline of her dress rubbed together in a sensual grating sound in his ear. Raúl's tie spilled out from behind the lapels of his jacket as he sensed an increase in his body temperature.

It was the anticipation of bawdy instances such as these that induced Raúl's almost nightly visits to Alegría's home. Even after a backbreaking ten or more hours on the docks, the young lion that roared in Raúl's loins when he thought of Alegría spurred on the regular callings without fail.

Raúl decided that the finest Tacajó dance palace would be where he would propose marriage to Alegría. After seeing the way her face lit up when she relayed stories told to her of the dance halls and their bands, he decided that it would be the perfect setting. Not this Saturday evening, of course, Raúl wanted to familiarize himself with the locale—not to mention complete the down payment on the ring he had picked out.

Raúl's mind had tuned out the spirited chatter coming from Alegría next to him. When he contemplated her, he saw not a girl but Mrs. Alegría Pérez. They turned a corner and came onto a hilly street that would lead them to *el parque*, more than halfway to the depot.

Raúl noted the funny way Alegría scrutinized him, realizing he had not heard her question. She repeated it, "What time is the bus to Tacajó?"

Before Raúl could answer, a steam whistle sounded off in the distance, twisting him around toward its point of origin—the docks. Two tugboat horns then sounded, and Raúl knew that a cargo ship was arriving. This ship was either late or early—either way, it had to be unloaded. Raúl calculated the hours it would take to unload in his head. Knowing the job would spill into Sunday, anyone who worked the unloading would receive bonus wages. He could use the money he earned from this ship for the payment release of Alegría's engagement ring.

Brimming with an inner excitement that presently spared no other feelings to his own self-committed plan for the betrothal of his girlfriend, Raúl unbuttoned and then removed his jacket, never taking his eyes off his intended date.

Alegría's face put the boatyard sounds and Raúl's shedding of his jacket together. She stood rigidly and speechless, her neck craning like a feathered bird's, gawking spellbound at Raúl.

"I can finish with double-time pay tomorrow morning on top of the time and half I'll start with tonight," said Raúl, holding Alegría's limp hand. Filled with an energizing confidence that told him he was acting on behalf of both of them, he continued, "We'll go next Saturday. I'll make it into something *real* special. I promise." Raúl peppered Alegría's hand with sputtering kisses.

"I love you, Alegría!" Raúl called back to her, running down the block. A car angrily beeped its horn, as it stopped short to avoid hitting the lunatic pedestrian attempting to usurp the right of way across the narrow cross street. "I love you!"

***

Too stunned to do anything else, Alegría continued to walk. After Raúl had left her sight, she walked a bit farther and entered the park at its far side entrance. She sat herself on the nearest bench, whiling away the time, her hands taking turns smoothing imagined wrinkles on her dress. Disregarding all passersby, she waited for some type of ire to rise from within, to fuel wrathful designs upon Raúl. But none were forthcoming.

There was just something too youthfully gallant about his unexpected desertion that she could not bring herself to condemn. Along with that, Raúl's departing words of lasting affection—even after being almost struck by a car—kept endearingly replaying in her mind.

Alegría rocked forward and stood up. Darkness had descended over the early evening. She decided to stop over Carmen's house. Maybe she would want to go to the movies.

Coming out of the park, she waited at the sidewalk for an oncoming car to pass. But the vehicle slowed to a halt on the street in front of her. It was a model-year white Buick Roadmaster convertible. The car was an eye-catcher; it had chrome piping along its exterior and red trim over its white wall tires.

The driver tooted the horn at Alegría to leave no doubt that he had stopped because of her. "*Adónde vas, preciosa?*" the driver asked, an arm casually leaning on the car's big, round steering wheel.

Alegría distinguished the accent immediately. The man was a Spaniard. He had dark hair and wore a dark suit.

A girl seated in the middle of the front seat waved. "Alegría, it's Rosa. *Hola.*"

Alegría relaxed at seeing the face of an acquaintance. She returned the girl's greeting. Rosa was two years older than Alegría. Margot and Alegría both did their nails with Rosa's mother, a fulltime homemaker and part-time manicurist. Rosa's mother had considerable conversational bragging rights lately over her daughter's courtship with one of the well-to-do Spaniards that had settled in town. Alegría reasoned he was the second gentleman in the front seat, his arm slung around Rosa. The picture of the young girl sandwiched between the two men appeared risqué even for Alegría's youthful sensibilities. As long as the man had money that benefitted the community, Alegría judgmentally supposed, the town's chaperone dictum could be overlooked.

"We are going to the dancing facilities out of town," said the driver to Alegría. "Would you like to join us?"

The driver took care in not making the invitation sound too brazen. He used the word 'us,' though it undeniably came across as 'me.' With his meaning audibly conveyed, he glanced over at Rosa for assistance.

"Have you ever been to the dance halls in Tacajó?" asked Rosa. "They are tremendous."

Alegría blinked with detectable interest at the words 'dance halls.'

"I can attest to that," said the man pressed beside Rosa. He grandly gesticulated one hand to indicate assurance. His hair was the color of wheat and long. Alegría was certain she had never seen a man with such real, grown out hair of such length.

Alegría felt all eyes on her, although only the men's eyes darted away from her face. They were both older men in comparison to Rosa and herself, the driver a few years the junior of the other.

Alegría's hesitation to decline gave the driver his interpreted opening. He held his hands apart. "Just try not to step on my feet during the Flamenco, *vale?*"

The sound of the foreign Spanish dance sparked a response from Alegría. "I'm a good dancer," she replied with slight umbrage.

The passenger door opened. "Well, you shall have your chance to prove it," said Rosa's apparent date.

Rosa followed him out of the car. "I'll be your chaperone," she said to Alegría lightheartedly before hopping in the backseat.

Rosa's date joined her in the back, and Alegría climbed in the car on the passenger side. "I can't come home too late," she said out loud for Rosa to hear, peeking over at the driver.

Rosa leaned forward. She fluttered a scarf with the tips of three fingers. "Take this for your hair. It's my spare. Oh, my manners are awful." She pointed to the driver. "Alegría, please meet Antonio Lorca de Vázquez." She then eased back in the seat, grabbing hold of her man's arm. "And this is my Eduardo."

"Eduardo Ricardo del Castillo," said the man in self-showy pronunciation.

Antonio leaned back, a hand on the steering wheel and a relaxed elbow jutting out from the car door. He stepped on the gas and the car motored ahead.

\*\*\*

Raúl interrupted his mother's reverie. "Ma," he said twice before he gained Alegría's notice. He crouched beside her, clothes changed and bathed. A new cotton patch dressing adorned his wrecked eye.

Alegría replaced the yellow dress in its box. "Did you take the aspirin?"

Raúl nodded. "Three."

"How's your head?"

"It hurts, but it's not killing me like before."

Alegría placed a loving hand to his cheek, her fingers gently gliding along the good side of his face.

"I'll put the suitcases we had packed in the car," said Raúl. "Yours, mine, and Momó's."

The one name's glaring omission unexpectedly caused them to hold each other's gazes in a desolate manner. Alegría turned away first, with a scratchy catch in her throat. "I want Momó to sew you a functional eye-patch."

They had purposely not turned on any lights in the house, except in the bathrooms. A glowing nightlight plugged into a nearby electrical socket on the wall provided the only other source of brightness. Sitting on her haunches, Alegría reached for the first box she had opened, forcing a smile as she lifted Raúl's clear-wrapped baby garment in her hand. "Look what I found, your christening gown."

Raúl snorted, his fingers touching the crinkled outer wrapping. "It looks like a dress."

"You slept through the whole thing," said Alegría, digging under the yellow dress through to the bottom of the second box. "Even when they poured that water on your head."

Alegría's face then grew sullen. She saw a garment similar to Raúl's at the bottom of the box, also wrapped in clear plastic with a label that was not required for Alegría to recognize it as Cira's hand-sewn christening gown. She pulled the small one-piece garment out slowly with one hand. Her unblinking eyes filled with tears as she scanned every inch of the cotton fabric.

Raúl placed his arm around his mother. Reaching out, he urged her to lower the baby dress back into the box. He then put his own nostalgic piece of clothing over it and covered both with the clothes Alegría had removed. He closed the cardboard box in a quarter-folded style and firmly pushed it aside.

Tugging on the towel wrapped around her, Alegría then said absently, "Those dresses have to be in one of these boxes."

Raúl squeezed his mother's bare shoulder. "I'll help you look for them, Ma."

***

Alegría found her two black dresses, one on top of the other in another packed box. She pulled them both out and, with a satisfactory nod, chose to wear the mod black mini dress with a white-color block.

Now exiting the home, Raúl's keychain jangled as he started to lock the front door. "Don't bother," said Alegría prior to walking off the front porch and out into the street. The message was clear. They were never coming back.

The street was dark, quiet, and completely devoid of any pedestrian or vehicular traffic like most middle-of-the-night residential streets. Alegría briskly walked over to the closest streetlight pole, her high heels clacking on the asphalt pavement. The night sounds of crickets' chirping immediately stopped, as did the hooting calls of a distant owl.

She leaped upward and landed in a sitting position on the arm of the light pole, her feet dangling off the side of the lighting overhang. The pole's extension was corrosively splotched with dried bird droppings that concerned Alegría enough into thinking the bottom of her dress would be permanently tarnished.

Raúl peered up through the spotlight of the incandescent streetlamp at his mother's swinging, stockinged legs. Then his lone eye's pupil expanded and the whites percolated with its abnormal cobalt-blue color, and he leaped upward. His impetus did not take him as far as he desired, but he managed to latch onto the lighting overhang with both of his arms. As a rising panic appeared to strike him, Alegría reached down and easily pulled her son up next to her. "Grab hold of me to keep steady," she instructed.

Raúl curled his arm around Alegría's waist and waited for his mother to speak.

"See if you can pick up a Docile scent."

Angling in three different directions, Raúl deeply inhaled the warm night air. Briefly meeting Alegría's eyes, he shook his head.

"They're out there somewhere. And so is Joshua."

"You can't pick up anything?" asked Raúl.

"No. This close to the cobalt moon, a vampire's sense of smell starts fading, until it's not much better than a Purebred's. One of the supernatural checks and balances of the Equilibrium. My eyesight is going to degrade too, back to 20/20. But y*our* senses will gradually heighten through tomorrow night." Alegría then stuck out her arm, palm-up, and ran the rigid tips of her long-nailed fingers across her forearm. The pointy nails acted like tiny knives and broke Alegría's skin. Blood dribbled out, falling from her arm and plopping down on the sidewalk like heavy raindrops that arrive in advance of an imminent downpour.

"What gives, Ma?" asked a perplexed Raúl.

"I'm trying to see if I can get a leg up on things," Alegría replied as the carmine-colored droplets continued staining the sidewalk below.

Alegría let her arm bleed for a good fifteen minutes, sitting on top of the streetlight with Raúl. Several times she had to reopen the wound as her skin miraculously mended itself during the process. Finally, she decided to come down. She grabbed hold of Raúl and descended to the pavement, avoiding the large puddle of blood running off the sidewalk. She handed Raúl the handkerchief she had borrowed to wipe clean her arm.

"Maybe it was too much of a long shot," she said with a tinge of disappointment as she brushed off her fanny. "Damn bird shit. Make sure it's all off."

Raúl examined his mother's *derrière*, finding fault with some portions of the dirty fabric covering it. With Alegría tilting forward at the waist, Raúl's rigid hand bounced off his mother's hard cheeks in a repetitive slapping exercise that resembled—and sounded like—spanking, until the whitish residue fell completely away.

Pacified, Alegría headed for Raúl's car, her high heels click-clacking noisily with each strident step. Suddenly, she stopped and motioned Raúl to also be still. Alegría's head wheeled in cranked angles, trying to determine the direction of the sound she heard.

Stepping in and then out from under the shine of a streetlamp at the end of the street, a youthful figure made his presence known. From that distance, it appeared to be two blue pinpoints glowing from his shadowy face. The figure surged forward toward Alegría. Raúl intercepted him without much difficulty in front of his mother. He was a young man, Raúl's age, of similar height but with a slighter build.

Alegría placed a placating hand on her son's shoulder and Raúl released the constraining grip he had imposed on the teenager. The distinct blue color faded from his eyes.

The teenager appraised Alegría with restrained regard. He smoothed his silver button-down shirt, slid the heels of his palms against his temples, and cupped his hands over the high-crested ridges of his hair, all in a composing manner. "Mistress," said the pompadour boy, "my name is Lane."

Lane then faced Raúl, trying not to stare at the bandage over his eye. He pointed two prominent fingers downward, revealing a yellowed tincture on each nail, which prompted Raúl to silently question his mother.

"Sorry, darling. With all that's happened, I haven't had a chance yet—" Alegría cut herself off to better explain. "Lane is offering you the Hostile half-vampire greeting. Two fingers of the hand, pointing down in a *V*. Offer it back to him."

Raúl obeyed. He studied Lane, not altogether hiding the poor assessment he formed of him, based on his too-tight corduroys, too-shiny shirt, and too-high hair. The next words out of Lane's mouth made Raúl like him even less.

"My mother is not as young—or as pretty as you, mistress." Alegría's lips pursed in a pleased but cautious manner.

"Yeah, neither is mine," said a female voice from the shadows. Making her presence known among the trio was a dyed blond with stringy hair in a jacquard-check skater dress. Her large, round choker beads jangled around her neck as she came to a bouncy halt, wiggling two fingers downward. "I'm Miranda."

Raúl introduced himself to the pair after returning Miranda's yellow-nailed digital greeting.

Raúl caught Lane's eyes wandering over Alegría's body when he asked him, "And where is your mother now?" A furrowed brow and cock of the head by Raúl questioned Lane over his strayed focus.

Lane straightened and coughed into his hand, his cheeks flushing. "My mother is traveling out of the country with my father on his private yacht."

"His dad also has a private plane," volunteered Miranda. "My old lady is in San Francisco, in case you're wondering. She went to check out the Haight-Ashbury scene a few weeks ago."

"Have you scouts picked up any Docile scents?" asked Alegría.

"Is that what we are, Lane? Scouts?" asked an amused Miranda.

Lane gazed directly into Alegría's eyes. "Mistress, we hit the mother lode."

Alegría's eyebrow arched with interest. "What are you driving, Lane?"

"My father's jag. It's around the corner."

"Raúl, darling, I'm going with Lane. You two follow us." Alegría hooked onto Lane's bicep and began leading him down the street. "Now, what exactly do you mean by mother lode?"

Raúl watched his mother walking away arm-in-arm with Lane, fighting the twinge of jealousy circulating through him. He resigned himself to the fact that his mother knew what she was doing. Miranda then skipped up beside him.

"What happened to your eye?"

\*\*\*

A few minutes since the withdrawal of the shepherd back to his vessel, the stadium remained abuzz from the man's short but exhilarating speech, many spectators remaining on their feet. Sitting next to Milagros, Joshua took a breath and said, "Sorry I was obnoxious with your friend."

Milagros half turned to survey Joshua. Everything about him—the wide eyes, the passive posture, and the genuine regret—conveyed a helpless sincerity that made Milagros want to jump on top of him and hug him with all her might. Just as she thought she would not be able to control her bubbly feeling, Laz tapped her on the shoulder. "Let's go see my pop."

Laz led the gang along the lane of the retaining wall, closer to where the shepherd's vessel was stationed. There was a gathering of kids ahead, waving and trying to win the attention of the sailboat. Someone identified Laz as the 'shepherd's son' and the gathered crowd peeled back in deference to him and his trailing friends. The boat raised anchor and its motors started up. The half circle around the quartet collapsed as more teenagers surged forward at the sound of the boat's intentions.

The craft made a slow, sharp turn and pulled alongside the barrier wall, in between mooring pilings. In their excitement, a few followers fell, or were accidentally pushed, into the water near the turning boat. The boat idled to a stop, at a gate section of the two-and-a-half foot retaining wall railing that unhinged and swung open. One of the yacht's white-jacketed crewmen assisted the foursome—under quick fire instructions from Laz— aboard the boat. The crewman refused access to any other of the shrieking, pleading youths jostling around the plank way.

Once aboard, Laz gestured at everyone to keep stepping behind him and walked them into the main cabin below as the boat eased away from the pickup area. With familiarity, Laz opened the cabin door. Seated at a round, wooden table, having removed his Nehru jacket and cravat, the shepherd was busily fixing himself something to drink. He glanced up momentarily at the youths but was too involved with his own activity to stop and offer a greeting. A long neck bottle of *malta*, or wheat soda, a can of condensed milk and a tall soda fountain glass were evenly lined up in front of him.

Lázaro Candela, a/k/a the shepherd, popped the bottle's lid with a can opener and attentively poured the dark malt into the glass he held tilted, as one would with any carbonated beverage to avoid accumulating a foamy head. He then flipped the double-sided can opener in his hand and punched three triangular holes into the top of the can. He leaned the punctured can over the glass, extricating a thick, creamy pour from the multiple openings. The shepherd let the sweet milk accumulate a three-inch foundation at the bottom of the glass before he stopped the displacing flow into the dark liquid. He rimmed the excess milk from the lip of the can with his thumb, running it satisfyingly along the tip of his tongue. He took hold of a long spoon and began to stir the drink briskly until it transformed into a frothy, caramel-colored blend.

Heartily, he blew away the top of the foamy head that had formed from the stirring, a backlash of spume landing on the tip of his nose. He buried his sudsy nose into the large glass and began greedily downing the contents. He drank the entire milkshake-like drink in continuous gulps. He drained every last drop and ceremoniously put the glass down on the table, unable, or unwilling, to suppress a very pleasurable "aahh" sound from his frothy, mustache-framed mouth.

The shepherd reached for a napkin to wipe his upper lip and mouth as Laz and Milagros walked over to him. He stood and offered Laz a warm hug but placed both hands on Milagros' shoulders, apparently put off from the emanating effects of the garlic bath she had taken. "*Milagritos*," he said enthusiastically. "*Qué tal?*"

"Still liking that *malta* and *leche condensada*, I see, Señor Candela," Milagros said playfully.

"Oh, you know me. I can't resist," answered the shepherd. "And it's *so* calorie-rich," he added in a defeatist tone, summing up his disclosed guilty pleasure.

"Tell me about it. I feel two pounds heavier after watching you drink it."

The shepherd let out a large guffaw that caught even him by surprise. "Oh, Milagros. You and your wonderful sense of humor. It is good to see you again. And who are your friends?"

Milagros introduced Joshua and Jerry, and after a pause, Laz said, "They all engaged a she-devil a few hours ago."

The shepherd evaluated everyone with renewed interest. "This close to the cobalt moon?" He picked up a hand cloth and wiped the table area dampened by dissolved foam. He folded the cloth in his hands. "It is written in the ancient parchments that all lords and mistresses of the underworld must make themselves scarce by yesterday's eve."

"Well, we know someone who didn't get sent the scroll," said Jerry.

Joshua nudged Milagros. "You mean to tell me the fathers of all those kids out there are going to turn their backs on them? When the kids most need them?"

Milagros answered Joshua dispassionately, "The fathers of all those kids are ashamed of them. Think about it. Do you think we are some source of pride to our fathers? We are all nothing but a genetically weak litter of a super race of beings."

"A super race of *evil* beings," articulated the shepherd. "Evil beings with evil offspring that we will not permit to conquer us." The shepherd reached for his Nehru jacket hanging on the back of a chair and put it on. "All is ready for the migration to begin in a few hours. I must inform my flock. We leave from here at 9:00 a.m. sharp."

Milagros and Joshua gave each other simultaneous looks of doubt which did not bypass the shepherd.

"What's the matter?" he asked, holding his unwound neckerchief. "Do you have something better to do in the morning?"

# Chapter Five

Lane manned the wheel of the cherry-red, model-year Jaguar E-Type coupe as it cruised along Biscayne Blvd, passing through a stretch of one and two-story boxy motels. He never felt his male pride as inflated as it was with Alegría sitting in the passenger seat next to him. Through his side window, he saw a neon-light sign reading, VAGABOND MOTEL, and flashing with availability of rooms. Rivaling neon signs with kitschy motel names that were supposed to charm vacationing tourists in their motoring station wagons periodically beckoned on either side of the street.

The comfort-forging black leather interior seating of the luxury car clearly agreed with Alegría; she had modified the bucket seat to where she could stretch out her feet and adjusted the air-conditioning vents to her direct benefit. One arm lay casually over the armrest attached to the five-speed gearshift console in between herself and her young driver. "Lane, describe to me again your encounter with the Dociles tonight."

There was enough consistent light from the bright main street for Lane to share in the steady, delineating image of Alegría's relaxed form. Every time Lane shifted gears, he fabricated a look down at the gearshift in order to sneak a peek at Alegría's stockinged legs, which were disinterestedly parted in front of her in a way that flared craving hormonal sensors below his belt.

Lane breathed in deeply, enjoying the swirl of pleasurable sensations Alegría's perfume directed to his brain. He began, "The three of us were feeling antsy and we went out, not expecting to get into *too* much trouble. Marvis—I told you about him—he goes to Coral Gables High with me and Miranda. He first smelled the two of them from out the window where you're sitting."

Lane scanned his passenger; she seemed deep in thought, listening attentively. His eyes skirted over her susceptible-appearing body. Her hand lay listlessly in her lap, her fingers extending past the short-end fabric of her dress, lightly caressing the inside of her thigh. Lane's foot accelerated on the gas pedal but pulled back as soon as he returned his sight to the road.

"We followed the scent. I picked it up too, and so did Miranda, who was sitting in the backseat there. After we found them, we tormented them for a good while until I decided to let them go. Even the darkie Purebred who was with them. He came at me with a fancy, shiny crucifix, but I taught him a lesson."

Alegría spoke without betraying her calm demeanor. "The girl...she had dark, curly hair? And the other boy, dark hair and a dimpled chin?"

"Yeah. The girl was stupid enough to challenge me with a knife. I disarmed her in no time. The other one smelled a little off, but he didn't try anything after he saw how I handled the girl. It was all fun and games, messing with them after that."

"But you didn't harm them?"

"No. But with *the calling* boiling over all three of us, it was hard to resist. I had to put my foot down with Marvis and Miranda. Point out to them that the pups were no good to us until tonight."

Alegría's hand slid up and around her abdomen as if she were trying to settle an upset stomach. She dragged one foot back and began absently waggling her knee, widening the hidden space between her shapely legs. Lane immediately noticed. With every rhythmic, wagging motion of her knee, the hem of Alegría's skirt alternately pulled tight across her legs and then slackened into a V-shaped depression between her inner thighs.

"I got the idea to follow them when I saw them pull off in their car," said Lane, struggling to keep his eyes on the road.

\*\*\*

"Wouldn't it be a gas if we followed them, I said." Miranda bobbed her head as if it were a requirement to expel her words. "Lane smiled and Marvis said, 'Real *gassy*'—and we all laughed. Marvis is like that. And the next thing I know, we are tailing them across the causeway to Virginia Key."

Seated in Raúl's Corvair, traveling right behind Lane's father's Jaguar on Biscayne Boulevard, Miranda tugged on the large, round choker beads around her neck as she continued. "There wasn't a lot of traffic, so we could stay back and still see where they headed. We stayed out on the exit road after we saw them pull into the stadium parking lot. That's when we all breathed in your mom's blood aroma. Lane made Marvis stay with the Dociles, and we came back to town and found you guys. I for one was glad to be rid of Marvis. He never let me ride in the front seat. It is mighty cramped in the backseat of Lane's Jag."

"Me and Lane, we're not going together, in case you're wondering," Miranda said in a conversation deviation that seemed natural to her speech patterns. "Oh, and that kid Marvis I've been talking about, him neither. We're all just friends from the same high school. You don't talk much, huh? I guess you'd be what they call the strong, silent type. Lane calls me a flap jaw."

Miranda trailed off briefly. "Why are they pulling over?" she inquired as Raúl veered off the road behind the Jaguar. "Why is *she* talking to them?"

Raúl recognized this part of Biscayne Boulevard where the motels became more spendthrift and their lighting much more subdued. Raúl observed the girl with a short skirt and tight blouse Miranda had pointed out, speaking into the open passenger window. Then, taking a vigilant glance around her, she climbed into the expensive European import.

Raúl assessed Miranda and informed, "My mother must be hungry."

*** 

In the backseat, the lady of the evening neatly folded the bills Alegría had given her inside of her blouse. "Park closer to the shop, honey," she said. "The room is included in what you gave me."

Lane had pulled to a stop away from the mostly empty parking spaces in front of the cheap-looking motel building and out of range of the single bulb lighting fixtures attached to the walls outside. Ignoring her, Lane put the car into park.

"Didn't you hear me?" asked the woman, listing to the side over her drawn-up knees in the cramped backseat. "In front. Over there."

Alegría turned around in a manner that urged the streetwalker to tone down the authoritativeness in her voice. "Evie, that was your name?" she asked. "Evie, my nephew and I would like to remain in the car with you. I would appreciate it if you humored us."

Evie shrugged, her agitation subsiding. "Lucky for you, I'm a pretty limber person." She leaned back and reclined as best as she could. "Jeez, I'll bet the Apollo astronauts have more room than this. A girl could get, you know, claustrophobic back here."

"No, you come up in front," said Alegría.

Raúl's car passed alongside of them and pulled into one of the empty parking spaces in front of the motel. Lane glanced at Alegría, making sure that she had also seen him.

Evie twisted her body around to swing a long leg with a high-heeled shoe over the front seat. "Okay. But don't blame me if the horn starts a honkin' by accident."

Alegría grabbed Evie's arm. "Not him," she said.

Evie stopped and absorbed the implied request. "It's not going to be much of a show in the dark, honey," she said with a glimpse toward Lane as she reversed her position and sat on Alegría's lap. With her skirt hiked up practically around her waist and her face a few inches from her customer, Evie said, "I suppose you'll want me to start?"

Alegría raised her middle finger. "No, I will." After a few disarming light scratches over Evie's collar and neck, she passively inserted her sharp-nailed finger into the working girl's ear. Twisting her finger, blood squirted out from Evie's ear and she screamed. Alegría clamped onto Evie's head, keeping her finger boring through her ear canal, inciting her to pass out from the intense pain.

Eventually, Alegría withdrew her intrusively fatal digit. The deepness of its insertion produced a suction sound as the finger emerged from the ear passageway slick with blood and pink membrane tissue clinging to the nail. Salivating with expectation, Alegría pushed her victim against the dashboard. "There's nothing like a fresh kill," she said to Lane. "The blood's warm and still rich with oxygen. Now go and tell my son to get his trunk ready."

Completely enraptured by the proceedings he had witnessed—from the sight of one woman climbing on the lap of another to the easily disabling act of violence perpetrated by Alegría—Lane responded lethargically to the order until a baleful stare from his mistress spurred him to fling open his door.

Lane hopped out of the car but could not avoid a withdrawing glance into the revealed interior. Lane saw Alegría rip open the insentient Evie's blouse, popping buttons that ricocheted wildly off the vehicle's featured templates. He watched her take back the bills Evie had tucked into her brassiere and pluck a key ring from the same hiding place. When Alegría buried her face between Evie's ample breasts, Lane drew in two quick breaths. As Alegría's fangs penetrated Evie's prominent chest, Lane experienced a heightened sensation over his entire body.

Not moving her feeding face from her pickup's cleavage, Alegría, with one arm cradled around Evie's waist, pointed with the other, demanding Lane's complete withdrawal—now. Lane shut the car door, expelling a deep breath. The warm night air did not help his overheated state, evidenced most strikingly by the bulge he noticed in his crotch.

***

Alegría gorged on Evie, unbothered by her lack of self-control, psychologically driven by her depressed state.

When she had finished, she opened the passenger door and Evie half fell out, arms hanging down from a topless torso, her hair falling over the back of her head, showing the black roots of her dye job. Raúl grabbed hold of the dead woman and quickly carried her over to his car, dropping her in the open trunk, with Lane slamming shut the hood.

As he did so, a door in the motel building opened and a bright-shirted man with a short-skirted woman came out. The man's shirt was arbitrarily buttoned, revealing a tank top undershirt. He wore a Panama hat, and he discarded the remains of a cigarette butt as he waited for the woman to lock the door.

He did no more than glance at Raúl and Lane, who were transferring the suitcases pulled out from the trunk to the backseat. The man offered an impersonal goodbye to the woman as he climbed into his car parked near the door from which he had emerged. The car hurriedly reversed out of the parking space and left the motel's parking lot.

Showing her business sense, among other attributes, the short-skirted woman sauntered toward Raúl and Lane. Raúl hid his hands stained with Evie's blood behind his back.

About fifty feet away, watching from inside the Jaguar, Alegría's eyes gleamed their murderous black and gold color, ready to spring into action upon the first prying sign of trouble.

About to begin a negotiation, the working girl became startled by Miranda, sticking her head out of the Corvair. "It's getting awfully lonely in here, boys," she said.

After a quick further appraisal of the situation, the short-skirted woman visibly decided that her company would not be desired if offered. She walked away from the youngsters, in a path through the parking lot, cutting back to the boulevard.

As soon as the short-skirted woman was out of range, Alegría whisked right over, the lower half of her back-to-human face smeared with blood, as was most of her neck. She pulled out the key ring she had taken from Evie's bra. "Little miss," she said to Miranda, "would you care to freshen up?"

Miranda, who did not use much makeup, jumped at being asked. "Certainly, mistress."

Alegría walked up to the numbered room etched on the key ring. "You can dump the body into the bay from the foot of the causeway," she said, turning back to Raúl.

"We're heading to Virginia Key as soon as I put my face back on. In case you don't know, we have a lead on Joshua."

\*\*\*

Toni, her hair badly rumpled, had been the first to spot him as she came up for air behind one of the rectangular concession cutouts on the second floor. Revealing himself from under the counter, Peter then raised up beside her, holding her slim headband in two fingers, which Toni immediately snatched back.

Peter snuggled close to Toni, his face pecking at her bare neck, indicating he had only reluctantly accepted the break in their make-out session. Toni initiated a mild protest but then more urgently poked Peter's shoulder, causing him to curb his amorous display. Pulling out his glasses, he swiped the front of the lenses against his tie-dyed shirt and put them on. The leather-vested boy came into sharpened view, walking conspicuously through the parking lot, his hands shoved too innocently in his front pockets. The moon and stars provided no cover for him. The sporadic cheering and applause from inside the marine stadium drowned out the visitor's quickening footsteps.

Peter and Toni watched in silence as the leather-vested boy reached the multi-step walk-up of the stadium. They heard the roar of the teenage crowd reverberate through the concrete structure again. Intensely scratching both of his shoulders with crossed arms, the whites of the trespassing boy's eyes flashed a cobalt-blue color as the rising chant of '*Shepherd! Shepherd! Shepherd!*' filled their ears. Peter and Toni matched shock demeanors. They lost sight of him as he crossed into the pavilion directly below. But soon, he appeared on the second-floor walkway, bounding over the railing, his eyes quickly reverting to normal.

Peter and Toni popped up from behind the counter as he wandered in front of their concession. "Got a ticket?" asked Peter.

With eyes locked on the startled leather-vested boy, Peter slowly brought out his hand and extended two fingers...downward. The boy relaxed.

"I heard some Hostiles get the scratchies before the big night," said Toni, adjusting her headband while holding apart two fingers in an upside-down *V*.

\*\*\*

Everyone in the audience was so enthralled by the man with the bullhorn that no one seemed to be aware of the three misfits. From one end of the stadium, they climbed unnoticed up to the top row of seats and scampered onto the catwalk suspended over the grandstand, leading to the announcer's booth connected to a fold in the cantilever roof.

As the enthralled audience chanted another loud chorus of '*Shepherd! Shepherd! Shepherd*,' Peter, Toni, and Marvis surveyed the scene from the window openings of the announcer's booth.

Peter reached into his pants' pocket and pulled out a small dark blue jar. He twisted off the cap and handed the jar to Marvis. "Stick a couple of gobs in your nose. It'll neutralize the smell of the garlic on us and in the air."

Marvis accepted the jar without too much thought and scooped out with one finger a generous dab of the jar's whipped ointment. He stuck the anointed finger into one nostril and repeated the application to the other. He sniffed hard with each application of the mentholated rub and then gave the jar back to Peter with a subdued nod of gratitude.

When the mania below had subsided with the retreat of the bullhorn speaker, the three squatted down and concealed from the crowd. Some commotion a short time later aroused the trio. Peeking out from their perch again, they witnessed the boat maneuvering to the edge of the stadium's retaining wall. A collapsing ring of excited followers jockeyed alongside the craft, waving and yelling with a mixture of admiration and self-promotion.

"What's all the hullabaloo now?" asked Peter.

"Oh, look," observed an amused Toni as two teenagers jumped or fell into the water. "I hope they don't get hit by the boat."

"I know those three." Marvis pointed downward. "The girl and the two behind her."

"Yeah?" asked Peter with budding interest as he scoped in on Milagros, Joshua, and Jerry. "So do we."

"There's a mistress around—according to them," said Toni.

"There is," asserted Marvis with a willingness to disclose more information, which he did. "We all smelled her blood. The other Hostiles who were with me tonight. A guy and a girl. They went to try and find her. I volunteered to stay with the two Dociles. My friends will be back for me."

"Just remember the Docile greeting," Peter said to Marvis. "Two upward fingers."

"Like the peace sign," chimed in Toni with a broader visual demonstration than Peter's.

Surveying the congregation below, a devious smile invaded Peter's face as he spoke what he construed as an amusing play on words.

"By tomorrow, they'll all be in *pieces*."

\*\*\*

Satiated with blood, Alegría fell asleep on the ride to Virginia Key. Her taxed mind careened, in those few minutes of rest, from place to place and time period to time period until it settled back into the first ritzy vehicle, she had ever ridden on…

\*\*\*

"… I would never have stood you up like your date did this evening," said Antonio to Alegría, helping her out of his white Buick Roadmaster.

Alegría feigned ignorance. "What do you mean?"

"Oh, come on now," rebutted Antonio. "The way you are dressed." Alegría could hear the music coming from the lot of the square-block building with a wooden façade into which Antonio had parked his car. Taking in every detail surrounding her, the building had no side windows facing the parking lot but had double delivery doors that opened from the inside. Two solitary lampposts at the back of the lot provided the only light. A parking attendant assisted with the positioning of the vehicles. Adjacent to the lot, a two-story brick building with off-colored lights, dimmed behind several shade-drawn windows, hinted at the activity inside.

Avoiding a small pothole in the asphalt as they walked, Antonio extended a crooked arm in which Alegría lightly placed her hand. Eduardo and Rosa marched behind them in a much more familiar step.

"This is the biggest and best dance palace in town," Antonio divulged.

Circular canopies adorned the multiple windows of the front of the dancehall. A faded-red gable canopy covered the area leading to the front door. The sign on a post with replaceable lettering read: *Hoy y Manaña Se Presenta Dámaso Pérez Prado y Su Orquesta*. It was the last thing Alegría read before she was ushered through the greeting doors and into the sweeping wash of orchestra rhythms inside.

The two Spaniards reconciled the cover-charge fee with a man holding a fist full of bills at the door and checked in their hats in a booth across from the entrance. While the girls waited, Rosa smiled at Alegría, moving her shoulders to the distinctly Cuban beat of the music playing. Fold-up chairs lined the walls of the establishment but few were occupied. Movable alcohol stands situated along each of the three walls, patronized by mostly men who were purchasing drinks in pairs, did brisk business.

"This must be a new band. I never heard of them," said Rosa in a loud-enough voice to be heard over the music. "Last week they had a band from Spain—or at least they said they were. They played Spanish songs with real castañets. We danced Flamenco and drank sangria."

Alegría scoped out the orchestra. It carried a partisan arrangement of saxophone and trumpet musicians along with conga players in front. A man of small build with dark hair above a prominent forehead and a small black mustache, including a growth of hair beneath his lower lip, stood out as the obvious conductor. He wore a light gray three-piece tailcoat suit and white bowtie. Alegría appraised the man's skin tone as the exact color of the café con leche she drank every morning.

The orchestra number ended to polite applause, and the conductor motioned for the commencement of another. Instantly, brass arrangements let loose and the band leader let out a tempo cry of what sounded like a grunt, cueing rhythmic percussions that filled the wide dance floor with invading couples from all directions. The two girls fell eagerly in line with their pulling dates.

"Vale, now you can show me how good a dancer you are," said Antonio to Alegría in a voice trying to rise above the instrumentals.

Alegría took on the challenge and in no time was flaunting her wares to the stimulating beats of music that she had never heard before, but that suddenly made her feel wonderfully invigorated.

Antonio was light on his feet, and he held his own as he and Alegría sashayed to the syncopated rhythms governing their fluid arm and leg motions.

"How old are you?" asked Antonio.

Alegría recalled something her mother had told her and she relayed it in between a well-executed shuffle step. "Few women admit their age…"

"And few men act theirs," interposed Antonio. "Yes, I know that one. Believe me, I have the acting wisdom of the ages—I mean of age."

Alegría did not know what to make of the stealthy smile that crept over Antonio's face. But it quickly faded, and he guided her back to the marvelously danceable pulses of music flowing through her body. "What's the name of this music? It's so lively."

"It's something new—it's called *Mambo*."

A flurry of horns finished the song and left Alegría and Antonio very close to each other. Being so close, Antonio easily enveloped his dance partner in his arms and boldly kissed her. Alegría fought—but not as hard as she could—to break the impassioned embrace. When Antonio finally released her, Alegría stared at Antonio with suppressed anger and a heaving chest that was not entirely the result of her dancing. Alegría's chest rose with another deep breath.

But it quickly deflated with the awareness that she had been awakened by Lane nudging her shoulder.

"We're coming up to the stadium, mistress."

\*\*\*

"It's totally out of the question," said the shepherd. "I can see no worthwhile outcome in returning to that escaped place of terror you described."

"What about saving someone's life?" Joshua strongly posed. "Isn't that worthwhile?"

The shepherd deliberated, scrutinizing the faces of everyone seated around the table with him. "Your concern for your friend is commendable, but what about the risks, not only for yourself but for Milagros and Jerry?"

"In the morning, the risks are minimal," Joshua responded.

"In the morning, the buses arrive—for all of us," the shepherd said with an increased firmness. "You just heard me finish telling everyone out there about that."

The shepherd rose from his chair. He was wearing his Nehru jacket but had untied his cravat, fresh from his second appearance in front of his followers. He crossed his arms and walked over to the porthole in the cabin and peered out. The narrow opening offered him a snapshot of the now-subdued scene outside.

The stadium crowd appeared appreciably reduced from its former size. Some of his supporters had come prepared with their own sleeping bags or rolled-up mats and had laid them out in between the rows of flipped-up seats. Despite the late hour, few, if any, had yet been struck by the desire to sleep, continuing to outwardly unwind from the previous wild excitement. Some, he supposed, had gone back to their cars to relax and grab their shut eye before the morning. An enterprising few had staked a claim on the floating stage to camp out on for the reminder of the night.

The shepherd turned back to his one reluctant follower. "We cannot wait for you," he said dispassionately to Joshua.

Joshua answered similarly. "No one's asking you to."

Milagros spoke, "Where are we going, Señor Candela?"

"I cannot tell you, my dear. Only that it is a safe place where the cobalt moon will rise and set over us without harm."

Jerry plopped his hand on the table and straightened in his chair. "A road trip is out for me. I've got Saturday-morning chores to take care of. My momma will skin my hide if I shuck 'em. Plus, baseball practice…" Jerry shot Joshua a regretful glance that the shepherd did not fully comprehend.

"Can't we—Joshua and I—meet up with you?" asked Milagros.

The shepherd released a drawn-out breath before responding. "If I made an exception for you, how would that look to the others?"

"No one has to find out, pop," lobbied Laz.

"Why tempt the fates again?" asked the shepherd of Milagros and Joshua. "What if this rogue somehow forces the better angels from your nature? *That* can compromise the life of every person out there, every person depending on me?"

"We would never betray you," Milagros replied in earnest.

The shepherd lowered his chin. "I'm sorry, but the answer is—" His brain registered the color-drained, horrified frowns of Milagros and Joshua, the blanch undertone that rose up from Jerry's fright-riddled face, and the bug-eyed alarm from the countenance of Laz. The projected dismay and terrorized screams of his disciples dictated the shepherd's reactionary head-twisting movement.

From the other side of the porthole, glaring directly into the cabin, he saw two hideous black and gold eyes fiendishly moving from side to side like an untamed animal on the loose and eager to pounce.

\*\*\*

With its headlights off, the Lane-chauffeured vehicle stopped near the waiting boy. Raúl's car entered the parking lot gate in the same manner following the Jaguar.

Everyone exited the vehicles and eventually joined together. Lane waved over the boy, who eyed Alegría with some reservation. "Say something," Lane said.

"Hello," Marvis timidly said to Alegría. "You should know it stinks in there. You should also know—"

"Where are they?" she interrupted.

"The two Dociles," the boy answered with a quick head toss to one side. "On the boat. Inside."

Alegría's eyes briefly turned toward the stadium and then back to Raúl. "Take everyone back with you, and pick up some extra food."

"What about my revenge?" asked Raúl.

Wearing her black capelet, Alegría studied her son for several seconds before responding. "Vengeance is mine."

She waited for the cars to leave and then strode forward with shorter steps than usual, the points of her high heels tapping the asphalt in a scratchy, foreboding cadence.

As she neared the stadium, an expressionless Alegría maneuvered through the rows of parked cars near the entrance. She spied sleeping teenagers inside some vehicles with their windows partially or completely lowered. But her eyes were inevitably drawn to the unique structure looming in front of her. Then, as she walked, she heard a whistle. The distinctively wolfish whistle of a male extoling the virtues of a shapely female from afar; it was directed at her. Alegría spun around; she saw no one, nor heard any rustling from within any of the vehicles. Not everyone was sleeping, evidently.

Alegría scaled the steps to the plaza and strode through the closest entrance way. Coming out on the curved ramp that spilled into one end of the stadium, she spotted the anchored yacht. She marched the length of the retaining wall's railing in front of the first rows of seating facing the water, a breeze fluttering the length of her capelet. As she walked, she heard a variety of music emanating from transistor radios that were playing in lowered volume. Several boys along the way jackknifed up from their reclined positions to confirm, if not admire, her presence.

An unhurried Alegría had practically ignored everything and everyone around her to this point, although she could no longer hide the fact that some type of nasal affliction had overtaken her.

She did not arouse suspicion from any of the young, tired eyes who glimpsed her sedate behavior. The last person any of the young attendees would have expected to see strolling into their midst would have been a mother vampire, she rationalized, especially during the early hours of the cobalt moon's rising.

But with the object of her desire presumably in the sailing vessel moored out in front of her in the water, Alegría had no choice but to tip her hand. Short of breath from the insufferable scent around her, she stood nearly touching the two-and-a-half-foot railing. The basin waters gently lapped against the retaining wall directly beneath her feet, the staining water marks from the shifting tides apparent on the exposed face of the wall. A whoosh in the air supplanted the gentle lapping sound, as Alegría lifted off the wall and over to the sailboat.

The previous outward calm demeanor and inner peace exhibited by Alegría, until her breathing had become labored, disappeared in a flash. She landed portside on the vessel with altered face and fangs drawn. The light from inside the cabin attracted her. She bent over to peer inside the porthole.

\*\*\*

Milagros rushed to lock the door. They were trapped like rats—or so it seemed.

"She's here!" Milagros warned the shepherd. *"The mother vampire! On the boat! Outside!"*

Joshua and Jerry sent their chairs tumbling back from their enormous fright. Laz instinctively ran over to his father, who struggled to gather his composure. "This can't be," said the shepherd. "The ancient parchments forbid it."

Then the sudden cold reality of what *was* confronting them arrived at the door of the cabin with a loud, concentrated bang, generating more screams from those inside. The shepherd opened a drawer, pulled out a string of garlic cloves, and placed them around his son's neck like a Hawaiian lei.

Another penetrating bang hit the door, shaking the cabin and cowering all with a collective cry of despair. "I have a crucifix, holy water, and a redwood carved stake," said the shepherd in one continuous breath. The expectation he raised in Milagros' eyes obliged him to add disappointingly, "They're in my cabin. Next door."

Milagros understood the only implied way to access the shepherd's cabin was out through the sole door being currently assailed.

The door of their cabin was made of oak, and it was not flimsy. But another bash from Alegría shattered a chunk in the center and allowed her to poke her violent fist inside. Through the splintered opening, Alegría's abominable face—making guttural sounds and showing her fangs menacingly—was revealed when she pulled back her arm. Then she turned simply rabid with successive pummels upon the decaying door.

Joshua and Jerry grabbed each other's arms near the shoulders. The cramping fear of the evil entity about to breach the barrier between them choked their breathing.

The shepherd hurried over to the skylight window facing the bow of the sailboat and slid it open. Everyone hastened over to it, except Milagros.

"Get out through here!" shouted the shepherd.

Boosted by his father, Laz was the first one to crawl through the tight opening. In his rush, the garlic chain snapped and fell from around his neck. Joshua nodded to Jerry to go next, and Jerry obliged.

A terrific blow then knocked the top hinge off the door. Alegría was practically within their confined space.

"Go Joshua!" yelled Milagros.

"You go!" spat back Joshua.

"*I* can't make it through there!"

Joshua hesitated, understanding her plight. "I'm not leaving you again," he then said firmly into her eyes.

Milagros' breath caught in her throat at the committed words.

The cabin door then crashed to the ground in a broken heap. And the seething miscreation stepped into the room.

\*\*\*

On the bow's deck, Laz began yelling and waving his arms. "A mistress of the undead is here! A mistress of the undead is here!" His piercing voice gained the attention of everyone on the floating stage and many of those along the water's edge alongside of the stadium. Laz then stumbled over something. Impulsively glancing at what had instigated his fall, he saw one of the white-jacketed crewmen. His throat had been ripped out, his dull eyes were open, and his head was connected to his shoulders by only the cowl of his neck. Laz startled back, kicking away from the man and paddling his hands underneath him.

Jerry stopped him. "You wouldn't happen to have flare gun handy?"

"Probably down below somewhere."

Jerry spied a fishing net half-sprawled out over a storage chest. It was a nylon-cast net. He grabbed hold of it. He also picked up a shiny cigarette lighter he spotted near the dead body, lying amid broken cigarettes that lay scattered around their crumpled carton. Quickly opening the chest, inside he found only two portable gasoline containers filled with fuel.

"Take one," Jerry said to Laz, "and pray we're not too late."

\*\*\*

The skylight window was not big enough for the shepherd either. In a desperate act, he tried to flip over the table as an obstacle for Alegría. Milagros and Joshua joined in overturning and pushing the table from the underside.

Alegría let out a hateful yell and struck a mighty blow into the center of the furniture with her forearm, splitting the table in two and knocking everyone back in a temporarily incapacitated state. Joshua fell to the floor, against the wall, as did Milagros. The dazed shepherd dropped to his knees. Alegría stepped over to the kneeling man and, with her hands, exerted a centralized push downward on the shepherd's shoulders with such force that it crushed his spine, mashing his lumbar vertebrae and causing his immediate death. He fell backward in a sitting position, not far from the cabin's porthole. Milagros emitted a pained sigh and turned her throbbing head away after witnessing the brutal liquidation. Alegría then walked over to the half-dazed Joshua just as he was forcing his fingers to tighten into a fist. She stepped hard on his wrist, which coerced his fingers to stiffly fan out in pain in his open palm.

All appeared lost now. The vile vampiress appeared she would have her misguided revenge.

Joshua's other hand crawled over and found Milagros' accepting fingers for one final squeeze of shared emotion.

In a last summoned moment of courage, Joshua met Alegría's odious eyes as she raised her homicidal hand at him, her gaping, fang-exposed mouth releasing a gravelly, drawn-out growl of satisfaction. Then suddenly, she shuddered and her head shook from side to side. Drawing normal breaths became difficult and she began loudly wheezing. As her face returned to human form, she exhibited the more visible signs of an allergic seizure. Her eyes became watery and swollen to the point of nearly closing. Her lips swelled as if stung by bees. Abruptly, she was smashed in the face by the bunched wreath of garlic, the bulbs splintering off her forehead and cheeks. With agonizing disdain, her hands scrubbed away the residue of the pungent plant from her face. Unable to fill her lungs with sufficient air, Alegría—*incredibly*—retreated.

Wiping her hands and getting to her feet, Milagros said, "Our garlic shield kicked in."

Joshua stood up next to her, a disbelieving half smile infiltrating his face. He could not fathom the miraculous reprieve which had just occurred. "Nice throw," he disconnectedly said.

Milagros examined the shepherd, his crooked neck forcing an upward silly gaze at nothing. She closed her eyes, heavily exhaled, and nodded at the door's opening.

"Stay close behind me. Remember, we're toxic to her."

\*\*\*

Standing over the door leading to the compartments below, a harried Jerry spread out the casting net to get a feel for its size. The door opened unexpectedly. A gasping Alegría rushed out, catching her flailing hand in a piece of the netting.

The sound of the door opening and the figure of Alegría right underneath him naturally frightened Jerry; he lost his balance, dropping straight down to the deck below. The first thing he saw when he opened his eyes was the other white-jacketed crewman lying on deck, pinned back against the boat's stern. He looked like a discarded ragdoll, with arms and legs distortedly spread out and his chin tucked in over red-stained collars and lapels. Then the foreboding presence hovering over him captured his undivided attention. Without moving his head, Jerry's eyes shifted and beheld Alegría. All Jerry could do was swallow hard at the luckless occurrence that had plopped him at her unmerciful feet.

Alegría drew her fangs and prepared to break Jerry in two with one swing of her raised hand. But at the last instant, her physiology betrayed her. Her puffy eyes and lips bulged some more and she strained to breathe. She moved off, gasping for breath and uncoordinatedly pestered by the portion of netting that had snagged in the bejeweled fingers of her hand.

Astonished, Jerry delayed briefly. Upon moving, he slung the trailing end of the net on the deck over the disoriented Alegría. The unearthly being entwined herself within the net by twisting hastily around. A fast reeling noise cut off Alegría's yelping protestations, and the tight pull from the braided-end rope flapped close the net and knocked her off her high heels. The braided-end rope had been tied and hooked by Laz on the top deck to the mast rigging. The rope's recoil hoisted a thrashing Alegría up and swung her back over the bow.

Milagros and Joshua emerged cautiously through the same door Alegría had burst out from. Laz jumped down to meet them. He searched each of their grave faces for an answer as to the whereabouts of his father, his intent to head below stopped by Milagros and Joshua.

"You can't help him and we have to get out of here!" Milagros said.

As Laz slumped his shoulders, Jerry jumped back up to the top deck. "Up here!" he yelled. He purposely toppled over one of the two cans of gasoline, spilling some of the contents on the deck. Picking up the can, he shook out the rest of the flammable liquid in a circle beneath the suspended Alegría. Without hesitation, he pulled out the crewman's cigarette lighter and flicked the flint. The instant the small, blue flame appeared, he let the lighter drop. A line of flames spread into a ring of fire under the thrashing captive. With her capelet wrapped clumsily around her, Alegría was trapped in the net on her back with her legs up in the air.

"Who you gonna hunt down and torture now? *Huh*?" said Jerry defiantly. "Oh, no, not *my* family!"

Alegría kicked more vehemently. She groaned and squirmed, trying to keep her clothes from catching fire.

The other survivors joined Jerry. The teenagers watched with a perverse curiosity as the flames grew taller around the confined female beast, strung up like a jungle animal snared by a trip-wire booby trap.

Alegría grew frantic; she thrashed and thrashed. Exhausting that approach, she wriggled her fingers to pull in a clump of netting closer to her face. She began to gnaw at the net with her teeth, specifically with her canines. The razor-sharp points of her teeth started to cut through the meshed web of the strong nylon threads immobilizing her.

The first to notice, Milagros exclaimed, *"God help us! She's biting through the net!"*

Joshua picked up the other red can of gasoline. "Let's blow it."

Laz nodded. "The gas tanks."

Laz and Joshua jumped down to the lower deck. Laz pushed a button on the steering console to start the engines. He then throttled the boat's controls to a maximum idling capacity, while Joshua splashed the clear, odorous liquid all around, finally throwing the near-empty container through the door leading to the cabins.

Alegría was munching faster. A small tearing sound in the nylon followed by a wider one could be distinctly heard. "Hurry!" yelled Milagros as the boys scampered back to the burning top deck.

Frustratingly, no one had a combustible agent, so Laz took off his shirt and set a sleeve to the fire near them. With minor hesitation, he dropped the flaming shirt through the doorway to the cabins. In a matter of seconds, crisscrossing walls of bright orange flames fanned across both decks of the ship, quickly consuming the dead crewmen.

In rapid succession, the boys and the girl dove off the ship into the water—except Jerry.

The sailboat's overheating engines were revving loudly and smoke from the fire on board began spewing out of the exhausts.

***

In the water, as everyone came up to the surface, the unaccounted-for Jerry gathered attention. Spotting Jerry still on the boat, Joshua and Milagros voiced inexplicable consternations at their friend.

"I can't swim!" he called back.

"She's gonna blow any second!" said Laz, treading water beside Joshua and Milagros. "We've got to get to shore."

Strung up to the mast, with flames accosting her from every way, the struggling Alegría urgently continued her own life-or-death struggle in the face of the grim situation. Her teeth picked methodically through the netting like a forest animal boring down on a hardtack nutriment. A small piece of netting then tore, allowing her arm to stretch out through the ripped opening, but an encroaching flame licked Alegría's freed hand, causing a frightening screech and withdrawal of her fingers.

It was only then that one greater fear overcame another. Jerry spied the empty red gas can close to him. He picked it up, clutched it to his chest, and jumped overboard.

Following his plunge, Jerry bobbed up to the surface, tightly holding the plastic floating can, his fingers wrapped around the round, black screw-on top he had replaced.

"Just kick with your feet," instructed Joshua, coming up alongside of him. "We're right here. Don't worry."

Swimming ahead, Laz was helped up over the retaining wall by the waiting team of Teddy and Tommy. The struggling Jerry was pulled up next, followed by Milagros and then Joshua.

In a simultaneous reaction, the out-of-breath teens half-ducked in unison at the explosion that then burst from the sailboat. A booming eruption from the belly of the ship spewed a black, orange, and yellow mushroom cloud of destruction into the night air. Shielding his eyes, Jerry felt engulfed by the expanding heat generated. Smoking flying fragments of machinery shot out from the boat like wayward skyrockets, while smoldering embers of smaller fabricated accessories flitted into the water and onto the nearby floating stage, which had been vacated by its homesteaders.

Everyone in the stadium witnessed the end of the ship as the bubbling waters tugged its tattered carcass into the unseen darkness below. The sailboat sank quickly and all but disappeared except for the tip of its tallest mast which stayed above the surface, amid the flotsam, like a nautical grave marker in the shallow basin.

All of the milling teenagers were on their feet. "We saw her," said Teddy, breaking the silence.

"She walked right in front of us and just jumped over to the boat," disclosed Tommy.

With the danger apparently passed, a collection of apprehensive Docile teenagers, who had tactically retreated to a higher grandstand location, descended from their position. Many took giant leaps downward, the whites of their eyes glittering a light blue color. Most landed smoothly on their feet, though one or two dropped down awkwardly.

What began first as whispers elevated into fervently repeated questions from the gathering swarm. "*Where's the shepherd? What happened to the shepherd?*"

Milagros put her arm around a visibly-affected Laz. She squeezed him tightly as if trying to transfer some of her inner strength to him.

The white-undershirted Laz lifted his head and delivered the bad news. "The shepherd is dead," he quaveringly said, evoking a stunned hush from everyone within earshot. "He died protecting us from a mistress of the undead. She killed our yachtsmen."

In certain sectors of the gathered teenagers, an unsettled chatter arose. *"Mistress of the undead? I told you. How did she find us? What does she want with us? It's against the doctrines."*

"He brought the mistress," someone accusatorily said, pointing at Joshua. Peter stepped forward to be more fully seen. "He jeopardized all of our lives."

"Cool it, you," Milagros said.

Toni joined the verbal attack with Peter. "He didn't even know the Docile signal," she stated impassionedly.

"Or will you deny that?" Peter asked Milagros directly.

There was more uncertain buzzing from the impressionable teens, which veered toward short pronouncements leaning in Peter's favor.

"Is this how you will honor my father?" Laz asked the shifting crowd. "My *dead* father? With suspicion and malice toward your fellow brethren?"

The mention of the stunning loss of the shepherd spawned a guilt-invoking, subduing effect on most. Then Joshua put a hand on Laz's shoulder. "Peter's right," he said. "The vampire came for me. It's all my fault."

The declared admission agitated everyone again. Peter seized the opportunity.

"What are you going to tell the coast guard?" he asked Laz. "They're sure to be here soon. Or hadn't you thought of that?"

Caught off guard, Laz did not answer right away.

"I want to be led by someone who thinks ahead. Don't all of you?" Peter asked, followed by a rising chorus of agreement.

"We want Peter," Toni chirped, which was instantly seconded.

Someone else cried, "Let Peter lead us." And then the chant of '*We Want Peter*' took root, the majority of the surrounding cabal casting their lot with the bespectacled teenager.

As a smiling Peter accepted congratulatory slaps and pats on the back with vigor, Laz plodded away. He sat dejectedly in a fold-down seat away from the masses that
had rejected him, his clothes dripping intermittently with saltwater through the slats of the seat to the concrete ground.

His three soaked supporters angled around him. "You can come with us," said Milagros.

Laz raised his eye level. "I have to stay here. For the coast guard and for the police. And you both have to return in the morning to catch the buses."

Joshua hooked his arm around Milagros', and the two slowly slogged toward the curved exit ramp of the stadium.

"Hang loose," Jerry said to Laz. He followed a few paces behind his weary friends, finally letting drop the empty red gas can he had seized from the sunken sailboat.

# Chapter Six

The Equilibrium hovered over the inert body on the littered sea floor. Equin uttered the first words followed in equally balanced, interconnected speech order by Libor and Umber.

"The blast was not strong enough…"

"To kill her. It only served…"

"To save her from the fire."

Alegría lay concussed on the sludgy seabed after the sailboat explosion.

Equin and Umber directed their next complementing comments toward Libor. "Her manner of interference…"

"Has exceeded all boundaries."

"She was warned. Her meddling…"

"Has threatened the supernatural order."

"We must act to…"

"Nullify her at once."

Libor pondered his response to the pointed commentary. "That is a serious proposal…"

"Which must be considered. What…"

"Other alternative do we have?"

In his dry transdimensional state, Libor inserted his hands into the gold-encircled cuffs of his shiny satin lavender-blue jacket. His next pronouncement, posed in the form of a trailing question, prompted reflective responses from his associates. "The very essence of Equilibrium is…"

"Order through balance. For every imbalance…"

"An equal counterbalance must be found."

A pleased curl displayed over Libor's lips. "It is agreed. An…"

"Equal counterbalance for this…"

"Heedless daughter of darkness."

The underwater light around each of them increased sharply and then faded until it was completely gone, vanishing the ghostly triumvirate with it.

\*\*\*

Alegría began stirring in the disappearing light. The explosion had thrown her yards from the main wreckage, the casting net in shreds around her. She slipped away from it, kicking up a cloud of dirty bottom sediment all around her. She undid the tying string of her tattered capelet and swam with undulating grace over to the skeletal remains of the sunken ship, following the tallest mast of the schooner upward to the surface of the water.

There were police boats with whirling spotlights circling around her. She discerned a much more well-lit stadium crowded with uniformed men. She ducked down just in time to avoid a spotlight from one of the patrol boats that shined right at the top of the mast, peeking atop the water like a submarine's periscope.

"I thought I saw something," said the voice conducting the spotlight on the trolling police boat.

"Probably a piece of floating debris," answered his police companion at his side.

Convinced she had not been seen, Alegría swam like a fish under the water to the far shore of the basin. She came up into the darkened mangrove undetected. She bent over and began expelling the saltwater that had filled her lungs. The water spewed out of her mouth in a rush like that of a well pump following pent-up hand cranks.

"I am really beginning to hate the water," Alegría coughed aloud with mild disgust. She then cut through the mangrove until she reached the other side, where she dove into the bay and swam away.

***

Rosa swept through the wide swing doors that led from the emergency room annex to the OR elevators and the main floors of the hospital. Sensing *something* had occurred, she hurried over and hugged Milagros tightly. In quick, short bursts in Spanish, she inquired about Milagros' health and her most recent whereabouts, her eyes questioning her daughter's damp clothing.

Milagros answered that she was fine and that her mother need not worry. "How's Manolín?"

"Resting," answered Rosa.

"Ten minutes," the woman at the emergency room admittance desk said.

As Joshua and Jerry tried to follow Rosa and Milagros back through the swing doors, the desk attendant called after them, "Immediate family only."

Stopped by the edict, the gender-divided pairs parted ways.

Rosa led Milagros upstairs to the bedside of her wounded cousin.

*"Primo,"* Milagros said caringly, taking his hand in hers as if in a handshake. His eyes were closed, his breathing from the rhythmic rise and fall of his hospital gown even. She carefully placed his hand down on the bed. Milagros nodded at her aunt and her husband—her tía Clara and tío Manolo—whom she had greeted with commiserating hugs moments ago. They were seated in chairs close to their son's bed.

Milagros subtly signaled her mother as she turned for the door. Rosa followed her out of the room.

In the deserted hallway outside of Manolín's room, Milagros bluntly said, "Juan's death has been avenged. Alegría is dead."

Rosa stared at Milagros as if she was expecting her to say something more. She calmly blinked and asked softly, "Who is dead?"

Milagros hesitated. "The one Juan called the serpent of Satan. The mother vampire I told you about. With the kids who go to our high school?"

"Kids?" Rosa asked with interest. "You told me she had a daughter in your grade. The one whose birthday party you went to."

"*Si,* that's the one."

"You never told me she had more than one child," stated Rosa, stepping back. "And you never told me her name…"

*Alegría is dead. Alegría is dead. Alegría is dead.* The statement ricocheted through the temporal lobe of Rosa's brain, into the hippocampus—the brain's memory storage unit. Each repetition rang more pronounced, echoing through a chamber of suppressed memory. It was a name she had not heard in more than fifteen years, a name Rosa could not easily bring herself to repeat. "Is this…unholy one's other child a boy…named Raúl?"

Milagros nodded several times robotically. "I just met him two days ago."

Rosa half turned, and with an unseeing stare away from Milagros, her mind was ushered back to a time seventeen years in the past…

\*\*\*

Cranky already, Milagros became more upset with the first trickle of water to streak her small forehead. She shook her tiny fists and kicked her white and pink baby booties in response to her displeasure. Another tumble of water onto Milagros' head frowned her cheeky, wide-eyed infant face and came followed by a second invocation from the clergyman. She quivered antagonistically in her mother's steady hands; her eyes shut into even slits, her reddening face and her gummy mouth opening to release a naturally indignant cry.

Rosa rocked Milagros in her arms, offering indecipherable chirps of comfort. The crying baby's ill-tempered disposition did not nudge the priest forward any faster in the ceremony. He remained professionally committed to his principal role. Raising his voice to be better heard over the objections of baby Milagros, he completed the final invocation and the directed final cerebral pouring of the holy water. "May the gift of the Holy Spirit always remain alive in your soul, Milagros Ricardo Benítez."

Standing as godmother, Rosa's sister Clara handed her a white hand towel which Rosa used to softly wipe her infant daughter's forehead with. "Let me take her now," said Clara.

As she obliged her sister, the priest politely pulled Rosa away from her congratulating family. "I've spoken to the archdiocese in Santiago. We can begin the annulment proceedings anytime. You need to only sign a few papers. You can come see me tomorrow if you wish."

"That will be of great relief to me and my family, Father Torres," Rosa replied.

The priest's demeanor brightened. "It is good to be able to preside over ceremonies that celebrate rebirth," he said, waving a hand alluding to his just-completed solemn rite. "I have had my fill of vigil masses for the *desaparecidos.*"

Rosa understood the priest's meaning well, having attended many of the religious ceremonies for those who had been dubbed the…*disappeared* of Antilla. "How can ordinary people simply vanish from the streets of their own town?"

"All coinciding with the arrival and departure period of those swindling Spaniards," Father Torres responded. "I heard back from the Spanish consulate in Havana. The names Antonio Lorca de Vázquez and Eduardo Ricardo del Castillo were thoroughly researched and found to be Spanish aristocrats of the nineteenth century. Their identities were obviously pilfered by our Spanish imposters."

The man of the cloth drifted off as some personal acquaintances gathered around Rosa, a smiling Alegría and cordial Raúl, holding in one strong arm his fifteen-month-old namesake son. "Look how big this young man has gotten," Rosa said, shaking the carried boy's wrist. The toddler swung the back of his hand and barely missed hitting Rosa in the face.

Springing back surprised, Rosa said, "Isn't he a feisty one?" as she adjusted the dislodged veil on her head.

Raúl grabbed his son's hand in a scolding exercise as he offered an impotent glance at his wife.

Alegría cradled in her arms her three-month-old-baby Cira, and Rosa dutifully conveyed her affection. "What an angel!" she gushed, a finger caressing the rosy cheek of the baby. "And look at those eyelashes… She's going to be a model or a movie star."

The expressions of unanimous pleasure were interrupted by the opening of the front doors of the church, pushed creakingly back wide at the same time. A long slab of sunlight spilled into the baptistery from outside. Standing in the doorway, casting an elongated shadow, stood a black-silhouetted man.

The beam of sunlight projecting into the dimly lit church made most squint or shield their eyes; it forced Alegría to cringingly turn away. "Raúl," she called out in mild distress, "my sunglasses."

Raúl deftly opened his wife's purse hanging from her arm. He pulled out her sunglasses and all but placed them over her nose for her.

Rosa thought Alegría's reaction was peculiar, as she now found as peculiar the long-sleeved dress she fully noticed Alegría wearing and the folded parasol she held at her side like a cane. But the black-silhouetted man respectfully taking off his floppy hat diverted Rosa's immediate attention. Instinctively, she reached for her baby, taking Milagros from Clara, who had gravitated toward her. The man at the door was not dressed for church; he wore baggy pants and a loose-fitting, sweat-stained pullover shirt. He spotted the figure of authority and walked toward him. As he did, the unexpected visitor's face came into distinguishing view to all.

"It's Juan Montes," someone identified.

"What can that heathen want with Father Torres?" asked another. Rosa understood the inference. Rosa knew Juan in passing. His father ran a furniture repair shop on *Calle* Aguilera. In the past, Juan and his father had been to the Benítez home to pick up and then deliver re-upholstered chairs and seat cushions for the residence. A young man in his mid-twenties, Juan, much to the dismay of his family, had found a spiritual substitute to Catholicism in the teachings of the Yoruba religion.

"He should not be permitted inside the church," stated another woman with rising indignity, a voice Rosa distinguished as her own mother's.

"Is not everyone welcomed under this roof?" Father Torres said for all to hear.

Meeting Juan in the center aisle, he placed a solemn hand on his shoulder and allowed Juan to whisper something in his ear. Making eye-contact with Juan again, the priest then excused himself with the assurance of an immediate return and quickly shuffled past his parishioners, ignoring their pleas and gestures for information. "I must get a few things," he said, disappearing into a hidden vestibule of the church.

Head down, Juan began walking out of the church, twisting his hat in his hands. Suddenly, a voice called out his name. He turned and marched back in its direction, passing several attendees along the way. As all of the veil-shrouded women gawked at him, his eyes lingered on Alegría longer than anyone else, until he fixed upon the source of the call.

"What is it?" asked Rosa, with the sleeping Milagros in her rocking arms.

Juan permitted himself a glimpse of the baby before answering. "I was with my father collecting pinewood in the timberland when we found it. A mass grave with all of the bodies of the disappeared."

***

Juan pulled out the felling ax he had driven into the trunk of the pine tree he was cutting down in tandem with his father and rested it over his shoulder. The incited squeals and snorts coming from an area not too far away from their position kept growing louder.

"Wild hogs fighting over something," his father said.

"I'm going to go see," said Juan.

Without a strenuous objection from his father, Juan followed his curiosity toward the pig noises. The forestry area they were in outside of Antilla was known as *el júcaro,* a mountainous, uncultivated zone dense with pine trees and populated by exotic wildlife. A good eight-mile hike outside of town, el júcaro received few visitors, except adventurous boys on bicycles or entrepreneurial men like Juan Montes and his father, who reaped some commercial benefit from an excursion to the isolated pines. As he neared a substantial clearing stretching deep inside the forest, beams of hazy, golden sunlight slanted through foliage breaks in the trees. Juan slapped at his sweaty neck, trying to swat away a large buzzing insect.

While stepping through thick underbrush, a fast-moving hog crossed his path and startled him. Though the movement of the

121

hog surprised him, it was what the brown-skinned animal clenched in its mouth that totally jolted Juan and nearly instigated a complete loss of balance. A grimy, gnawed human forearm unmistakably dangled from the omnivore's snout. Close enough to see that two fingers of the hand had been chewed off completely, Juan determined from its size that it was a female arm. The hog stopped momentarily, shook its head at Juan as if in a selfish display to its claim, and scurried off on its short, fast-moving feet.

The clearing he entered bore the appearance of being excavated, unnaturally carved out within the surrounding tree-pervading landscape. Juan then zeroed in on the chorus of high-pitched noises. There were seven or eight fat hogs with dark brown or black hides trampling in one area, squealing with delight or puffing with impatient-sounding snorts. The squat animals, to Juan's horror, had partially pulled free from a shallow burial the torso of a headless cadaver.

The yell rose from deep inside Juan's chest, and he chased it forward without thinking. Swinging his ax with the flat side out, he rushed the scrounging animals. The hogs screeched wildly and dispersed in different directions. With a backswing, Juan hit one hog with the butt of the ax and toppled him over. The squealing swine quickly righted itself and ran away into the woods as if all creation were nipping at its feet.

After all the pigs had scattered, Juan let his ax drop as his father appeared beside him. Standing together, they surveyed the terrain in front of them. A long, wide layer of unhardened topsoil stretched over a far-reaching swath of ground.

*"When we dug up some of the loose dirt, we unearthed more human remains. That's when we knew. That's when my father sent me back to town, while he stayed on guard."*

Juan had lost count as to how many times he had told the story. But this was the first time he had told it to Rosa face-to-face. Almost a year had passed since the terrible discovery on

Milagros' christening day, and Juan and Rosa were on their first date together. They were at the small recreational site north of town that spilled off from Banes Bay and that the townspeople referred to as *la playita.* The area was nothing more than a spit of pebbly shoreline within a small cove into which one could wade or swim.

"Imagine," said Rosa, lounging on a blanket under the partial shade of gently swaying palm trees, "the remains of more than seventy of Antilla's residents were dug out of that mass grave."

"And even more from the towns of Nicaro and Preston across Nipe Bay," said Juan. "All buried in the one isolated spot."

Juan took a bite out of the sandwich he held in his hand. "How's yours?"

Rosa bit into her lunch and answered pleasingly with her face.

Juan took a swig from his open bottle of malta. "The sun did not bother you?"

Rosa put down her half-eaten sandwich and shrugged. Her black hair blew loosely in the steady breeze. She negligibly lowered the shoulder strap of her one-piece bathing suit. "I will have a few tan lines. It's to be expected."

Juan pulled out a small bottle shaped like a perfume atomizer. "Let me wet your fingers before you take another bite."

Rosa modestly extended her hand and allowed Juan to sprinkle out some water from the bottle onto her fingers. The tips of Juan's massaging fingers lightly rubbed the moisture over Rosa's palm. Juan was thorough in the deed and Rosa seemed to enjoy the sensation she derived from his touch. "I'm feeling like a noble woman who dips her fingers into a water bowl before beginning the next course of a sumptuous meal."

"The water was pleasant?" asked Juan.

"Why yes, it was, Juan," answered Rosa.

Juan sighed deeply, nodding with assurance to himself. He then flung his arms around the surprised girl, patting her back and shaking her by the shoulders. "That was holy water I poured on your hand. I asked Father Torres for some. You ate from the sandwich with garlic and the sun has no adverse effect on you." Juan's intoned voice projected his pleasure, as did the cementing together of his steepled fingers.

He bounced to one knee and squeezed a puzzled Rosa's hand. "You've been spared, Rosa. You've been spared!" he relayed loudly.

To Juan's expressed regret, the exuberant sounds awakened the child with them. Rosa immediately reached for Milagros, who had been asleep on her belly on their shared blanket. She tried to comfort the wailing toddler, lovingly patting the sweaty curls of dark hair that clung to the side of her cheek that was reddened from her tummy-side-down *siesta.*

Juan scanned Rosa and then Milagros. "Well, not completely spared," he said with a sigh of resignation.

***

"The bodies in the grave were all drained of blood. They had gouges of torn flesh—and it wasn't from any wild animals. I was part of the exhumation party. I saw them all."

As Juan tried to put across his fantastic supposition to Rosa, she exhibited a natural resistance to his eerie claims. A now-wide-awake Milagros toddled nearby, and Rosa pulled her close to her chest, piously evoking the name of the Virgin of Charity of El Cobre in a merciful plea. Milagros, for her part, resented being smothered by her mother at that instant. Fussily trying to squirm away from Rosa's grip, the child wanted to continue dawdling around the couple's blanket, collecting pebbles or other small objects that her young eye found interesting.

"The *babalawo*—our high priest—confirmed it," divulged Juan.

"Ay, Juan. Must you keep bringing that up?"

"You asked me."

Milagros began to loudly protest over her restriction, forcing Rosa to yield and let go of her. The quieted child nearly stepped on the sparse remains of Rosa's sandwich, following her release as she teetered off.

"Your...*practices*. My mother almost had a heart attack when I told her I was coming here with you, you know."

"It's an accepted part of my life, Rosa. I accept you with your faith. And I would never try to impose my beliefs on you...or Milagritos."

The bare-chested Juan edged closer to Rosa, hoping the sincerity of his words had touched her. In his hand appeared a flower—a white ginger lily—that he handed to Rosa. Although originally from India, everyone knew this bulbous plant had been adopted by Cubans as their national flower. The natives called the flower *mariposa* because its spreading petals resembled butterfly wings. When Rosa finished appreciating the elegant beauty of the delicate flower and gazed up to thank Juan, her lips let out a soft sigh as they were converged upon by his blanketing mouth. Not too rushed, not too stiff, and not too long, the end result could have been categorized as a perfect first kiss.

Rosa's head came to rest on Juan's shoulder. She posed a question and then straightened up to receive his reply. "Why did you look at my baby when you said I was not completely spared?"

Juan waited a few seconds before he answered, as if allowing Rosa to brace herself over what he was about to say. "According to a sub-segment of our teachings, dealing with the occult, this beautiful fruit of your prior union stands a chance at being damned."

As Rosa's eyes searched Juan's, her head trembled in disbelief over the ominous words. She wanted to reach out to Milagros again, as if the act of clutching the child to her bosom would offer her foolproof protection from a danger Rosa did not completely understand. In her state of arisen anxiety, she did not feel or pay mind to the flower being stolen from her hand. But then she relaxed at the soothing, sympathetic touch of Juan's fingers curling loose locks of her hair around the flap of her ear.

"But we are going to make sure that does not happen," said Juan, threading the stem of the white ginger lily into the twined hair around her ear.

***

The evening Caribbean sky was charged with its usual panoply of glitter. Sparkling stars filled the blue-black expanse of night in an arbitrary array of infused brilliance.

"It's good to see the old traditions coming to life again," said Rosa. "The lights, the flags, the ornaments…it's a wonderful sight."

"The cobalt moon rises in two nights," said Juan, looking up past the decorated treetops of the park at the bright, near-full circle of the moon.

Rosa barely glanced at the moon, preferring to tighten her grip around Juan's arm instead and proceed with their stroll in the park. "Tomorrow is the first night of carnaval—the first carnaval since…"

"The Spaniards left," finished Juan. "I mention the cobalt moon because of Milagritos. It will be her first."

As always, with the correlating mention of her young daughter, Rosa's interest in the occult subject matter piqued. "Must we do something for her? Take her to church?"

"No," said Juan. "She is safe for the next sixteen years."

"I bring it up because of your friend Alegría."

"Alegría?" asked Rosa, trying to come up with a tie-in. "Why, the poor thing has been bedridden for months. The doctors aren't sure what's wrong with her."

"When did you see her last?"

Rosa paused in thought. "A few weeks ago. My mother went over to her house to do her nails, to try and lift her from her malaise. I went along and took Milagritos."

"How did she look?"

"Very pale."

"She had contact with the other Spaniard, did she not?"

Rosa loosened her grip on Juan. "Well, yes. I told you about that evening we went dancing in Tacajó."

The couple reached the park's mermaid fountain, interrupting the clamor of a several teens loitering about. One of the teens had scaled the back of the nearest mermaid sculpture to honk her carved breasts and was reveling in the success. At the sight of Juan and Rosa, the boy briskly slipped down off the unoffended statute and ran off with his two chortling cohorts, averting a near collision with another couple who had come into the area from the opposite end.

Juan placed a firm hand on her arm. "It takes a full cycle of the cobalt moon to complete the change for one who has been...cursed. Your friend Alegría has been slowly converting for the past two and a half years. The transmutation will be complete in two more days."

Rosa became flustered. "Transmutation? Such an ugly word. Really, Juan, now I don't know what to think."

Juan did not speak until he held Rosa's undivided attention. "If I'm right, Alegría has the evil strain, and she has passed it to her children." Rosa silently tolerated Juan's fingers digging into her arm. "Tomorrow is the day I must prevent this town from reliving another tragic nightmare," stated Juan.

"Tomorrow is the day I must kill Alegría Pérez. And you're going to help me..."

"Do not seek to blame yourself," said Rosa with a consoling stroke of her daughter's arm.

"If I had given Juan more information…" Milagros said, staring down at the small glass of juice front of her, "if he had known he was dealing with someone from his past…things may have turned out differently. If I had told you about the boy who destroyed my science project." She, Rosa, and the boys had returned to their home from the hospital and were seated around the kitchen table.

"Our fates are written in advance… That's what Juan would say," replied her mother.

Deeply troubled by her own, what could be characterized, oversights, Milagros could not push away the self-blame presently consuming her. She had never fully informed her mother—or Juan—about Alegría's identity. She never mentioned Alegría by name. It was for no reason other than the fact that it did not seem important and that a name bestowed a humanizing quality to Alegría, something Milagros, influenced by Juan in this area, never sought to do. "Another tipoff could have been Raúl or Cira. I never discussed them in any detail with you either. The night of Cira's birthday party, I was more focused on the fact that I had been asked to a party by Joshua than *whose* party I was attending."

"They weren't in your circle of friends," said an intervening Joshua. "You just met them through me a couple of days ago. You couldn't have known."

Rosa drained the last few drops of coffee from her cup and gently placed it in her saucer's circular indentation. "If anyone is to blame, it's me. I've shielded you too much."

"So, you were all tikes back in the day with Raúl and Cira," said Jerry. "Ain't that a kick in the noggin?" Rattling the small cup and saucer at his fingertips, Jerry then let out a wide yawn, his hand late in covering his gaping mouth. He glanced at the kitchen wall clock, and involuntarily everyone else did, too. Almost 5:30, it read. No one could consider his actions as impolite.

Feeling a need to shake her doldrums, Milagros rose from her chair and moved over to the stove. "I'm going to make breakfast," she said. "The sun will be up soon and we need to maintain our strength for the busy day ahead."

"That's music to my ears," said Jerry.

A few minutes later, Milagros, assisted by her mother, had whipped up some eggs with ham and toasted sliced bread for all. The women reseated themselves at the table. The hot breakfast was well received by all, evidenced by Jerry's steady shoveling of the main dish into his mouth.

Joshua paused before biting into a piece of buttered toast. Studying Rosa, he asked, "When was the last time you saw my mother?"

Rosa wiped her mouth with a napkin. "I… I would have to think for a moment."

Reaching for her mug of café con leche, Milagros interestedly watched her mother. Then, Milagros' hand trembled and some of the warm milk with coffee splashed from the shaking mug onto her plate, dousing the remainder of her omelet. She then jerked back, sitting straight up in her chair, but only for an instant. Racked again by a spasm, her body lifted out of her chair. Before Rosa could clutch her arm, Milagros was slammed into the refrigerator and then raked across the stove and counter, knocking over the milk pot, two frying pans, and an opened five-pound bag of sugar that had been used to fill the nearby sugar jar. Milagros screamed in terror, forcefully carried by an invisible power to the kitchen doorway where Joshua tried to encase her with his arms, blocking her intended path out.

\*\*\*

The force possessing Milagros powerfully shook the two of them as Joshua desperately tried to keep Milagros from lifting any higher off the floor. He very quickly reached a point where he could no longer hang onto her. "Grab her legs!" Joshua screamed at Jerry, who arrived—but too late.

Milagros flew out of the kitchen into the interior of house. Rosa followed shouting after her in fear. Jerry was left holding one of Milagros' shoes and offered Joshua a helpless look before the pair took off after her.

Joshua and Jerry followed the sounds of household fixtures overturning or breaking, and of hard thumping sounds against the walls. Reaching the front door, they saw Rosa draped over Milagros who was pinned to it face-front a good foot above the floor. Milagros spasmed and sprang back from the door toward Joshua and Jerry—and then abruptly stopped, her feet swinging in midair; she desperately stretched out her arms at Joshua but then she slingshot back to the door, flipping around with a punishing thud to her back and shoulders.

Rosa yelled with a pained lack of understanding, "What is this?! What is happening?!" She tugged at as much of her daughter's body as she could, unable to peel her off.

"Open the door," Milagros groggily pleaded, trying to point with her arm.

Before he could reach her, Milagros' back arched, indicating she was about to be thrown again. Joshua ducked the human pinball as she propelled off the door and flew past him.

"Hurry," exhorted a panicky Rosa as the anxious Joshua fumbled with the dead bolt lock.

Equaling her prior distance away from the door, Milagros was yanked back with a ferocious recoil that left her legs kicking out in front of her.

"Here she comes!" yelled Jerry. Finally, and without a second to spare, Joshua flung open the door, the flying figure of Milagros shooting through it.

Everyone ran outside. In sharp contrast to the injurious treatment she received inside the home, Milagros, to everyone's amazement, descended magically and softly on the sidewalk in front of her house as if her body were light as a feather. She was immediately embraced by Rosa who showered her with motherly words of concern.

Joshua's one uttered word conveyed his alarm, consternation, and affection: "*Milá.*"

Milagros' eyes shone clear and she gave all indication of being uninjured and of gaining control of her former self.

"What the hell just happened?" asked Jerry, holding out to Milagros her shoe.

Milagros took her foot apparel from Jerry and put it on. "Now I know what a crash dummy feels like." She took a deep breath and looked up at the perceptibly eroded night sky. The glow of the new day could be detected along the faraway landscape to the east.

Milagros shrugged her shoulders and addressed all. "It's the supernatural checks and balances at work—in a sporting sort of way. It is the dawn of the cobalt moon. No Docile half-vampire is permitted to stay within the sanctuary of their home."

# Chapter Seven

Sheila Landis had never been inside a police station. After pulling open one of the front double doors and walking inside, it crossed her mind that it was not unlike the ones she had glimpsed on television shows—at least at the outset. At the end of a short entrance corridor, a uniformed officer sat behind a high front desk. As she fully walked inside, Sheila detected a muskiness in the air.

Sheila garnered the attention of the seated uniformed officer as she did most men. Her polished breeding exceeded a ramrod straight posture with pinned-back shoulders and head locked unswervingly ahead when she walked, which tended to be eye-catching with both sexes. And the smart wardrobe at her disposal never failed to provide a stylish flourish to her exterior bearing.

For this break-of-dawn trip to the station, Sheila had opted to wear a simple slim violet skirt and white blouse. Her hair was swept up and clamped together in a tasteful but imperfect mode that suggested casual sophistication. Far from an expert on uniform rank, she had seen enough of the three-striped arrow insignia adorning the blue-sleeved arms of the officer to know his station. "Sergeant," she said, directly addressing the officer, "my daughter and husband are missing. Please help me."

The sergeant, whose name tag identified him as 'Foster,' folded his hands in front of him. "We're a little short-handed now, ma'am. There's been a reported disturbance over on Virginia Key; all spare units have been dispatched to the area."

Sheila remained silent, clutching her pocket purse in front of her. Harkening again to television-crime dramas, she had expected to be told that there was not much the police could do for her presently because an insufficient amount of time had elapsed in the unaccounted-for status of the family members. But the sergeant shuffled some papers on his desk and found an empty clipboard. He fastened a single sheet of form stationery to it and glanced at his wristwatch. "The seven-o'clock shift should be coming in soon," he said and handed the clipboard to Sheila. "Fill out this missing-persons report."

Sheila accepted the clipboard from the uniformed man. "Thank you, Sergeant Foster," she said with genuine gratitude.

"You can sit down over there." The sergeant pointed to a set of chairs bunched together against the side wall. "You said there were two people missing?"

"My husband went searching for our daughter hours ago; he hasn't come home or called."

The sergeant nodded slightly. "Put both of their names down on the form."

Just then, the phone on the sergeant's desk rang. As he answered it, Sheila drifted toward the chairs which she assessed as suitable to arrange around a card table and nothing more. As she sat down over only the front edge of the thinly cushioned seat, she heard the sergeant say, *"Detective Gregory is not in. May I take a message?"*

She then pulled off one of the white gloves she wore, yanking at the pointer finger first and the thumb last. Retrieving a pen from her purse, she directed her attention to the sheet of paper on the rigid clipboard in her hand.

\*\*\*

Lacey awoke at the first light of day. Although not altogether a sound sleep she had sustained through the night, it was restful enough to provide her body with the much-needed regeneration it craved. Lacey had not had anywhere near a decent night's rest, much less sleep, for three days since her late-night abduction from her bed by Alegría. It was the very bed she now stretched stiff limbs out over with a reveling feeling of comfort.

She took a sleepy-eyed moment to enjoy a long closed-mouth inhale with her head firmly nestled on her familiar pillow and strands of disheveled hair lightly brushing her cheeks. The fingertips of Lacey's outstretched hands caressed the smooth cotton threads of her bed sheet to a satisfying sensation of personal belonging and safety—guarded safety.

Lacey doubted that she would ever feel completely safe in her own bed again until the threat of Alegría was eliminated. The meddling intervals of anxious slumber she encountered through the just-concluded night, recalling the trying and torturous experiences she had survived, were clear proof of that to her.

Following her drawn-out breath, Lacey opened her eyes with a wide clarity; they moved from the overhead fan circulating from the ceiling above her to the familiar walls and furniture of her room. The early morning sunlight streaking the room's window shadowed a hand-sized something stuck to the glass outside and detained her aimless gaze. She peered at its boxy outline through the drawn shade a second or two longer before kicking off whatever portion of bed sheet that remained covering her.

At the window—a window her father had made sure to lock tightly and fortify with side jambs—she removed the inside stops and unlocked the pane. She reached her arm outside and detached the folded envelope scotch-taped to the glass with her name written on it. She knew it had to be from Jerry.

Lacey pulled out the single sheet of lined paper folded into a square and read its contents:

*Lacey Sweets,*

*I just wanted to let you know I'm thinking about you and can't wait to hugaliciously hold you in my arms again.*

*Me and the gang are lying low. Don't worry.*
*As soon as you read this, please call Detective Gregory, Miami PD—number on back.*
*Tell him to get to Vizcaya right away.*

*Your Jerry Berry*

Lacey smiled at Jerry's cutesy sentiments, a much-needed smile, as she slid back to her bed and sat down. She remembered the name Gregory as being the person her father eventually called at the police department last night after her return. She gathered he was the one handling her case from the exchanges between her father and mother.

Lacey picked up the beige rotary phone on her night table and poked her index finger into a dial circle above a corresponding number. She drew the plastic dial around to the finger stop, and after each return of the spinning dial, she repeated the exercise with the other numbers Jerry had written for her.

The voice picking up the line on the other end came unmistakably through the receiver in her ear: *"Miami Police Department. Sergeant Foster speaking."*

\*\*\*

Detective Phillip Gregory casually came through the front doors of the police station. He made pleasant eye-contact with Sergeant Foster and glimpsed a blond woman sitting with folded white-gloved hands in her lap, probably awaiting a husband or brother to be released from the drunk tank. The woman acknowledged Gregory with a slight movement of her head.

"How's the guardian of the graveyard gate?" asked Gregory with his usual wordplay on the overnight shift Foster worked.

"'Morning, Phil," said Sergeant Foster, making a patting search of papers on his desk. "Message for you."

Gregory accepted the small square sheet of paper that Foster handed to him. "The Hayes girl?" he queried after seeing the name.

"Less than half an hour ago. You've got a two-o'clock appointment with her today, in case you didn't know."

"Thanks, the lieutenant rang me up late last night and told me. A happy ending with a missing teen. I'll take it no matter what the circumstances." Gregory half turned to walk inside. "All quiet on the western front?"

"Not too quiet," apprised Foster. "Some hullabaloo over on Virginia Key a few hours ago. A lot of kids and a boat that went up in flames."

"Kids?" asked Gregory, twisting back. He reflexively glanced at his watch. "A few hours ago?" Gregory instantly thought of his teenage son who spent Friday evening bowling and returned home around midnight.

"Kids," confirmed the sergeant with a shrug of his husky shoulders. "And, uh, speaking of kids," he added with a nod toward the station's early-morning visitor, "this lady has made a report on two members of her immediate family that she has not seen since yesterday. One is a minor."

The blond woman rose from her seat. "My daughter, detective. And my husband."

Gregory appraised the woman standing in front of him, her gloved fingers tightly clenching the top of her hand purse. He regretted his early misplaced thought describing the reason for her presence. He scanned the sergeant as if to ask if there was some alternative person available. The sergeant respectfully avoided his gaze. Gregory absorbed the woman's clear blue eyes and the swirling torment they displayed in stark contrast to her strikingly composed exterior. He also noticed the puffiness around her mascaraed-eyelids. As a regular midnight-shift man early in his career, he knew too well the weary eyes of someone who had not slept all night. Then her next words struck a chord.

"My daughter Dawn Landis attends West Side High, and she would never miss curfew without calling."

*West Side High School.* Gregory took off his hat. "Forgive me," he said, extending his hand and introducing himself. "Won't you follow me?"

Sergeant Foster appeared at his side, delaying Gregory's first step. He handed him the report Sheila had filled out. Gregory nodded with appreciation, and the sergeant walked away, favoring a leg.

"He lost four toes to frostbite in the Korean War," explained Gregory.

The detective led Sheila through a maze of mostly empty desks to his own. The blades of overhead ceiling fans spun leisurely above them. Multiple half-opened, square-shaped windows on the walls encased the expansive room, providing the wide area with toned natural lighting. Gregory stopped at a desk which abutted his and rolled over its empty chair for Sheila to sit in. "My partner Pat's desk," he said reflectively.

Gregory sat down. "Would you like some coffee, Mrs. Landis?"

Sheila shook her head. "No, thank you."

Gregory glanced down at the report he had been handed. "Will you allow me to make one call before we start?"

Sheila offered a tight-lipped nod, her eyes closing briefly.

Gregory dialed the Hayes residence, giving the rotary dial of his phone quick, hard spins. Lacey herself picked up on the other end. She did not allow for any pleasantries before reeling off the purpose of her call. "*My boyfriend Jerry told me to call you— Jerry Porter. He told me to tell you—he left me a note to tell you—to go to Vizcaya right away.*"

Pen in hand, Gregory enunciated Vizcaya as the principal word in her spurt of words he wrote down.

Sheila sat even straighter in her seat. "Vizcaya," she said. A desperation came over her face and voice. "That is where my daughter went last night with her boyfriend. My husband went looking for her there in the middle of the night. They did not come home." Sheila opened her purse and pulled out a handkerchief to hide her failing composure.

Sheila's reaction prompted Gregory to end the conversation with Lacey prematurely, but confirming his knowledge of their scheduled appointment for later in the day. Two thoughts rushed into Gregory's mind almost simultaneously. One was to offer the distressed woman a glass of water. But it was the other police-instinctive query that spilled forth. "Does your daughter have a boyfriend?" he asked routinely.

Sheila plugged up a runny nostril as discriminatingly as she could with her embroidered handkerchief. "Why, yes. Raúl," she sniffed. "Raúl Purrez. There were so many Purrezes in the phonebook…"

"That Vizcaya place; it's the estate home and gardens in South Miami?" Gregory inquired.

"Yes. I drove past there before coming here. It was dark. I saw no sign of anyone from the exterior."

"I'll, uh—I'll arrange for a squad car to go out there before they open up."

"Your face altered expressions when I mentioned that boy's name. I don't know where he lives, or my husband and I would have gone to his house ourselves. The school principal said he could not give out students' addresses. My daughter is fifteen."

After hearing the connection with the Pérez boy, Gregory decided to take, at least, preliminary action on this woman's case. "I happen to know where your daughter's boyfriend lives—if it's the same boy. I'll be happy to take a quick ride out to his home for you."

Sheila became almost cheerful. "You do! Thank you. Oh heavens! My husband suspected he was a juvenile delinquent. I must go with you. *Please.*"

Riding with a civilian was not regular police procedure, but it was not against protocol either. The Landis woman could be of help in corroborating Raúl's identity, if nothing else. Gregory nodded his agreement.

"What about the Vizcaya locality?" asked Sheila, returning the used hanky into her purse and then clicking it shut. "It is completely walled with an imposing wrought-iron front entrance gate."

Gregory rose from his chair and waited for Sheila to do the same. "I'll have the sergeant look for a curator's phone number or security detail information. Maybe somebody can get down there to open up early."

\*\*\*

Sheila overheard a colleague say to Detective Gregory that the collective crime scene was the most gruesome he had seen in all of his twenty-plus years on the force. Surpassing even the murder-suicide of that family of four in Wynwood eight years ago, she remembered reading about at the time. Gregory had swung past the Pérez home with Sheila. With the driveway empty and no one answering the front door, it appeared no one was home. While knocking on neighbors' doors in search of investigative information about the residence and its occupants,

Gregory had been summoned to the Vizcaya scene on his car's police radio. Waiting in the vehicle, Sheila alerted him to the crackling wireless call.

Sheila had been held back at the oval forecourt of the mansion's north entrance.

"We found two men," Gregory now said to her after he had returned from inside. "They are deceased."

Sheila blinked rapidly and clung to her hand purse. She nodded at Gregory, and he led her forward through the pink marble, horse-shoe-shaped gateway, past the sunken swimming pool, and up the steps to the East Terrace.

The remarkable vista opened up to Sheila. Separated now from the horizon, the new day's sun had shaken off its orange glow. The unmistakably defined ball of dazzling radiance delivered a brilliant slanting sheen over the aquamarine surface of Biscayne Bay. Far in the distance, a smattering of puffy flat-bottomed clouds glided listlessly in the panoramic sky. The salty breeze from the bay seeped invigoratingly through Sheila's lungs. Because of the shroud of unspeakable acts she conceived that hung over the premises, Sheila fought the urge to soak up the beautiful morning feel at the palatial estate.

On the oblong East Terrace, men with police or medical badges folded outward from shirt and jacket pockets scurried about. She paced through their crisscrossing movements, as rapidly as her constrictive skirt permitted, over to two covered bodies near the promenade steps. The bodies lay side by side. Large rocks pinned down the ends of white medical sheets overlaying their lumpy forms.

Gregory gestured to a couple of forensics men casually talking to one another. Their eyes veered toward Sheila until one flicked away an unfiltered cigarette that he had sucked into near oblivion.

Standing over the dead bodies, Sheila vacillated, releasing measured breaths through her nose. Unpredictably, a stiff breeze rippled over the sheets of the cadavers. A corner flap from one of the sheets fluttered loose and folded back, exposing the face of one of the bodies.

Bloated and stained with the unmistakable pall of gray death, the face jolted Sheila and elicited a gasp as she took in the cadaver's black eye socket hole above the cheek.

Gregory steadied her, and she shook her head at him. "They pulled this one out of the water. Looks like he was in there for hours."

"The fishies started in on him," said one of the forensics men, crouching to cover the exposed portion of the body. "At least one of them pecked out his eye."

"Mrs. Landis' husband was believed to be in the vicinity last evening," Gregory said to the man who shrank a little, understanding Gregory's meaning.

Maintaining his squatting position, the forensics man edged over to the other body. Moving aside the weighing rock from one of the top corners of the sheet, he glanced up at Sheila and then at Gregory. Sheila stood frozen, her eyes glued to the hidden facial outline under the thin sheet until Gregory gave the nod.

The forensics man slowly uncovered the pale, lifeless face. Sheila's lips parted, but no breath escaped them. *He could have been sleeping,* she thought, *except for the chunk of gaping flesh missing from his throat.* Sheila turned away. "That's my Randy," she said, muffling an anguished cry. The forensics man empathetically brought back the sheet over Randall's face and attentively tacked down the corner with the rock.

Sheila fumbled with her purse, trying to retrieve a needed tissue. She forced herself to take deep, even breaths. She reached down for all the self-control her well-bred background could muster. She did not ask who, why, or how. Her thoughts instead raced out to her daughter.

Gregory seemed to read her mind. "There were two other…girls," he said to Sheila. "We found some IDs among the clothes. The good news is we don't think either is your daughter. But we'd still like you to…have a look."

"A look?" asked Sheila, the rims of her teary eyes stained with displaced mascara.

"At the bodies. Just their faces."

"Bodies?" Sheila wondered out loud before becoming increasingly concerned.

Gregory breathed in deeply through his nose. "Mrs. Landis, a terrible thing has happened here…"

A uniformed policeman interrupted Gregory. "Detective, excuse me. You're wanted out at the far end of the gardens. Marine patrol found *parts* of another body."

The detective's face commanded more from the young officer.

"The body's hacked up—arms and legs chopped off."

Sheila nearly swooned, requiring Gregory once again to provide a ballast for the close-to-overcome woman.

Straining to compose herself, Sheila, with Gregory's help, navigated into the courtyard through the East-Loggia entrance, tiptoeing around shattered glass and ducking under yellow police-caution tape. Following Gregory's silent command, the young cop who had reported the discovery of the dismembered body accompanied them. Under Gregory's orders to 'find her something to sit on,' he extemporaneously pulled a chair from a nearby room. Sheila gratefully sank into the plush burgundy and gold trim-cushioned seating of the wooden chair.

Sheila distinctly heard Gregory give another order to the young cop to 'find her some water.' Gregory then left. The young cop returned with water in an elaborate china cup rimmed with sterling silver. A yacht burgee and the word NEPENTHE were also part of the cup's unique identifying features.

After a first few satisfying sips, Sheila drank sporadically from the china cup. Her eyes lingered over two stains a few feet apart, of what she determined to be dried blood on the coral-stoned courtyard floor. Orange traffic cones were placed around the affected areas. She refused to speculate whose blood had been spilled, but something told her it was her husband's.

***

A woman shortly thereafter appeared at the North Arcade. Facing in that direction, Sheila had been one of the first to become aware of her. From behind sizable round-rimmed glasses, she surveyed everyone moving around with varying degrees of contempt in her eyes. She wore a plain gray skirt that covered her knees and a high-collared mohair jacket with a frilly white under blouse. Her predominantly gray hair was tied tightly in a bun at the top of her head. In a clear tangent moment, rising above her currently despondent brainwaves, Sheila typecast the woman as a head librarian.

Staring indignantly, the woman stepped down into the courtyard, veering around the marked off circles of dried blood. She then focused on Sheila and came walking purposely toward her with a handbag hooked over a bent arm. "What may I ask are you doing?" she posed.

Not expecting the snooty opening, Sheila remained tongue-tied.

"That is Cauldon England bone china you are holding. It is part of the china from the original owner's eighty-foot yacht and certainly not for common use."

The young cop, who had stayed with Sheila without having to have been told, interceded. "May I help you?"

"You may if you can tell me why this woman is sitting on a seventeenth-century intarsia-decorated Italian chair that has obviously been relocated from its rightful place in the banquet hall."

Sheila innocently inspected herself and the chair. She was too emotionally distraught to feel insulted. Emotionless, she rose from the chair, offering the china cup in her hand to the woman who made no gesture to accept it.

The young cop confronted the pushy woman. His body language implied both irritation and a shortage of patience with her conduct. Before he could verbalize his sentiments, the woman spoke again, adjusting her shoulders into a rigid posture.

"My name is Mildred Crawford. I am the curator of this museum. I wish to speak to the person in charge."

The person in charge arrived before he had to be summoned. Coincidentally, within seconds of the curator's assertive request, Detective Gregory came back into the courtyard.

"Here he is now," the young cop told the curator.

In the brief interim, the curator had opened her purse and airily pulled out a pair of slate-gray gloves. She deftly slipped one glove and then the other over the fingers of each hand, tugging tightly down the tapered ends to well below her wrists.

"This is the curator, Mildred…" the young cop informed Gregory.

"Crawford," said the curator. She only extended her hand when Gregory held out his. "I was expecting someone of higher rank."

"I'm a first-grade detective," Gregory stated without pretense. He then turned to Sheila. "There's no cause for further alarm with the new…discovery."

Sheila nodded gratefully, her head weighing heavily on her shoulders.

Gregory readdressed the other woman. "Mrs. Crawford—"

"*Miss,*" corrected the curator.

"*Miss* Crawford, I'd like you to unlock all the bottom-floor entrances for my men and accompany me through every room in this house, in case any ancillary doors need unlocking." Gregory's eyes scanned upward as he finished.

"Most of the upstairs rooms are only roped off to the public, detective. There's no need to lock anything. Now, has a burglary taken place?"

"It's far worse than that. We have several people dead on the premises, I'm afraid." Gregory briefly touched the back of Sheila's shoulder in a display of sensitivity.

The curator half spun around and showed her first hint of concern. "It would be prudent to take an inventory."

\*\*\*

Miss Crawford was appalled. First, some uncouth intruder had left a soda-pop bottle on the Louis XVI table in the master bedroom. The same person or persons, no doubt, had torn most of the bed canopy curtain down, leaving only a ripped portion of drooping drapery.

The 'do-not-touch' restriction imposed by the authorities prevented her from removing the bottle and immediately formulated a contesting, grim premonition. *That's a silk-embroidered landscape panel set into a four-hundred-year-old tabletop. Do you know what a ringed soda stain is going to do to it?"*

From inside the master bathroom, with the breeze from the bay blowing pleasantly through the open loggia doors, she had seen the dried blood on the loggia flooring. Miss Crawford had told herself that the floor could be pressure cleaned to remove all traces of the puddled and smeared mess she beheld. But the worst of it by far was the wanton destruction of the wall panel and Watteau painting inside the Espagnolette bedroom. She could not conceive of the depraved mind that would want to demolish such exquisite craftsmanship.

Miss Crawford wanted to draw the drapes that had been drawn back from the room's east-facing windows. *"This Tabriz rug should at all times avoid direct sunlight."* Both of her conservation petitions were met with unshared distress by the crime-scene technicians who prevented her from touching anything. The galled woman huffed out of the Espagnolette bedroom. Her cultural art world turned completely upside down.

On the second floor's east gallery, Miss Crawford searched for and found Detective Gregory at the far end of the gallery, being spoken to by another detective.

"Have we seen all the rooms to this place?" Gregory posed as Miss Crawford approached.

"I've given you the same tour our guides give to visitors, detective," answered the curator.

From the end of the south gallery, someone whistled at Gregory and called him over. Trailed by Miss Crawford and the young cop, Gregory walked over to one of the two uniformed officers. "Looks like there's another passageway down through here, detective," said the shorter of the two officers.

"There is nothing back there," Miss Crawford interposed as the two cops pushed back a solid stage wall. "It's nothing but a service passage leading to what were the servant's quarters. We have it blocked off at both ends."

"More rooms?" inquired Gregory.

Miss Crawford found the light switch for them just inside the darkened passageway. Gregory told the taller of the two cops to stay put while he, Miss Crawford, and the other two officers walked through.

"I haven't been back here in ages," said Miss Crawford, a quarter of the way in.

Inside the empty passage, the investigators came upon two doors apart from each other. Gregory, in the lead, tried the door closest to him; it opened, leading deeper inside the engaging complex. The young cop swerved off with Gregory's assent to

146

open the other door, but it was locked. Everyone shifted in Miss Crawford's direction.

"It's the first servant's quarters," advised the curator. "I do not carry the keys for these doors. The maintenance company does. The rooms remain locked and only opened twice a year for airing and cleaning."

Gregory proceeded through the other unlocked door. It was dark, and once again he sought the curator to assist with finding the lighting switch.

"I'll be glad to lead you from here," said Miss Crawford. "Though I hope you are not planning on spending a great deal of time in here, detective. It's quite stuffy."

Gregory remained quiet, drawn instead to a staircase opening that cropped up in front of them.

"The servant's stairwell," disclosed Miss Crawford.

The detective motioned for the shorter-in-stature officer to head down the stairs in a clear fact-finding mission. "Check it out."

The remaining three led by Gregory slinked down a short corridor and through an open doorway off to the side. Muted light from a wide shuttered window at the far wall of the empty rectangular room bounced against the faded hardwood floor and cast the room with a sepia tone.

At the doorway, Miss Crawford peeked in and offered verbal context to their location. The woman stepped further into the room the more she spoke. "This was the gathering place of the staff. This is where they took their meals. On a table, I'm sure, perpendicularly placed near that window."

Both men of authority then heard something through the room's other doorway. Gregory signaled Miss Crawford to remain stationary while he and the young cop unholstered their weapons.

\*\*\*

One may have easily characterized the decision to stay at Vizcaya as utterly foolish, if not entirely reckless, Alegría evaluated. But not only had she stayed, she had daringly taken refuge in one of the servant's rooms not twenty feet from where she now perceived Detective Gregory and company had reached.

"We'll leave the door, as it is locked from the outside," she had told Raúl and her mother. "I'll scale from the outside, force open the window, and bring Momó, you, and your catatonic girlfriend up the same way. And we'll set up a diversion, just in case, with the three Hostiles."

Inside the room with Alegría, standing like sentinels on the other side of the door were Raúl and Margot. Raúl held Randall's shotgun reloaded with the casings he took from his overalls. Margot flaunted the spear-gun that had targeted her earlier, loaded with a recovered lone spear. The other spears, Alegría recalled, had wildly scattered when she began her brutalization of the white-clad corpse. The grandmother and grandson stood motionless, awaiting further developments from the voices they heard outside. In the only chair in the sparse room sat Dawn; she stared blankly out through glazed eyes, blinking intermittently.

"If discovery is imminent," Alegría had directed her followers, "plan *B* is to fire multiple volleys through the door and negotiate a standoff until nightfall."

Alegría lay on the room's single mattress bed, pushed into a corner where ambient sunlight was filtered out by the eight-fold Coromandel screen purloined from the breakfast room. Lying face-up on the bare mattress with eyes closed, Alegría appeared as if she were sleeping. Her finely plucked eyebrows and rose-painted mouth twitched from time to time, a telltale sign of unrestful slumber or dreaming.

Nearby, Raúl's shoulder's straightened in nothing more than posture relief for his back muscles. But in doing so, his shifting weight pressured the hardwood floorboard with his foot and caused it to creak.

Raúl and Margot stared at each other with deep concern, and then their eyes crept back to the shielded bed where Alegría lay, where Alegría's dreams persisted beneath her uneasy sleep…

\*\*\*

"… I think Eduardo wants to pop the question."

"What?" said Alegría with a mixture of surprise and elation.

The two girls had just come out of the ladies' room, and Rosa had lightly grabbed Alegría's arm before they headed back into the dancehall.

"Will you permit us some time alone if the situation arises?"

"Certainly…but isn't this rather sudden?"

"Yes, it is. It's only been a month since Eduardo saw me in the crowd at the carnaval. Eduardo made inquiries about me, he said, the minute he stepped off his grand marshal float." Rosa swung her shoulders back and forth, her hands pinned against the sides of her dress. *"Fue amor a primera vista."*

Alegría smiled, but her eyes displayed some reservation.

Rosa addressed it. "I know," she said with a half-bow of her head. "He's older than me…by maybe twenty years."

"Don't you know?"

"I haven't asked. And what about you? Don't think I did not see you and Antonio kissing on the dance floor. He's at least twenty-eight."

Alegría became guarded. She tried to push the recollection of the familiar *exchange* with Antonio from her mind.

"Oh, don't worry," said Rosa, flapping a hand. "I won't tell anyone."

"I'm just here for the dancing," said Alegría, straightening her back.

"There won't be any more dancing until the top of the hour," said Antonio, startling Alegría. "The band is on break."

Eduardo also appeared as if out of nowhere and nestled himself at Rosa's elbow. The gentlemen carried small fruity drink cups in their hands which they handed to their dates. The girls graciously accepted.

"Why don't we go for a quick ride," Eduardo asked Rosa directly, "until the band is ready to return?"

With the cup to her lips, Rosa's eyes rolled to one side at Alegría, trading a disguised signal. "A ride would be splendid," answered Rosa, letting Eduardo take the drink from her hand.

Antonio addressed Alegría. "Let us step outside and enjoy the night as well."

Disposing of the drinks, the couples exited the dancehall. There was considerable activity outside, with well-dressed men and women milling about with lit cigarettes in their hands. In the parking lot, a few cars passed the pair, the lot's flashlight-waving attendant guiding the vehicles out. Soon, the Roadmaster convertible with a relaxed Eduardo at the wheel and Rosa nuzzled under his outstretched arm departed from the lot, leaving Alegría and Antonio waving with halfhearted farewells after them.

Antonio gently clasped Alegría's elbow. "Why don't we go over there? From the roof, we can see when they return."

Alegría's face questioned the direction Antonio proposed. *The two-story building on the other side of the lot?* She let herself be guided toward the building because it was not at an overly disconnecting distance from the dancehall and because she did not think Antonio would be able to get inside.

At a side door etched into the brick building, Antonio found the doorknob uncooperative. He smiled back at Alegría, tried again, and, releasing the wobbly knob, pushed open the grimy door with his palm.

"We cannot go in there," said a wary Alegría. She glanced upward at the shade-drawn windows snuffing out most of the light behind them and indicating, more than likely, the presence of some people. "What if we are caught?"

"We will tell the truth," answered Antonio coolly. "That the door was open and we just wanted to find a cool place for a few minutes…higher up. Vale."

The simple and what Alegría accepted as an all-around honest statement allowed the mischief of youth to bubble within her, which quickly gave rise to a streak of daring. She entered through the door which Antonio closed gently behind her. Immediately inside, Alegría discerned the camouflaged cruelty that lay within. She heard the grunts and oinks of what she identified as confined pigs and breathed the smell of slaughter in the air. She had been around enough pig butcherings during the seasons of *Nochebuena* to know they were in a slaughterhouse. The dirty floor was slick, holding traces of long-lost absorbing sawdust.

They veered away from closed double doors in front of them and toward a nearby iron staircase. "Do you know where you are going?" Alegría asked as they began climbing, shoes clanking on the wrought-iron steps.

The couple hesitated at an open swing door near the second-floor landing. Alegría heard the idle chatter of various men inside while battered by the associated smell of blood and intestinal odors of freshly killed animals that had been sliced open. She acknowledged Antonio's signal to stay quiet and accepted his offered hand.

"It's just a skeleton crew working some extra hours," he stated. Then he jutted out his chin away from the open door, directing their path toward an upward extension of the staircase.

Alegría could not avoid stealing a look into the large, not well-lit room as she scooted past the door. She glimpsed three engaged men, all wearing vinyl aprons slick with blood. One, with a glowing cigarette in his lips, swung a meat cleaver down on a table of slimy entrails. The other two worked at properly hanging from a rolling meat hook a gutted pig over a blood-draining trough. The blood-dripping pig bumped two other martyred constituents, hanging from their own metal gaffes.

The sharply angled fire-escape-like extension of the staircase met a skylight which presumably opened to the roof. The hunched pair held onto the low railings as they climbed the short distance to the top. Alegría took care to step gingerly on the narrow steps, but looking up, she nearly slipped and lost her balance. A lightning-fast reaction from Antonio, reaching back to grab her wrist, kept her from falling.

Antonio flapped open the skylight window and stepped out onto the roof, assisting Alegría behind him.

Alegría found the fresh air filling her lungs a welcomed change from the stifling animal stink inside the building. She gazed upward. Glittering stars blanketed the night sky above her, upstaging the dwindled brightness of the quarter moon which hung dejectedly low amid its surrounding incandescent splendor.

Unexpectedly, Antonio grabbed Alegría and whisked her out of sight behind the skylight fixture. He wrapped her in a protective and also self-indulging embrace as the noise they had heard repeated and the skylight door flapped open. Alegría's heart raced in her chest, doubly stimulated from the fear of being discovered and the closeness of her body to Antonio's. She remained rigid, refusing to meet Antonio's eyes.

The investigating man poked his head out a few feet from the roof access. He must have heard Alegría's suppressed exclamation from her slip on the stairs, she surmised. The man leaned out with one hand on the sooty roof. He gazed in all directions allowed by his position, which prevented a reverse sweep. Sufficiently assured, he brought the skylight flap down. A firm latching sound conveyed the closing shut of the window frame.

Alegría exhaled, and her eyes reflexively sought Antonio's. Before her lips could fully stretch out a smile of relief, Antonio smothered her with a kiss. The fingers of his hand slid up the back of her neck and burrowed into her wavy hair until he clasped a thick-enough entanglement of locks to keep her lips fixed to his hungry mouth. Alegría detected pressure from her passionate admirer's other hand at the small of her back which arched her frame harder into his.

Alegría resisted only briefly. Then, after an ardent interlude of open-mouth kissing, she succumbed to the combination of romantic forces coercing her all evening. She succumbed to the foreign appeal of Antonio, to the luxurious ride of the gleaming roadster, to the exhilarating music and dance movements, and to the mystical stars suddenly swirling above her. Shortly after realizing she was breathing through an unencumbered mouth, her knees trembled as her hands reached down over her dress and found Antonio, his head slinking under the flouncy layers of her skirt.

The stars then seemed to sway in unison above her, becoming brighter and brighter with each illusionary swing until they blurred into one shining and explosive spectacle of light that spun Alegría's consciousness into a feathery darkness.

\*\*\*

Later, Alegría could not remember coming down from the rooftop of the meat-packing plant. She could not remember the couple having skipped the orchestra's second set. She could not remember the drive home to Antilla from the dancehall. All she remembered, at a time too late to change anything, were bits of a confusing conversation she overheard between Eduardo and Antonio while semiconscious in the backseat of the Roadmaster convertible.

"She is Rosa's friend!"

153

"I could not resist. She is enchanting."

"I'll bet. You are always thinking with your fangs!"

"Look who is talking. Courting and then proposing marriage to a Purebred."

"I told you this fraud would take at least a year. What better cover to prove our commitment to the town and neighboring areas?"

"Fine. But what else could I do? I could not drain her? How would we have explained *that* to your new fiancée?"

"There is a cobalt moon in September. We will still be here, and she will start feeling some effects."

"What does it matter? By the time she experiences a full cycle of the cobalt moon in three more years, we will be long gone."

With her eyes fluttering half open and close, another familiar voice recognized by Alegría in her semiconscious state joined the other two.

"I'm back," said Rosa, wiggling the fingers of one hand, the hand which had one finger newly adorned with a sparkling engagement ring. "I just couldn't resist showing off a little inside."

Eduardo took his betrothed's hand and kissed it prior to helping her into the car.

Rosa sat in the back and placed Alegría's head on her shoulder. "The poor thing," she said. "It must have been all the dancing. I'm sure she will never forget this night."

# Chapter Eight

With the warming temperatures following the break of dawn, the smell of rancid garlic became too unbearable. First one dove in. Then a pair jumped into the water, methodically followed by all the Dociles. Some of the boys took off their shirts first. A few brazen girls did the same. One or two of the more spirited young ladies even removed their brassieres. Many of the bathers—sharing bars of soap—opted to splash in along the side embankment of the stadium whose grandstand jutted out over the water like a geometric forty-five-degree right triangle. The aggregate action of the teenagers baffled all of the police officers mingling about, who were powerless to stop the systematic self-dunkings occurring in the basin of the marine stadium. One of the police officers present unsuccessfully resorted to blowing a whistle to try and halt the watery migration.

In no time, everyone under the age of twenty was in the water—except Laz. Standing next to a police officer with hands on his hips, he watched his father's flock engage in body-scrubbing bathing rituals to shed the residue of scent-cloaking garlic from their bodies. One bewildered cop near them tilted the hat back from his forehead and scratched his head, staring at all the kids bobbing in the water. The crews of the marine patrol boats anchored away from the shore stopped their fact-finding tasks to also gawk at the unusual proceedings. Laz just smiled innocently at the cop at his side.

"Aren't you part of this bunch, kid?" asked the cop with his hands akimbo. "Or are you just not into communal bathing?"

Another cop ambled over to his colleague. "I thought hippies didn't like the water," he said. "Even junior ones."

"We're not junior hippies, officer," said Laz. "We're just high-school kids."

The officer closest to Laz eyeballed him sternly. "High-school kids that stayed out all night...on their own."

Laz stayed silent. He had agreed to lie to the police, in a scheme concocted with Peter before the authorities arrived, with the expressed intent of continuing the mission of his father. If the police found out his father had been killed, along with the two crew members, the ensuing investigation would certainly jeopardize the expedition set for this morning. At least that was what Peter had told him, and Laz had buckled under the peer pressure of support backing Peter at the time.

Yet another cop walked up to the threesome, the oldest, in years, of three uniformed officers strolling about. He spoke directly to Laz. "You the kid that took the schooner out for a midnight sail...which somehow ended up exploding and sinking right out there?"

Laz nodded. He bowed his head when he heard the other officer inject, "It was his old man's boat, Dave."

"You couldn't have handled a craft of that size on your own," said Officer Dave, followed with a casual point out toward the young bathers. "Which one of those duckies helped you?"

The officer waited for an answer, but instead received suppressed whimpering from Laz, his head down and instantly overcome with emotion. The two officers on either side of Laz blamelessly squinted at each other before Officer Dave's colleague said, "Probably thinking of the beating his old man is going to give him."

***

Rosa gently squeezed the pistol nozzle of a garden hose, generating the intended soft, wide spray over Milagros who was standing a few feet away. In the backyard of their home, against a back wall, Milagros had shed her blouse and skirt and was rinsing off from a quick soaping she had given herself. "I guess this is what's known as an *al fresco* shower, huh, *mamá*?"

"Make sure the saltwater and any garlic remains are all off," said Rosa. Wrapping a towel around Milagros, she briefly offered a helping hand to dry her before handing over a folded stack of clothes on the ground which included a fresh pair of undergarments.

"Joshua is obviously ready to hear about his mother now," said Milagros, slipping on her underwear. "Is there something, anything you can tell him, besides the fact she became a passing acquaintance? How about his father? I'd like to know myself." Milagros finished buttoning her blouse and turned around to face her mother. "And, God, what happened when you and Juan tried to kill Alegría initially?"

"Ay, so many questions," answered Rosa. "Sixteen years it's been, *mija*."

The pair walked along the side of the house to the front yard, where they found Joshua sitting with his head tucked inside folded arms and resting on bent knees.

"He's exhausted," said Milagros.

"You all must be," said her mother. "Where will you get your rest before tonight?"

"On the bus," answered Milagros.

Jerry then came skipping out through the front door. Catching sight of Milagros and Rosa, he smiled. "Thanks, y'all, for use of your shower."

Milagros raised a finger halfway to her lips, tilting her head at Joshua.

Jerry did not heed Milagros' call for restrain. He unsympathetically bumped the outwardly snoozing Joshua with his foot. "C'mon, Jay. It's your turn. Don't worry, there's plenty hot water left." When Joshua did not budge, Jerry kicked him a little harder. "I have to get going. I promised momma. Saturday chores. Then it's off to see Lacey this afternoon. I'll call you guys tomorrow...after this *thing* of yours." He broke out successive Docile half-vampire and human greetings with one hand in an intentionally lighthearted way that made Milagros chuckle.

"You know we're going to drop you off," Milagros stated.

"Thought you'd never offer, my sister," replied an appreciative Jerry.

Finally lifting his head slowly, Joshua peered up at Jerry, revealing puffy, runny eyes and lips swollen to twice their normal size. His repugnant face alarmed everyone. His labored breathing released wheezing sounds. His shoulders shuddered, and his head trembled.

"Get him to the backyard!" yelled Milagros. "It's the leftover garlic."

Because of the traces of garlic, Milagros stayed a distance behind as Jerry and Rosa rushed Joshua to the back. "Hurry, take off his shirt and hose him down," she instructed.

Jerry pulled off Joshua's shirt and grimaced at the blotchy skin of Joshua's neck and chest. He took the offered garden hose and pointed at Joshua. Squeezing the pistol nozzle, a concentrated gush of water blasted Joshua in the face. Raising his hands and deflecting some of the jetstream, Joshua staggered against the back wall of the house, disoriented by the unrelenting discharge of water.

"Don't let up, Jerry," Milagros said forcefully.

Jerry saturated Joshua until he motioned his arms, signaling his capitulation. Jerry glanced at Milagros who nodded before releasing his hand from around the nozzle.

Joshua placed his hands on his knees. Everyone stepped closer to him and let out a sigh of relief as he lifted his head, his face no longer distorted. The previous epidermal blotches on his neck and chest had also remarkably dissipated.

Putting a hand on Joshua's shoulder, Jerry said, "I didn't mean to go all Bull Connor on you, Jay, but you were looking stinkin' ugly. A lot like Alegría coming out of the cabin on the boat…and when she got a whiff of me."

Joshua straightened up and skimmed off whatever excess water he could from his person. Rosa handed him a towel. "That sure woke me up," he said.

Milagros put a hand on her hip. "The supernatural convergence is in full motion. All half-vampires, Dociles and Hostiles, begin to shoulder the traits of a vampire on the day of the cobalt moon. That garlic residue was poison to you."

Jerry rubbed his chin and took a wary step back. "Are you going to start craving blood anytime soon?"

"It won't come to that, Jerry. We are going to sequester ourselves." A beaming Milagros then reached for Joshua's hand, holding it loosely in hers. "I'm glad to see you are finally coming around, Mr. Puig. First the garlic…and now your nails."

Casting his eyes downward, Joshua lingered a bit over the fingertips of his hand before holding out the rigid digits.

He suddenly shivered, Milagros uncertain if the chill had been caused from the air or the sight of his crusty yellow fingernail color.

\*\*\*

"Shouldn't you take off your blouse?" he asked, arching his eyebrows.

"In front of all these people, Peter?" responded Toni, pretending to be offended.

Peter kicked his feet and spread his arms through the water to move up closer to his girlfriend, bobbing in front of him. "Purely to keep up the act, my sweet." Peter summoned a broad grin that cracked his mouth.

"There's nothing pure about that," said Toni, playfully splashing him.

Peter spit out the saltwater that flew into his grinning mouth, energetically pedaling his feet to keep his chin above the water's surface. The pair had jumped into the water like everyone else, and none too soon. The light application of garlic they had spread over themselves for pretense purposes was becoming stingingly unendurable, finally breaking down the previous nullifying menthol agent.

For the most part, around them, there was little obtrusive splashing or carrying on among the assembly of cleansing teenagers—although not everyone could refrain from hijinks amid the coed bathing. A splinter group of boys had floated over to a tight circle of buoyant females, which counted among them two topless free-spirits. A mischievous pair of boys outside the ring dove straight down and came up in the middle of the ensemble of girls, spurring irritated yelps and stiff orders of expulsion.

Quickly recovered from the face splash, Peter swam over to Toni. She did not protest when he slung both of his arms around her. He slid his tinted prescription glasses from their position at the top of his head to the accustomed bridge of his nose. Through water-spotted lenses, Laz and the police came into better focus for the near-sighted swimmer. After tonight, Peter told himself, his visual impairment would be a thing of the past and he could rid himself of his detracting eyeglasses forever. When Peter noticed what appeared to be Laz breaking down, he motioned Toni to swim in with him.

The morning tide had swelled the basin and the new elevated waterline made it easier for Peter to pull himself up at the concrete lip of the retaining wall. He then helped Toni up and over the low, scalable railing. He reached for his orange-tie-dyed T-shirt that he had slung over the retaining wall railing and put it on as he walked over to Laz and the men of authority. Toni followed, her soaked peasant blouse clinging to her torso.

"Laz," said Peter, "everything cool?"

"You two know each other?" asked the older officer.

"We just met tonight," replied Peter who courteously volunteered his name.

"Did you see who came in with him on the schooner that blew up?"

Peter shook his head.

"Do you know what triggered the explosion on the schooner?"

Peter unwaveringly held the policeman's cross-examining eyes. "Maybe a boiler plate blew in the engine room."

The older officer clasped his hands to his belt. "Engine room," he said with a smirk. "It's not a battleship, kid."

"Same with the other kids I spoke to, Dave," said one of the officers. "No one knows anything. And everybody's got the same story. They're all here as part of an outdoor sleepover for a weekend fieldtrip upstate, sponsored by a Christian ministry organization."

The veteran policeman decided on a different tactic with Toni. He asked her name, and she divulged it. His next question was: "Does your mother know you are here?"

Toni blinked once and said, "My mother has been preparing me for this weekend my whole life."

One of the officers nudged the senior officer's arm enough to slide away into a three-way side conference. "Not for anything, Dave, and I know it's your call. But there's no sign of vandalism. Are we going to book eighty, ninety kids for trespassing? Wait all morning for their parents to come and claim them?"

The youngest-looking of the officers interjected passively. "I'm not one to turn my nose up at OT, but my kid's got a little league game at ten."

Hiding the fact he had been listening attentively, Peter watched as the older officer surveyed the scene on the water. The impromptu bathers were almost all back onto dry land, or dry concrete as it were. The anchored police boats were spread out in all directions in the basin. Scorch marks where burning debris had landed on the floating stage before snuffing out were patently visible. The slanted tip of the schooner's mast stuck less prominently out from underneath the blue-green water due to the arriving tide.

One of the uniformed colleagues leaned closer to Officer Dave's ear. "Marine patrol's got jurisdiction over the boat," he stated in another swaying argument for dismissal.

Latched onto the front of his belt with both hands, the veteran officer said, "We can't leave these kids without adult supervision."

A fourth officer then emerged from the curved entrance ramp into the stadium, walking leisurely toward them, his jaw working diligently on obvious foodstuff in his mouth. Tall and rather gangly, his buttoned uniform collar hung loose around his skinny neck. He carried a half-eaten, high-domed muffin in his hand. After making unceremonious eye-contact with his fellow officers, the associate addressed Officer Dave. "Two buses just pulled up in the parking lot," he said, barely finishing a swallow. "They're here for the kids."

Officer Dave and the others peered at the tall, gangly officer. Their interest seemed to be as much on the information delivered as to what he was eating.

Sensing the dual scrutiny, the gangly officer meekly raised the decimated muffin in his hand. "The buses came loaded with breakfast."

*** 

Inside the Impala, Milagros pulled out a sheet of paper and handed it to her mother. "I counted back the cobalt moons," she said. "The night Eduardo proposed to you was in March 1949. That was also the night you think Alegría…"

"Yes, that was the night," stated Rosa. "By Antonio."

"The cobalt moon came in September that year," Milagros continued, facing her mother sitting in the passenger seat. "Not a sufficiently long enough cycle to change Alegría after Antonio's bite. The next cobalt moon came in May 1952. That was the month Alegría converted and escaped from you and Juan. That also had to be the night that Joshua's father converted. Although we don't know when he was bitten."

Joshua and Jerry arched forward in the backseat. Jerry spoke up first. "So if Jay's pops wasn't a vamp yet, how did Jay, uh…get his bat wings?"

Milagros suppressed a smile and answered, "Joshua's father had to have had the vampire strain in his blood before he conceived Joshua. He had to have been bitten before he married Joshua's mother. He passed the Docile strain to Joshua like a hereditary trait, the same way Alegría passed it to both of her kids before she fully converted."

"Yes, the strain is passed from parent to child," said Rosa. "That is exactly how Juan explained it to me."

"Miss Rosa," said Jerry, bringing a mock claw of his fingertips to the side of his neck. "I guess you sure were lucky not to get the big hickey yourself."

The hand gesture helped Rosa express her understanding with a faint smile. "Eduardo and I were engaged for five months before we married. We were together as man and wife for eight more months before he and Antonio left. He traveled often during that time. When he was home, he was always up before sunrise, never to return until sunset. I tried to understand. Never questioned him too much. Just as I never questioned him when he told me our photographer had been assaulted and all the photos from our wedding stolen. Yet, I do believe some part of Eduardo loved me. That is why, how do you say, no big hickey for me."

Milagros and Joshua made eye-contact. He barely nodded and then sat back in the seat. "Joshua wants to know about his mother. But first…tell us what happened when you and Juan tried to kill Alegría."

As Milagros turned the ignition, she noticed her mother glance down at the slip of paper with dates Milagros had prepared. Rosa crumpled the paper in her hand as it seemed she was being swept back to the very time she was trying to choke off in her fist.

***

*"The plan was hatched by Juan and his babalawo,"* Rosa said. *"The man had been a champion arm wrestler in the province before he found his alternative spiritual calling. Juan and I would lure Alegría to Juan's woodworking shop to see the bunk beds he had custom made for her children. At night, Alegría was not as rundown physically as she had been by the daylight hours. The only problem was what to do with Raúl."*

*"Juan opened the store. He did not turn on the lights. It was after hours and dark inside, with little filtered light from the street."*

"This way," Juan said in the semi-darkness.

Alegría and Raúl were drawn inside by his friendly voice.

Then from an obscured region, a hand appeared. It rose up holding a club. Raúl responded to the whirl behind him, but not quickly enough. The truncheon struck him on the side of the head and dropped him to the floor with a heavy thump. Alegría screamed. She called out Raúl's name and then Juan and Rosa's. The figure appeared from the shadows; his long arms and broad chest swallowed up Alegría and pulled her deeper into the darkness. The restricted Alegría could not flail with her arms, but her feet kicked wildly as she demanded to be released. She knocked over a stack of small cans of primer that were on display on top of a wooden stand.

Deeper inside, it turned pitch-black. When artificial light flooded the darkness, the high priest was ominously revealed, ceasing Alegría's screams. He was broad-shouldered and lean, with an unlit chewed cigar clenched in his teeth. A cowrie-shell necklace and an Ifá divination chain made from one-inch long ikin seed rattled around his neck. The man's skin was the color of coal and his teeth brighter than the white *guayabera* shirt that draped over him.

Rosa stood at the far wall, her hand having raised a lever which brought the room and all of its equipment to life. They were in the back workshop of the furniture store, with Alegría plopped on her back on a plywood board above the floor. Working fast with Juan, the high priest tied Alegría's arms and feet to the board with an electrical cord. She lost one of her shoes in the struggle. Making eye-contact with Rosa, she asked incredulously, "What are you doing?"

"The end of days is here for you," the babalawo declared, placing around Alegría's neck a wreath string of garlic bulbs. He nodded at Juan, now positioned at the end of a long double-sided workbench. Juan flipped a switch beneath the tabletop, powering the saw blade that protruded from the flat surface at his end. The thin disk spun speedily in place, blurring the sharp serrated edges all around its whirring exterior. "Your kind has delivered us enough pain and suffering," said the ebony capturer.

Bothered by the garlic necklace, Alegría shook her head disagreeably from side to side with a shortness of breath. "What do you mean my kind?"

Looming above Alegría's face, the high priest pulled the cigar from his mouth, his eyes narrowing with menace. "You must die before you become undead."

At a right angle to the table, the board Alegría lay upon began to shake—to move. Support trusses with wheels beneath the board facilitated the sliding movement. The horror in her eyes became evident when she realized her entire body was sliding toward the buzz saw—her neck on an intersecting course with the blade!

"Rosa!" Alegría yelled. The captive woman's eyes searched for her friend, but she had vanished from her previous stationary spot.

"The bucket!" shouted the church leader to Juan.

"Right here," Juan answered, holding up a metal pale in an ominous display of their barbarous intent.

The sight of the pale filled Alegría with more dread. As she began screaming for random assistance, her eyes glowed with a golden luster. The high priest became alarmed and shrieked another command at Juan: "Hood!"

Juan slapped a burlap covering into his master's open hand. Clutching the coarse head covering, the religious leader stuffed it over Alegría's head despite her objections.

Then the rolling plywood board cracked at Alegría's feet, and Alegría's leg started coming free. Rosa screamed from somewhere near the table.

The teacher again called to his pupil. "We must hurry!" He moved to the other side of the rolling board. "Help me push," he instructed Juan who joined him.

The high priest and Juan began coaxing forward the rolling board to its appointed intersection with the buzz saw. "Not too fast," cautioned Juan. "If it's not a clean cut, the blade may stall."

Alegría was no more than a foot away from decapitation when Raúl came up from behind the two would-be assassins and punched the high priest in the kidney with a well-placed haymaker. The disabling blow crumpled the man to his knees.

The revived husband grabbed Juan by the shirt and spun him violently into the closest wall. Juan banged his shoulders against the wall's shelf casing and slumped down on his rear end, several tools falling from the quivering shelves above him. A dislodged tool box nearly struck Juan, falling to the floor and spilling much of its contents in a clamorous jumble. As he attempted to stand, a power tool struck Juan flush on the head, knocking him semiconscious.

As the hooded Alegría inched toward her head-severing execution, Raúl called out, "I'm here, honey," as he frantically sought to find the saw blade's mechanical switch.

"Raúl! Raúl!" came Alegría's muffled shouts through her head covering.

The would-be deliverer spotted the red switch beneath the tabletop and thumbed it off. The saw's floor motor purred to a halt and the lethally spinning disk bluntly stopped, revealing all of its razor-sharp edges only inches from Alegría's crooked neck.

Raúl gently stroked his wife's immobilized arms. "It's over, baby," he said, reaching to remove his wife's hood. But a strong black forearm wrapped around his neck, stopping him. His breath choked off. Raúl pushed back hard with his feet, and both men careened into a wall, knocking down two by fours and other pre-cut pieces of wood that were on racked display.

Raúl squirmed out of the religious man's grip. But in doing so, his attacker slipped his hands around Raúl's neck and attempted to strangle the life out of him. The aggressor bent Raúl back on a worktable against the back wall, leveraging his weight to pin his opponent down. Raúl swung with weak fists at the man, visibly overwhelmed by his upper-body muscle strength.

One of Raúl's weakened arms dropped outstretched on the table, his fingers grazing a power drill lying randomly within reach. He tried grabbing it as soon as he realized its potential. The eyes of the high priest read Raúl's intent and he snatched the electric tool first, which was plugged into a table socket. The drill powered on. Latching onto the high priest's wrist, Raúl desperately tried to keep the deadly instrument away from his face. The drill chuck protruded a long coiling truss screw whose sharp point whirled inches from his Raúl's cheek. Holding on for dear life, Raúl twisted out of his submissive position and rose up.

The standing combatants spun once around, with the power drill disappearing between them. Then one of the men cried out, a spasm wracking his body. The loud boring sound tapered off into a sloppy shredding noise, and the aspiring murderer dropped to the floor, holding his perforated stomach, seeped in blood. As if to make himself more comfortable for the death he knew was imminent, he sat himself up against some shelving.

Raúl stared at him, receiving from the mortally wounded man a venomous look in reply as he took his last breaths. Regaining his faculties, Raúl hurried over to free Alegría. For the second time in a matter of minutes, he stretched a hand to remove the hood from his wife's head. And for the second time, he was prevented from completing his aim, this time fatally so. The first nail pierced Raúl's neck above his Adam's apple. The second nail struck him below the jawline. Both nails smashed arteries and veins in his neck that sent spurts of blood pouring forth in different directions. Raúl tried to cry out, but his voice was stifled by regurgitating blood coming out from the sides of his mouth.

Looking in the direction of the fired mini-missiles, Raúl, in his last living act, raised his arm with an accusatory point of his fingers at the religious chieftain who had in his possession the nail gun that had hit Juan on the head. The fired nail gun slipped out of the limp fingers of the dying man's hand to the floor beside him.

As Rosa helped a dazed Juan to his feet, she became aware of Alegría shaking off her hood which Raúl had lifted over her face. Alegría cried out, "Rosa, help me! Please!"

After a cold glare from Rosa indicated that she was not interested in assisting her, Alegría's mien changed from fearful and powerless to enraged and emboldened. Her tears instantly dried as her eyes altered to their earlier golden hue. A concerted exertion from her lower body coerced the cracked plywood board to break in two pieces. Her tied lower extremities hit the floor, feet first. *Alegría was breaking free! I pulled Juan by the arm and we got going—*

"Get going!" yelled the driver, followed by two honks of his car horn, interrupting the memory sequence in Rosa's mind.

"Ay, all right already," said Milagros, stepping on the accelerator. "Don't get your knickers in a twist."

The impatient car behind them at the stop light passed the Impala with rapid-fire tooting. "What's the hurry, Murray?!" Jerry shouted through the backseat window.

"What did the police say about the deaths of Raúl and the babalawo in Juan's store, Señora?" asked Joshua.

Rosa delayed responding until her daughter's eyes shifted away from her to fix back upon the road. She moved her fingers along the V-neckline pointed collar of her shirtwaist dress and then smoothed the same hand over her full skirt. "They were dismayed, of course."

"But didn't Alegría cause a problem for you?" asked Joshua. "I mean, over the ambush and trying to kill her and her husband's death?"

Rosa cast her eyes out at the road. "It would have been her word against ours—mine and Juan's. We blamed it on the santero chieftain. Raúl and he died at each other's hands while Juan and I fled."

"And Alegría?"

Rosa turned her head to look out the passenger window. "In another day, she became what she became and left Antilla with her family. No one knew where."

Milagros again stole brief attention away from the road. "I guess the authorities didn't have much to go on when Alegría vanished, huh, mamá?"

"Yes, they closed the case quickly. Who would want to investigate two more killings on the opening night of the carnaval? Killings that weren't suspicious, I mean. Why risk reopening old wounds."

"But two innocent people died—Alegría's husband and the high priest," said Joshua.

"The innocent are not always spared," Rosa said with a calm firmness.

In a few minutes, they had arrived at Jerry's house. Jerry raised his hand and Joshua responded by extending his palm for his bud to scrape. "Swing only with a righteous sword, my man," said Jerry.

Joshua subtlety acknowledged, conjecturing that the tidbit of advice came from the repertoire of Jerry's mother.

Jerry then interchanged ringing hand slaps with Milagros in the front seat. "Take care of my boy," he said. "And watch your own back, too."

"You know it, Jeremiah."

Jerry acknowledged Milagros' mother. "Miss Rosa," he said, nodding politely.

Joshua watched Jerry hop out of the car and jog up to his front door. As the Impala drove away, he edged closer to Rosa. "You said my mother was a bridesmaid at your wedding?"

# Chapter Nine

Alegría's restless repose continued in her hiding place. She jerked her shoulders and her head tossed from side to side. Her eyes remained closed, but her subconscious mind was a veritable movie reel of past events, of occurrences being unearthed in a rearward excavation of memory brought on by the strenuous circumstances accosting her, especially over the last twelve hours.

Standing at the door with their wielded weapons were the statue-like Raúl and Margot. Raúl's curtailed, anxious breathing heaved his chest in abridged surges. Margot assumed the stationary posture of a beast of the wild whose protective maternal instincts were about to be tested.

Well aware of these two cherished remainders of her family, Alegría registered their unease along with the precariousness of her surroundings. Yet the potentially calamitous situation was not enough to awaken her, not enough to pull her away from the optical path into which her subconscious had led her. She became especially agitated at the materialization of the church, the biggest in Antilla, arising clearly in her mind on a day that was seventeen years in the past…

\*\*\*

*"May the gift of the Holy Spirit always remain alive in your soul, Milagros Ricardo Benítez."*

Sitting next to Raúl and Raulito, Alegría held three-month-old Cira. She watched as Rosa, cradling her baby in her arms, accepted a white hand towel from another familiar woman.

The door opened and a beam of blinding light spilled into the church. The black-silhouetted man with the floppy hat retraced his steps slowly, his gaze lingering on hers.

1. Then they were out of the church and in a car. Rosa leaned forward. *"My manners are awful… This is my Eduardo."*
   *"Eduardo Ricardo del Castillo."*
   The names ran together and then repeated in an edited version in Alegría's mind: Milagros Ricardo Benítez. Eduardo Ricardo del Castillo…Milagros Ricardo…Eduardo Ricardo.

2. A rapid return to Cira's seventeenth birthday party: *"And that's Millie,"* said Cira. *"Millie,"* repeated Alegría. *"Punch?"* In the kitchen conference with her children. *"Millie is a Docile. I can smell her."*

3. The fragmented scene quickly changed. She and Raúl were seated again in his Corvair outside of Jerry's house, vigilantly waiting for him on a night he never showed up:
   *"They just teamed up—him and that Millie girl."*
   *"What's Millie's last name?"*

4. And back to Cira's party. An overheard comment to Raul:
   *"I'm Milagros… Joshua's date."*

5. Then the black-silhouetted man with the floppy hat again, dressed differently. He was trying to do her harm with another crazed man, a buzz saw loudly ringing in her ear.

6. Then the face of the black-silhouetted man was older, and he could no longer do her harm. He was dead, lying on the limestone floor at Vizcaya with a meat clever in his back.
   The snippets of memory kept recycling through Alegría's heated hippocampus. To the stakeout in front of Jerry's house: *"I want to take care of Puig."*

*"Puig is Joshua's last name?"* Alegría drifts off. *"That's right. You did mention it at the party. Your sister never did."*

7. Then the scene changed from night to day, and years in the past, in an instant. It changed to a teenage Alegría pushing her first baby carriage, her trusted friend Carmen at her side. *"Now, tell me all about Rodolfo."*

*"Well, his full name is Rodolfo Puig,"* answered Carmen. *"He works at the shoe store across from the movie theater."*

8. *"Puig is Joshua's last name?"*

Rodolfo Puig…Milagros Ricardo…Puig…Joshua Puig… *JOSHUA.*

Alegría sat up in bed, her eyes wide and filled with rage.

\*\*\*

Having heard the floorboard noise, Gregory had his revolver drawn as he moved ahead in the corridor with the young cop. Miss Crawford had taken a few discretionary steps backward. The police officials encountered two doors on either side of them. The doors were to adjacent rooms, tucked into the northwest corner block of the second-floor servants' rooms, disguised from the main mansion.

Gregory tried conventionally opening the door to his right first. To his surprise, the knob turned all the way. His eyes flashed a signal at the young cop and he swung open the door. The two men entered with weapons drawn, assuming stooped positions.

The room had a sheetless twin bed and a small writing desk as its only decorative furnishings. But the focus fell on the youngsters huddled together in one corner. They rushed the policemen with open arms. *"Help us! Save us! There's a killer loose!"*

"It's okay," said the young cop, putting away his gun. "You're safe now."

173

"What happened here?" asked Gregory. None of the three answered. Instead, they tightened their grips around the men. Two of them had fastened around the young cop. One of the trio was nearly Gregory's height. Gregory stepped back, and the young cop took his cue, severing the close contact. Strangely, one of the boys began vigorously scratching his arm.

Miss Crawford encroached the scene. She did not display the same kindly disposition as the officers. "Are these the little hoodlums who broke into my museum? I expect them to be fully prosecuted under the law, detective."

The faces of the three teenagers, the girl specifically, sniffling and trembling exuded a frightened innocence mixed with genuine fear.

"Take 'em away," instructed Gregory. "But not too far. I want some answers."

Miss Crawford grumpily followed the young cop and the teenagers out of the room.

Taking one last look around, Gregory also left the room. He exited but did not follow the others right away. Standing by the other uninviting door, he stared at the knob. A uniformed officer came through as he stretched out his hand. Gregory held off and waited for the officer to speak.

"The parents of two of the deceased teenagers have arrived," said the officer, removing his hat.

Gregory bowed his head and turned away from the door as if to follow the retreating officer. The detective then stopped and reached back.

The aged brass doorknob he tried to turn held firm in its locked setting.

***

"In August 1949, Eduardo and I tied the knot. The honorable Reverendo Alfonso Torres presided over the after-dusk ceremony. The reception followed immediately at *el Náutico.* You remember, Joshua, our town's pier restaurant?"

"Oh, yeah," answered Joshua. "It stood on stilts and jutted over the water of the bay. Everyone said it was the best place to see the seaplanes landing before they taxied over to the waterfront hotel around the bend."

"I'm sure you were beautiful in your wedding gown," smiled Milagros.

Rosa softly closed her eyes, the pleasant recall overrunning her thoughts.

\*\*\*

Mrs. Eduardo Ricardo del Castillo admiringly pressed her hand to the *décolletage* of her strapless floral lace dress. With a half twirl, she stepped back from the mirror in el Náutico's bathroom, glad to be free of the sweep train of her wedding gown. She carefully placed her marriage veil into an open box carton on the sink. "No more hiding my face."

"You look radiant," said Carmen.

Rosa beamed. "I do, don't I?"

Alegría then came charging into the bathroom. Wearing the same dress as Carmen, she headed quickly into one of the bathroom stalls and threw up not loudly or extendedly. It was just a solitary heave-ho. In a few seconds, she came out of the stall, clenching a bathroom tissue to her lips. "I can't deal with all the food smells," she said, walking over to the sink, her baby bump noticeable through her bridesmaid dress. After rinsing her mouth, she replaced the glove she had removed over her hand and slipped a mint into her mouth. She walked over to the bride and gently tapped her wrist. "Eduardo is waiting for you to come out so that you can be formally introduced as Mr. and Mrs."

"You girls go ahead," Rosa instructed. "I want to retouch my makeup."

Rosa dallied at the mirror after the girls had gone, making sure her makeup and hair were to her satisfaction.

At last ready for her big entrance, she pushed open the swing door of the ladies' room, the revved-up sound of the playing music engulfing her. Slipping out unnoticed, Rosa happened to catch sight of the coat-tailed man and woman dancing…spiritedly dancing. The woman was wearing the carnation pink-color design of the bridesmaid dresses and the man—the wheat-colored maned man in the formal coattails—was her less-than-an-hour-old husband! Through unblinking eyes, she followed Carmen whirling gleefully in Eduardo's arms on the small dance floor. As if she were spying through a looking glass, Carmen and Eduardo became larger with the sparkling joy in Carmen's eyes and the brilliance of Eduardo's smile pouring out in simultaneous satisfaction with the other. A bubbling vexation overcame Rosa, her breathing becoming more pronounced. The music chords from the band sounded louder and harsher in her suddenly throbbing temples.

The music stopped. Eduardo bowed gallantly in front of Carmen and kissed her hand. The polite applause for the band that had all but ceased picked up with greater vigor at the ascertained debut of the bride. Rosa paid the applause little mind as she steamrolled right for Carmen. Eduardo stepped in her path, cutting her off. He gracefully whisked his bride away in his arms, signaling the band to strike up an appropriate number. The handclapping from guests seated, and standing, grew louder as the leader of the band which staked out a cramped space in front of one of the wide picture windows facing the bay formally introduced the bride and groom by name.

Eduardo clutched Rosa tightly to his chest and led her through two sweeping paces on the dance floor. "I suggest you show your pearly whites, my dear," he said affably, "as all eyes are upon us."

"What was *she* doing draped all over you?"

Eduardo kept in step with the music. "It was harmless and meant nothing."

"I believe the first dance belongs to the bride's father, does it not?"

Eduardo came to a curt halt, bowed slightly, and yielded Rosa.

"May I?" asked Miguel Benítez, Rosa's father.

Rosa began dancing with her proud father as the band leader announced them to another round of handclapping. They were soon joined by a handful of other couples on the floor who had been seated around tables arranged in a semicircle.

"My heart is swelling with pride for you, daughter," Miguel Benítez said.

A disengaged Rosa failed to fully absorb the profound compliment. Instead, she seemed more interested in scanning the other couples on the dance floor. During a quick pass, she spotted him—and then she took the in-step lead from her baffled father over to her target, brushing the elbows and shoulders of other revolving couples and downright ruffling the feathers of another.

"Oh, hello, you two," said Rosa, trying to act casually after banging into Antonio and one of her other bridesmaids. "Marisol, why don't we switch partners?"

"Switch?" asked her father. "But the song is not over."

"Come now, Papa," replied Rosa. "You cut in on Eduardo."

The older man tried to hide his hurt as Rosa squeezed in between Marisol and Antonio much to the former's chagrin. Rosa raised her arms in the starting dance position. Antonio tugged on his silver cummerbund, dipped his chin at Rosa, and took hold of her hands. They fluidly pranced away, leaving the awkwardly matched pair of Marisol and her father to their own devices.

"You look very beautiful, Rosita," said Antonio.

"*Gracias*. You look very handsome yourself." Antonio's hand slipped away from her waist as he took one step back. Holding onto his other hand, Rosa let herself be twirled before recoupling again. "I know someone else who thinks you look very handsome."

"Oh?" responded Antonio, trying to sound uninterested. "And who is that?"

"My bridesmaid Carmen," Rosa whispered.

\*\*\*

"And that's how I most remember your mother, Joshua," Rosa said. "Dancing practically non-stop with your father at my reception."

Inside the car, Rosa peered right at Joshua, expecting the false smile on her face would mask any infiltrating deceit in her eyes.

\*\*\*

As soon as the Impala pulled to a stop across from his house, Joshua hopped out of the vehicle, pleasantly reflecting on Rosa's just-completed account of his young parents' twirling around the dance floor. The family's cream-colored 1965 Ford Galaxie 500 in the driveway partially obscured the gaping garage door. Joshua could see Thomas puttering around inside the garage.

A bicycle he knew well rested outside of the garage door. The Garvins had given it to him during his first Christmas with the adoptive couple. It was a snazzy metallic-blue Stingray five-speed model with ape hanger handlebars and metal-flaked grips. In Joshua's mind, it was the best gift the Garvins had ever given him, and he had treasured it for years. But he had outgrown it now.

Joshua could have bypassed him into the house via the front door, but he knew better. Still wearing his work clothes with the familiar rectangular Holsum uniform patch sewn to his shirt, Joshua understood that Thomas had skipped his normal routine of hitting the sack after his long nightshift and was purposely waiting for him to come home. Joshua approached the garage but did not step inside.

Thomas spoke without engaging him directly. "Weren't you supposed to take that bike down to St. Mary's for donation?"

"Yes," answered Joshua, uncomfortably reminded that he had shirked an agreed-upon task.

Thomas now moved closer to Joshua, wiping a small towel over his hands. His eyes were bloodshot—magnified by his near-sighted lenses—and the pouches under them appeared more pronounced than normal. Dense threads of disorderly hair were scattered over his forehead. "You think while I'm out working twelve-hour shifts, you can come and go as you please? Leave Katherine alone all night? Have anybody you want stay overnight?"

A rebellious rumbling surged up from Joshua's chest. He peered intensely at his foster father. *Let me tell you about my night, Thomas. While you were baking bread, my friends and I barely avoided dying at the hands of a fiendish monstrosity that would make you shit your pants the minute you made eye-contact.*

"No, sir," answered Joshua.

Thomas brought one fisted hand to rest on his hip, the towel draped at his side. "Twice in one week now, I've had to interrupt my sleep schedule because of you, be dragged down to your principal's office, and get hit with a big time out of pocket expense. And you're out and about whenever you want, without a worry in the world."

179

Joshua fixed his eyes on Thomas. He was indebted to this man, Joshua reasoned, and Thomas deserved his measure of respect even if he was boorish at times.

"You're not becoming…what do you call—*anti-*establishment, are you?"

Joshua suppressed an inclination to roll his eyes. *Make that boorish,* most *of the time.* "No, Thomas. I'm not turning anti-establishment."

Sufficiently reassured, Thomas motioned off to the side. "This floor is overdue for a good cleaning. After sweeping everything out, get a bucket of soap and water and wash her down. Anything on the floor that we don't use anymore, throw out. And then take care of the bicycle—down to St. Mary's *today.*"

About to plead to the authority figure to grant him until tomorrow to take care of the punitive chore, his foster parent prevented it.

"What happened to your face and shirt?" asked Thomas, pointing to the remnant facial and fabric scuffs and stains from Joshua's horrible night.

Joshua unintentionally glanced back at the waiting car. Milagros had parked across the street, her driver-side window lying open to Joshua's side of the house.

The older man took immediate interest. "You keeping time with a girl, boy?" he asked, ducking out of the garage and taking several steps down the driveway.

"No, I'm not," answered Joshua, trying not to seem obvious in his desire to keep Thomas from advancing toward the sidewalk.

Thomas wheeled and grabbed Joshua's arm. "Did she do this to you? What did you do to her?"

His voice took on such a sordid characteristic that it left Joshua wordless.

"You better not be letting any girl get the best of you, hear me?"

Joshua could not remember Thomas aggressively laying a hand on him before now. Angered by his unsavory insinuations, Joshua yanked himself free and stomped away.

"Where do you think you're going? Have you lost your senses, boy?"

Joshua ignored his guardian and kept striding toward his waiting ride. Thomas hurried up to the sidewalk. "You leave now—you leave for good. You hear that? I mean it."

Joshua hopped into the backseat. The car's wheels were in motion before he slammed close the door. Sitting rigidly in the backseat of the moving car, he glanced back over his shoulder. Through the window, he focused not on Thomas but on a concerned Katherine who had come out of the house halfway down the driveway, an arm wrapped around her waist and a hand pressed to her flushed cheek.

"What about the fibrinogen?" asked Milagros.

Joshua attempted to put on a more agreeable face for the sake of Milagros and Rosa in the front seat. "I'll do without for now," he answered with a stiff lip.

Rosa turned around. "Deep down, I'm sure he only wants to protect you. A parent will take whatever measures, even if they are extreme, to keep their child from harm." She then rigidly faced front.

Joshua scooted up to the edge of the backseat. "So, are we taking a ride to you-know-where?"

\*\*\*

The room was quiet enough to hear a pin drop as Alegría's head cocked to one side, her eyes spasming wide. She would not have required her superior auditory perception to hear the hand twisting fruitlessly on the locked doorknob from the outside.

When the knob's jiggling ceased, her agitated state on the bed eased. She could only assume the trump cards of Lane, Miranda, and Marvis had been played to her anticipating fullest.

From behind the fold-out screen, Alegría closed her eyes, initiating another round of restless, memory-filled slumber…

***

*"… You must die before you become undead."*

"Rosa!" Alegría yelled. But her friend was nowhere to be seen.

*"The bucket!"* her assailant demanded.

The garlic clove wreath around Alegría's neck pounded her senses like noxious fumes. Yet through its dizzying effects, beyond her bound state on the tremulous sideboard and above the piercing sound of the buzz saw in her ear, she could interpret the called-out intentions. The *bucket* was to be used as a receptacle for her soon-to-be-severed head!

Alegría screamed for mercy and help. Then all went black— but she maintained her awareness. She heard the stranger and Juan, their exchanged speech short and homicidal. And then she deciphered the commenced violent struggle followed by the salvation in Raúl's voice—joyfully without the whining interference from the buzz saw. *"It's over, baby."* She perceived his touch on her confined arms and his intended removal of the hood that had put her terrifyingly in the dark.

Then the sightless Alegría heard more violent sparring unquestionably involving Raúl again. She shook her head forcefully, trying to shed the partially dislodged hood from her head. As all came to a relative calm again and she was able to shake the coarse hood off, she almost wished she hadn't. She witnessed her husband experience the closing seconds of an agonizing death. Right in front of her eyes, two thin metal projectiles stuck out from Raúl's punctured throat, promoting a

182

bubbly leakage of blood from the irreparably damaged cardiovascular grid of his neck. His eye-contact with her conveyed his powerless and painful end before he doubled over on the floor.

Alegría strained mightily, trying to comprehend how this mindboggling devastation had befallen her. Through teary eyes, she glimpsed her friend. *"Rosa, help me! Please!"*

Rosa ceased apparent attempts to fully revive Juan on the floor and appeared over Alegría. A great relief washed over the captive woman until she examined Rosa's face which did not harbor any trace of rescuer about it.

"Tomorrow, when the moon climbs to its highest point in the night sky, you will become a vampire," she told Alegría with an impassive face. "Your children will become vampires as teenagers. I want you to promise me that you and your children will never harm me, Milagros, or Juan."

Alegría shut her eyes, trying to make sense of the words she was hearing.

"You are changing," said Rosa. "The effects of the sun. Your nausea. These garlic cloves." Rosa lifted the pungent clumps closer to Alegría's face, and the action compelled Alegría to twist her face away as if the cloves were red hot irons. "Promise me you and your children will not hurt my family and I will let you live."

"I won't hurt anyone," sobbed a squirming Alegría. "*We* won't."

Rosa's face did not change expression. It remained cold and completely uninterested in offering assistance. "I don't trust you," she said, reaching down to push the button beneath the tabletop, activating the buzz saw.

Tiny bits of sawdust kicked up in a small cloud around the energized blade. The strong motor below initiated a trembling movement from the plywood board supporting Alegría, inching it toward its very short rendezvous with the saw. "No!" Alegría cried out.

"Swear to me that you and yours will not harm my child or my family."

The whining noise of the saw intensified in Alegría's ear. Feeling the hot air of the buzz saw at her neck and knowing that at any second the unforgiving blade would tear through her fragile exterior, she screamed: "I swear! I swear!"

The whining noise of the saw intensified in her ear...

***

Alegría tried to scream as she had at that horrifying instant on that night years ago. She tried to move her immobile arms. But Margot, who covered her daughter's mouth in her cupped hand, prevented any vocal cry. Then Alegría realized that her arms were being held down on the bed in her sequestered room by Raúl. When she displayed a calmer outward bearing, Margot and Raúl released their restraining grips.

"Looks like you were having a rough dream, Ma."

***

A sideways parked police cruiser blocked the stone-pillar entrance of Vizcaya. A yellow police caution strip ran across the two drawn back wrought-iron doors. A police officer guided traffic along South Miami Avenue in front of the walled enclave.

"We're too late," said Joshua, looking out from the window of the passing Impala.

"I'd hate to be a member of the chamber of commerce starting today," said Milagros, peeking toward the police crowd control barricades being set up along the sidewalk.

Milagros made a left turn into a street that took her onto the grounds of the Museum of Science and Natural History.

"Remember the Vizcaya handbook?" she asked. "It said this parcel of land used to be part of the Deering Estate."

"What do you two expect to accomplish?" asked Rosa as soon as the vehicle halted in the parking lot.

Milagros' lowered gaze veered toward Joshua.

"One of our classmates," said Joshua. "Alegría had her. She may have been left behind."

Rosa shook her head unconvincingly. "Don't you...both have to leave this morning?"

"Si, and we're running late. The causeway isn't far from here. Please take a ride to the marine stadium. Remember my friend Laz from Jackson High? He's there. Talk to him. If the buses won't wait, find out where they are going from him. And then come back for us. We'll figure things out from there. Please do this last thing for us. For me."

Milagros had grabbed a pressing hold of her mother's hands, with Rosa squeezing back. "As long as you don't separate from each other, promise you will stay together."

"We're a team, Joshua and I. Nothing is going to break us apart."

"Through thick and thin," said Joshua, opening the backdoor.

Milagros kissed and hugged her mother. "Laz's father is dead. He was to be our shepherd. Alegría killed him." Leaving her mother speechless, she then followed after Joshua.

The pair came out onto South Miami Avenue and crossed the street. Against traffic, they followed the police barricades toward the entrance, Joshua in the lead the whole way.

"Let's go over what we are going to say," said Milagros, quickstepping next to him. "We can't say anything remotely incriminating. Nothing that's going to give the police reason to question us at length or hold us. Understand?"

Joshua paused to regard Milagros, his eyes warmly supportive and lips gently pursed in the most benevolent

185

manner. Milagros inhaled pleasantly. Joshua, she determined, had now come full circle. She judged that she and Joshua were finally on the same page, that she and he had a chance at becoming, yes, more than kindred spirits. Milagros' smiling eyes danced over Joshua's face and then her eyes glazed over and her jaw dropped in disbelief over what she heard him say to the policeman who stopped them on the edge of the sidewalk near the entrance.

"I was here last night."

***

Surveying the splendid scenery of the main gardens from the second-floor-breakfast-room balcony, Detective Gregory wondered what could have possessed someone to bring such destruction to the sculptures in the walkways at either side of the gardens. Perplexed at not having found any signs of heavy tools or machinery, he could not reconcile the murdered teens as having perpetrated the devastation, which meant to him that there had to be others involved—besides the three they found alive. He seriously doubted any of those three kids could have wielded anything the size and strength required to reduce the statues he saw to their near-rubble state.

In the foreground, he briefly honed in on the curator, stepping carefully through one of the statue walkways, her arms flapping in the air in histrionical dismay. He faintly heard her pained voice in the pleasant wafting breeze. *"This can't be. This can't be."*

Gregory held the swimming pool's white life preserver that had been left in the room by the presumed gang of intruders. He had been told that no prints could be gotten from the hard Styrofoam composition. It was part of the strange collection of articles discovered on site by the investigative team, along with a portable cooler, scattered fishing spears, a ripped-apart leg holster, and a gold-plated crucifix. He turned around, barely paying attention to one of the antique cross-legged, life-sized oriental figurines positioned near him. He hung the safety instrument over one of the high-back chairs surrounding the round table in the center of the room. The three teenagers seated at the table all shot looks of speculative curiosity at the round flotation device.

"All right," said Gregory, "I'm sure this has been extremely difficult for all of you, but can somebody offer a clue as to what happened here?"

"There was a killer," said Lane.

As the other two teenagers nodded affirmatively, Gregory eased a chair back from the head of the table and sat down. He pulled out a small notepad from his inside jacket pocket. "What did he look like?"

"We didn't see."

Miranda simultaneously spoke out over Lane's answer, "Tall."

Lane cast a swift disparaging glance at the contradicting girl that Gregory did not miss. Miranda lowered her eyes and took a sip from the cup of water in front of her on the table. Marvis also took the opportunity to drink from a similar cup.

"He might have been tall," said Lane. "We only caught a shadowy glimpse of him. We went into hiding when we heard the first screams."

Gregory put his pen down. "How did the three of you get in here?"

"By boat. We rented a boat to take us here." Lane's eyes sought each of his companions' in a furtive roll that raised Gregory's police antennae.

The young police officer entered the room, waving a small piece of paper.

"There's no answer at any of these kids' homes."

"None of the three?" asked Gregory.

The young officer shook his head. "Just keeps ringing and ringing."

Gregory scrutinized the rescued threesome. They each offered an expression of faultless ignorance.

"Try again in a short while."

The young cop nodded and folded the paper into his shirt pocket.

One of the cops from earlier then appeared at the arched doorway. "Detective, believe it or not, we've got two more party crashers from last night."

***

Joshua and Milagros walked into the room to the utter surprise of Lane and his cronies. Also caught unawares, Joshua and Milagros recovered and stared intently at the three former muggers. As they walked around the table, Milagros' piercing look at Lane made him involuntarily swallow.

Joshua's attention lingered on the life preserver with the frayed-end rope hitched over a chair as he and Milagros sat facing the three interrogees.

The announcing officer handed the plainclothes policeman two index cards. He stood and introduced himself as a detective prior to scanning the cards. "Joshua Poo-ig...*West Side High*...Mill-agros Ricardo...*West Side High*... Your school is not going to be one to envy come Monday. You were here last night?"

"I was—she wasn't," answered Joshua quickly.

"Yes, *we* were," nodded Milagros, verbally and visually rebutting Joshua which ruffled the detective's feathers.

The pair glanced uncomfortably at their interrogator who had to absorb snickering from Lane and Miranda. The detective laid one hand over the other, crossing his wrists. "Tell me what you know so what happened here will never happen again."

Joshua took the lead. "We scaled the walls after the last security guard left. One girl who died fell off the balcony—it was an accident."

"What girl?" asked Gregory. "What balcony?" Gregory traded a questioning look with the announcing cop who was standing with his arms crossed.

The young cop then interrupted the proceedings. "Detective," he said, taking two steps into the room, "we need you."

Gregory met the young cop halfway inside the room. "All kinds of press are here," he informed. "And they are getting antsy."

"Stay here, Nelson," Gregory said to the announcing cop. "No one talks to each other…understand?" Gregory's eyes met those of the seated teenagers for emphasis. Before he stepped from the room with the young cop, Gregory could be heard wondering out loud to his young charge, "What crazy fad could possibly compel girls *and* boys to paint their nails such an ugly, yellow color?"

# Chapter Ten

Rosa parked as close as she could to the buses. Exiting her vehicle, she walked over to several police officers and two uniformed men, apparently the bus drivers. She pinpointed Laz among the teenagers around the men. After making eye-contact with him, Rosa heard one of the police officers say to a blond-haired boy with tinted glasses, "I don't care what type of schedule you're on. No one gets on these buses without an adult."

"Problem solved," said Laz, motioning to Rosa, joining them. Laz gave Peter a defiant look prior to greeting Rosa with a kiss on her cheek. "Here is our counselor for the trip."

Rosa read DAVIDSON on the officer's nametag as he tugged on the shiny brim of his policeman's cap. "Ma'am. Are you accompanying this group?"

Rosa nodded.

"And you are?"

"Rosa Montes."

The officer accepted a clipboard given to him by one of the drivers. He thumbed through pages of names.

"She's at the end," said Laz helpfully.

"My daughter should be on there. Milagros Ricardo."

"Okay, I see it. Rosa Mon-tez." Officer Davidson turned to the bus drivers. "This congregation employ either of you before?"

One driver scrunched his face with uncertainty. The other said, "Can't personally recall if they have. From what the boss said, everything was prepaid. My-am-uh to Mary-an-uh. Overnight stay and back in the morning. Lodgings for me and Otis included."

"That's right," said Otis, the bus driver. "Sure, was counting on the extra jack—wages, that is."

A buzz spread through the assembly of teenagers milling behind the huddled adults, touched off when the first bus driver said, "Miami to Marianna." The word *Marianna* leaped from teenagers' mouth to mouth.

"It's a lot of kids for one adult," Officer Davidson said.

"There will be more counselors at the camp," tendered Laz. "The paperwork is all there."

After a final perusal of everyone's faces, the officer handed the clipboard back to the first bus driver. "Have a safe trip…"

Those young people closest to the officer let out a cheer, quickly echoed by other nearby packs of happy teens. Someone yelled, "Way to go, Laz!" in witnessed appreciation for his effort in securing their discharge.

"… Except *you*." Officer Davidson's pronouncement dashed Laz's brightened disposition. "You're staying to see this boat issue through."

"Our boat marina confirmed everything you needed to know, officer," Laz stated. "You said my mother and uncle were on the way down."

"Exactly why I need you here." The officer put a commiserating hand on Laz's shoulder. "Son, I can't let the only link to that sunken boat out there leave."

***

The hushed words spilled from Milagros and Lane's lips at the same time: "Why are you here?" The synchronous speech

191

noticeably vexed both of them, but the close-by police presence tempered their displeasure.

"How long have you guys been here?" asked Joshua in a low voice.

"Long enough," answered Lane.

"Did you see a girl? Sandy blond hair."

"*Joshua*," a miffed Milagros interrupted.

"The mistress said you'd be back for her," a resentful-sounding Miranda uttered.

"Mistress?" asked Joshua.

"What mistress?" Milagros immediately questioned.

Lane smiled smugly. "As if you didn't know."

Miranda followed his lead, puckering her lips at Joshua with sarcastic affection.

Marvis let out a high-pitched giggle. "She's alive," he said, trying to sound spookily dramatic. He then noisily scratched the back of his neck.

Striding into the center of the room from his guard position at the door, Officer Nelson broke off the chat. "If I hear another word, I'll personally stick all of you in separate rooms. There's plenty here to do it." The officer's stern warning succeeded in muffling any more exchanges but could not completely erase the silly grins from the faces of Miranda and Marvis.

Staring contemptuously at their opposites, Milagros and Joshua, taking her lead, lifted two fingers in front of their chests. The other stern-faced kids inverted two fingers in the opposite direction in a defiant show of their allegiance.

Milagros nudged Joshua with her knee. "We're not going to get anything out of them. *Nos vamos*?" Joshua reluctantly nodded as officer Nelson crept closer.

"I have to go to the ladies' room," Milagros told the officer.

"Me too," voiced Miranda with a scornful mouth twist at Milagros.

The officer rubbed a hand over his chin. "Wait there," he said. Walking over to the doorway, Officer Nelson stepped out onto the wide first step. He peeked back at the group of five. Milagros and Miranda were standing, watching him.

The officer scoped out both ends of the gallery, called over an unseen colleague, and waited for his closer presence.

"What's up, Nelly?" asked the greeting officer.

Officer Nelson thumbed his hand back into the room. "The girls want to take a tinkle. Have any idea where the closest john is?"

"What girls?" asked the colleague.

***

In the brief interlude, Joshua rose quietly from his chair and slipped with Milagros over to the balcony, followed in the same stealth manner by the opposing troupe.

Without breaking stride, Joshua and Milagros hopped over the railing and descended onto the South Terrace. Marvis similarly scaled the railing and dropped down beside the pair, Joshua noticing the different shade of blue rising in the escaping Hostile and Milagros' eyes.

"Get lost if you know what's good for you!" Milagros warned Marvis as soon as they landed.

Joshua glanced up to see Lane and Miranda had chosen a different breakout route—upward. He noted the similar change in their eye color as Marvis as they shimmied up one of the balustrades to the lip of the slanted roof and peered downward. They pulled themselves up and scampered over to the other slanting side of the tiled-roof's peak, out of sight.

Joshua, Milagros, and Marvis raced around the mansion's southeast corner and into the East Terrace, Joshua remembering well how he had chugged into the same area carrying Dawn the night before, preluding his dramatic escape. "Get out of here, you," insisted Milagros with a stiff forearm to Marvis' chin.

The boy's face angered and he showed cropped-up fangs to Milagros. Forced to divert her attention from Marvis to the wide-armed police officer who suddenly rushed up in front of her, Milagros lowered her shoulder and knocked the public servant on his keister. The officer's crouched stance had been weakened prior to the impact from the unnatural sight of Milagros' radiating light blue eyes.

Marvis issued a satisfied half-growl, half-gurgle sound at the toppled public official two seconds before his head whipped to one side from the force of a beautifully delivered right cross flush on the chin from Joshua. Marvis staggered backward. His fangs withdrew and his eyes reverted to normal.

Joshua, with his back to Milagros, heard a gasp and something break. Concentrated on the sound, he saw a shattered cup and saucer at the feet of a woman standing outside the arched doors of the East Terrace. The woman, in a slim violet skirt and white blouse, frozenly stared at Joshua. From behind her streamed out half dozen or more police officers.

"This way!" yelled Milagros, pointing down at the East-Terrace steps. The sea which had provided their liberation from this very place the previous evening once again beckoned.

In the lead, Milagros and Joshua whooshed past two coroner's office attendees who were lifting a black body bag onto a wheeled stretcher, with a second bulging body bag on the ground close by. Both attendees impotently observed the teenagers fleeing from the whistle-blowing, pursuing policemen.

There were two boats tied to the gondola moorings of the Sea Wall, the recognized fishing vessel and a Miami Marine Patrol boat. The fishing boat was unoccupied; the other was not. Joshua and Milagros went for the fast boat. On the Sea Wall Promenade, in front of the patrol boat, a short-sleeve-shirted marine officer sipped from the unscrewed top of the thermos he held in one hand. Another officer on the boat languished near the controls.

The front officer cut short a swallow when he saw the approaching teens. They were upon him in no time, much faster than he could have imagined possible from the disbelief registered in his eyes. Milagros arrived first. The surprised officer dropped his thermos to reach for the girl who leaped to one side, almost completely over him. The marine officer's outstretched hand, however, clipped Milagros' foot, causing her to land awkwardly on the boat and tumble over.

Joshua swooped in and snatched the front officer by the wrist and spun him around once and into the water. Joshua jumped on the patrol boat and found Milagros pinned to the floor, alongside the armchair helm seat by a now-billy-club brandishing official. Without much impetus, Joshua charged the man, a broad-shouldered hulk with bulging forearms sticking out from under his white short-sleeved shirt. Ready for the lunge, the marine cop raised the billy club from across Milagros' back and jammed it into Joshua's stomach, doubling him over.

The muscular cop pressed the club back over the sprawled Milagros. "Whoa! There girlie," he said, with his bent knee leaning into the small of her back. "You sure are one strong filly."

Marvis then flew feet-first into the side of the head of the muscular marine officer, knocking him backwards and rocking the helm chair violently.

Milagros got up and turned the ignition key, with Joshua, on his feet and holding the side of his stomach, untying the mooring line. Milagros pushed the throttle up and the boat departed with a roar, leaving the chasing battalion of officers frustrated on the seawall steps. Despite staggering under the boat's swerving movement, Joshua, with help from Marvis, pushed the off-balance marine officer over the side.

A second patrol boat unexpectedly appeared in front of them. Milagros hit the horn button, firmly indicating that she was not disposed to yield the right of way. The second patrol boat swerved and smacked off the side of the stone barge. Milagros then opened up the throttle. The heavy-powered outboard engines surged the boat forward, lifting the front end out of the water. In the wide, foaming wake, Joshua saw the bobbing head of the muscular cop and the second boat break off pursuit to pick up their comrade.

The accelerated pace of the speedboat whipped the wind all around them. Recreational boats were spread out in the distance on the scenic waterway. None seemed to be moving close to them. Joshua inched up to Milagros at the controls. "There has to be an easier way out of that place."

Milagros smiled. "Virginia Key's right over there," she said before pointing due east with her finger.

"We're going back to the stadium?" asked Joshua. "You heard Miranda. Dawn's alive."

"And so is Alegría," replied Milagros, holding the steering wheel firmly. "We're leaving town, remember?"

"There won't be any need for Alegría to keep Dawn alive after today—you know that. Are you just going to let that happen?"

Milagros clenched her teeth and let out an exhausted sigh. She throttled back on the controls, bringing the boat to a swaying standstill. "Don't put that on me! You wanted to go back—*we* went back. It's not my fault we couldn't find her. And yeah, if it comes to the survival of your pinup girl or me, guess who I'm picking?"

Joshua's mouth pruned. "Fine," he said. "Drop me off on shore somewhere. I'll do what I have to do."

"You're not serious?" answered Milagros, sticking a fisted hand on her hip. "If you don't get far away from this city before nightfall, you'll be all alone. Not only against Alegría and Raúl but against who knows how many more like Raúl."

The other passenger in the boat spoke up for the first time. "Why don't you just swim to shore if you want to go back so bad?"

In no mood to hear third-party advice and chafed by the irritating giggle that punctuated it, Joshua moved intimidatingly toward Marvis. "Why don't you show me?"

"Joshua," called out Milagros. "Leave him alone."

"He can't come with us," responded Joshua, grabbing Marvis by the shoulders. "We have to get rid of him."

"I helped you escape," reminded Marvis. "Or did you forget that already?"

Milagros' next words were calmly spoken. "If *that* one wants to accompany us to meet a hundred Docile half-vampires…why not let him?"

Smiling deviously, Joshua understood. He then felt his eyes roll back in his head but nothing more, as his body collapsed on boat's floorboards.

***

"We can't leave yet," said Rosa. "I have to go back for Milagros and Joshua."

Laz pulled Rosa toward the front of the bus. "We're behind schedule as it is, Mrs. Montes. Not to mention being on shaky ground with the police." Laz stared down at his feet. "I know as a Docile's mother, you're not supposed to be involved in any of this. I don't know how you convinced my father to let you come along."

Rosa pushed back her shoulders and gazed directly at Laz. "I became involved long ago and I've never stopped being involved." She placed a hand on his shoulder. "I'm so sorry about your father. I can't tell you how much I appreciate his not

197

informing Milagros of my plans." She hugged the boy warmly. "What's a few minutes longer, Lazarito?"

As Rosa drifted toward Officer Davidson, Laz nodded almost helplessly, tracking slowly after her. Laz wanted to tell Rosa something more, but because it involved his dead father, he had trouble bringing it out. Eventually, scuba divers would be submerging through the boat wreckage and what was left of the bodies of his father and the crewmen were sure to be discovered, a discovery that would stop this trip in its tracks.

"Officer," said Rosa to the uniformed man, "my daughter and her friend are fifteen minutes away from here. I have to go and get them."

Officer Davidson sought out one of the bus drivers standing nearby. "I and Horace ain't getting paid by the hour anyway," said the shrugging driver. He then boarded the bus and flopped unbothered into his seat.

One of the cops from earlier entered the conversation. "Are we going to be sticking around much longer?"

Officer Davidson stretched out his neck at his brother-in-arms. "Call it a shift. Get a ride back to the station with the other unit. I'm going to stay here and tie up the loose ends with the boat."

Peter, with a clingy Toni at his side, made his presence known. "What's going on?" he asked with a dose of bluster.

"A couple in your crew is late apparently," answered the head policeman. "The misses is going for them."

Expecting Peter to contest the issue, if nothing more than to continue undermining his practices, Laz braced for some kind of fake outrage from the student to incite the anxious kids, some of them already on board the buses.

Peter raised his hands above his head in front of everyone. "So, we have to wait for two of Laz's lost sheep—well, I say…we can wait." Many in the awaiting assembly put down the travel bags, in one form or another that they carried, without much objection.

Laz was dumbstruck at Peter's cooperation in the matter.

As a more-relaxed Rosa headed in the direction of her car, the first bus driver's honking horn halted her. He pointed toward the front entrance of the parking lot, it seemed at first, at the four police cruisers simultaneously leaving the premises. As the last of the departing squad cars steered away, the three arrivals seemed to materialize for all to see. It did not take long for Laz to ascertain that one of them was Milagros and the other was Joshua.

Laz did not give the other unidentified person much thought, as he and Rosa, ahead of him, hurried to meet them.

***

Milagros brought the boat along a thin strip of uncultivated beach on the south side of Virginia Key. In clear sight of the stadium, from the rear, she guided the landing, approaching the small island from the opposite side of the bay. Joshua had revived mostly under his own power.

"You fainted," said Marvis in between insufferable giggles. "Looks like all the grown-up excitement got to you."

"He's been through a lot more excitement than just now," Milagros informed. "Ask your mistress…"

Joshua stood up, exhibiting weak assurance of his fitness. "So much for doing without my shot of medicine."

Near the shore, Milagros settled the throttle in lowest gear. Signaling everyone, the three slipped over the side into waist-deep water and waded in the rest of the way onto a pebbly strip of beach harboring a range of moss-covered rocks farther removed from the narrow shoreline. Turned around, facing the open water, the police boat puttered out into the bay.

Leaving the beach, they passed through a row of trees and came right out to the main roadway, opposite the entrance to the marine stadium parking lot. They hurried across the double causeway road which maintained light vehicle traffic in either direction.

"Is not taking your medicine going to be an issue?" asked Milagros before attempting to dart across the first division of lanes.

"Not in the short term," said Joshua. "As long as I don't bruise or cut myself too deep."

A car horn threateningly sounded as a vehicle whizzed past. The three hustled across the roadway and entered the stadium parking lot through the main vehicle entrance.

"I can't wait to introduce you to everyone," said Milagros to Marvis.

Marvis tried to put on a brave face, but his concern was quite perceptible. He managed a difficult swallow. "You won't hurt me. It's against your nature…isn't it?"

A wily smile from Milagros left Marvis to his own uncertain imagination as she and Joshua quickened their pace to greet the spotted Rosa and Laz.

Rosa embraced her daughter. "Mija," she said tenderly while acknowledging Joshua rather impartially.

"Fashionably late as usual," said Laz with a big grin. "Just to get all the attention."

"It's just the prima donna in me," quipped Milagros.

Laz gave Joshua a welcoming pat on the arm and then asked, "Who's he?"

"Him?" replied Milagros with an off-handed look at Marvis. "He's just a Hostile half-vampire we picked up."

\*\*\*

On her way back to the mansion, the curator was drawn by the rush of activity outside the East Terrace door. With a magnet-like quality, her eyes immediately fixed on the broken china cup and saucer at the feet of Sheila. "What have you done?" she asked, drawing closer.

"I'm sorry," said Sheila, weakly pointing with her finger. "The girl…the boys…their eyes…"

Mrs. Crawford crouched down, delicately collecting the broken pieces of china.

"This is irreplaceable. How could you?"

Following the excitement, Gregory and the accompanying officer arrived on the East Terrace, stopping near the two women. Miss Crawford stood facing the detective with the broken porcelain pieces in her cupped hands. "The set will never be the same. Never."

Sheila again tried apologizing, this time to Gregory, when she was superseded by Officer Nelson. "They're all gone. The five of them," panted the officer. "Two of them told me they had to take a leak. I went outside the room for two seconds. When I turned around…they jumped out the window somehow."

"Looks like three of them, uh, commandeered a patrol boat," said the young cop, joining the convened men. "The other two…we don't know what happened to them."

Gregory responded to the improbable occurrence not with anger or panic but with an exhibited calm and a broader assessment of the situation. "Send some men to do a sweep of the woods," he instructed. "We'll leave it to marine patrol to deal with the other three."

"Those three kids have a head start. Two officers were tossed in the drink."

Gregory could see a patrol boat with ugly dents and scrapes along its fiberglass hull returning to the Sea Wall Promenade, a congregation of officers welcoming it. His eyes then broke away from the scene. He took a few uncertain steps and craned his neck up at the mansion.

"How is it not one of those kids broke their necks getting out?"

*\*\*\**

Having witnessed the arrival of the absent teens, Officer Davidson decided to check on the progress of his seafaring associates. Emerging from the curved entrance ramp of the stadium, he became perplexed at the dearth of patrol boats in the basin. There had been six, by his count, not long ago. Now there was one remaining, stationed along the retaining wall, preparing to unfasten lines to shove off.

"Where'd everybody go?" asked the Miami police officer.

"All called away," said a sunglasses-wearing officer. "Sam and I are going to guard the mouth of the lagoon—to keep the curious ones out." The *lagoon*, Davidson had learned, was how marine patrol referred to the stadium's basin—which Davidson also found out was the length of the Washington Mall.

The unoccupied officer in the boat called back as the boat pulled away, "Get this—three kids took one of our boats out for a joyride. They're out on the bay at last report."

Silent alarms went off in Davidson's brain. "Hey! Hey!" he called as the rumbling engines from the withdrawing vessel opened up. Both maritime law enforcement officers had their backs to him and did not hear his shouts over the engines. Sliding alongside the retaining wall, Davidson yelled until he dropped his hands in futility as the vessel's powerful engines parted the waters in a foamy trail of dissolving agitation. The boat picked up speed and shrank in size, moving farther and farther away from him.

*\*\*\**

Brought into the colony of Docile half-vampires, Marvis' perceptive senses were raging, especially his sense of smell. There were quite a few students still loitering along the sides of the buses, a few with transistor radios glued to their ears, a couple of others sneaking cigarettes. Marvis' head spun in the direction of three cute girls expressively critiquing their outerwear—the full, pleasing visual of which involuntarily sprang forth fangs over his lower lip. He slapped a panicked hand to his mouth to muzzle his spontaneous reaction. His alarmed eyes rolled from side to side to see if he had been compromised. It appeared no one had seen the predatory lapse.

Peter edged in at his side. "I didn't expect to see you back so soon." The teen did not give Marvis a chance to answer. His eyes grew wide with excitement behind his tinted prescription glasses. "I have big news; we know our destination. I know where the Dociles' hiding place is going to be. It's too late for your mistress, but the others with you can benefit with us."

"Why is it too late for the mistress?"

The question reigned in Peter's expressiveness. "Remember the boat? After you left, it exploded and sank. Your mistress was aboard…"

Marvis curled his lips. "The mistress survived. She's resting. She'll be coming back for me here after sundown. She's going to be pleased with your news."

Surprised and gladdened, Peter exclaimed, "Wow! If she can survive that…it means we are going to be *superfiendishly* indestructible!"

Before he could fully share in Peter's revelry, Marvis turned sullen.

"What's your name?" asked Officer Davidson, his intimidating frame casting a shadow over the alarmed boy. "How'd you get your pants wet? Those two you came in with, how did you all get here?" Countering the officer's advance,

Marvis took several steps backward but stopped with the final question. Instead of speaking, he ran off.

***

Officer Davidson hurried after Marvis whose breakaway speed left the law enforcer in the dust. During that witnessing phase, all Peter could construe was that the cop would stop the trip, prevent his analyzed passage to uncomplicated supervillainhood…and destroy his much-anticipated emancipation from his accursed prescription glasses. Pushing back his spectacles on the bridge of his sweaty nose, he called over to those hanging around outside the buses.

"Everyone on board, now!" he said, winching his arms in a shooing motion. Weaving his way between the heavy transportation vehicles, he emphasized, "C'mon, let's go! Everybody, prepare to head out."

Seeing his instructions being heeded, he told Toni to wait for his return. He then turned toward the stadium and raced off. With his supernatural fervor up, he caught up to and tackled the half-jogging policeman in the stadium's vacant ground-floor concessions area.

Instinctively, the knocked-down officer grabbed for his holstered gun, but it was too late. The officer rose to his feet in a stooped position, staring at the snub-nose barrel end of his own service revolver. "Put it down," he said, motioning gently with his hand. "This is not what you want to do."

After a silent standoff of several seconds or more, Marvis came running out from somewhere and hitched alongside Peter.

"You shoot and every cop in there is going to hear it," said Officer Dave.

"All the cop boats are gone," Marvis reported to the gun-toting Peter.

"And you sent everyone else in your squad home," said Peter, clicking back the revolver's hammer. His finger curled around the trigger… The round fired—but erratically.

Landing on the armed teenager from the second-floor walkway, Joshua's impact produced the errant discharge and knocked Peter to the ground, the gun spinning away on the concrete flooring. Milagros also jumped down with Joshua. She raced for the wayward gun, but Marvis beat her to it. Marvis waved the weapon indiscriminately, freezing everyone. Eventually, he leveled the .38 at Officer Davidson.

"Shoot him!" yelled Peter, on one knee, straightening the bent out-of-shape glasses on his face. "Shoot him!"

A nervous Marvis instructed the officer to 'turn around,' ignoring the pleas for restraint and calm from Joshua and Milagros.

"Is this the way you want your life to turn?" asked the officer as he slowly complied. "Think about your future, kid."

"Our future is exactly what we're thinking about," Peter said coldly. "Shoot now!" he exhorted.

After a few agitated breaths, with the cold, hard steel in his hand, a quivering Marvis rushed up and struck the policeman on the back of the head as hard as he could.

\*\*\*

Horace, the driver, sat on the bottom step of the door of his bus, whittling. From inside the bus could be heard a cacophony of idle chatter mixed with popular music playing. When the shot rang out from the stadium, Horace glanced up and then went back to his wood paring. The echo of the shot, nullified by the noise inside the bus, did not garner an abundance of attention from the preoccupied students.

The other driver stepped off his bus and called over. "Did you hear that, Horace?"

"Yep," said Horace. The apathetic man remained concentrated on his miniature carving. "Sounded to me like a gunshot."

"Yeah, me too," said Otis before nonchalantly climbing back aboard his bus.

Waiting for Peter off the bus, Toni chose to investigate, trailed by a mistrustful Rosa. When the pair arrived in the determined vicinity of the heard shot, the area was empty.

Quickly spotting a vigilant Peter near the entrance of a restroom, Toni scampered over and draped an arm around him. Disregarding Rosa as if she were invisible, Peter brought Toni inside where she saw the unresponsive public servant latched to the piping under one of the sinks.

"Is he…?" asked Toni timorously.

Peter shook his head with disdain. "Would he be handcuffed if he was? I knocked him out with his own piece."

Marvis frowned over Peter's comment as Rosa quickened past him over to Milagros. A bare-chested Joshua had his shirt pulled off at Milagros' apparent insistence. Her daughter's fingers lightly touched the red and purple contusions covering his abdomen.

"Must have been from the nightstick to the stomach before our boat ride," Joshua submitted. A red welt along the side of Joshua's neck seemingly sprang up as he was being examined, as did noticeable black and blue marks along Joshua's forearm and bicep. "That's where I came down on our friend Peter here. Something told me our running after Marvis and the policeman was not going to end agreeably."

"You've got more bruises than a banana," Toni blurted out to the sole amusement of Marvis.

\*\*\*

Peter took quivering aim at the unconscious Officer Davidson.

"What are you doing?" asked Milagros in a rising voice.

"Kiss off," said the nervous Peter. "He knows where we're going. When he's found, he'll call ahead to stop us."

Marvis bobbed his head up and down in agreement. "I dig it."

Toni put her hands over her eyes and then decided better use for them would be to plug her ears. Shutting her eyes, she said, "Anytime you're ready, Peter."

Rosa said something in Spanish and made the sign of the cross for the benefit of the condemned man. Since having seen the incapacitated police authority on the floor, Rosa had stayed observantly quiet. She noticed the captured man's police belt with the empty holster had been removed and placed into one of the service sinks. In another sink, his smashed police radio had been deposited.

"There's another way," said Milagros.

Comprehending the intervening girl's meaning, Peter snorted a few deep breaths through his nose. His face angered as he switched the position of the gun in his hand and commenced pistol-whipping the defenseless Officer Davidson across the head and face.

As the battered officer's head thrashed back and forth, spitting out blood aimlessly, Milagros yelled, "That's enough!"

Breathing heavily, Peter jumped back admiringly. His head hanging down immobile, the officer's spittle merged into a drool of blood from his nose and mouth, stretching to the floor.

"He'll be out for hours," said Milagros. "Even after they find him."

Rosa uttered what everyone accepted as the next course of action. "We must go."

Outside the bathroom, Milagros passed a stern judgment on Marvis. "It's the end of the line for you, Mister Tagalong."

"Maybe we can find a storage closet or something to lock him in," said Joshua.

"Leave him to me," said Peter, pointing the pilfered handgun in its most lethal manner.

"What are you planning to do?" asked Milagros.

"He's a Hostile, isn't he?"

Milagros leaned closer to Peter without appearing aggressive. "I never told you that."

Peter sniffed exaggeratedly. "Well...take a whiff of him." Peter scrutinized everyone, much more edgy than a few seconds ago.

Marvis, for his part, did not seem very concerned. His thumbs were stuck loosely into his leather vest pockets.

"What else can he be if you want to get rid of him?" When no one answered, Peter assertively asked, "Well, is he or isn't he a Hostile?"

"Yeah, he's a Hostile," relented Milagros. "A Hostile I noticed you became rather chummy with. Why don't you let me take a closer whiff of you?"

Peter glanced at Toni whose eyes widened unnaturally. He crooked the elbow of his free arm and showed his armpit area. "Be my guest," Peter said to Milagros, pulling down his short sleeve to reveal a sweaty, sandy tuft of underarm hair. When Milagros did not move, he motioned with his gun for Marvis to start walking. Marvis did so. Coming out of the bathroom, he looked like a prisoner with Peter and Toni following behind him.

Rosa tried to lightly steer Milagros in the opposite direction, but her daughter resisted. "He's the enemy," she said, nodding at Marvis. "He knows too much."

Milagros cast a questioning gaze at her mother, causing her to divert her eyes.

"We can't let him do it," Joshua said, buttoning his shirt. "It would be no different than the cop."

"Go back outside," said Milagros to Rosa. "Make sure we are ready to leave the minute we come out."

Rosa watched Joshua and Milagros catch up with the splintered group before anxiously turning around to head back to the parking lot.

# Chapter Eleven

The five teenagers passed through the horseshoe-shaped entryway at the end of the public area plaza, taking them underneath the stadium grandstand. Here, in the underbelly of the structure, a framework of four-sided concrete pylons extended deep into the basin waters, supporting the sizable construction.

Peter sent Toni down the ramp along the side of the stadium to peek into the basin. "Make sure the cops are gone," he directed.

At the bottom of the ramp, some pieces of floating refuse from the yacht's explosion remained littered over the calm waters near the shore.

"Coast is clear," Toni said, prancing back up the ramp. "They must all be on coffee break," she flightily pronounced.

Peter allowed his irritation at the comment to show. He ordered Marvis, under the dominion of his gun, to turn around and face him. Then he menaced Joshua and Milagros with the weapon. "I know you two are meaning to stop me, but I wouldn't do anything stupid if I were you. I have to be a real hero with the other followers. And I need more than my ditz of a girlfriend as witness."

Peter returned the gun's aim on the previous target. At this point, Marvis—standing flush against the waist-high railing, with the blue-green basin water a short drop below—became a little disconcerted. "This play-acting stuff is starting to freak me out," he said, putting his hands down.

"Killing a Hostile would cement my leadership role," Peter declared, his grip tightening around the revolver. "I may even get you two barred for bringing him here," he contended, glancing at Joshua and Milagros.

"Maybe we should—"

The bullet fired by Peter struck Marvis below his left shoulder blade, cutting off his speech. Toni screamed. Joshua and Milagros charged Peter.

Struggling briefly, with Joshua's hands clutched around the interlocked fingers of Peter's firing hand, the pair managed to rip the revolver from Peter's grasp after smacking his wrist twice against the guardrail. The gun fell into the water.

As a yelping Toni flung herself on Milagros' back, Peter hit Joshua in the side of the face with his elbow, knocking him back. Peter then snatched hold of Marvis who had slung an arm around the middle tube rail to keep himself partially upright. Peter tried to push Marvis through the safety rail opening, but Marvis resisted. Exerting greater force, Peter succeeded in stuffing Marvis, who was bleeding heavily through his nose and mouth, through the rail's spacing. But Marvis latched onto the bottom rail with both hands, preventing his hanging body from falling into the water. Peter kicked once and then twice on Marvis' knuckles. A third kick delivered a painful removal of the battered hand.

Marvis held on with only five fingers now. Glancing behind him, Peter glimpsed Joshua, trying to shake the effects of the elbow to the face while Milagros literally peeled Toni off her back. With a closed fist, Peter banged hard on Marvis' vulnerable hand, eliciting another anguished cry from the badly wounded boy. Peter's eye composition changed to a cobalt blue, and he wound up and brought down his fist like a sledgehammer.

Marvis' own eyes shimmered with a cobalt-blue tone as he timed Peter's intended blow, simultaneously releasing his hand from the rail, replacing it with the other. Peter struck the bare metal rail, sending an intense shooting pain from the crunched carpal bones of his wrist up through the ligaments of his arm. While Peter dealt with the stinging pain, Marvis hooked a free hand around Peter's ankle. Knocked off balance, Peter slid to the ground and was pulled through the railing by a falling Marvis.

***

Toni dove for Peter, barely grazing his fingers as he dropped into the water with Marvis. Sticking her shoulders in between the railing, she shouted out his name. She waited, for what seemed like an interminable time, for Peter to bob up. At the point of entry, escaping air bubbles popped at the surface inside a widening stain of dark red water.

Toni began to cry. She stomped her feet petulantly at Milagros, now bent over the railing, looking down. "*Do something!*" she implored.

Joshua staggered forward, holding his head. When Milagros saw him, any inclination of trying to save Peter or the Hostile fled from her mind. Gently coaxing his hand down, Milagros gasped at the sight of the contusion on Joshua's swollen cheekbone, which was a clump of raised purple skin. She asked, "What is happening to you?"

"It must be all the roughhousing," Joshua replied. "Without my daily medicine, I'm at risk."

"What kind of risk?"

"I told you," Joshua answered with an almost dismissive wave of his hand. "Bruising, for one thing. Internally, I could bleed into my joints—that causes a lot of pain and swelling. Collect blood in my urine. Spontaneous nosebleeds. Oh, and suffer a gastrointestinal hemorrhage."

"*Joshua*!" Milagros exclaimed in a pronouncement steeped in reprimand and dread. After a reflective pause, Milagros spoke again. "Your hemophilia. It's the monkey wrench in all of this for you. It must be why you were such a late Docile bloomer. Now it's working against you, it seems."

"If I could get my medicine," Joshua said. "I had a big bruise earlier this week that healed fast. It disappeared completely over couple of days."

"No medicine works that fast."

"Maybe the medicine combined with what I am pulls out the monkey wrench?"

Before Milagros could respond, a near-hysterical Toni attracted attention by running down the ramp and hopping on a loading platform. With clenched fists, she loudly urged Peter's resurrection from the water. She then straightened, took a deep breath, and jumped in feet-first.

\*\*\*

Peter had been dragged by his foot to the bottom by Marvis. They were two descending weights pulling against each other with opposite purpose, one struggling for survival and the other determined to prevent it down to his dying breath. When the cobalt-blue glimmer in Marvis' eyes finally extinguished, Peter broke free, and Marvis sank slowly backward, settling on the bottom of the sandy seafloor near a bed of brown seaweed. As his arms fell gently at his sides, the mist of blood rising from his chest mixed with the dust tossed up from his landing and turned into a maroon cloud.

Peter came up for air and then swam underwater away from the place of his fall. His glasses having fallen off, his eyes burned with a cobalt-blue varnish through the water's moderate visibility. He heard the sounds of a splashing Toni crying out his name and bobbed up behind her. Happily relieved, she let herself be steered away from her jump off point. The reunited pair settled behind a pylon deep underneath the grandstand far enough from the others to remain undetectable.

Gulping in deep breaths of air and shaking, Toni held on to Peter, his eyes back to a normal state. "You gave me such a scare," Toni said.

"Now, now," said Peter, pulling her close to him. "All is well."

"Oh, did you lose your glasses?"

"No matter. I'm actually seeing better…the approach of the cobalt moon."

"We'd better get back to tell everybody how you saved them from a Hostile."

Peter remained afloat without moving, to Toni's surprise. "I don't care about that, you twit."

Toni frowned at the verbal slight. "But…you wanted to be a hero to the other followers."

"I want to be a hero alright. But not to *them* or you. I want to be a hero to that mistress Marvis said is still out there."

Toni spun away from him in a tiff. As she started to swim off, Peter snared her by the shoulders and forced her under the water. Peter's eyes percolated with their cobalt-blue aura as he used all of his strength to keep his girlfriend from coming up. Toni's hands managed one or two weak and fruitless splashes before she succumbed to the unimaginable betrayal.

***

Standing alongside one of the buses, Laz and Rosa saw them emerge from the front of the stadium and rushed to meet them. Milagros slipped out from under Joshua's dependent arm and into her mother's loving embrace. Rosa grimaced at the bruised and blotched sight of Joshua.

Laz placed a hand on Milagros and offered a sympathetic look at Joshua's swollen face without comment.

"We heard another shot," said Laz.

"Peter shot Marvis," Milagros explained. "They fell in the water and never came back up. Toni jumped in… We never saw her again." Changing the subject, she continued, slapping her fist into her palm for emphasis. "You have to help Joshua. Get him his medicine from his parents' house and then catch up with the buses."

Walking slowly, Joshua said, "Thomas won't give him anything. He's a stranger."

Milagros took a breath. "Jerry then. You have to find Jerry."

"Tell Jerry I need my shaving kit," said Joshua. "He'll know what I mean." Milagros led Joshua toward the bus drivers. One had his arms crossed, shooting the breeze with the other.

Two of several kids with their heads stuck out of the bus windows asked, "Where's Peter?"

When Joshua and Milagros all but ignored them, the same two, along with a couple of others who had previously voiced support for Peter, came down on the steps of the bus. The question was repeated. "Where's Peter?" The crowding friends seemed intent on impeding Joshua and Milagros' climb aboard.

"He's dead!" answered Milagros with steely eyes—and in earshot of the bus drivers. "And so is his girlfriend. Peter drowned. Toni jumped in after him and never came up. We shouted after them…waited as long as we could."

"You're kidding," came the lead response.

"Do I look like we're playing a joke?" shot back Joshua. With his statement, he made sure to angle the bruised side of his face for everyone to see. He lifted his shirt up to reveal his harshly discolored abdomen for additional emphasis.

One by one, the opposers lost their boldness and retreated back to their seats inside the bus.

"What about that other kid that was with you?" asked one unrelenting teen.

"He was a Hostile," said Milagros. "Do you really want to know what happened to him?"

As the shocking revelation stunned everyone into silence, Joshua and Milagros awaited the responses of the two drivers.

"Did you hear what the gal said?" asked Otis.

Horace pulled a small tin from his back pocket. Twisting off the lid, he pinched a snuff of tobacco and stuffed it under his lip. "Yep," he said calmly. "Now here's what I think. Ol' Peter and his hunny bunny maybe just decided a fieldtrip on their own might be more educational."

Otis' brief smile displayed a prominent missing upper tooth. "And that one? Looks like somebody took him out behind the woodshed."

"Maybe he got fresh with Peter's gal."

Otis tilted his head with uncertainty. "But what about that last shot?"

"You heard the girl. The other boy got hos-*tile.* The cop maybe had to do his duty." Horace sauntered over to Milagros. "What about the cop?"

"He'll be alright," said Milagros.

After he received a reassuring nod from Joshua, Horace bounced a blank look at Otis and asked out loud, "Are we ready to go here?"

"Ready," Milagros confirmed. She then spoke to her mother. "You get on the second bus. Joshua and I can manage those on this one now." She proffered Laz a goodbye hug. "You're the best, Lazarito. Your father would be proud."

Choking back a rush of emotions, Laz stepped back with his head bowed and eyes tightly closed. When his eyes opened, Joshua was standing in front of him with his hand extended.

"I won't forget this," said Joshua.

"Like I'm going to let you," answered Laz, completing a hearty shake.

Laz watched Joshua and Milagros climb aboard the bus, the door closing in a squeaky huff.

Horace released the airbrake and the bus hissed its consent for forward movement. It slowly rolled off, followed by its companion conveyance. The buses curved around the parking lot's dual fountain circular and exited through the main gate.

With a heavy heart and drooping chin, Laz walked back to the familiar car which had arrived earlier. As he neared the luxury family vehicle, he rushed over to his mother standing beside it and permitted himself to be consumed by her smothering embrace.

"I have to run home to change," he said, partially breaking their clinch, "and I have to borrow the car."

\*\*\*

Peter slogged up on the boat ramp, soaking wet and short of breath. After hiding from Joshua and Milagros behind one of the concrete pillars until they left, he had made three dives before he found it lying on the soft basin ground amid sunken cans and bottles dropped carelessly or purposely into the water by boaters and stadium spectators alike. He relished how his improved eyesight had permitted the discovery.

He sat down and opened the ammunition cylinder of the recovered police-service revolver. Removing the four remaining bullets from their firing chambers, he placed the small projectiles beside the gun and lay back on the hard cement floor, waiting for everything to dry. After a short rest, he sat up and inspected the gun. He shook it and then reinserted the lethal cartridges in the chamber holes. He reunited the firing cylinder and barrel with a quick flip of the wrist.

On his feet, Peter turned into the exterior walkway. Hearing a groan—he perceived from a heightened sense of hearing—coming from inside the bathroom, he marched over to investigate. On the floor, the pummeled Officer Davidson had regained a level of consciousness, more than enough for the trapped man to recognize with dread the silver-plated barrel of his own service weapon pointing down at him. The officer raised one hand in a pacifying gesture and then changing expressions, he began yanking furiously on the handcuffed other hand, rattling the sturdy piping beneath the sink.

Peter came out of the bathroom with the second of his two fired shots ringing in his ears. He hurried back underneath the stadium and dropped the gun into the water near where he and Marvis had originally fallen in.

Quickly leaving the stadium, he ran back along the shoreline into an adjacent tract of undeveloped property.

***

Still amped up from his fraught-filled night and the nitroglycerin-like amount of Cuban coffee he had consumed, Jerry finished his Saturday-morning chores in record time. He cleaned his shared room including picking up after his younger brother. He separated their dirty clothes into manageable piles for his sister to wash. He polished the furniture, agreeably commenting over the lemony scent the new can of furniture polish gave off. He filed the coiled blades of the push reel lawnmower and cut the patch of grass behind his house. He ran down to the meat market to pay an outstanding bill and pick up meaty cuts of pork chops for the family's planned Sunday dinner. All was done per his mother's post payday instructions. And he called Lacey, setting up a hopeful get-together at her house later in the afternoon. Lacey confirmed she had found his

218

clandestine and sentimentally appreciated note and had followed its instructions.

After finishing his obligations, Jerry diligently changed into his baseball uniform and completed Saturday practice at West Side High, dragging at the end. On the walk home, his eyelids reminded him of his lack of sleep, often drooping over his line of vision. Halfway to his house, the urgent beeping of an automobile horn jerked him wide-awake. Approaching the vehicle—a model-year black Lincoln Continental—Jerry recognized the driver through the lowered passenger window.

"Your sister told me you'd be around here," said Laz. "Joshua gave me your address. He's hurt—or more like hurting. There was some trouble at the marine stadium, but Joshua, Milagros, and all the flock managed to leave town."

"You say Jay was *hurting*?"

"He's bruised up bad. He said you could help him."

"How?"

"He said he needed…his shaving kit."

Jerry had barely repeated the object of the strange-sounding request to himself when the coded association became clear. "Turn around and take me back to the school."

"Maybe the coach is still in his office," said Jerry, arriving at the school grounds. But a trip around the teacher's empty parking lot led him to believe Coach Toney had already headed home after practice. "Pull up to the front," he then told Laz. "Maybe there's a janitor on duty." Laz parked the car close to the main school building.

"I sure appreciate what you're doing for Jay," said Jerry as the two walked up to the three gothic arched doors. "Especially after what you've gone through. Your loss, I mean."

Laz took a deep breath. "I had some grief time with my mother at home. I told her I had to finish carrying on my father's calling, and she understood. I'll feel better when this night is over and everyone has emerged safely as the shepherd intended."

After finding all the main doors were locked securely, the two began knocking on other ancillary double-wooden doors with small casement windows. "It's no good," said Jerry. "Let's go around."

Jerry led Laz around a side of the school. There was a row of windows running close to the ground. Jerry dropped to one knee and pondered the situation. "The cafeteria's freezers and storage units are down there. We can slip through but you may not like this... We're going to have to—"

Before Jerry could detail the scenario he had in mind, Laz sent a heavy rock crashing through one of the frosted windows. The action staggered Jerry.

"That was the plan, right?" asked Laz.

"More or less," answered Jerry.

The rock left a hole in the tempered glass, and the boys carefully kicked and plucked out all of the jagged pieces until all edges along the frame were smoothed out. Slipping through the ground-floor window, the boys gained their desired access. With Jerry covertly in the lead, they made their way through the annex of classroom-filled corridors.

"Jay's locker is over here," said Jerry, eventually stopping in front of one non-descript locker amid a compressed column of non-descript lockers.

Laz nearly panicked when he saw the built-in combination lock on the door. "Tell me you know the numbers."

"Don't sweat it, *Laz-a-ree-toe*," assured Jerry as his fingers worked their magic on the single-dial lock. Jerry swung the locker door open and reached for the utility kit Joshua had shown him earlier in the week. He unzipped it for Laz to see the medicinal paraphernalia. Laz nodded with increased comprehension.

Jerry closed shut the metal locker door, giving the dial lock a casual spin, all without taking his eyes off Laz. "We splittin' or sittin'?" he asked. Jerry then read the redirected focus in Laz's eyes and, sensing a presence behind him, turned around.

The tall custodian dressed in coveralls held a wrench in one hand and a wet mop handle in the other.

"We did knock," said Jerry meekly.

***

Blowing through the half-lowered window of the bus into his face, the temperate wind moderately displaced the short-combed hairs of Joshua's head. The soothing current of air promoted in Joshua a pleasantly lethargic state, a welcomed physical respite from the chaotic chain of events that had upended his life over the past few days.

The bus had been on the road for a several hours, and Milagros had fallen asleep, her head sometimes resting on Joshua's shoulder. Making its first rest stop just before the bus pulled off the main roadway, Joshua saw a sign that read: LAKE BUENA VISTA FUTURE HOME OF WALT DISNEY WORLD. He did not pay it much thought as the bus began to come alive with restless kids.

Milagros awoke. She immediately checked Joshua's bruised face. "How do you feel?" she asked.

"Lousy," answered Joshua.

"You look it." Milagros pulled out her compact and inspected herself. "I should talk," she said, dabbing the case's small, flat powder puff above her cheeks.

The kids eagerly descended upon the food establishments dotting the rest stop. Most opted for the fast-food joints. Joshua, Milagros, and Rosa ended up in a Howard Johnson's, which many of the students eventually wound up patronizing for its decadent dessert menu featuring twenty-eight ice-cream flavors.

As they were leaving the Hojo to re-board the bus, Joshua noticed a newspaper vending machine outside. The front-page headline captured Joshua attention along with his companions. He dropped a five-cent coin in the slot and reached for the edition. Folding the newspaper under his arm, he walked to the bus in silence with Milagros and her mother.

A cluster of about ten to twelve high-school-age kids Joshua had not seen before crowded around their bus.

"This here group says they are fixin' to join us," Horace said to Rosa, the adult, as the three walked up.

The collective eyes of the new recruits did not fail to observe Joshua's battered appearance. Among them was a tallish boy, with purple-and-orange-striped bell-bottom pants supported by a wide white belt and a petite blond with a macramé headband, wearing a fringe vest and matching fringe-ankle boots, who made hesitant eye-contact with Joshua. She passed along a whispered comment—obviously about Joshua—to a strawberry-blond with heart-shaped glasses standing at her side. Next to those two was a brunette in a halter-top, wearing a flower tiara. Another girl donned a floppy hat and an abundance of beads around her neck.

Milagros assumed charge. "Are you regional?"

The tallish boy answered, "Kissimmee." He lifted his hand, sticking up two fingers.

Another in the pack said, "Ocala."

The two blonds said in unison: "Orlando." They each raised the two main fingers of their hands. There came other identifying calls of Central Florida towns until all the new travelers had their hands displaying the Docile half-vampire sign.

Milagros reciprocated with her fingers, and so did Joshua. "We had some trouble before leaving Miami," she said, trying to explain Joshua's appearance.

"What kind of trouble?" asked the tallish boy.

"Double trouble, you might say," replied Milagros. She peered into his eyes. "We ran into some Hostiles…and a mother vampire. We nearly killed her."

The words *mother vampire* spread with hushed alarm off the lips of many of the new recruits. "Right on," said the tallish boy, offering a subdued fist pump.

Squinting from one side of his face, Horace answered Otis' curious expression. "It's this new flower-power generation. Just more confusing code words."

"We've got to check off their names from the manifest," said Milagros to Rosa. "I'll take half in my bus. The rest can go with you."

Joshua hopped on his bus with the others, the new passengers boarding in the end one by one. The brunette in the halter-top wore small ankle bells sown into her jeans' flared bottoms and the jingling sound from her pace drew conspicuous looks from everyone. Settling in his seat, he parted the newspaper, appeasing a strong itch that developed on his forearm as he began to read. He then folded the afternoon daily back in half and stuck it into the side of his seat, as a surge of all-too-fresh memories from the sensational page-one story flooded his mind.

It was not long afterward, as Horace eased the bus out of the rest stop, with the second bus following close behind, that Joshua restlessly pulled out the newspaper again.

He held open the broad front to Milagros, having retaken her seat next to him. "Look at the headline and sub-headline." He began speedily thumbing through the newssheets to reach the page where the story continued. "Pete, Chris, Rachel, Vicky…Cira. That's five, not four students."

Milagros twisted herself more upright in her seat. "Alegría removed Cira's body."

"Okay. Then what three men? It's the same number the detective said. There was Juan…" Joshua halted briefly when he

223

spoke the name, out of respect to Milagros and his memory. "A charter boat captain. What about the other body?" Joshua read silently for several seconds and then snapped closed the newspaper, showing some distress. Opening the crinkled broadsheet to the same page again, he read out loud the information that had temporarily halted his reading. *"'A second corpse was found barbarically dismembered, its body parts floating in the waters just behind the lush gardens.'"* Joshua ceased his reading to look at Milagros, but she avoided the eye-contact by turning her head toward the window. *"'A third man identified as Randall Landis of Miami was found with a crushed larynx and deep gashes along his neck.'"*

"Dawn's father," said Milagros in a lower tone.

"He came looking for his daughter." Joshua sagged back in his seat, crumpling the newspaper in his lap. "And now he's dead. Dawn's father is dead."

Milagros clutched the seat divide, her brow wrinkling from the castigation in her uttered words. "Don't you dare, Joshua—don't you dare think of taking on any blame for that."

"He was probably in one of those body bags we saw at Vizcaya." Joshua lay his head back; his eyes closed as if trying to shut out his spoken thoughts. "Dawn's probably dead, too. Alegría won't stop until she finds me. From now on, every night for the rest of my life will be a cobalt-moon night. Running. Cowering. Looking over my shoulder at every turn. For what purpose? To have innocent people die in my wake."

"After tonight, we'll find a new way to regroup. We can find a way to level the playing field against Ale—"

The fatalistic manner in which Joshua raised his hand over the side of his face stopped Milagros mid-word. "Save the pep talk," he said. "If I don't get my medicine soon, with these injuries…cobalt moon or no cobalt moon, I won't make it to morning."

Joshua's head listed to one side, facing Milagros. After his hand fell back, he felt the rivulet of warm liquid from his ear canal sliding down his neck and a similar trickle of fluid leaking from his nose over his lips, chin, and down his neck. It was not until he reflexively wiped his hand over his face and heard Milagros distressingly articulate his name that he realized he was bleeding from two places.

*"Oh, Joshua."*

# Chapter Twelve

Gregory brought Sheila back to headquarters, debating whether to divulge the disturbing news he had received from one of the boys who had somehow escaped their detention earlier. *One girl who died fell off the balcony—it was an accident.* There were bloodspots consistent with two different wounds seeped into the limestone of the East Terrace, one directly below the second-floor balcony. He decided to wait until all the blood analysis came back, to draw more definitive conclusions.

"I'm going to order sandwiches," Gregory told Sheila as he pulled into the station. "You're welcome to share a bite with me." *It was a bit beyond normal protocol, but not out of line,* Gregory told himself.

Sheila seemed gladdened by the invitation. "Thank you, detective," she gratefully said. "I would welcome that." She inhaled deeply, preparing to speak again. "I'm going to have to make funeral arrangements…for my husband."

"Yes, for your husband," said Gregory. "Because his death was ruled a homicide, an autopsy must be conducted first before his body can be released by the coroner's office."

A far cry from the quiet building the pair had left early that morning, the stationhouse was buzzing with activity after Gregory and Sheila returned. Phones could be heard ringing throughout. Upon arrival, an initially surprised Gregory received a handful of message slips from the besieged dayshift desk sergeant. In between placing successive telephone calls on hold,

226

the desk sergeant had made an overwhelmed gesture and said, "All off-duty personnel have been called into service. The chief wants to be brought up to speed ASAP. He's meeting with the mayor and the city commissioners. The out-of-town papers are calling every five minutes. Plus AP, UPI, Reuters even. You've got the messages there in your hand."

Gregory offered his gratitude and turned away, with Sheila at his side. Behind him, he heard the desk sergeant answer a new incoming call. *"I'm not authorized to give out any information... I can take a message for the lead detective..."*

Gregory reached his workstation. There were more messages sticking out from his desk pad, placed there by colleagues or support personnel. One such colleague approached the desk and handed Gregory a large mailing envelope with the Dade County Courthouse seal showing in one corner. "This came for you a little while ago," said the clean-cut detective dressed in a white shirt and thin, dark tie.

Gregory did not have to open the legal-size envelope to know what was inside. It was his search warrant to enter the Pérez home. At Vizcaya, Gregory had questioned all of the victims' parents about their children's friends—male and female. The common gender links were the Pérez siblings, a suspect in one murder who was more than likely at the scene of multiple others. This was an extraordinary coincidence. He needed to move on this. He needed to find this kid Raúl's whereabouts. "Thanks," Gregory simply said.

"Was it really as bad as they say out there?" asked the clean-cut man.

Gregory peeked over at Sheila and then back at the lower-grade detective, exhaling uneasily. "I'll share my report with you later, Paul."

Assigned to the Robbery Squad, Paul shot an awkward glance at Sheila, and then retreated rather self-consciously.

Another detective who had been on the grounds at Vizcaya weaved toward Gregory's desk. "We reached the parents of one of the five kids. The one that came in later with the girl. Joshua Poo-ig. Seems he's got foster parents. According to the old man, the kid doesn't live with them anymore—get this, as of yesterday. The old man told me they had 'a parting of the ways.'" The detective handed Gregory another sheet of paper. "Still a dead end with the first three kids you found hiding. No phone pickup and no one's home at any of the residences. Patrol units confirmed it."

Gregory briefly scanned the paper before placing it off to the side of his desk.

"The names and addresses the kids gave us check with public records?"

The detective nodded with a tight-lipped curl of his lips and lumbered away. A third detective circled near Gregory's desk. "I heard on the police radio that a uni was gunned down. Name of Henry Davidson, twenty-three years on the beat."

Gregory straightened and swiveled in his chair to keep up with the detective's movements. The loss of one of their own struck a particularly tragic chord with everyone in the law-enforcement community. None deeper than with fellow men in blue.

"Where? How?"

The third detective flopped into the chair at his desk not far from Gregory's. He picked up his phone. Before dialing, he answered, "Over on Virginia Key. The marine stadium. He was handcuffed to a bathroom sink and shot in cold blood. Marine patrol found him."

*Virginia Key*, remembered Gregory. There had been a commotion there last night, along with a heavy congregation of young people. Gregory swiveled back to face Sheila.

"Ah, as you can see this may not be the best of time after all…"

Sheila pressed her lips together in an understanding manner and rose. Gregory did likewise.

The desk sergeant came up to them. "Detective."

"Yes, sergeant," answered Gregory, trying not to sound irritated.

"Your two o'clock is here."

Gregory checked his watch. He made an apologetic gesture to Sheila. "I guess I can walk you out."

Gregory thanked the desk sergeant with a firm, inoffensive meeting of the eyes and escorted Sheila up to the front where a civilian manned the front desk. There, the Hayes girl sat with her parents. Gregory's eyes returned to Lacey as she promptly jumped out of her chair. She shouted: *"Jerry!"*

Through the front doors, a uniformed officer brought in two handcuffed boys. Gregory recognized one of them as Jerry Porter.

\*\*\*

Lacey hugged Jerry, though he could not reciprocate because of his restrained condition. Lacey's parents were put off by the combination of their daughter's displayed affection and the sight of the handcuffed Jerry in his baseball pants and long-sleeved undershirt.

"What happened?" asked the concerned girl.

The arresting officer answered for Jerry—to Gregory and not Lacey. "A B&E over at West Side High. The janitor nabbed them—with this." The arresting officer handed Gregory the utility kit.

"Detective Gregory," Jerry said, holding the detective's gaze.

Gregory was familiar with such looks, brimming with information wanting to be divulged—in private.

Lacey spoke up. "Jerry's the one who told me to call you this morning about Vizcaya."

Sheila had circumnavigated the scene and was about to leave through the corridor leading to the front doors when the final word of Lacey's sentence stopped her. She turned around with interest.

Gregory saw her out of the corner of his eye. "How bad was it with these two?"

"A busted window," replied the arresting officer.

"Would you mind leaving them with me and holding off on filing a report?"

"Okay by me, detective," said the arresting officer. "I'd rather be out there looking for a cop killer." He unlocked the handcuffs of the two boys.

Gregory signaled for everyone to follow him. "Just the young folk, Mr. and Mrs. Hayes, please." Gregory nodded his assent at the entreating Sheila to join them.

He found chairs for the three teenagers while Sheila retook her previous seat.

"He's Laz," said Jerry to Lacey who offered a smile. "He's cool."

Noting her conspicuous presence, Gregory introduced Sheila to the boys and Lacey. "This is Mrs. Landis."

Jerry's head whirled in her direction, Gregory noting the reaction. Taking a breath, he placed a hand, palm down, on his desk. "Last night, something terrible happened in our city. For the sake of all that is good and decent, you have to tell me everything you know."

Jerry received a sideways glance from his fellow male teen. His eyes wandered upward at the large ceiling fan rotating above him and then to the detective at the occupied desk nearest them. Caught eavesdropping, the detective quickly began shuffling paperwork around, pretending to be engaged. Coaxing back his attention, Lacey warmheartedly took hold of Jerry's hand. He finally met Detective Gregory's patient stare. "Raúl Pérez and his mother are responsible for everything. They're evil. The mother kidnapped Lacey."

Lacey was already nodding when Gregory's eyes located hers. "I wasn't originally honest because I didn't think anyone would believe me. But the mother kidnapped me. Jerry and his friends rescued me."

"What friends?"

"Jay—I mean, Joshua…Milagros, her cousin Manny, and her stepfather. He was killed."

Gregory studied the third teen. "I wasn't there," said the boy, who then pointed at the utility kit on Gregory's desk. "Joshua needs that. It's got his medicine inside."

Gregory pulled out a legal-sized yellow notepad and let it drop heavily on the desk. He clicked the top of his ballpoint pen. "Okay, let's start with your name."

"Lazaro Candela, Jr."

As Gregory wrote, Jerry leaned over the detective's desk, his spoken words carrying a sense of urgency. "Laz says Joshua really needs his medicine. He's taken some shots to the body. I've seen how he gets when that happens."

Gregory stopped writing to shuffle through some papers. "Joshua…yes, I've got that name here. I met him earlier, as a matter of fact." Gregory deliberately folded over to a clean page of his yellow notepad. "Where can I find this, Josh—"

The interrupting words flowed out from Jerry in one even breath. "There isn't time, detective. Raúl's mother is a vampire. She kidnapped Lacey, and she has your daughter, Mrs. Landis."

Sheila's eyes widened. "You saw my daughter Dawn? When?"

The detective sitting not far away cleared his throat in a skeptical manner, pushed back his chair noisily, and stood up. "I'm going to hit the john," he said, for all to know.

"Mrs. Landis...please," said Gregory, putting down his pen. "Jerry, you disappoint me."

Jerry ignored Gregory to respectfully answer Sheila. "Last night, at the big house on the bay, Dawn almost got away with us, but Alegría, uh, the mother vampire, she snatched her at the last minute. There was nothing we could do."

Sheila pressed down on the clasp of her purse. "Do you know where Dawn could be now?" Before Jerry could answer, she followed with, "Did you say mother *vampire*?"

"Yes, ma'am."

Sheila sat back in her chair, her eyes closed; she raised a hand to her temple as if she were experiencing the onset of a migraine headache.

Gregory aimed his displeasure at Jerry and Laz. "All right, you two. You want to play it that way; it's fingerprint time."

"No," cried Lacey. "He's telling the truth. I was kidnapped by Alegría. Her daughter was going to become a vampire, too. The whites of her eyes turned blue. I saw it."

Sheila sighed loudly, her purse tumbling out of her hands onto the floor. Gregory jumped up, thinking she was about to faint and slide out of her chair.

*\*\*\**

Sheila sipped from the glass of water Gregory had requested from a subordinate. What she had passed off as the sun's rays playing tricks with her fatigued mind came rushing back to her, the absconding youngsters she had briefly encountered at Vizcaya, specifically one boy—his blue-stained eyes peering right at her.

"You must hear the children out, detective," Sheila said, handing the water glass back to Gregory. "It is what incited me drop the china cup earlier, a rare lapse on my part. Those three fleeing boys and girl. I saw their eyes. I swear to you now that one boy who looked at me—his eyes were the same color as the pair of sapphire quartz dangling earrings I have in my jewelry box at home."

Putting the water cup down on his desk, Gregory remained standing. "What are you saying? That you actually believe…"

"I believe what I saw. And I saw the same thing this child said she saw." Sheila reached for Lacey, sitting closest to her, and wrapped her fingers around the girl's hand.

Gregory addressed Laz. "What's your role in all of this?"

"Support," Laz said with a negligible twitch of his shoulder.

"Mrs. Landis," said Gregory, trying to sound unruffled as he walked back around his desk. "I think it's best if you took a step back. These boys will be detained for a while until a parent or guardian comes for them. Lacey, you can call me next week if you decide that you have something more concrete to tell me, or I'll consider your case closed without prejudice. That means nothing was fully resolved, but no one got hurt." Gregory motioned for the students to rise. "Okay, kids, I've got a search warrant to execute."

No one stood as Gregory called across the room to the clean-cut detective. Sheila noticed the dejection on the—as she called them—*children's* faces. "I'll make restitution for the damages incurred from the boys' breaking into the school," she said. "I'll write a check right now in good faith payable to the school, and you can release the boys into my custody."

Jerry lifted his hanging head. "It was a window. That's all we broke."

"It doesn't work that way, Mrs. Landis. The boys have to answer—"

"Why, I am answering for them," Sheila said, being as gentle and restrained as an interrupting person could be. "I thought I was being clear in that regard." Nimbly, she extracted her checkbook from her purse.

The clean-cut detective appeared. "You want me to take them to booking?"

Gregory hesitated, scanning everyone's unassertive faces. He replied, "No. Looks like this is their lucky day. Sorry to trouble you, Paul."

The teenagers stirred optimistically in their chairs. Sheila unfastened the top of her writing pen. Gregory put up his hand in a stopping motion. "I trust you to check with the school and make amends on your own, Mrs. Landis."

"Thank you, kindly detective." Sheila closed the gold snap clasp of her purse and stood. "Shall we, children?"

"You can't take them," said Gregory.

"Why not?" countered Sheila. "Are the boys not free to go?"

Jerry reached across Gregory's desk for the utility kit, but the detective interceded. "Is that your property?"

"No."

"Then I can't give it to you."

"Our friend really needs it," petitioned Laz.

"Then your friend can come in and claim it."

"But, *detective*…you don't understand."

Jerry and Laz tried to silently convey to Sheila the importance of the utility pouch, but she sided with the unbending Gregory. "I do believe Detective Gregory has been most accommodating up to this point, and we would not want to appear ungrateful. Will you kindly escort us out, detective?"

Gregory reached for his hat and the large manila envelope. "I'm on my way out myself."

Several steps toward the front desk, Sheila halted her stride. "Oh, allow me a final swallow of water, detective," she said. Gregory nodded, crowded by the jabbering teenagers in his pulling orbit of authority.

Sheila quickly walked back to his desk. As she raised the glass to her lips, the utility kit conspicuously caught her eye.

***

"Thanks for believing us, Mrs. Landis," said Jerry, holding up Joshua's medicinal kit in his hand, the kit Sheila had lifted from Gregory's desk under the pretext of quenching her thirst.

"It may be more accurate to say that I believe *in* the two of you. Your story is quite fantastic," said Sheila, driving her car, with Jerry and Laz seated next to her. "However, after seeing for myself the phantom-like eyes of those three particular children... I hesitate to rule out any manner of unconvention at this juncture."

Shortly thereafter, directed by the boys, Sheila pulled her Ford Fairlane into the parking lot of West Side High, navigating her vehicle to a spot specifically alongside another. "My, what a beautiful automobile!" Sheila commented as Laz jangled proprietary keys.

"It's my father's," answered Laz, lowering his eyes.

"You must be a responsible young man to have your father's confidence with such an expensive motorcar."

Laz nodded, not lifting his head much. An induced silence spread through the car that Sheila handled with ease. "Well," she said to Jerry, "I can't express enough how grateful I am for the encouraging information that you have passed along about my daughter."

Jerry remained uncommonly quiet, only blinking back an acknowledgment.

"Your lack of speech goes beyond the usual inarticulate awkwardness of youth," said Sheila. "If you have something more to say about *my Dawn*, I beseech you to do so."

Jerry answered Sheila's appeal. "Somehow, somewhere, tonight Alegría is going to come after my friend Joshua."

"You don't know that for sure," injected Laz. "The she-devil doesn't know where..."

235

"She found us at the stadium, didn't she?" responded Jerry. He then addressed Sheila with an apologetic smile. "My friend Joshua is as sweet as can be on your daughter, ma'am, and he saved your Dawn's life last night. The she-devil, um, Alegría, blames Joshua for the accidental death of *her* daughter. She's coming for Joshua tonight, and she's going to have Dawn with her. And, oh, by the way, Joshua is a half-vampire, but the good kind."

Sheila did not break eye-contact with Jerry for a few beats until her hands folded over her lap and she gazed out the windshield. Solemnly exhaling, she faced Jerry again. "I expect you'll wish to change out of your uniform attire before we deliver this medication to Joshua."

***

The cold-blooded deed he had perpetrated was what Peter most recalled as he whiled away the day, inside an empty container trailer in the plot of uncultivated land next to the stadium. He repeatedly conjured a scene where the last two shots he fired were heard by the marine patrol officers, whose boat had returned after the buses left. He pictured one or two going to investigate and finding the dead officer.

Around lunchtime, he grew hungry and walked to a convenience store he came upon less than a mile away. Peter bought a premade sandwich and drink. A contemporary poster of a hand demonstrating the peace symbol hanging on display attracted his attention. He smiled to himself, purchased the anti-war placard, and returned to his earlier hideout.

About an hour before sunset, he left the trailer and began walking, eventually passing the stadium; its entrance continued to be blocked by police cars with flashing lights. Other cars originally intent on entering the parking lot were being turned back around. A speaker on top of one of the patrol cars crackled,

*"Tonight's concert has been canceled,"* in a repetitive, scratchy tone that sounded as if it had been pre-recorded.

On the opposite side of the roadway, Peter kept walking, the poster held out in front of him like he was picketing a jobsite. It was not long before intermittent honks from car horns rang out at him. One car slowed down enough for someone to stick his head out the window and yell, "It's upside down, stupid!"

But Peter paid no heed to the beeping or occasional heckles and eventually stationed himself in as visible a place to oncoming traffic as he could.

***

From behind the eight-panel Coromandel screen, Alegría sat up in bed calculating her predicament. Based on the dull tone of light coloring the ceiling and corners of the room, she estimated it was less than an hour until sundown. A door opened on her side of the room—the bathroom door. From it emerged Dawn, accompanied by Margot. Walking past Alegría's bed, the younger girl's face remained impassive, with expressionless eyes staring straight ahead. The stylish dress she had given her as a change of outerwear improved immensely her previous decaying state of clothing, Alegria noted to herself.

Margot, who like Dawn, had freshened up with a late-night bath at the functional mansion and a change of clothes, came back around the oriental-lacquer screen. She sat next to her daughter, now sitting on the side of the bed. Eyes averted, she waited for Alegría to speak.

"*Mima*, you were right," Alegría said softly. "The man you killed last night. He was the santero from Antilla. Rosa's husband. So much has come back to me...about the past." Alegría placed her chin on her mother's shoulder, the comfort she drew from the woman demonstrated in her deep inhales and exhales. "Would you get my other black dress out for today, and

237

a hooded capelet?" she asked, eyes closed, unzipping her mod black mini dress with white-colored blocks. "We'll have to leave the suitcases."

Raúl curved around the screen as Margot left to do her daughter's bidding. Standing, Alegría wriggled her back and let her dress fall from her shoulders to the floor. Stepping out of the dress at her feet, wearing only a bra and panties, she nonchalantly faced her son.

"*Mijo*," Alegría said in a greeting, pausing to cup her son's face prior to turning toward the bathroom.

Raúl reached for a towel to raise behind his scantily clad mother as she stepped into the indirect outdoor light between the end of the screen and the bathroom door. His body and the unfurled towel cast a complete shadow at Alegría's back. "We drew water for the baths before sunrise. But we haven't been flushing since the cops got here," warned Raúl. "The noise from the pipes…"

"The police?" Alegría asked as she glided into the bathroom without closing the door.

"Not nearly as many as earlier." Raúl slung the towel over his shoulder and leaned back against the outside wall. "We got through the day right under their noses. That took a lot of *cojones*, Ma. Relying on that little guide booklet you picked up."

"It's almost time," Alegría said calmly as she sat on the toilet with her lowered panties bunched around her ankles. "We have to be ready to move quickly."

Margot dropped off the requested dress without speaking. Alegría glanced up at her departing mother crossing in front of Raúl, the cascading stream of her urine filling everyone's ears.

*** 

238

Outside, on the sloping red-clay-tiled roof above the family's hiding place reclined Lane and Miranda, hidden from detection, under a small overhang of the Northwest Tower.

"My throat's parched," said Lane whose pompadour was matted down with sweat, his silver shirt unbuttoned.

"Mine, too," agreed Miranda, resting against the exterior tower wall. Her jacquard-check skater dress clung uncomfortably to her perspiring torso. "Why didn't you leave more water up here knowing we'd be here all day?"

"Why didn't you?" snapped Lane.

"I'm not the one that made the plan."

"Well, neither did I."

"Some mistress…she was supposed to kill those two Dociles at the stadium, and she didn't. They got the better of her obviously. You could see it in her face after she swam back here. We shouldn't have come back here with them. We should have stayed at the stadium. It was crawling with Dociles."

"How long do you think we could have lasted there, *alone*, with that putrid smell smothering us? The mistress was right about the two Dociles coming back here, wasn't she?"

Unable to contest Lane's words, Miranda quieted before engaging Lane again. "I hope Marvis is all right. Do you think he made it?"

"Yeah. They were way out in front of the cops on the water. He'll be waiting for us as the mistress planned." Lane began to button his shirt. "In a few more hours, the cobalt moon will rise. The mistress has promised us an easy conversion."

"I hope so."

Soon afterward, the slanting rays of the orange sun disappeared behind the tall trees to the west. "The time has come," said Lane.

"Finally."

"The time has come for me—not you." Lane clamped a hand behind a perplexed Miranda's neck and rammed her face

239

into the rigid roof tiles...several times. The first forced impact crushed Miranda's nose cartilage and sent blood pouring out of her flattened nostrils. The second traumatized the frontal lobe of her brain, causing massive internal bleeding. The third cracked the skull in the center of her forehead. All sentient faculties had left her body forever as Lane let her slide headfirst off the roof and into the courtyard.

Miranda landed a few feet away from the young cop who was standing near the North Arcade. The youthful officer turned over Miranda's inert body, cringing when he saw her bloody, broken face. He pulled out his whistle and sounded the alarm. Police officers swarmed out from the mansion around the body like ants drawn to a crippled predator.

***

Lane let himself be spotted, running nimbly across the center ridge peak of the roof and scaling the Northeast Tower. Facing the picturesque bay, he began kicking at a row of clay tile with the heel of his shoe—the cobalt blue burnish of his eyes strikingly evident with each kick. Two dislodged barrel tiles fell and smashed apart near the feet of another officer below.

Looking up, the officer was astounded to see Lane balancing himself on the tower's roof. Ducking away, a crouched Lane then hurriedly retraced his steps back toward the Northwest Tower out of the eye-line of those below. Reaching the western façade and holding onto the edge of the slanted roof, Lane purposely dangled his body off the side of the building. A window opened, and he was pulled inside the hideout room by Alegría.

"You have your diversion, mistress," said Lane, admiring the black drop-waist scooter mini dress with gold zippers and gold hem piping that Alegría wore.

Alegría nodded at Lane with restrained approval. "Take her," she said to Raúl, pointing at the torpid Dawn. "I'll take Momó. Leave the weapons—except the knives."

They all jumped out the window of the hideout room and landed firmly on the ground, a cobalt-blue-eyed Raúl carrying Dawn and Alegría with her mother wrapped around her back. The escapees slithered around the parked patrol vehicles in the deserted Arrival Court and ran into the woods alongside the Entry Piazza. As if she had been drugged, Dawn, her eyes half closed, endured the rough treading through the thick brush without a sound. Margot stoically accepted the piggyback-style ride provided by her daughter. After scaling the perimeter wall to the east, the fugitives found themselves conspicuously outside the grounds.

"They must have towed away the cars," said Raúl, evaluating the trampled brush of the vacant side street.

"Come with me down this way," said Alegría.

Raúl left Dawn with his grandmother. Blinking intermittently, her head tilted in an odd manner.

"I guess she's still out there, wherever that may be," said an appraising Lane. He cranked his hand up and down in front of Dawn's face. Margot slapped it away, the stern rebuke in her eyes dissuading any further attempt at engagement.

A Cadillac Eldorado soon poked its way out of the discrete, upscale residential street adjacent the great villa and picked up the idle pedestrians.

"Nice jacking," praised Lane, hopping into the backseat with Dawn and Margot. Behind the wheel, Raúl pulled the vehicle up to the corner. A small police presence was visible down in front of the main gate. Making a slow right turn, Raúl guided the car onto South Miami Avenue, away from the great house.

"Back across the causeway," instructed Alegría, as Raúl flipped on the car's headlights. She twisted around to speak to

Lane in the backseat. "I hope your friend is as reliable as you have proven."

Lane bounced up to the edge of his seat. "Yes, mistress," he said, his hand grazing Alegría's elbow. "Thank you, mistress."

They sat in silence through the short trip back to the marine stadium. Alegría's next utterance—"Stop!"—did not come until she saw the blond-haired boy holding the poster on the side of the road.

The boy approached the car after it deviated onto the shoulder of the roadway. Alegría rolled down the window and inspected the *upside-down* psychedelic-style poster of a human hand displaying the peace sign—a blow-up imitation of the Hostile half-vampire greeting. Her eyes approvingly swept over the boy.

"Clever," she said, accepting his subservient nod.

"Mistress, my name is Peter," said the boy, flinging away the poster board.

***

Lane was stone-faced with jealousy over Peter's attained seating next to Alegría.

"How did you infiltrate the Dociles?" she asked him.

"My stupid girlfriend," replied Peter. "She tricked one of her stupid classmates. They had been friends for years."

"The same girlfriend you said you almost lost your life trying to save from drowning?"

The newly picked-up passenger hesitated and then nodded his head twice. "The Dociles tried to drown all three of us, Marvis included. Only I was able to get away."

"How'd you stand the smell of garlic?" inquired Lane.

Peter pulled out of his pocket a small jar of menthol rub and twisted it open. "Apply generous doses into each nostril. Toni had her own, too. We shared with Marvis."

Though sitting in the backseat, Lane sensed Alegría grinding her teeth at Peter's revelation. But she quickly shook her inward displeasure. "You've provided me with crucial information on Joshua and the Dociles," she said, and pleasingly pinched Peter's chin. "Well done."

Alegría addressed her other loyal follower. "Lane, dear, where does your jet-setting father keep his private plane?"

"He keeps it at Opa Locka Airport."

"With a pilot on twenty-four-hour call?"

"Two pilots. One for the weekends."

"Marvelous." Alegría stretched back her arm, placing her hand on Lane's leg, squeezing his thigh. "Do you think you can make the arrangements for a quick pleasure trip to Marianna?"

"Pleasure trip?" Lane cleared his throat, as neural impulses heated his thigh in a widening direction. "I'm sure it could be arranged."

"Wonderful," said Alegría with one final squeezing shake. "Raúl…"

"I know. Opa Locka Airport."

"But first stop at a drugstore. I want to pick up a Sunshine State tourism map."

\*\*\*

In the airplane hangar, Alegría crumpled the unfolded tourism pamphlet in her hand. "Well selected," she said with grudging admiration. "It's a perfect hiding spot…or should I say *was* a perfect hiding spot."

"Provided his information is correct," Raúl said cynically.

"It is," said Peter. "I'm sure of it. It's Marianna."

"We've got them," Alegría said convincingly. "Now be ready to take Dawn and Momó aboard the plane. I'd like to leave within the hour."

"Within the hour?" asked Raúl. "The pilot's not here yet. And the plane has to be refueled."

Alegría did not respond, accepting she would not be getting off the ground as soon as she hoped. Unbothered, she pointed over Lane's shoulder at two large transportation vehicles on the other side of the hangar. "I take it those two RVs over there belong to your father?"

Lane nodded.

"Walk with me," she said. "You too, Peter, dear."

The breeze picked up as they reached the open aircraft hangar door. Lights, some blinking, symmetrically dotted the darkened municipal landing field outside.

"Do you know any other Hostiles?" she posed to the boys.

"Maybe two or three from the drive-in."

"Yeah, there are at least two from the club, I know."

"Contact them. Get them here. And tell them to bring every other Hostile they know. And all Hostiles those Hostiles know. I want to pack those RVs with our kind. Rip out the interior for more space if you need to. Do you understand?"

"Yes, mistress."

"Yes, mistress."

"Wait! Not yet."

The evacuating boys halted to await further instruction. Alegría guided the boys away from the revealing hangar light and more into the shadows. "You've both served me well," she said, grazing each of their proud faces with her hand. Her sharp-nailed fingers enticingly scratched Lane's chin.

"You first," she told him, raising the hem of her short skirt with her thumb. "Kneel down in front of me."

Lane quickly complied, his eyes riveted to Alegría's sexually vulnerable area. An attentive Peter exhaled enviously, eliciting a momentary look from Alegría that the absorbed boy failed to see.

"Give me your fingers," ordered Alegría. "Don't be nervous," she said, clasping Lane's raised, quivering wrist. "Now…cut my thigh with your fingernail. Be careful not to slice my garter strap."

Lane glanced up. Alegría released his wrist, and the more composed boy did as instructed. His middle finger slowly slid across Alegría's tawny thigh, leaving a thin red trail of fleshy, horizontally sliced skin.

"That's far enough," said Alegría, intercepting Lane's precision advancement between her legs. "The wound will start to heal. You will have to keep reopening it. My fragrance will carry well in this open space and mild wind. Between those Hostiles we attract here with this bloodletting and those you two are able to summon, we should produce a sizable force."

"Yes, mistress."

"Yes, mistress."

Alegría initiated a second revealing adjustment to her skirt line. "Peter, dear, you do see I have two thighs…"

# Chapter Thirteen

Carmen Puig Sánchez strolled pensively along *el Malecón,* the famed seawall esplanade bordering metropolitan Havana in a curving trajectory along the city's natural coastline. The breeze was constant, and the night sky an ostentatious show of stars typical of a cloudless, tropical spring night.

An aged street hawker meekly approached, offering trinkets from his movable stand. Stopping at Carmen's side, he raised a baseball cap from his head in salutation. "The stars and moon have never been so visibly bright over Havana as they are now," he said, glancing upward. "Havana, at night, used to be a pageant of electric lights. Now, with all the commerce and tourist activities extinguished, the capital's only significant nightlight comes from the heavens above." His sightline changed, and he remarked, "However, some customs from the past will never be stamped out completely."

Following his gaze, Carmen understood his meaning as she glimpsed the young lovers, with their limbs entwined, sitting on a seawall dark spot in between the streetlamps. The couple was oblivious to their surroundings, except when the rising tide's rolling waves, blunted by the seawall, sprinkled ocean water over them to their exuded mutual delight. Carmen pulled a coin from her purse and handed it to the scraggly vender. "Something for the girl," said Carmen before moving away. "Make it seem the boy has purchased it."

Passing a point farther along the seafront boulevard, the tumble of the swelling waves smashing into the base of the seawall lightly sprayed Carmen's face and shapeless gray dress with misty seawater. As if her nose were stuffed up, she could not smell the salt in the air as she usually did; her keen sense of smell had begun fading yesterday as it always did during the infrequent occurrences of the cobalt moon. The reduction of her perceptive senses, for one day, had always been nothing more than a minor inconvenience. But today's cobalt moon was different. Acutely aware that this cobalt moon—her seventh since her condemnation into the underworld of perpetual damnation—also marked the defining cobalt moon cycle for her son and a night Carmen had been dreading for his sake.

Her heart had been in tatters since her forced separation from little Rodolfo many years ago. Not a day passed when she did not think of him, when she did not draw from the only memories she had of him—as a newborn and then months-old child, how he felt snuggled in her arms, how he smelled, and that cute nick he had in his chin—the inherited cleft of his father—that looked like someone had marked his chin ever so lightly with a fine pencil. *How much more pronounced that indentation must be now?* Carmen wondered as she had an untold number of times before. Was it melded into a chin that suggested connection to a strong and chiseled jawline in the making—similar to his father?

Carmen had come out to the seawall with the expectation of trying to feel less anxious and less anguished, hoping the sea air would have a mollifying effect on her state of physical agitation and heartache. But with the agreeable sea breeze acting as no placating consequence to Carmen, she decided to return to her apartment.

Reaching her second-floor walk-up in old Havana, she flicked on the light in the sparsely furnished flat, dropped her purse on the all-purpose table, and sat down on a teal vinyl chrome chair underneath a whirring ceiling fan. Crossing her feet at the ankles, she lifted them onto a matching chair. Nailed to the wall in front of her, a flipped-down calendar displayed neatly crossed-out days of the month in lined rows interrupted by two circled ones. Carmen stared at the modest wall decoration for an undetermined time until her eyes closed and a slideshow of life-altering memories clicked forward in her mind…

***

"… The door's ajar," said Rodolfo, his hand pushing open the glass door of Juan's furniture refurbishing store. "Someone must be inside. The backlight is on."

"I should wait out here," said Carmen.

They were both struck by the sound of loud machinery coming from the back of the store. "Sounds like Juan's putting the finishing touches on something," said Rodolfo, coaxing Carmen all the way inside and closing the door. "Besides, he'll never know the door is open if we don't tell him. With all the traffic from the carnaval out here, I'm sure he'll appreciate it."

In the semidarkness, Carmen nearly stumbled over cans of primer scattered on the floor. The whining machinery sound grew louder as they neared the light at the back of the store. Peeking into the brightness, Carmen's senses were bombarded with unexpected horror. Three bodies lay on the floor, Rosa's spouse, Juan, and two with permanently distorted faces and stained with copious amounts of blood, one of whom she recognized as Alegría's husband, Raúl. The smell of cut lumber mixed with the reek of sweat and blood from the fatal wounds combined to stifle the breathing space within the woodshop.

The whine of the buzz saw surpassed in intensity by a shrill scream careened through Carmen's skull like the screeching sound of hard-applied automobile brakes.

248

*"I swear! I swear!"*

*"Swear that you will help me kill Carmen and her son."*

Carmen thought she had misheard the woman she had identified as Rosa standing over the buzz saw.

*"Carmen is doomed to the underworld—like you. And her son is cursed like your children."*

Rodolfo sprang forward as the whine of the motor reached a screeching crescendo. Carmen remained frozen, her wide eyes fixed on her restrained friend Alegría.

A second after Carmen saw Alegría faint, the mechanical whining stopped, the teeth of the buzz saw millimeters from her neck.

Rosa spun around to see Rodolfo holding up the buzz saw's pulled-out electrical cord in his hand. "Have you gone mad?" he asked with disbelief. "Oh, lord, look at this carnage."

Carmen stepped out from the shadows, her face etched with pained bewilderment. "Why do you want to kill me and my son?" she asked Rosa with a touch of frightened sadness.

Rosa showed her hand from underneath the woodcutting table and fired the nail gun twice at Rodolfo. One thin, speeding projectile settled more than halfway deep along the side of Rodolfo's neck, ahead of the second, which tore underneath his chin and shattered his larynx, eliciting the heaviest streams of blood. Carmen screamed and Rosa fired a third time. The nail flew into Rodolfo's open mouth, lodging in the back of his throat and dropping him to the floor. Carmen rushed over to him.

Rosa hurried around the cutting table over to meet her. With Carmen's arms cradling her unresponsive husband, Rosa pointed the nail gun at her bowed head. Alegría then revived and, seeing the cutting blade's hot serrated edges at her throat, summoned a burst of concentrated strength that finished breaking in two the cracked sliding table she lay upon. Her feet hit the ground, and she stood upright. The captive shook free of the binds that loosened around her from the splintered wood. She made a move toward escaping but intuitively glanced back at Rosa first, who had targeted the nail gun on her.

The first shot missed. The deadly nail whistled passed, fluttering the tips of swaying hair along the side of Alegría's head. With the second fired shot, the speeding nail skimmed Alegría's face, tracing a thin red crease under her cheekbone to her earlobe. Rosa fired once more but missed completely as Alegría vanished into the dark store. Rosa started after her, but hearing the rowdy displacement of furniture, the sound of tumbling items, and then the rough opening of the front door, she gave up on the idea.

Though anguishing over the dead Rodolfo in her arms, Carmen perceived Rosa hovering over her again. Tilting her shoulders to one side to warily raise her eyelevel, Carmen did not have much time to contemplate the small round barrel of the nail gun pointed at her forehead before Rosa pulled the trigger. An empty chamber click rang out loudly in the quiet bloody room. Then came another click, and then another in rapid fashion. The gun had exhausted its artillery.

An angry Rosa raised the gun high in the air and brought the barrel end crashing down over Carmen's right temple.

Carmen welcomed the blackness descending over, hoping beyond all hope that she would emerge from what was the worst nightmare of her life and reawaken into the warm familial embrace of her husband and child.

***

Carmen came to, feeling her body in a state of tottering forward motion. Dank traces of plantain husks filled her nose, but her eyes could not discern anything in the shadowy gloom encapsulating her. She tried moving her hands but found her wrists were stuck together in a prayerful clasp to her chest. Her legs were bent at the knees with her feet constrained at the ankles. Involuntarily, she thrust out with her hands, puffing out in two places what she now determined to be a plantain sack. Her mouth, taped shut, prevented attempts to scream.

She started scratching at the sticky ply covering her lips. Then, sensing a fluttering above her, she stopped. Several fingers poked through the sutured twine at the top of the sack, dropping the widened opening around Carmen's head and shoulders.

A frightened Carmen distinguished Juan as the one who opened the sack, with Rosa at his side. With the nighttime sky above her, a strong wind whipped Carmen's hair wildly around her face. Bound and gagged, she saw she was being transported on a wheelbarrow.

Carmen clawed at the electrician's tape covering her mouth, finally able to painfully peel most of the adhesive strip from her lips. "Rosa—oh my God!" Carmen spat out in a breathless exhale. Then Carmen remembered the last face she had seen before she had blacked out—no, before she had been *knocked* out. She remembered because Rosa now duplicated the same inscrutable and pitilessly facial expression she had prior to hitting Carmen with the nail gun. Carmen asked a succession of questions, each bordering on the edge of panic. "What are we doing up here? Why am I tied up? Why did you…*Rodolfo!*"

A strong hand landed on Carmen's shoulder—Juan's hand; its forcefulness demanded she stop squirming about. "Why?" was all Carmen could say before she bowed her head and began to cry.

"You are going to become a vampire tomorrow night— thanks to Antonio," Rosa stated as Carmen raised her head, stupefied. "If we don't kill you before then, the town can never be safe. *We* will never be safe."

"I would never hurt anyone," said Carmen.

"No? Not even after what I did to your husband?" Rosa slapped the loosened piece of tape back over Carmen's mouth and pushed her head down.

Juan pulled the sack up over her and retied the crisscrossing twine. "She never showed the signs Alegría did…the babalawo cautioned that blood disorders can sabotage the depraved progression. A vampire's blood mingles most potently with normal platelets."

"We've been over this," replied Rosa. "Some pregnant women don't get morning sickness or swollen ankles. It doesn't change their condition. Just because Carmen seems normal, it doesn't change what she or her son will become."

"A generational dilution of the $X$ chromosome in Carmen's offspring may bring out a different kind of Hostile half-vampire. The babalawo would not discard that possibility, even though he knew of no prior precedents."

The wheelbarrow lifted slightly from the handle end, precipitating more forward movement. Carmen continued to hear her captors' conversation.

"I'm not killing the child," Juan said.

"He'll be a threat to Milagros."

"When, and if, the time comes, then we'll deal with it. But not now. Not a one-year-old baby. *No.*"

Terrified from the overheard threat to her boy, Carmen pitched hard to one side of the rolling wheelbarrow. The bulky fruit bag fell onto the ground, with Carmen jabbing and kicking violently from within.

"Grab one end," said Juan.

Feeling lifted off the ground and carried, Carmen punched and kicked, puffing out different sections of the sack with each blow. Her combativeness resulted in her feet falling to the ground, one end of the sack obviously dropped.

"Stop kicking," Rosa demanded.

With half her body on the ground, she squirmed free of the hands that supported her shoulders and instinctually rolled completely over once. She pulled off the muffling tape over her mouth once more. "Don't do this!" Carmen shouted out. "Let me go! Please!"

Carmen felt the shoving from different hands, forcing her to roll over several times, disorienting her. Then a foot with a sharp heel pushed her into a half roll. First came the sudden, sharp falling sensation as if the ground had disappeared, instantly incrementing into a headlong tumble. Hurtling through blackened space, a deep unbridled scream from Carmen drowned out the whistling cyclonic air that buffeted her burlap sack.

On the rapid plunge downward, Carmen's feet struck something, chiseled but blunted, deviating her careening descent. Then her fall stopped, and her body experienced the weighty sensation of hanging. Within moments, the burdened seams at the bottom of the sack split open and Carmen dropped out in a rush and landed crumpled on a small ridge carved about halfway up along the face of the cliff.

Beneath the expansive nocturnal theater of innumerable stars and a bright moon, the eternal coastal trade winds swirled around the frightened and dazed Carmen, exposing a sweeping and deadly panorama. At sea level, at least one hundred and fifty dizzying feet below her, wave after ocean wave crashed into a shoreline of jagged rocks in a synchronized tow. Carmen credited her struggling as preventing the original designs of Juan and Rosa of heaving her over the bluff, forcing her to be pushed off instead, closer to the edge of the cliff than intended.

For hours, Carmen drifted in and out of consciousness, her head aching, the epicenter of pain emanating from where the butt of the nail gun had impacted her above her temple. In one of her lucid stretches, she spotted a small low-flying plane and watched its blinking red light grow smaller as it moved away.

But the engine drone stayed with her even as the aircraft passed out of sight…

***

The seaplane landed right in front of el Náutico's bay windows to the delighted fancy of the inside spectators. Almost everyone had been brought to their feet by the sighting of the fuselage-landing flying craft with pontoon skis attached to each wing. Eduardo held up his hand in an attention-gaining manner as the plane curled back alongside an outside dock. "Our ride to the stars and back is here," he said for Rosa's benefit.

Antonio let out an enthusiastic yell. Bridesmaid Marisol seemed enthralled by the prospect and moved closer to Antonio. Raúl grabbed Alegría's hand and gravitated closer to the bride and groom. As Alegría hooked Carmen's arm to make it a threesome, Carmen thought it odd to see the exuberance decorating Rosa's face suddenly replaced with a blank, calculating stare.

"You're not really thinking of going," Rosa said with her hand half raised at Alegría. "After that sloppy incident in the bathroom earlier."

Alegría bloated her cheeks and mimicked enough with her hand for Raúl to understand. "I feel fine," she said to Rosa.

"Do you really want to risk it? In your condition?"

Raúl tugged on Alegría's arm. "Maybe it's not a good idea."

With a wooden smile, Rosa left her newlywed husband's side. "Are you ready for some adventure?" she asked Carmen, dragging her bridesmaid with her to the Sánchez guest table. Reading Rosa's over-the-shoulder gesturing toward the bay windows, Carmen deferred to her father.

"I think it's best if she not," said Carmen's father Benigno. "Unescorted as she is and all." He bowed his head at Carmen and sat down.

"Then you come with her, Señor Sánchez," said Rosa.

Benigno appeared perturbed by the unexpected suggestion. "Out of the question," he answered.

"I'll go with Carmen!" said Felita, her innocent joy immediately and harshly soured by her father's dismissive frown and Carmen's huffed disdain.

Carmen's mother Benita softly slinked her hand around her husband's arm. "Are you going to refuse a bride's wish on her wedding day? Carmen won't be alone."

Benigno made a minute relenting gesture that the young women picked up on.

"Let's go," said Rosa.

Carmen followed but quickly stopped when they came upon Marisol. "It looks like you're the fifth wheel, Mari," said Rosa. "You can't come."

The ladies left the resentful girl and shuffled over with Eduardo and Antonio to the pilot—a man who so dressed the part that Carmen assumed his black leather aviator hat, pulled-up goggles, and white scarf came part and parcel with the seaplane rental. Rosa snuck her arm around Eduardo's. "It's just the four of us."

"Very well," said Eduardo after a short inquiry over his wife's face and a quick dart of his eyes at a blameless Carmen. Eduardo mindfully introduced his new bride to the pilot who smacked the heels of his boots together and raised Rosa's hand to his lips.

"Can we leave immediately, captain?" Rosa asked with a less-than-genuine smile.

"If you wish," answered the man, who presented himself as Humberto and as the bride's obedient servant.

Rosa had not waited for the pilot's complete reply; she walked ahead instead, pulling Eduardo with her. Humberto lowered the goggles over his eyes, loosely snapped his chinstrap together, and followed the bride and groom. Tickled by the pilot's getup right down to his baggy-knee trousers, Carmen clasped her hand around the bicep of Antonio who had offered his arm to the girl in a cavalier manner. Carmen could not resist an inclination to peek behind her as she accompanied him out. A look of concern absorbed Alegría's face unmistakably focused in her direction.

In the air, the seaplane swerved to the south, over Nipe Bay, to the twinkling town of Preston. Carmen could see belching gray smoke from the silos of the great sugar mill processing centers spread along the flat landscape.

"That's the United Fruit Company over there," said Antonio over the drone of the engines.

"When demand is high, the mills operate on a twenty-four-hour basis," replied Carmen, who showed her knowledge of the subject. "On cloudless days, we can see the smoke from Antilla."

Antonio's seatbelt was unbuckled, and he had convinced Carmen to push back the armrest in between their seats under the guise of being better able to describe the aerial vistas outside their window.

Carmen sat with her hands folded, looking out of the blister side window. The interior of the seaplane had two rows of seating, a pair of seats on each side. Other couples could have been easily accommodated. Room, however, became a prime issue as Carmen now became uncomfortable with Antonio's crowding overtures. About to put an end to Antonio's squeeze play, the plane hit an air pocket and dipped suddenly. A startled Carmen yelped and reached out with her hands involuntarily.

Antonio was there to capture one of them; he then brought both of Carmen's hands into his cupped palms. "There now, just a bump in the skyway road," he said with reassurance.

Rosa lifted her head over one of the seats in front of Carmen and Antonio. "I think I felt my wedding cake come up." Her eyebrow rose at the ostensible hand-holding she spied. She withdrew behind the backrest, the whimsy remaining evident in her tone. "Oops. Sorry, you two. Act as if I wasn't here."

Carmen pulled her hands away. "Please," she said. "I am fine. And if you wish a better view, I will be glad to change seats with you."

"The only better view I would like," said Antonio, inching closer, "is of your eyes." Antonio leaned all the way in and kissed Carmen on the mouth. The overwhelmed girl tried to push Antonio away, but her hands could not budge his immovable shoulders. Forcing Antonio to downshift, she managed to turn her face and break the imposed kiss. The offended Carmen slapped Antonio across the cheek.

Initially stunned, the retaliation by Carmen then angered Antonio. With a menacing shift in his seat, he backed her against the window. His neck-grabbing hand cut off Carmen's attempted scream. Helpless, Carmen found herself flipped around by the stimulated Antonio, her nose pressed to the window, short emissions of her breath fogging the glass. Out of the corner of her eye, she gathered in between the spacing of the seats in front of her the impervious newlyweds engaged in a passionate arm-entwining embrace.

Carmen felt her dress lifted from behind and the invasion of intrusive fingers clambering up her legs. Antonio's visible hand tightened around her neck, squeezing the breath from her lungs. She distinguished the soft cartilage of Antonio's nose nudge between the back of her trembling thighs. A prickly sensation below her right buttocks induced Carmen's body to twitch in advance of the gray haze of unconsciousness that enveloped her.

\*\*\*

Carmen's fingers glided over her haunches, touching through her skirt the place Antonio had bitten her. The passing plane had triggered a memory that still ran deep after all these years. The human bite marks had left small circular scars, Carmen remembered, covered by the white cotton handkerchief Antonio had tied around her, placed like an unspeakably high garter around her leg. She had thrown the stained handkerchief away the next morning after awakening. Felita told her that the family had come straight home after her seaplane ride because the wobbly Carmen had gotten airsick.

She was too ashamed by the incident to tell anyone. She avoided Rosa for months, which was not that difficult due to her married station. And thankfully, she never saw Antonio again. Nine months later, she met Rodolfo at the shoe store and married him a few months after that. Her husband had accepted the made-up reason behind the raised blemishes as hornet stings sustained from an unlucky log sitting during a family picnic.

Her husband...her *dead* Rodolfo.

Feeling absolutely powerless, she curled up in fetal position and closed her eyes, the whistling ocean breeze a ceaseless reminder to her present perilous predicament.

\*\*\*

Judging from the sun, near noon the next day, she awoke with functioning clarity and with it a greater, desperate self-awareness of her treacherous situation. She was slouched on a narrow lip of flat rock not much longer than the length of her body. The wind blew in unremitting gusts, ruffling her hair into unruly disarray. For as far as she could see, the ocean rolled out like a long turquoise carpet to the far edge of the horizon. Below, the rising tide had covered much of the rocky coast but made the drop no less terrorizing.

Carmen struggled to break free of the bonds around her ankles and wrists but could not. With her head tilted back, she spotted a jagged, jutting chunk of rock above her. Twisting around and inclining against the rocky wall, she managed to stand. Forcing herself not to look down, Carmen lifted her hands. The jutting point was too far away. She took a hop step closer and then another. She was nearly there. Then something hit her face—frightening her—causing her to lose her balance. Carmen fell on her back blinded, the wind rippling through her ears like the sound of bed sheets flapping on a clothesline prior to a summer storm. Carmen shook her head twice and the plantain sack flew off her face, chaotically carried away by an indiscriminate air current. She spotted a tree branch sticking out from the side of the cliff above her. She surmised the used plantain sack's twined top had snagged on the tree branch, halting her fall and saving her life prior to the bottom splitting open. The sack had finally dislodged in the wind all these hours later.

When Carmen refocused her eyes, she froze in terror, realizing her new placement on the rocky shelving. The joined sky and sea and fatal coastline below rocked in unison, in a vertigo effect, as she nearly tipped over the edge of her crescent perch. With the fastest reflex she could rally, the ashen-faced Carmen spun back away from the hazardous point. Breathing heavily against the promontory's rugged wall, she wished for a way to chisel out a deeper hollow in the rock to fit inside, shielded from the sun and wind.

Carmen lay prone for hours, praying and pleading for deliverance and wondering what she could have done at her age to deserve such despicable condemnation from Rosa and Juan.

\*\*\*

The sun had long since angled behind the cliff and daylight had given way to darkness. Paralyzed by fear, her bound feet and wrists burdened Carmen with an added tormenting sense of vulnerability. Mentally drained, she lay curled up on the imprisoning outcrop, facing away from the sea.

259

Then for no apparent reason, Carmen lifted her head off the dirty ground. Strands of her hair filled with earthy dust stuck to her cheek. Stretching over her, the night sky appeared resplendent with a claustrophobic collection of stars thrust into brilliant fellowship through their sheer numbers. The moon was a perfect chalky circle dappled with shadows of millennia of galactic excavation. Carmen's eyes were immediately drawn to it. She could not take her eyes away from this enchanting orb of the zodiac. Transfixed by its gaudy brightness, Carmen stared at the moon…until her breathing became more pronounced and she raised her shoulders, sitting up with a revitalized bearing.

Carmen greedily sucked in the swirling air around her, her chest fiercely rising and falling with each maximally circulated breath. She noticed a small tear had developed across the binding tape in between her wrists. With little exertion, she broke free by her own hands. An instant later, she snapped her feet apart, breaking their prior tight confines. Astounded at the ease in which she was able to free herself, Carmen jumped to her feet and stepped to the very lip of the ledge. She gazed outward, completely unfazed by the imposing menace of nature in her face, completely unfazed and unafraid. Carmen felt strong; every fiber of her being had shed its prior enfeebling sheath of fear. She felt in harmony with the cosmos!

She swiveled her head with a canvassing look at the rocky cliff behind her. Her eyes beamed with a golden light. Carmen then turned on a dime, causing a chunk of the lip of igneous rock she was standing on to break off and audibly fall into a reunifying encounter with similar rocks far below. She had moved too quickly to have fallen or to have even lost her balance. Before the broken fragment crashed through the sea waves, Carmen was already scaling the bluff. Insect-like, she moved up the face of the cliff, grasping with her hands and digging with her toes through the irregularities of the steep slope until she reached the top. On the way up, Carmen sided along the half-broken tree branch that had stopped her fall. Its roots had been so weakened previously by Carmen's weight that they slid out from its stony foundation with the slightest tug. From there, she completed her nearly effortless climb to the summit.

She rushed ahead and breached the forest in no time. Carmen theorized Rosa and Juan had climbed deep into the wild of el júcaro. Although bare-footed, she experienced no discomfort on the bottoms of her feet as she zigzagged through the rough wooded terrain. She was still hungry and thirsty but not as debilitating so as earlier.

Carmen heard something in the distance; it was the frantic squeal of a trapped hog. She hurried toward the sound which came from much farther away than she originally thought.

Arriving a few feet away from the furor, Carmen distinguished a human figure squatting over the squealing animal, holding it down. A fleeting determination in Carmen's mind told her the landscape appeared much too dark for her to be able to see as sharply she did. The hunched-over figure, wearing familiar clothes to Carmen, brought down a hand which cracked the animal's skull with a distinct crunch and abruptly silenced its squealing. The figure then ripped open the stilled wild pig's fat underbelly—with bare hand.

Carmen deeply inhaled the fetid musk filling the air. The fresh slaughter set off a myriad of sensors in her brain, all intensely craving every feral composition of the dead swine. Carmen irresistibly stepped forward.

The trapper heard her, and a pair of gold and black eyes flashed with recognition upon Carmen. Without saying a word, Carmen came up and dropped to her knees alongside the huntress.

Carmen stuck her hands into the squishy open belly of the wild beast and pulled out gooey entrails, which she shoved into her ravenous mouth. She then yanked off the butchered animal's hind leg and began eating it like an overblown turkey leg. She ripped into the black bristly skin with her teeth, tearing off a chunk of the gamey flesh and cramming it into her chomping mouth with two rigid fingers. Carmen could not have been eating more industriously had she been wearing a feeding bag.

She observed her dining partner. The woman had ripped off the hog's head at the neck; one hand held the whiskered snout, its flapping bottom jaw revealing an even row of yellow teeth. The woman bit off an ear and spat it away. She began munching at the top of the animal's head; her hard teeth pierced the cracked cranium, sounding as if she was crunching ice cubes in her mouth. Her fingers shucked away the shattered bone pieces and exposed the wrinkled gray matter. As she sunk her teeth into the organ's soft tissue, Carmen's cheeks split open with a blood-saturated smile.

Alegría had always been fond of pigs' brain, she remembered.

\*\*\*

In the projection screen of Carmen's mind, the mental imagery of the gluttonous Alegría that eventful night turned grainy and began to dissolve and then disintegrate like brittle celluloid film. A steady, rapid knocking finished snapping her back to the present. She rose from the chair and, with gathered momentum, flung open the front door.

Initially, Carmen stood unmoving in front of the woman in the sleeveless brown gingham dress. Then she inhaled deeply several times as if she was absorbing the woman's presence with her lungs. The woman soaked Carmen in, just as expressively, with each one of her expanding breaths.

Uttering *"Hermana"* simultaneously, the women fell into each other's arms.

After the swell of emotion had subsided, Felita asked, "How are you?"

Carmen smiled broadly. After a not-unpleasant duration of silence, all she could bring herself to say was: "I'll make café."

Scanning the premises, Felita sat down on one of the teal, vinyl chrome chairs of the Formica table. A modest sofa and a twelve-inch television set off to one corner on a stand were the only furnishings in the main living area. "Is this where you stay…unbothered?"

Carmen understood Felita's underlying curiosity. "During the day I stay inside Morro Castle, the old Spanish fort at the mouth of the harbor. It's no longer a sightseeing attraction." Carmen set down a glass of water in front of her sister. "How's mother?"

"She's hanging in there." The inquisitiveness in Carmen's eyes begged more information. Felita took a sip from the glass. "Papá died almost a year now. High blood pressure. He was never the same after losing his district manager post to a military officer."

Carmen tried to hide her emotions. "Well, now he's free of the misery I brought to him."

"Don't talk like that."

Carmen straightened her posture. "Have you forgotten how he disowned me? How he forbade all contact between me and my son? Called me an abomination for what I had become?"

Felita reached for one of her sister's wrists. "You can come back now. To see mother, at least. She was always against telling Rodolfito you were dead. I'm sorry I played a part in it for all those years. Papá played on our fears over what had happened to you, and we just weren't strong enough to stand up to him."

Carmen pulled back her hand. "It doesn't matter now." She snapped the calendar off the wall and dropped it in front of Felita, the circled date unmistakable. "Tonight is seventh cycle of the cobalt moon since I gave birth. In a few hours, my son, wherever he is, will become a monster…like his mother."

"Wherever he is…" said Felita, her voice trailing off. "We tried as best we could to find him for years, to get him a message, to let him know we hadn't forgotten about him. The government stonewalled us at every turn. I know that awful airport manager was behind it, branding Rodolfito as a counterrevolutionary on his permanent records. Remember, your phone call to me on the night he left, I told you about the trouble that manager made for us at the airport."

"Ah, yes," Carmen said with a brief pause. "Señor…Guerrero, wasn't it?"

"Oh, I hate even recalling that name."

"I looked him up when I settled in Havana. Coincidentally, it turned out to be his last day on the job."

"Ay, hermana," sighed Felita.

"I'm happy to say ever since then, I've only concentrated on feeding on members of *el partido*."

"How quickly before you work your way all the way up to the top?" grinned Felita.

Carmen's eyes danced with amusement. "Not quickly enough, I'm afraid," she replied, immediately overcome by melancholy. "I know you're wondering why I asked you here. Why I called you for the first time in so many years."

"Truthfully, my only thoughts were of seeing you again after so much time."

"Ever since Papá excommunicated me, I've traveled through the provinces, staying mostly in the bigger cities until, as I said, I settled here in the capital. Now, I've decided to stop. I've given up on my dreams of reuniting with my son. I no longer yearn to know what happened to Alegría."

"But I thought you couldn't stop. I mean you have to…in order to survive."

"I do," answered Carmen with a piercing look. "I called you here to help me commit suicide by sunlight."

"Absolutely not," said Felita with rising indignity.

Carmen spoke calmly as if explaining an already-practiced routine. "We'll sit on the wall of el Malecón and await the dawn. You just brush my ashes into the sea afterwards…"

"I can't believe what you are saying and trying to make me a part of it." Felita stood up. "What about Rodolfito?"

"He thinks I'm dead, remember?" replied Carmen, locking onto her sister's eyes.

"I've been racked with guilt for so long. That's why I've never attempted to leave to find him. Now, I simply can't live with the thought of my son blaming me for his cursed rebirth."

Before another word could be spoken, a brightness, Carmen initially perceived as a spotlight, bounced off the walls of her small apartment. The light expanded into a blinding exposition of colored particles of energy swirling around like a shaken snow globe. As the energy particles settled, three human-shaped figures appeared inside her apartment!

Carmen did not feel threatened as the three figures materialized before her eyes—their multi-colored funky wardrobe just would not permit it. When the tallest of the three stepped forward to speak, Carmen noticed that she could see none of the trio's feet due to the length of their trousers cuffs.

"Greetings, daughter of darkness…"

"We bid you well…"

"… We are the Equilibrium."

Felita's eyes rolled back and she fainted, dropping in place to the floor.

"Is it my Judgment Day?" Carmen asked passively.

The female among them responded first. "We would rather…"

"Call it a…"

"Day of reckoning."

"Would you like to see your son…"

"In exchange for helping us correct an…"

"Imbalance in the supernatural order of things?"

Carmen's face did not shift from one to the other, attempting to follow their connecting speech pattern. She stayed fixed on the female who had initiated the gripping question. "My son…" Carmen said in a low trailing voice.

The tallest male apparition addressed Carmen. "The reunion we propose will…"

"Be more than familial. It…"

"Will, we expect, be vindictive."

Drawing a deep breath through her nose, Carmen said, "Take me to my son."

As the blinding light started ricocheting all around them, Carmen closed her eyes and peacefully let herself be assimilated by colorful energy flecks whirling around her. As her body took on the same abstract qualities of her visitors, she could hear the call of the metaphysical beings echoing down an unchartered corridor of her mind:

"Come with us…"

"Daughter of darkness…"

"Come with us."

# Chapter Fourteen

Looking out the window of the bus, Joshua could not help being impressed by the antebellum homes and Victorian buildings he saw along the road. The bus had entered the sleepy town of Marianna with a population of less than six thousand according to its 'city-limits' welcoming sign.

Milagros too was captivated by the nineteenth-century structures bathed in the glow of the late afternoon sun. "The old south sure has some lovely architecture," she said, sitting next to him.

She held Joshua's hand in her lap like she was his caregiver. Joshua had had another episode of nose bleeding during the trip but no more loss of blood from either ear. He placed his free hand over the other entwined fingers. "Rosa's timeline doesn't add up," he said. "My mother and father hadn't met when your parents married. They never danced together at the reception in el Náutico. Why would your mother make that up?"

Milagros seemed to be crunching numbers in her head. "Your dad's family could very easily have been invited…"

"No," said Joshua firmly. "I know exactly when my parents began dating, and it was right after they first met for the first time in May 1950. Just a couple of months later, they married. You're seven months older than me. I'm four months younger than Cira and eighteen months younger than Raúl."

Joshua withdrew his hands from the lap of a quieted Milagros.

The pair remained uncommunicative until after sundown when the buses pulled through the low-lying stonewall entrance of the park, flagpoles on either side flapping with the flags of the United States, the state of Florida, and the confederacy.

Outside the visitor's center, a two-story building of limestone construction, there were half a dozen people waiting to greet the arriving travelers. They all wore the same light gray polo shirt with the emblem of the state park above the breast pocket. By far, the oldest of welcomers came up to cheerfully meet them, assessing the long line of teenagers that had spilled out from the buses.

"Welcome to Florida Caverns State Park," he said with a ceramic smile as white as the snowy tuft of hair on his head. The park administrator checked the opened page of the portfolio binder he carried. "I was expecting a Mister Can-deluh. Lah-zarrow Can-deluh."

"He didn't make it," said Milagros.

The news barely dimmed the man's enthusiasm. "Well," he said, shifting over to Rosa, "are you Mrs. Can-deluh per chance?"

Rosa shook her head politely. Stumped, the man scanned the other young travelers, lingering on Joshua's bruised face. A comment seemed forth coming, but the presence of the other uniformed greeters stifled him. "Allow me to introduce myself," he said with a newly drawn breath, "I'm Roger, park director. And these here are Ferguson, Cooper, Daniel, Melanie, and Cynthia. They are your assigned counselors for the duration of your short stay."

Roger leaned toward Rosa. "Accommodations have been prepared, Mrs....?"

"Montes."

Roger did not attempt to repeat the name. "Ah, yes. Mr. Can-deluh's assistant," pointing to the binder page. He smiled and rerouted his attention. "I trust the gentlemen drivers found the parking area to their satisfaction. Your buses will be safely housed." Horace and Otis nodded. "We have a room for you two gentlemen," Roger assured the drivers.

"Is there a pay phone I can use?" asked a girl with a red bandana and heart-shaped rose-tinted glasses of one of the smiling counselors.

The overheard request sounded an alarm in Milagros. "Nobody makes any calls. You should know that." Milagros confronted the girl. "You're part of the group that came aboard at the rest stop." The girl responded with an almost contemptuous shrug of the shoulder. Finally, Milagros asked, "Do I have to pry your name out of your mouth?"

"Meg," said the girl with the red bandana, peeking over her glasses.

"I take it you and the others checked in with Rosa on the bus."

Catching her mother's attention, Rosa nudged in between them. "Margaret," Rosa said, lifting her chin at Meg, "and there was Bradley and three others whose names I wrote down."

Roger attempted to gain everyone's attention. "I know everyone must be hungry. We're prepared to remedy that over in the recreation center. The counselors will show you to your cabins first. Boys this way. Girls that way." The final instruction brought out a mock groan of protest from the boys' present, as well as some unpolished flirtatious comments. Roger paid no attention. Taking a closer notice of Joshua, he expressed, "Say now, this young man does not look fit for activities to me. We have a physician in town I can contact."

"It's not as bad as it looks," said Joshua.

"Well, around here, we like to brag that there's nothing better than the clean night air of the country to rejuvenate a person's body and soul." Roger gave Joshua's shoulder a reassuring pat. "I'll bet you will feel reborn in the morning."

"I hope we all will," said Milagros.

***

"This was to be Mister Can-deluh's room," said Roger, opening the cabin door for Rosa and Milagros. "I suppose you can have it now, Mrs. M." A small double bed with a small round writing table off to the side took up most of the one-room accommodation.

"Your daughter can take your assigned cabin next door. No bathroom hardships that way." Roger gestured to the narrow, open bathroom door in the corner.

"My daughter and I will stay together here," said Rosa.

Smiling gratefully, Milagros eased the door close behind Roger as he departed. Standing with her back to the door and her smile evaporated, she asked her mother pointblank, "Why did you lie to Joshua about his mother and father at your wedding?"

Rosa's eyes widened defensively. "Mija," she said, avoiding her daughter's gaze. "What a thing to say to me!"

"How did you escape Alegría's wrath after she converted?"

Suddenly, Rosa felt she had little space to maneuver in the bed-dominated room. She inhaled twice through tightened lips. "We fled the very next day after the cobalt moon. Juan, myself, and you. We told no one. We moved from place to place for several years until we left Cuba on the freedom flights. We convinced my sister and her husband to go into hiding with Manolín. They eventually joined us here." Rosa sat down on the edge of the bed.

"No wonder I don't remember Joshua as a child. Have no memory of him—or Antilla." Milagros folded her arms. "But all that talk about returning to Cuba to see my *abuelos* and Juan getting his furniture store back and...and Manolín's pony."

The words shot out of Rosa's mouth as harshly as her focused glare. "Alegría murdered my parents *and* Juan's parents...in retaliation for Raúl and what we tried to do to her. We all knew we could never go back as long as she and her children remained alive. We had to keep up the pretense to fit in with the other exiles." Rosa clasped her hands together to recapture her composure. "Hand me my overnight bag, please."

Milagros complied, her mother's travel satchel weighing in her hand. "You had a bag packed and a room reserved. You planned on coming with us all along. Why didn't you tell me?"

"Yes, I made an arrangement with Señor Candela. It was just in case I was needed. Nothing was definite."

"What about the story with Joshua's mother and father at your reception?"

Rosa flapped a hand. "Oh, that. What was the harm? After all, Carmen *was* there. She *was* one of my bridesmaids." Her facial muscles then grew taut. "What does it matter who she danced with? Eduardo? Antonio?"

"It doesn't seem right, to play with a person's feelings like that. Especially about one's mother and father."

"Get me a glass of water. I want to take a sedative. And pour one for yourself."

Milagros emerged from the bathroom sipping one of the two glasses three-quartered filled with water. "I guess Antonio and Eduardo were tied at the hip," she said, sitting on the bed. "I've rarely ever heard you mention one without the other. When you first saw them the first night of the carnival, when they took you and Alegría dancing. when they danced with Joshua's mother at your wedding."

"Who said anything about dancing with Joshua's mother?"

"You did. *What does it matter who she danced with? Eduardo? Antonio?*"

Rosa assumed the glasses from her inquiring daughter and placed them on the writing table. "Grab my bottle. I left it in my bag."

As Milagros searched her mother's bag on the other side of the bed, Rosa pulled out from her skirt a small cylindrical plastic bottle and popped it open. Shielding her actions, she dumped a powdery substance into the glass from which Milagros had been sipping, whirlpooling the water with shakes of her wrist until it dissolved. "Never mind," she said. "I had the bottle all along. It slipped my mind I pulled it out on the bus trip."

Milagros accepted back her glass. "I never understood why Joshua's father would leave him. Especially since Joshua was left without a mother." About to drink from the glass, a knock at the door stopped her.

Opening the door, one of the counselors, Ferguson, stood in the dark holding a lantern near his face. "Ready for the cavern tour? There's a subterranean surprise at every turn." The silly, happy face that Ferguson evoked under the shine of the lantern lent an air of buffoonery to the well-intentioned declarations.

Joshua then appeared and squeezed past Ferguson into the room. The oldest and heaviest of the five, aged 'twenty-something,' counselors they had seen, Ferguson followed him inside, commenting on Joshua's appearance. "Not for nothing, but this one here looks like he's been chewed up and spat out."

"He's right," Milagros said, offering Joshua her water. "You're looking worse."

"*Wait*," called out Rosa, drawing curious looks. "Get him another glass. You drank from that one, didn't you?"

"There are no other glasses," answered Milagros.

Joshua dismissively gulped down the water, leaving a cloudy trace of liquid at the bottom of the glass. "Water tastes kind of funny."

"Could be well water," replied Rosa, averting her eyes to all.

"Are we ready?" asked Ferguson.

Rosa lightly touched her daughter's arm. "You go ahead with Joshua. I will wait for you here. And then we'll go and eat."

"Are you sure?"

Rosa nodded. After closing the door softly behind the departing young people, she stepped over and sat on the bed, her face falling into her trembling hands.

*** 

They followed Ferguson down a moon-dappled wooded path to the sign-marked entrance of the cavern. The pudgy counselor faced the duo, raising his lantern shoulder-high. He spoke in a voice deeper than his own. "The Florida Peninsula is a plain of limestone formed over fifty million years ago. The fossilization and calcification of that limestone created the air-filled cavern you are about to enter. Here you will find a prehistoric world consisting of cave-drip formations of stalactites, stalagmites, and flowstones. Who's with me?" When no one moved an inch or uttered a peep, the deflated guide turned to walk down the incline of steps leading to the cavern, disappointed that he had failed to stir any anticipatory excitement. "Well, follow me," he said. "And don't stomp over one another in your obvious hysteria."

Interrupting, Meg came running up, a beam of light from her flashlight erratically jiggling in front of her. "Oh, goodie! I made it!" she proclaimed.

Milagros obstructed the girl. "This is a private tour."

"Oh, c'mon," said Meg who had ditched her sunglasses but not her bandana. "We all know you're scouting our digs for the night. What's the harm in my getting a sneak peek with you?"

"Are there any more coming?" asked Ferguson, popping back up from the mouth of the cavern.

"There better not be," Milagros said, eyeing Meg.

"*Solid*," said Ferguson, trying to sound cool. Walking back down the steps, he unlocked the heavy metal door at the cavern entrance using a key on a silver waist keychain clipped to his pants' belt loop.

Milagros spun and placed Meg in an encapsulating hold. Squeezing as tightly as she could, Milagros began sniffing the struggling girl.

"Get off of me!" Meg yelled. "Let me go or I'll…" Instantly, Meg's eyes tremored a powder-blue color and her resistance became stronger. Her eyes flashing the same color as Meg's, Milagros released her. "What's the big idea?" demanded the offended girl.

"You girls finished your 'wrasling?" asked Ferguson, not noticing the girls' fluctuating eye color.

"We're done," said Milagros. With Joshua in tow, she headed down the staircase of staggered steps with moss-covered stones on either side and verdant wild plants irregularly sprouting from the edges of the pebble-filled ground.

Ferguson cleared his throat. "The Florida Peninsula is—"

"You can fill her in later," said an interrupting Milagros.

"Well, forgive me for appreciating the wonders of the Earth," replied Ferguson, with a cold shoulder toward Milagros. "Flashlights on, explorers," he reluctantly extorted. "This way…and prepare to step back in time."

The heavy metal door opened and closed behind them. Milagros, who brought up the rear, ran her fingers over the door's inside push bar before following. She hit the bar with the heel of her palm, and the door opened.

The cavern immediately lived up to its other-epochal description, captivating everyone. Milagros, for one, had pictured a dark and dingy setting, but that image quickly fell pleasantly by the wayside as they walked through the serene but, nevertheless, mysterious underground chambers. Cave after cave the charmed explorers passed through contained a varying display of paleontological splendor, some with schematics of burned gold and phosphorescent lime-green colors encompassing the entire limestone deposit.

All the caves traversed within the cavern were lit to varying degrees by fixed lantern-type lamps.

"If you come across a dark spot or passageway, do not attempt to enter," warned Ferguson. "It could lead to potential flash flood-prone areas. We are below the floodplain. The Chipola River runs right through the campgrounds and its creeks can rise pretty fast. Especially on nights like tonight. Don't know if any of y'all are aware, but there is a full moon."

All eyes in the gallery darted over each other with no accompanying commentary.

Milagros' mind briefly played with the way Ferguson pronounced the word 'creek,' making it sound like 'crick.' She then easily returned to absorbing the amazing geological evolution around her. In one cave, Joshua scaled a lumpy mound of rock to touch the hard, scratchy configurations that grew down from the ceiling like pointy rods. In another, Meg caressed the cool, slippery spokes that rose from the ground like rail posts.

"Those earthen spikes from the top are called stalactites," advised Ferguson. "The ones pointing from the ground up are referred to as stalagmites."

"Are there any animals in these caves?" asked Meg.

Ferguson stopped. He repeated Meg's question, even though everyone had heard it. "I was coming to that, but since you asked, I am happy to inform you that we are in the habitat of certain amphibious creatures. Blind cave crayfish—small but cute little mongrel critters. Also salamanders. And yes, the water-filled caves have also been known to yield crawfish, or what's referred to in these parts as the poor man's lobster. Oh, and you'll find certain kinds of bats who call these caverns home. They should be rousing about now. After roosting inside the caves during the day, they leave to feed at night. Rest assured, they are not *those* types of bats. Our flying rodents have no bloodsucking tendencies."

The guide failed miserably in his attempt at adding closing scary sound effects, yet the teens could not contain various twinkles within their exchanged glances.

Meg wandered over to a side chamber marked with red-lettered DANGER signs. The chamber entrance, half-boarded up with crisscrossing two by fours, had heavy duty towing chains nailed taut in front of it. "What's through there?" asked Meg.

"Back away from the area," said Ferguson, beckoning with the underside of his palm as he came closer. "This area is completely off limits. There is a boiling hot spring through there. A fissure in the rock clear down to the earth's magma center formed it. Geologists from all over the world have come to study it."

"Is there any other way out of here except the door we came through?" Milagros casually asked Ferguson.

"Oh, there are other ways," said the guide, drawing everyone away from the prohibited area. "You just have to find them. Our Seminole bats and northern yellow bats fly in and out of a sparse number of crevices in the rocks at ground level above us. We don't even know where they all are. Too small for humans though."

Showing more interest in the accessible areas of the cavern, Milagros said to Joshua in a sidebar, "There's definitely enough room for everybody to spend the night. And we haven't seen everything. All we have to do is make sure that metal door leading in here is secured."

"The shepherd chose well," said Joshua before unexpectedly developing profuse nose bleeding and collapsing on the cold cavern floor.

***

The taxi rolled through the two-lane opening of the low-lying stonewall. Sliding into a spot in the side parking lot near two yellow school buses, the driver exited and opened the driver-side backdoor. "Well, sixty-seven minutes," he stated, yanking off his flat cap and placing it to his chest in an authentic gesture. "I said I could get you here from the airport in Tallahassee in an hour. I hope you won't trifle over those few extra ticks of the clock. Me and the misses could use the bonus stake you promised."

Under a shining bright moon, Alegría stretched a stockinged-leg out the vehicle, her hooded black capelet hiding her face until she tilted her gaze upward. "Thank you, driver. We won't be needing you any longer."

With Alegría uncomfortably close to him, the driver, a lean fellow, asked, "I can try and pull up closer to the campgrounds, if you like."

From the opened passenger door, Margot, wearing a scarf around her head and her dark cloak with the hood down, emerged with Dawn. From the other backseat door, Raúl and the two teenage Hostiles appeared.

"We'll walk," said Alegría placidly, her eyes not releasing the driver's. She pulled back her hood with the hint of smile and rammed the heel of her palm under the cabbie's chin, viciously snapping back his head and cervical spine and causing instantaneous death. Raúl caught the limp, livery driver from behind in his arms, his heavy head rolling from side to side in a contorted twirl.

"Don't leave him in the car," said Alegría, stopping Raúl and Lane's intentions. She peered around her, squinting her eyes. "Dammit, my eyes are on par with my sense of smell now. You three boys, look around. Find a body of water."

Peter was the first to call out. "Just up ahead!" Margot loudly shushed him, but his excitement overtook him. "My eyesight. I can see way up ahead—without glasses—like a telescope."

"It's temporary," advised Alegría, "until you complete the conversion. You should be feeling stronger as well. All of you." She gestured at Lane. "Grab him," she ordered, and Lane threw the lifeless driver over his shoulders. "Can you see the water?"

"This way," a nodding Lane said, taking the lead.

Alegría touched Raúl's shoulder. "You and Peter stay back. Do some reconnoitering. We'll keep going with Momó and Dawn."

Raúl glanced at his girlfriend, eyes rarely blinking and distant but not lacking full comprehension as she was led forward by the arm by his grandmother. "You think she's ever going to come out of it?" he asked Alegría. "I mean, is it permanent?"

"Does it matter?" replied his mother, turning toward the paved path away from the lot.

"How'd she get to be such a chatterbox?" snipped a grinning Peter as Dawn moved off with the others.

"How did you?" groused Raúl.

*** 

Farther ahead, detouring from the path, the foursome came to a clearing exposing a tributary surrounded on both sides by overhanging cypress trees. Next to a paved boat launching pad and walking dock, a posted sign prohibited swimming. Another, with the drawing of an alligator, warned of the lurking dangers associated with the semiaquatic reptile.

Without being told, Lane heaved the dead weight he carried from the jutting dock into the water. The splash disturbed a few birds reposing in the trees but otherwise made no lasting dent in the peaceful night setting. The taxi driver floated in a tight circle until he sank with barely a ripple beneath the water.

The searching quartet again found the path and followed its winding way to the visitors' center. Outside, two men in polo shirts were smoking. They stomped out their butts as they spotted the approaching visitors led by Alegría.

"Welcome," said the older, white-haired man, his hands out in half surprise. "We weren't, uh, expecting any more guests."

"We were just dropped off," said Alegría, flipping her cape back over her shoulders. "My mother, son, daughter, and I."

"Oh." The white-haired man's eyes strayed over the cut of Alegría's tony form. "Uh, my name is Roger... Roger Emerson. Park Director. My adjutant counselor, Cooper. We are stretched mightily thin as far as accommodations are concerned."

"Maybe they're the substitute chaperones," said Cooper. "For that band of teenagers."

After a bit of uncertain silence, Lane crowed, "That's my mom and grandma. *Chaperones*. They wouldn't let sis and I ride in a grungy bus all the way up from Miami. They baby us too much, if you ask me."

"A last-minute decision you might say," smiled Alegría.

"Ferguson's giving a late-night lantern tour of the big cave to the group leaders," advised Cooper. "You might still catch some of it."

"Group leaders?"

"A curly-haired girl and another kid kind of ran through the wash, if you get my drift."

Alegría inhaled pleasantly; she untied the string around her neck and let her hooded cape tumble from her shoulders. Effortlessly catching the falling mantle, she handed it to her mother. As she sauntered up to him, Roger's eyes lost the battle to remain at eye level with Alegría's. "Late-night lantern tour," she said, hooking an arm around Roger's. "That sounds...intriguing."

"Does it now? Well then, your druthers is my ruthers," said Roger, patting Alegría's hand in the crook of his arm and assuming a ramrod posture. "Allow me to lead the way. See to the ladies and gent, Cooper. Lickety split."

As the pair separated from the others, Alegría suppressed a giggle and said, "Roger, I find your Southern hospitality something simply to die for."

*** 

The pair of cobalt-blue eyes watched from a distance. In front of the fringe line of tall spruce pine trees from which they had emerged moments earlier, the four azurean eye sockets beamed with a fluorescent-like quality against the dark wooded background.

"See them?" asked Peter, who could see everyone sharply, the darkness nor the distance posing any impediment. He recognized Milagros and Joshua being pack-strap carried by another man, with another girl wearing a bandana.

Raúl nodded intently. He signaled for them to move parallel to the moving foursome.

"It's the Docile girl—and the kid. Looks like he's in trouble. Let's surprise 'em." Raúl halted Peter's movement forward.

"No. We'll follow. See where they go."

"We should capture them now, while we can, for the mistress," argued Peter.

Raúl's strong hand twisted the front of Peter's shirt. "No, I said."

For a second, Peter's innate aggressive nature spurred a challenge to his brain. But the devious boy smartly suppressed it and yanked himself away from Raúl's grip. His feelings bruised, Peter broke ranks and took off in the opposite direction of Raúl. He waited until the older Hostile tracked out of sight before crossing the open field, toward the area from which the other four came running. He followed the moon-dappled path until he spotted the sign pointing him to the staggered steps descending into the cavern.

Peter smiled wickedly and sped back across the field into the forest. He bypassed an active campground with several pitched tents, a large swimming pond hidden by dense ring of trees, and finally back to the parking lot area in the hopes of finding Alegría.

The headlights of a car slowly making its way through the park's entrance motivated him to take cover behind the taxi they had arrived in. He was only able to make out the blond-haired lady driver of the Ford Fairlane but not the two other passengers, as the car followed the path his mistress had earlier taken on foot.

*\*\*\**

Placing Joshua on the bed, Ferguson projected relief. "He plum gave out," said the counselor, wiping sweat from his face and issuing an expression of fatigue. "I might just do the same."

"He collapsed in the cave," expanded Milagros. "Get him some water, Mamá."

Rosa hesitated and then moved to carry out Milagros' mandate.

"I'll go back to base," said Ferguson. "Get one of our first-aid kits. Roger might insist on a doctor. Sure looks like it's more than a fainting spell to me. Though his breathing seems normal."

"Go with him," Milagros told Meg as Ferguson opened the cabin door to leave.

She obliged with a half salute and an utterance of, "Sure thing," before exiting with the counselor.

Milagros relieved Rosa of the glass she carried. She took a sip and splashed the rest of the water on Joshua's face. He remained unconscious. "He should be getting stronger, not weaker." Milagros left the glass on the bed. Heading toward the bathroom, she said, "I'll get him a wet towel."

With the bathroom door half closed, Rosa grabbed a pillow from the bed. Standing over Joshua, she unemotionally covered his face with it. The boy did not move as Rosa held the pillow down by the ends. Through tightened lips, Rosa inhaled and exhaled even, deep breaths as Joshua's own breathing was being snuffed out.

A sudden knock at the door startled Rosa, prompting her to strengthen her resolve. As the knocking continued, Rosa leaned in more, doing her utmost to deprive the suffocating boy of the last of his life-sustaining oxygen.

"Don't you hear the door?" called Milagros from the other room.

Through the sounds of the sink's running faucet and the repetitive knocking, Rosa did not waver from her murderous intent.

Only when the bathroom door swung completely open did Rosa slide off.

Milagros stomped out, heading toward the probing raps. "Are you not with it?" she irritatingly spat out. Glancing at her mother holding at her side one end of the pillow, Milagros slowed but did not stop until she answered the consistent knocking.

The cabin door opened to a smiling Jerry and Laz. A happy group hug ensued, followed by the appearance of a well-coiffed blond-haired woman introduced by the boys as 'Mrs. Landis.' The woman seemed to withdraw at the presentation of Milagros as Jerry and Laz greeted Rosa.

"I—I saw you at Vizcaya," said Mrs. Landis. "You with the other two boys. Your eyes…" She motioned toward the bed. "That's one of them. He looked right at me with those darker blue eyes."

Milagros' face quizzed Laz and Jerry. "She *knows*," said Laz, who then addressed the woman with an intended degree of reassurance. "Like we were telling you, Mrs. Landis, the changing eye colors are kind of the way they show their stripes."

The woman's doubt was overshadowed by the concern that spread over Jerry's face as he assessed Joshua. "That is not a healthy shade of white."

"He passed out," said Milagros.

Jerry pulled out from inside his shirt a black toiletry kit. "Maybe this is what he needs."

"It's Joshua's medicine," said Laz. "The *shaving kit* he asked for."

Milagros blinked with a smile, her eyes brimming with relief as she sat on the side of the bed. After a few energized breaths, she reached out and tugged on the pillow Rosa continued to hold at her side. "What were you doing with that?"

Rosa's face twitched, and she placed the pillow on the bed. "I was just seeing if Joshua would be more comfortable with an extra pillow for his head."

Jerry unzipped the case. "Who's going to do the honors?"

When no one spoke up, Mrs. Landis put her handbag down and yanked at the fingers of her gloves. "I undertook remedial nursing courses not long after my child was born."

\*\*\*

Joshua awoke to the cheery faces of Milagros, Jerry, and Laz hovering over his bedside. Gladdened by the sight, he said to Laz in a gravelly voice, "You made it."

"I'm a thrill-seeker," answered Laz.

Joshua noticed his medicinal kit lying next to him and a round Band-Aid in the middle of his arm.

"Mrs. Landis injected you," said Jerry. "She drove us all the way up here. She even carries her own Band-Aids."

Sitting up, Joshua cleared his throat. "Thank you," he said to the standing woman whom he recognized from earlier in the day but tried to conceal.

"From what Jerry has told me," said Sheila, her eyes hinting at their prior encounter, "the debt of gratitude belongs to me."

"You look loads better, Joshua," said Milagros. "I'd swear your swelling has gone down by the minute."

"You want some water?" asked Jerry, holding a glass.

Joshua shook his head. He was more interested in listening to Milagros who had nudged Laz off to the side. "We are all going to stay in the park cavern," he heard her say. "We've already checked it out." She placed a hand on his shoulder. "I need you and Jerry to help me move everyone underground before the cobalt moon's culmination."

Hearing his name, Jerry put the glass on the floor and inquired, "Culmination. What's that?"

"That refers to the highest point the moon rises over the horizon in its orbit," answered Laz. "When the Hostiles turn their deadliest."

"You'll lock us in," continued Milagros. "You can sleep in one of the vacated rooms with Jerry. Mrs. Landis can have her own room, and my mother can stay here."

"Your mom seems out of it," said Laz, nodding at Rosa sitting on a corner of the bed.

"Yeah, I guess it's all catching up to her." Then in a rush of emotion, Milagros blurted, "You're the brother I never had." She wrapped her arms around him. "I don't know how you've been able to hold up so well."

A benign knocking at the door could not interrupt the friends' warm embrace. Hands folded, sitting upright, Rosa did not move. Closer to Joshua than anyone, Jerry showed no desire to leave his friend's bedside.

Reading the inaction around her, Mrs. Landis reacted. "I'll get it."

"It's probably Ferguson," said Milagros.

The door's opening attracted the mild curiosity of everyone inside. From his bed, Joshua recognized Roger, his chest strangely waggling, an uncomfortable smile straining his face. "It's the camp director," he said with an informative wave.

"Come in," said Mrs. Landis.

*"May I come in, too?"*

The feminine voice filtered passively into Joshua's ears and exploded into his temples with a cognitive power that bulged his eyes and arrested his breathing. Jumping out of bed, he screamed in tandem with Milagros, Jerry, and Laz: *"Nooo!"* But it came too late; the exchange of frightful looks with one another delayed just enough the unison warning.

"Of course, you may," said Mrs. Landis, swinging the door wide open and stepping back.

A bone-crunching sound preceded Roger knocking over the writing table, sending a glass smashing to the floor as he fell inside. "You broke my arm!" he screamed in pain.

Following a short, leggy stride, Alegría stood among them.

# Chapter Fifteen

"Well, isn't this just groovy?" Alegría said, taking a non-menacing step. "Together again…for one last time."

Roger writhed on the floor. "My arm! Oh, my arm!"

"Raúl!" called Alegría, and her one-eyed son stepped through the door.

Sheila reacted first, cringing at the sight of Raúl's eye-patch. "Oh, dear. Raúl, where's my baby? Where's Dawn?"

"For the love of God, would somebody help me? *My arm! The pain. I can't—*"

"Would you take care of that?" Alegría ordered, annoyed.

Ignoring Sheila, Raúl stepped over to Roger and, with a cobalt-blue luster in his eye, delivered a jackhammer fist above the wailing man's ear. The blow rocketed the side of Roger's head into the floor, cracking his skull and leaving his unseeing eyes open. Sheila gasped, wobbling backward.

"That's better," said Alegría. "With all that noise, I couldn't hear myself think."

"How did she…find us?" whispered a dismayed Laz.

"She couldn't have followed us," answered Jerry softly. "We left in broad daylight."

Spying the bathroom door, Joshua elbowed Milagros. She shook her head.

"There's no way out of there."

Alegría strolled past an anxious Sheila, eyeing her from top to bottom. "Practical combination," she said. "But the colors are nowhere. And that hem? Much too nineteen-fifties."

The mini-dress-wearing villainess sauntered over to the bed, keeping an eye on the room's stunned standing occupants. With an easy flipping motion, she overturned the bed on its side, its mattress and springs landing upright against the back wall. "That's better, isn't it?" she asked. "Much more roomy." The action jarred Sheila back toward the others.

Alegría ambled to within inches of a trembling Rosa who had not moved since jumping up, following Alegría's shocking entrance. "*Que encanto…*Rosita*. After all these years," she said, followed by a purposeful pause. "You've put on weight." As she separated from her former friend, Alegría glanced over her shoulder and asked, "Done much table-sawing lately?"

The devilish diva strutted in front of the lined-up detainees, acting like a school superintendent about to chastise culpable students for some misdeed. Her eyes fell over each teenager as she spoke. "No holy water…no stakes…no spear gun…flare gun." She sniffed the air. "No garlic…and *no* crucifix that I see. I must say I am disappointed. And why aren't any of you shaking? Am I losing my gory revulsion?"

Sheila clicked a heel on the Maplewood floor. "I can no longer tolerate this unseemly behavior toward us, especially the children. Mrs. Purrez—I assume—I insist you cease your intimidating actions immediately and you or your son inform me as to the whereabouts of my daughter."

Alegría blinked twice. "Why, Katie Scarlett, have you been out riding without your bonnet again?" The pleasant Southern accent intonation Alegría assumed quickly faded, her face souring as she crept closer to Sheila. "Haven't you been paying attention?" she asked. "Didn't you see me flip that bed over like it was cot?" She pointed at Rosa. "See that woman over there? I'm going to decapitate her—like she once tried to decapitate me. Except I'm going to use a penknife and pocket mirror and make her watch."

Rosa bolted for the door but was corralled by Raúl who brought the squirming woman over to his mother. *"Suéltame, demonio!"* she cried.

In a quick, coordinated movement of her arms, Alegría clasped one hand around Rosa's neck and the other around Sheila's.

Raúl pulled out and shook a long carving knife, its sharp, pointy end dissuading any attempted assistance from the intimidated youths. "Don't try it. Any of you," he threatened.

"Let them go!" screamed Joshua and Milagros, clutching each other.

"Don't worry," said Alegría, facing Milagros. "I'm just going to choke Rosa into unconsciousness and have my fun with her later." As the oxygen-starved Rosa sank to her knees at Alegría's feet, Sheila rose higher in the grip the super-strengthened siren. Alegría seemed to relish holding the suffocating woman high above her as both of Sheila's shoes flew off her kicking feet.

At the door, three figures appeared, two feminine. Joshua stopped his hollering to observe the younger of the women. Her familiar face calmly absorbed the sadistic proceedings until her eyelids softly closed over her opaque eyes. Then her facial features and head began to twitch. After several seconds, she suddenly opened her eyes; no longer dulled, they shone fierce and combative.

As the word *mother!* roared out from her lungs, Dawn charged, as did the four undermatched youths and the middle-aged Margot and Lane.

***

"Not a moment to spare…" voiced one of the transcendental beings just outside the cabin.

"Go forth, daughter of darkness…"

"And counter the heedless one."

Carmen emerged from the bubble of colorful floating crystal particles surrounding her and the Equilibrium. At the door of the cabin, she witnessed Alegría drop the struggling woman she held high in her hand like a trophy and, in one rapid sweeping movement of her arm, knock down the assaulting teenagers like bowling pins.

Alegría picked up one of the boys off the ground and vertically raised him over her head like a weightlifter completing a routine. "I'm going to break you in two," she snarled.

The cleft in the boy's chin ever so briefly entranced Carmen—a smaller-scale carbon copy of her deceased husband. In a fleeting visual exchange, Carmen crammed the vulnerable boy's fervent gaze into her heart and answered with an expressive maternal tenderness. Her ensuing deep breath of confirmation was cut off by her own scream and surprised everyone in the room: "Alegría! *Let go of my son!*"

"Carmen?" uttered Alegría in her weightlifter's pose.

In one hand, Alegría bunched his pant legs together at the knees, the other clasped to his shirt beneath the collar. She raised her eyes at her human payload and then back level with Carmen's. "Your son's fate is sealed. He killed my Cira."

Carmen shot a glance back at the Equilibrium. A nodding Libor pointed his hand directly into the cabin.

"You…"

"Can…"

"Enter."

Carmen unhesitatingly shot forward as Alegría lifted her knee and yanked Joshua down. Interposing herself between her son and Alegría's lethal bent femur, Carmen took the brunt of the kneecap's mighty blow into her solar plexus. She doubled over on the floor, her son tumbling unharmed near her. He scrambled over to her as she caught her breath. "Is it really you?" he asked. "I thought you were—"

"I'm not, hijo," Carmen said, short of breath. "It's me. It's really me."

Alegría glanced out toward the Equilibrium's fading light and disdainfully declared, "Meddling fancy-pants-dressed weirdos."

As Carmen's hands lovingly caressed the sides of her son's face and pressed him close to her chest, her eyes were pulled to one of Alegría's other would-be victims. *Rosa.* She was being caringly assisted on the floor by the curly-haired teenage girl as she regained consciousness.

Immediately recognizing her, Rosa shook her head, leaning back with disbelief. "It can't be you," she said. *"It can't be you."* Carmen's incriminating gaze, coupled with Alegría's laser-like focus upon her, filled Rosa's eyes with a double dose of panic. Screaming, she furiously kicked her sliding heels on the Maplewood flooring until her back thumped against the nearest wall, preventing further retreat.

"I never did anything to deserve what you did to me and my family," Carmen said, peering at Rosa.

The back of her head pressed against the wall, Rosa's briefly aimless eyes settled back on Carmen. "I didn't know anything about what was going to happen to you. I didn't know who the Spaniards really were at the time. I thought if Antonio liked you, I wouldn't have had to worry... You shouldn't have been dancing with my Eduardo like that."

Carmen's head slightly shook, and her shoulders straightened as she incredulously searched Rosa's staunch face. "You were *jealous*...on your wedding day?"

With Raúl and Margot at her side, Alegría assumed her previous casual-but-in-control demeanor, interjecting, "Don't this beat all reunions between friends."

"I'm not your friend," said Rosa with contempt. She lowered her brow at Carmen and stood up defiantly. "Nor yours."

"You're right," said Carmen, also getting to her feet. "Friends don't try to kill each other—or murder each other's husbands."

"What?" cried the curly-haired girl.

"Milagros?" asked Carmen, clinging to her boy.

The girl acknowledged with a minimal squint and then pressed her mother for information. "What does she mean? Tell me."

At first, Rosa hesitated, but finally she succumbed to Milagros' silent insistence and, with a finishing burst of resentment, spat: "I killed Joshua's father. I shot him through the neck with a nail gun. It was right after we murdered Raúl, Alegría's husband. The same night, Juan and I thought we had killed Carmen by throwing her off a cliff."

Carmen scanned the others closest to Alegría—identifying those she knew had to be Raúl, Jr. and Margot. She watched Alegría take her puzzled son's hand, breaking the silence that descended upon the room.

"It was just recently that I put two and two together with the two of them and with Joshua," Alegría said. "So much happened so quickly; I never found the right moment to tell you. If it's any consolation, Momó killed Rosa's santero husband and I tore him to pieces later."

As Rosa grimaced over the revealed fate of her dead husband, Raúl lowered his chin and withdrew his hand from Alegría's. "It is," he said with leveled eyes. "But not enough." He wound back and whizzed the knife across the room, splitting Rosa across the chest.

\*\*\*

291

The execution of her mother ignited Milagros; she leaped at the murderer, but Raúl sidestepped, hooked her arm, and bear-hugged her and her flaring, powder-blue eyes into submission.

Shielding Joshua, Carmen stunned everyone by summoning her vampire teeth in a proposed standoff against her kindred opponent. "You're not touching him."

"I'm older than you," a measuring Alegría countered. "Stronger. You're weaker because of your abnormal blood...weak of heart, too. You never sought revenge with me over Rosa or the santero's family."

Sitting up, a resuscitated Sheila tightly embraced Dawn who dragged her mother outside the developing ring of combat. "Oh, my dear," said Sheila breathlessly to her offspring. "My *dear*."

Joshua tightened his grip on his mother's dress. "You're the vampire? Not my father?"

"Jeez, ma," grumbled Raúl. "How long were you gonna keep *that* from me?"

"I told you," Alegría replied. "I just recently figured out who's who in this nightmare."

"This is one bizarre freak circus," injected Jerry.

"That means..." verbalized Laz.

"I'm a *Hostile*," finished Joshua.

"A dead one," punctuated Alegría.

Quickly, Jerry fixed eyes on Laz. "Tabletop?"

Laz swiftly dropped on all fours behind Raúl. Milagros raised her knees as Jerry pushed into her, knocking Raúl backward and flipping onto the floor.

"Mijo," cried Alegría, but the threat from the fangs-drawn Carmen kept her from helping.

Margot reached into her pocketbook. Before she could reveal her intentions, Jerry smashed the water glass he had put on the floor over her head, sending the woman into a hardwood nosedive.

292

Seizing the opportunity, Milagros, on one knee, ordered two of the boys out. "Round everyone up. Get them into the cavern."

Jerry and Laz raced from the room, barreling past Lane, indecisive on whom to try and stop.

"After them!" shouted Alegría, redirecting Lane out of the room. "They're just Purebreds." Quickly returning her attention toward Carmen, she became more incensed with every clearly enunciated word. "No more chitchat. He dies *now*."

Carmen remained firmed. "Let's take it outside."

"You'd like that." Alegría motioned toward Joshua. "He's not acting the way he should be. His blood is weak, like yours."

"I can handle them, Ma," stated Raúl, standing back up. "It's just a female Docile and pantywaist Hostile."

"I'm not willing to risk it," replied Alegría. "Slide your grandmother out of the way and take the other carving knife from her purse." Her eyes, darting between Carmen's and the wary teens as Raúl complied, stopped on Dawn. "I see you're back with us, sweetheart."

Speaking in short breathy spurts, Dawn squeezed her mother. "She killed Daddy."

Alegría scoffed, unhesitatingly saying to her son, "Kill the gingerbread woman. Then hold the knife to Dawn's throat until I finish with my long-lost friend."

"In the name of all that's good and holy," said Sheila, understanding Alegría had targeted her.

Alegría read Joshua's rescue intentions. "Don't," she warned. "I'll rip Dawn's throat out and hand it to you before you reach her. Not even your mother is fast enough to prevent that."

Alegría's chilling words heightened the frightened squeals of Dawn and her mother until they were raised another decibel level by Raúl, who waved the pointy knife he had secured and demanded Dawn to 'move out of the way!'

*"What the blue blazes is going on in here?"* asked a dumbfounded Ferguson standing at the door with Meg.

The short diversion saved Sheila and set off simultaneous reactionary movements by the held-off individuals. Carmen's face metamorphed into a muddy, yellow-eyed, sharp-fanged, pointy-eared barbarity, emitting an ominous growling sound that provoked Alegría to respond with a replicated physical transformation.

Though in close quarters, Carmen and Alegría rammed each other with enough concussive force to knock everyone in the room off their feet. With arms locked, the two mutated women rocketed through the front wall of the cabin, shooting over the knocked-over Ferguson and Meg.

Joshua and Milagros quickly jumped on Raúl before he could get to his feet and began pummeling him with all their respective pent-up, eye-changed-induced might. On the floor, Raúl half rolled, the grip on his weapon loosening as the enraged teenagers reigned blow after afflicting blow on his head and upper body. Joshua jackknifed his elbow into Raúl's spine several times, the knife finally slipping from the half-vampire bully's quivering fingers. Milagros scrambled to her feet and kicked it away, and then kicked Raúl in the head and face, the cobalt-blue of his Cyclops eye completely regressing.

Curled up on the floor, the immobilized Raúl groaned beneath the standing out-of-breath assailers. He received another kick around his waist and spat up blood.

"Miserable little twerp," said an infuriated Dawn, pulling back her foot and staring down at him.

Joshua scrutinized Dawn's eyes, trying to confirm her wellbeing. Dawn returned no similar benevolence, which erased the trace of a smile that had crept out from the side of Joshua's mouth. "You are all deviant fiends," she said and pressed her face against Sheila's shoulder. "Let's hurry out of here, mother. Before those vampire devils return."

The rejection clearly stung Joshua. He backed over to Milagros who had sunk to her knees beside Rosa, brushing her fingers lightly over the eternally stilled body.

"I'm calling the sheriff," said a flabbergasted Ferguson near Roger's body. He attempted to collect some of the strewn contents of the first-aid kit he had carried into the room. "Although I don't rightly think he'll believe what I just saw."

"We shall accompany you," said Dawn's mother. Her attempted second foot forward clipped Margot's raised heel, wrecking her balance and spilling her onto the floor.

The revived woman held the kicked-away carving knife which had spun to a halt near her. With a banshee-like scream, Margot leaped and zeroed in on Joshua. In one fast, fluid motion, Milagros yanked Raúl's murder weapon from her mother's chest and stuck out it in front of Joshua. Margot plunged into the slanted blade, the room-piercing scream permanently silenced by her raspy last breath.

*** 

Jerry and Laz ran across the moonlit meadow trying to beat the advancing Lane into the cover of the woods. Disappearing into the forest, they took refuge behind a thick row of American beech trees. They detected Lane zigzagging his way toward them, his cobalt-blue eyes blinking like pocket-sized flashlights.

"I'll distract him," whispered Jerry. "You get your crew together and find that hiding place."

Just then, the treetops behind them began breaking off, splintered by a speeding missile descending on an angled path toward their position. The missile exploded through a tree a few feet above the roots and plowed into the open ground yards in front of them. Alegría and Carmen, in mostly human form, emerged from the cratered earth, rabidly scowling at each other in their yellow-eyed, serpent-toothed hideousness. Each trying to gain the upper hand, they parried with heavy tusks of broken tree bark, bashing each other repetitively.

"That is what I call fang to fang combat," declared Jerry.

"Let's go," said Laz.

"Where to fellas?" asked Lane with beady blue beacons staring down at the crouched pair.

Laz jumped up but Lane easily grabbed him by the collar and then hit Jerry hard above the ear to keep him off his feet. But then Lane was knocked over by another concussive wave created from a head-on collision by the main combatants nearby, which scattered dried leaves and dirt wildly in the air.

When the swirling dust settled, a hurt Carmen lay on her hands and knees on the ground, with a smug Alegría standing a few paces away.

Laz scrambled to his feet and took off. Jerry tackled Lane from behind as he prepared to follow. Lane assumed the upper hand and pinned Jerry to the ground. He raised his fist to hit Jerry, but instead, Lane was hurtled backward through the air. In a whoosh, he landed flush against a tree, dazed, with fallen leaves and dirt billowing around him.

The beast that had knocked away Lane swerved back as if to check on Jerry and then galloped away. Jerry recognized the gray dress of the interceding animal but had trouble reconciling in his mind the animal skin, hooved feet, and wiry spear-tipped tail.

Before he could blink, a second similar beast sped past him in hot pursuit of the first. The teenager associated all too well the black garment with gold piping that covered its torso.

Jerry obtained a head-start over Lane while he regained his wherewithal. He sprinted out of the woods through open ground, trying to find a path back to the main building. But Lane, once on his feet, reduced the gained ground between the two quickly. Jerry sprinted over a small footbridge, past empty picnic tables, and back into another patch of woods, with Lane closing in.

Slinking through a row of overhanging cypress trees, he checked behind him without slowing down. His footing gave way and he fell with a loud splash. Slapping around in the water, he struggled mightily from an inability to stay afloat.

Lane pounced on him, grabbing Jerry's shoulders and repeatedly dunking his head in and out of the water. With Jerry completely exhausted and gasping for breath, Lane eased over to the water's edge. "Sayonara, pal," he said and pushed Jerry under one more time and held him there, a slew of air bubbles rushing up from the submersion point.

The smile of satisfaction on Lane's face disappeared in an instant, replaced by one of sudden pain. Ripped away, Lane hit the water in a violent backflip and rotated on the surface—in the clamped jaws of an alligator. Screaming in the throes of death, Lane tried in vain to strike at the large reptile which engulfed his leg up to the waist. The alligator bounced and thrashed its ferocious jaws, cracking Lane's back in multiple places and extinguishing the brief shading of cobalt blue in his eyes.

Yards away, Jerry popped up gasping for air. He grabbed at rooted vines along the tributary's edge and pulled himself out. He lay on his side breathing hungrily, watching as the gator submerged with its surrendered catch.

\*\*\*

Milagros pushed Margot's slumping body off her and stood next to Joshua as Ferguson and Meg cautiously approached.

"Who's she?" asked Meg, fixed upon the face-up woman with the knife sticking out of her abdomen.

"I can definitely attest that to be an act of pure self-defense," said Ferguson with a respectful nod at Milagros. "Just like the earlier pummeling of that one over there…" He pointed irresolutely at Raúl. "But then there's Roger here. This looks like more of an ambush if you were to ask me."

"Isn't that your…?"

Not bothering to answer either of Meg's hanging questions, a grim-faced Milagros pulled a sheet from the overturned mattress and placed it over her mother. Milagros' head remained bowed for a moment.

"We've got to get out of here, mother," pleaded Dawn.

"This is utter insanity," said a distressed Sheila, back on her feet with the help of Dawn. "Young man, *please* lead us out of here."

Ferguson bobbed his head in agreement. "I don't reckon it'll do anyone much good to stay here, especially if those flying goblins decide to come back. *Let's skeddale.*"

The other polo-shirted counselors then spilled into the room, perplexed and stunned to various degrees at the property damage inside and outside, and the dead bodies lying about. One of the female counselors sought temporary comfort in the arms of a male associate upon seeing her dead park director.

"Looks like a wrecking ball came through here," said Cooper.

"We came to find Roger," said Daniel, peering at his fallen superior. "Tell him that one of the late arrivals is rounding up everyone."

"The girls, too," said Melanie.

Ferguson repositioned himself in front of his coworkers. "Rounding up? What for?"

"He asked for the park directory. They're all heading toward the big cave," answered Cooper. "Wouldn't pay us any mind about the hazards inside."

Ferguson tugged at his belt's keychain. "I don't see what they mean to accomplish. Only Roger and I have the key to the entrance. Only *I* carry it on me." He rubbed his chin. "'Course I wasn't able to lock things up after *that* one's fainting spell."

"Mother, we must leave," implored Dawn.

Sheila coincided. "Gentlemen and ladies, it is time we vacated these terrible premises."

While they all took the slightest pause to silently concur, Milagros intervened, her grief distinctly pushed aside. "I'm sorry, but you can't go out there. For your own safety," she said, placing herself in between the counselors and the front of the cabin. She had pulled the double-murder weapon from Margot's torso. The blood-smeared blade in her hand enhanced her menace. "Everyone in the bathroom—now."

"Bes' do what she says," said Ferguson, hands raised in a non-aggressive manner. "I saw her skewer that old lady there without blinking not two minutes ago."

"Why don't we just charge her?" proposed Daniel.

Joshua picked up the carving knife dropped by Margot and joined Milagros, muffling any more proposed challenges.

As the pair backed everyone toward the bathroom, Milagros yanked the keychain from Ferguson's belt. "Now how's that going to help?" asked the befuddled counselor.

One by one, they entered the cramp facilities. "We cannot all possibly fit in here," said Sheila.

"Not me, right?" questioned Meg, adjusting her bandana.

"No, of course not *you*," Milagros testily replied. Responding to Sheila, she suggested, "A couple of you will have to stand in the tub." After handing Ferguson's keychain to Joshua, Milagros reached around the door lock to pull out the key.

"If you do this, little lady, I just might forget about the self-defense testimony on your behalf…"

Milagros closed the door on Ferguson's feeble threat and locked the door from the outside. "Someone will let you out in the morning." Exhibiting tiredness, she purposely let the bathroom key fall on the floor.

***

"My mother," said Joshua, dropping his weapon. "Alive? Where did she come from? How did she get here?" Looking up and observing a blank-faced Milagros quieted Joshua. Putting aside his own unanswered questions, he readied a consoling shoulder, waiting for Milagros to cry. But she did not.

She eased toward him but not in search of comfort or solace. She chose her words deliberately. "I always suspected your physiology hampered your natural development, so to speak. Your lack of a blood-clotting agent sent everything haywire, I figure. It was all there in front of me. I just didn't see it right away. Why Juan's coconut shells were so confused with you. Why carrying the crucifix to Lacey's house bothered you? Why Miranda smelled you funny. Why you were scratching. Why your face blew up like Alegría's from the leftover garlic inside your clothes. Why you weren't pushed out of my house like I was this morning. And why Mrs. Landis said you looked right at her with those *darker* blue eyes."

Joshua moved his head sideways. "You mean you suspected I was a Hostile? And you still brought me here?"

"Whoa!" said Meg. "I'm about to wig out right now. Your *mother* was one of those heartless beings that flew out of here? You're a Hostile?" She began taking backward steps toward the front of the cabin. "So glad your bruises are all healed up there, Josh. Hope you and your mom get in some good quality time together. I think maybe I'll just leave you two alone now."

"*Hold it*," called Milagros.

Meg, who had turned to exit, stopped in her tracks.

"I'm coming with you," informed Milagros.

Meg dawdled back, with thumbs in her pockets. "What about him?" she asked, referring to Joshua.

"What about him?" replied Milagros prior to cocking back her arm. Instantly, the butt end of the knife struck the side of Meg's head—shocking and staggering her until she collapsed. The action furrowed Joshua's brow, and he shook his head.

Milagros stepped over to the battered Raúl lying in the same conquered spot on the floor. She reared back and kicked him in the spine. "You awake?" In a fetal position, Raúl's back straightened but gradually retracted again with a groan.

With an extended grimace showing bloodstained teeth, Raúl struggled to speak. "Wait till my mother comes back."

Milagros then grabbed Joshua's arm. "Don't let your sentimentality interfere. You heard Alegría. She's older. That makes her stronger. You've seen firsthand what Alegría can do. I'm sorry, but I wouldn't take odds on your mother surviving."

Joshua pulled his arm free and picked up the carving knife again. "I'm just going to have to improve those odds." He motioned to leave.

"Wait!" yelled Milagros, halting Joshua. She calmly circled back to Raúl, her arms limply at her side, the knife slipping out of her indifferent fingers. She sank to her knees, looking over at the covered remains of her mother and then back at Joshua, her face filled with such an uncharacteristic sadness that it pulled Joshua back in her direction. "Meg is for you," she said.

"For me…?"

Milagros' eyes shined a power-blue and, in twitchy movements that opened her mouth wide, tilted back her head revealing sprouted canine teeth. She bent down and buried her face into Raúl's neck. Raúl moaned and his body shuddered as Milagros tore into his flesh.

"Milá!" cried Joshua. *"Don't!"*

After a lurid combination of chomping, slurping, and suction sounds, Milagros raised her head. The deep perforation of Raúl's neck exposed his spinal column. Milagros wiped a slick coat of blood from her chin with the back of her hand. "I love that pet name—Milá. Did I ever tell you that?" Standing up, her eyes blazed a cobalt blue before turning solid gold with black irises. Slowly, she walked over to him, her cheeks, neck, and hair smeared with Raúl's blood. "We can be together now, Joshua. Together for a long, long time."

A disbelieving Joshua reached out and shook Milagros' shoulders, chasing the unsavory golden sheen from her eyes. "What have you done?"

Milagros wiggled free and picked up Meg by the arm as if she were a stuffed life-sized doll. Her fingernails slid across Meg's throat like red markers, leaving two fine lines of blood. *"Do it,"* she exhorted with a blend of intimidation and anger. "And we can help your mother—if it's not too late."

Swallowing hard and feeling his breathing constricted, Joshua struggled for words. Meeting his mother…the bombshell revelation of his true nature…the jolting conversion of Milagros—the convolution of shocking events was too overwhelming. He dropped the knife, spun around, and darted out of the cabin.

*** 

Carmen was injured. Alegría sensed it. The life or death pursuit had led to the park's floodplain swamp. Climbing up the split trunk of a bald cypress tupelo tree, a lurking Alegría waited for Carmen to trudge out of the brush and cross the shallow swamp. As Carmen appeared and passed underneath the split trunk of the massive tree, Alegría leaped on top of her. The grotesque cat-like creatures fought desperately in the murky bog and instigated a small tidal wave that washed them up on the other side of the plain.

On dry land, Carmen howled like a wounded animal, shook the excess water off her fur, and broke into a wobbly gallop. Alegría's yellow eyes sparkled as she took off after her. Not taking long to catch up, a charging Alegría bit down on Carmen's tail, bringing her to a skidding halt in the sloping glade into which they had emerged. She spun her prey around by the tail and flung her through the air, crashing on top of a rocky mound.

Lying prostrate, Carmen reverted to human form. Alegría hurried over, her own changed female figure latching onto Carmen. She jumped high and straight down into the small hill, with Carmen taking the brunt of the fall. Repeatedly, Alegría jumped up and directly downward, battering Carmen's body against the hard ground. One final time, Alegría soared and plummeted to earth with Carmen in her clutches. The hill's hardened soil broke from the extraordinary pounding, and the two crashed below into an ancient alcove of unique geological rock formation.

Bloodied and beaten, Carmen lay unable to defend herself as her weary victor stood over her.

*** 

Joshua encountered the moon-dappled path bottled up by a multitude of blanket-carrying, flashlight-waving, refreshed teens. He circumvented the long line, finally prying his way through to the front where he encountered Laz, guiding everyone into the cavern.

"Why are *you* here?" asked the wary Purebred.

"To give you something," answered Joshua. Only when Joshua pulled out the jangling keychain from his pocket did Laz relax. "Don't forget to lock it," he added, nodding at the cavern door.

Not far away, a disturbance could be heard as the ground trembled in recurring agitations.

"Get everyone inside, and good luck." Diverting his cobalt-blue seeping eyes, Joshua rushed away to the confused gasps of many surrounding Dociles.

***

A relaxing Peter spotted the RV pulling through the entrance as he listened to the radio in the taxi. He had lost his way in the park more than once, searching for his mistress and was only consistently able to find his original place of entry. He decided to rest a bit before trying again. But the sight of the RV and the trailing caravan of cars immediately extricated him from the auto. He flagged the big motor vehicle down, bringing it and the train of autos behind to a stop.

The forty-foot motorized trailer's door opened, and Peter gave the Hostile half-vampire salute to the young chauffeur who reciprocated. "Where's the other one?" Peter asked the exiting driver.

"It should be along soon," answered the teenager, tapping the front side of the vehicle. "Mine's got more horsepower under the hood."

A disembarking Hostile from one of the cars sniffed the air. "I smell Docile blood."

"Oh, their scent is sweeter than magnolias in the spring," said an inhaling female member. Her eyes tinged cobalt blue and dainty fangs sprang forth from her parted lips.

"You're beautiful when you're ravenous," said an apparent admirer.

Peter and the driver stared stiffly at each other. "Well, are we going to get our freak on or what?" asked the driver. "The moon's culmination is less than an hour away." A chorus of curt agreement emanated from most of the disembarked trekkers.

"Follow me," said Peter. He led the rank and file into the park through a wooded area with a broad assemblage of cypress knees and into a forest of tall spruce pine trees. Halting everyone at the fringe line, Peter could not believe their good fortune.

"Will you look at that," Peter asked the driver. "If it isn't the lambs being led to slaughter?"

From just inside the forest, a wide array of blinking blue pixels peered across the open field, zooming in on the brigade of unsuspecting Dociles marching along the cavern path.

# Chapter Sixteen

Inside the cavern chamber, a disheveled Alegría fluffed her hair, wiped mud off her arms, and patted dirt from her dress. "No amount of dry cleaning is going to fix this," she said, following the quick self-inspection.

"You always were so modest," said a grimacing Carmen.

"And you always were so stupidly irritating," Alegría shot back. "Why couldn't you accept things? You had the power to take your boy. You could have come to America with us. We could have raised our families side by side."

Carmen lifted her head at Alegría, standing over her. "Since I was different, I felt my son stood a chance to be different as well," she said, short of breath. "After seeing him, I know I was right. He's not the same as the others. You said so yourself."

"You're right," replied Alegría, crouching down. "He's not the same. And because of that, he'll be much easier to kill." She hoisted Carmen up and strode over to the largest stalagmite in the vicinity, jutting up a good three feet.

"But why?" cried Carmen.

"I told you. He killed my baby." Speaking the words filled Alegría with anger.

As she reared back with a shriek to impale Carmen on the stalagmite, what started as a low humming rumble from a dark antechamber erupted into a peal of high-pitched squeaking from an invasion of bats flying riotously through the terrestrial cave.

With bats zipping all around her, the flustered Alegría dropped Carmen. She fell face-up and chest-high on the huge sharp-pointed stalagmite, her painful last scream drowned out in the din.

Seconds after all the bats evacuated the cave through the excavated hole above, Joshua descended into the cave starkly alone with the soulless woman.

Alegría fixed her mussed hair. "Damn flying rats." She callously assessed Joshua staring at his skewered mother, her arms and legs dangling at her side above the ground.

"I must admit, my eyes were actually closed when I dropped her." She lightly touched the tip of the blood-streaked stalagmite penetrating through Carmen's trunk, careful not to step in the parabola of blood seeping from the column's sloping base. "There's room for two here. Although with you, I think perhaps more of a *sitting* position will do."

Joshua picked up a piece of one of the jagged-pointed stalactites that had fallen to the ground, following the roof implosion. He held it up like a stake.

Alegría tugged impatiently on her dress. "What is your hang-up, kid?"

She lunged at him, but Joshua, flashing eyes of cobalt blue, anticipated and avoided her, gaining more space between them. Alegría's expression changed for the worse. She bounded backward toward the darkened antechamber from where the bats flew out, landing on the rocky wall above it like a human spider—but could not hold the positioning. "I'm in no mood to chase through any underground tunnels," she said but then slipped, dropping ungracefully to the ground. "It's been a tiring evening," she offered with a heavy exhale.

Seeing Joshua scanning the opening above, Alegría peeked upward. Standing in front of the antechamber, she confidently surmised she could intercept him if he tried to exit the way he came in and thus had both avenues of possible escape presently cut off.

Taking another course of action, off to one side, a crouched Joshua slithered in between a range of stalagmite formations. His foot hooked on one, tumbling him into an open space between the geological configurations. Alegría launched. Joshua jumped back in between the tightly packed rows of stalagmites.

With a yell, the fast-dropping Alegría veered off at the last instant—preventing her impalement. He had done that on purpose, Alegría realized. Angered, she leaped high and smashed into the section of cave above Joshua, reigning down millennia-old chunks of rocky sedimentary. Had Joshua not sought cover within the stalagmite pickets whose points broke or blunted the larger falling pieces, he would have been crushed. Yet, enough displaced rock had pinned him in his place. He struggled to entangle his feet as Alegría landed in front of him. "Stay in that squatting position. It's just how I want you."

Alegría then heard someone jump into the cavern and shout her name. She recognized the voice. Concern seeped into her face as she turned and confronted Milagros and dried traces of blood present on her neck and clothes. The concern expanded into full-fledged anxiety when she spotted the black strip of cloth dangling in one hand. Milagros flung the cloth scornfully to one side.

Alegría did not take her eyes off it as she stepped, first slowly and then quickly toward it. She bent over and picked up Raúl's tattered eye patch. She raised the bloodied eye patch to her suddenly blanched face and wept.

* * *

Peter backtracked along the edge of the forest before he traversed the open field, the Docile scent infiltrating his brain like the aroma of a deliciously cooked meal being met by a hungry traveler. Invigorated by the high, brilliant moon above him and a clear, focused vision never known before, he barely felt his feet touching the ground in their energetic paces.

Peter targeted well beyond the end of the snaking line of Dociles in order to make it appear as if he was joining them on the path they were traveling. He casually linked with the end of the diminishing procession.

"No blanket?" asked one of the last in line.

"Uh, no," responded Peter with hands in his pockets.

"I've got an extra towel," said another. "Ah, borrowed from our cabin's bathroom. In case you don't feel like totally roughing it."

"Cool," replied Peter with an artificial smile, flipping the offered towel over his shoulder. "Thanks."

The remaining line moved quickly. The sight of Laz at the entrance to the cavern did not deter Peter. Holding a flashlight, the shepard's son directed everyone to keep an orderly flow through the heavy door he held open.

A girl in a red bandana, holding a hand to her neck, scooted past Peter and others, waving her arms in distress, *"Let me in! Let me in!"* She then uttered to Laz with some relief, "Whew! That girl—the one in charge—knocked me out but I came to and hightailed it here. There's a Hostile—and two mother vampires! They could be anywhere!"

Meg's declarations sent the remaining Dociles into a panicked push forward.

As Peter tried sneaking in with them, a halting light shone in his face.

*"You,"* said Laz, shining his flashlight at Peter. "You're here. You're supposed to be dead."

"Do I look dead?"

Laz impeded Peter's progress toward the entrance of the cavern. "Almost didn't recognize you without your glasses. How about your girlfriend?"

Peter stiffened. "Oh, *she's* dead." He yanked the towel from his shoulder and stuffed it into Laz's face, knocking him back into the door, slamming it shut.

Peter turned around, and his eyes bristled their cobalt color back over the open field, signaling the advance of the blue-eyed terror from the forest. Surging out from the trees, the Hostile horde charged across the moon-bathed field with emblazoned eyes and sharp, glinting teeth.

Seeing the approaching enemy, a terrified Laz tried to lock the door but Peter prevented it, knocking the keychain, flashlight, and Laz to the ground—which shook from the progressing stampede.

The Hostiles descended upon the cavern in a rabid frenzy, the first wave pushing aside a helpless Laz after being sniffed up and down and determined to be useless. Among the first arriving, the RV driver cranked open the metal entry. He entered the sanctuary with pigmented blue eyes blazing.

"*It's chow time!*" declared the abhorrent teenager.

One of the Dociles close by identified him and screamed, followed by another, igniting widespread hysteria inside.

*** 

The faces of the transcendental beings displayed a troubling displeasure in their metaphysical form above the escalating campground scene.

"Things are not proceeding according to plan…" said Umber.

"The rogue daughter of darkness has wrought…" continued Equin.

"Some unforeseen complications with her vengeful interference," concluded Libor, witnessing the mass of Hostiles breeching the Dociles' refuge site.

"Extraordinary measures must now be considered…"

"To counter the interference or risk…"

"An imbalance to the supernatural order."

Umber turned to Libor. "At this point, there is no…"

"Alternative to preventing the evil forces…"

"From obtaining an underserved, lasting advantage," concluded a nodding Libor.

"We are agreed…"

"You must summon…"

"Forth the *gargoyles!*" Libor raised a sweeping hand, causing an expanding ripple to form apart from their particular atmospheric bubble. A fissure in space developed from which sprang through in shrieking bursts a train of the leaden-colored winged creatures. Many dozens of the flying beasts spreading out into the natural atmosphere swooped high over and around the Equilibrium prior to executing a precision dive-bombing sortie to the cavern below.

The lead gargoyle slammed through the topsoil above the cave's entrance, paving the way for his companions to storm inside the cavern, ringing loudly with sounds of mayhem and terror. Winding through the cavern's antechambers, the gargoyles targeted the aggressive Hostiles as they hunted after the frightened Dociles. Time and again, cornered or knocked-to-the-ground Dociles were saved by the swooping, misshapen saviors.

Not as fortunate was a Docile female, being brutalized by the RV driver, who had captured her.

With the omnipresent Equilibrium observing, Equin empathized with the dying girl. "This was not her destiny…"

"But there were bound to…"

"Be casualties. We understood that." Libor closed his eyes, telepathically commanding a nearby gargoyle to extend his wing and speedily fly past a truss of hanging stalactites. The broken-off ancient limestone deposits fell like fast-dropping spears, several ripping through the back of the feasting RV driver, ending what turned into his last meal.

Eventually, all the seized Hostiles were rounded up and individually carried away thrashing and kicking with disapproval. Realizing the gargoyles had saved the day, the rescued and relieved Dociles clapped and cheered. The winged rescuers soared out of the cavern in a high, arching formation, an assembly line of their transporting silhouettes crossing in front of the cobalt moon high against the night sky.

Most of them carrying two Hostiles at a time in their clawed feet, the flapping creatures flew over the forest of tall trees, finding the area rich with cypress knees. The Hostile overheard by the Equilibrium who had likened the scent of Dociles in the air to a flower, upon her arrival, became one of the first to be deposited on the cone-shaped exterior root, nearly splitting her in two. Falling out of the sky, the Hostiles emitted short-term screams. Some landed face-up, others down, all with impaling force onto the varied collections of cypress knees, their incendiary cobalt-blue eyes shivering away forever.

Circling back in formation, the gargoyles then scooped up the corpses some two or three deep on the cone-shaped outgrowths. They fanned out far over the Chipola River and released the bodies one by one, letting them fall to their murky end.

\*\*\*

Joshua freed himself from his rocky trap. With Alegría stationary under the opening above, the darkened antechamber beckoned his and Milagros' next course of action. Before he entered, he offered fleeting final looks at his dead mother and Alegría. Carmen's gruesome end chilled him to the bone. Alegría, on the other hand, with her back to him and slowly sinking to her knees in expressed grief, extracted no pity from Joshua.

The length of the dark, stony passageway varied in height and width, compressing enough in size at one division to force them to tunnel through until they spilled out to a bigger artificially lit tunnel-like cave. Encountering a nest of cave salamanders in their crawling, the pair quickly helped pick and brush off the soft pencil-like subterranean creatures from each other's places of bodily entwinement once upright. Nearly finished, they heard the echoes of tumultuous pandemonium reverberating through a connecting passage.

"It's the main cave," said Milagros. She started forward and stopped, realizing Joshua was not at her side.

"I'm not running anymore," said Joshua, his feet cemented in place, "with *you.*" The indicting inflection in his voice matched the accusatory scowl on his face.

Milagros' suddenly glistening eyes searched his. "You've come too far. *We've* come too far, not to keep going now."

"Going where?" asked Joshua. "We've both seen our mothers brutally killed." Joshua raised the heel of his palm to his temple. "This is crazy. Look what you've done to yourself. For what? Why won't you see it? I don't know what I am, but I'm not like the rest."

Milagros hastily wiped away a renegade tear from her cheek. "If you want to make a stand, I'll make it with you. But not here. Come with me a little farther. We'll have a better chance."

Delving deeper into Milagros' pleading eyes, a more-composed Joshua accepted the girl's petition for continued trust.

The sounds of panic ahead seemed to be lessening even as Milagros urged, "Keep following the screams!" Scanning all around her as she ran, Milagros slowed and motioned with shared recognition to Joshua, the previously encountered side chamber rendered off-limits by signs, cut lumber, and chains.

She tore down the two DANGER signs outside the vaulted catacomb, handing the first one to Joshua. "We're going to lead Alegría in here," said Milagros, climbing over the chains and twisting through the wooden deterrence. "A vampire's sensory perception is reduced tonight."

Joshua's cobalt-blue eyes illuminated some of the dark interior. Several yards of stony soil separated the entrance from an underground precipice. Across the expanse, a barren wall of sheer rock enclosed everything. Cautiously, Joshua flipped the aluminum sign into the deep hollowed-out earth. After a few seconds of silence, the falling sign clanking once off the side of the rocky wall plopped to a liquid-sounding end, immediately followed by a dissolving hissing sound. Then Joshua noticed Milagros' eyes—blackened pupils surrounded by a burned gold color. "How about *your* senses?"

"I'm a newbie. All my senses are heightened. That's why we might balance the scales against Alegría in here."

Stepping back outside, Joshua said, "I'll do it. She'll chase me in for sure."

"She'll chase either one of us in, now that she knows we…"

Joshua heard the low fluttering sounds building quickly until they turned into a screeching wave steamrolling through the cave. Emerging from the winding passageway they had followed, a squadron of hurrying bats flew past them, making an undulating turn into a smaller secondary chamber. Straightening after their passing, Joshua had only a split-second to read the peril in Milagros' face before the stunning impact of a deranged Alegría—bursting through the same winding passageway— knocked both of them backward, shattering the wood planks and ripping the chains from their nailed tethers.

Joshua fought to stay conscious amid the darkness of the catacomb and the physical trauma numbing his motor nerves. He felt himself picked up and carried outside, his feet dragging over splintered wood and chains. He realized Alegría hauled him and

Milagros by the nape of their necks like intended sporting mantle trophies.

Alegría's face foamed with rage. "I'm going to chop you into little pieces below the waist and force-feed you to each other!"

To everyone's surprise, Meg came running through the opposite chamber. She froze at the wrathful sight of Alegría and her bagged prey. No sooner did she scream than a teenage boy barged in and tackled her to the ground. The boy went for Meg's neck. Joshua swapped a look with Milagros, bleeding from the scalp. Alegría rammed both of their faces into the ground. "Stop squirming!" she commanded.

From the corner of a bruised eye, the next thing distinguished by Joshua was the pumping bluish-gray wing appearing so graceful in its perceived slow-motion flapping. His focus, though, could not escape the misshapen body attached to the wing, the smallish head, bird-like eyes, and longish legs of the flying creature. A visible bruise stood out disagreeably around its neck. Then Joshua's senses reset, returning to real-time awareness, and the wing flap hurriedly increased. With a baritone yelp, the winged beast's clawed feet hooked onto the boy assaulting Meg and flung him up into a row of stalactites. Impaled in several places over his body, gravity pulled the dead Hostile back to the ground.

As the flying creature circled the cave, passing level with Alegría, one of its dark gray eyes gleamed with recognition. On its way to completing another pass, it dove straight for her. Dropping Joshua and Milagros, Alegría yelled with anticipated savagery and jumped at the gargoyle. The underworld monstrosities fought with one another in a midair dance to the death. Exerting all the apparent force she could summon, a maniacal Alegría clamped onto one of its wings at the shoulder until it cracked loudly and cleanly. The gargoyle howled with pain and fell straight to the ground with Alegría.

Extricating herself from the tangle, Alegría tore the broken wing from the gargoyle's exoskeleton, leaving it convulsing in agony, sweeping up ancient dirt from the cave floor with its remaining now-deficient wing. Alegría stomped hard on its stomach, rendering it motionless. Her wrath tempered by the disabling act, she turned toward Joshua and Milagros, asking with a smirk, "Now, what was I *slaying*? Ah, yes, little pieces."

All the furor had dislodged the second DANGER sign Milagros had previously tried to hide by sticking it into a stony crevice. It lay face-up on the ground. As Joshua helped Milagros to her feet, Alegría's foot stepped on the sign, crunching it into the dirt.

"Take the chains," said Milagros.

Joshua scooped up the heavy iron links, handing one to her, and ducked inside the catacomb, the sensation of Alegría's hot breath on the back of his neck.

\*\*\*

One of the last to enter the cave, Peter managed to flee when he witnessed the table-turning invasion of the gargoyles. He raced back down the path, cutting through a hiking trail and headed back toward the parking lot. He did not evade the detection of the Equilibrium, however.

Umber was the first to refer to the new related circumstance. "The *others* are here…"

"The counterbalance must be…"

"Complete. So be it," finished Libor, closing his eyes and deviating a gargoyle in flight to give chase after Peter.

Reaching the parking lot, a frantic Peter saw and flagged down the expected second RV rolling through the entrance gate. He ran up to the motorized vehicle, banging on its side to be let in. Once inside, he screamed in a state of panic, "Get out of here now!"

The hesitant driver did not have a chance to question anything because the pursuing gargoyle crashed through the windshield and snatched and flung him from his seat, sending out petrified shrieks from the inhabitants of the long vehicle. Peter jumped into the driver's chair and turned the trailer around. Screeching back onto the main road outside the park, he floored the gas pedal. The gargoyle made several close passes, with Peter frantically trying to keep the steering wheel straight. The gargoyle landed with a thud on the cab above him, bending over to peek inside with squinting eyes and a yowling black-tongued mouth. Its jolting appearance compounded by the terror-stricken screams of the passengers caused Peter to lose control.

The RV zigzagged sharply over the yellow line dividing the roadway and overturned violently into the opposite embankment. Not two seconds later, a fiery explosion consumed the vehicle and all of its occupants.

The gargoyle retrieved the tossed-out RV driver's body from the road and dropped the still-alive boy into the flaming vehicle. It then winged back to the park. As the Equilibrium dematerialized, it followed its disappearing brethren through the atmospheric rupture in the sky.

*** 

Alegría's gold eyes glowed dully inside the catacomb, the outside cavelight at her back providing sparse visibility. Breathing heavily with sagging shoulders, she tentatively surveyed the distance between herself and the located precipice. From out of the blackness, a cobalt-blue-eyed Joshua swung with the first chain, coiling it tightly around her neck. From the other side, a golden-eyed Milagros whipped her iron manacle at Alegría's feet, wrapping it around one of her tormentor's ankles, causing her to fall.

Joshua and Milagros hurriedly dragged Alegría toward the precipice. About two feet from the edge, Alegría kicked free of the chain around her ankle, Milagros sliding off to the side. She yanked at the chain wound around her neck, pulling Joshua's face within frightful inches of hers. Choked by her putrid breath, Joshua leaned back from the bestial, spittle-dripping fanged face. Alegría savagely smacked him away with the back of her fist, sending him into a tumbling roll.

As if she had eyes in the back of her head, Alegría ducked as Milagros swung the loosed chain at her head. Straightening, Alegría grabbed an off-balance Milagros by the throat and lifted her in the air. She hesitated at the close-up sight of the gold tint in Milagros' eyes. Quivering, she said, "I'm going to rip your head off!"

Milagros' strength quickly faded in Alegría's deadly grip. She released the chain; her arms capitulated at her sides like straight, falling rods. Then a baritone yelp filled the antechamber, and a woozy Joshua felt a rush of wind brush his side.

The injured gargoyle attacked, forcing Alegría to drop Milagros, the girl gasping for life-giving air. Skidding backward toward the cliff with the flapping single-winged liberator, Alegría took control of the situation with vicious body blows that folded the disadvantaged gargoyle into itself. Preparing to throw it over the precipice, one of the creature's lower extremities reached up and hooked the end of the weighty chain around Alegría's neck and jerked her down and over the cliff with it.

Hearing nothing, while shaking off the cobwebs, Joshua crawled over to the edge. When he peeked over the side, a long finger-nailed hand appeared and clamped onto the tapered edge of the rim, startling him. A choking Alegría held on with one hand, with the hooked gargoyle dangling upside down at her feet, trying to dislodge her with all of its remaining strength.

Immediately, Joshua initiated a furious pounding of Alegría's hand with his fists, but the devil incarnate's fingers remained affixed. "Too weak to float up, aren't you?" he yelled during his barrage. He alarmingly noticed Alegría's bejeweled fingers were bloodying his pummeling fists.

Then a semi-revived Milagros joined the frantic effort to end the princess of evil's existence once and for all. The heel of her shoe kicked at the hardened earth around Alegría's hand while Joshua continued his incessant pounding. The strategy wrought some success as the unbending hand began to slide back in the loosened ground. But just as it did, a suffocating Alegría finished unwinding the steel bonds from around her neck, sending the gargoyle plummeting to a howling, incinerated death below. She then quickly clamped her other hand on the rim and reached up and snagged Milagros' foot.

In the instant that followed, Joshua's panic-filled eyes met Milagros', finding the signaled finality in their defeated state. In her vulnerable position, she communicated the vice-like grip Alegría had attained spelled doom. Rather than be cast over the side, Milagros jumped.

She landed around Alegría's shoulders, wrestling mightily to loosen the demon woman's tenuous grip.

"If I fall, she falls with me, Joshua!" an anxious Alegría called out.

A paralyzed Joshua watched in horror. Now slipping to Alegría's waist, Milagros tried to pull the odious creature down, shaking herself from side to side, her gold-toned eyes opening and shutting tightly. "Milá! Please! Can't you levitate up?!"

"She'll grab me if I try and float up with me!" answered Milagros.

Alegría became more desperate, her two-handed grip weakening. "Pull me up, Joshua, and she comes up with me!"

After initially hesitating, Joshua grabbed Alegría's cold wrist and pulled.

"No, Joshua!" cried Milagros. "No!"

Stoically, Joshua helped Alegría to bring her elbows over the ledge. As Joshua bent over the side to extend a hand to Milagros, the godless female kicked back with her feet like a mule, striking the fastened girl's midsection and sending her falling into the blackened pit. Horrified, Joshua watched until Milagros disappeared into the black vacuum and then rolled over on his back, cringing at the sound of the brave girl's painfully disintegrating body.

"What kind of Hostile half-vampire are you?" Alegría contemptuously asked, kneeling over him. "You're not supposed to have a heart." She wound back a clawed hand. "So allow me to relieve you of yours."

Joshua never took his passive eyes from hers, almost lulling her into lowering her guard. With the blinding quickness of a gunslinger from a classic western, Joshua drew from his back pocket the broken-off stalactite from earlier and pierced Alegría's chest with it. "As you were *slaying*," mocked Joshua, releasing his bloody grip from the granite stake.

Before the fiendish femme fatale could complete her shocked scream, Joshua kicked her with both feet over the edge and, with closed eyes, listened satisfyingly to her agonizing demise.

# Epilogue

Joshua stayed awake the whole trip home, in the backseat of Mrs. Landis' car. When Milagros did not monopolize his thoughts, he recalled coming out of the deadly catacomb and finding a hiding Meg, frightened and superficially bleeding from the neck.

"Get away from me!" she initially cried.

Wiping his own bloodied hands, he slowly convinced her that he did not pose a threat and eventually coaxed her into letting him convert her bandana into a scarf to conceal the multiple cuts on her neck. He then persuaded her to retrace her steps back to the others.

Thereafter, Joshua dumped the dead Hostile into the molten pit and hurried back for his mother. Fighting back tears, he freed her from her death spike and carried and dragged, when necessary, her body back to the catacomb. Letting her fall into the death pit was an act, he equated, as an alternative method of cremation.

He wound his way back to the main cave populated with Dociles, many still worried-looking or shaken. He spotted two familiar faces—Teddy and Tommy. Among the first Dociles he had met, they traded subtle, silent acknowledgments indicating a mutual gladness over having survived unscathed. Around other milling Dociles, he saw Meg being treated for her neck lesions. She fluttered, with diminished mistrust, the red bandana in her hand at him as he walked past.

The gladdest face encountered, Laz soon turned somber when he noticed Joshua's missing sidekick. Exchanging unvoiced confirmation of the worst, Joshua sighed heavily. Then he said, "Alegría's dead."

"The mother…and the son?" inquired Laz.

Joshua bobbed his head with conviction.

"Your mother?" Laz waited a few beats as Joshua averted his eyes. "I'm sorry," he offered, walking together now. "The gargoyles saved us. That means we're safe for rest of the night, *doesn't it*?"

With a half-smile creeping over his lips, Joshua put Laz's mind at ease. "Yes. I'm not staying."

"Listen," counseled Laz. "Let the police investigate the camp director's death all they want. But get rid of any other bodies. In the end, all they can do is bill us for the damage."

With drooping chin, Joshua plodded out of the cavern feeling much the way he did now in the car, staring down at his lap at the fibrinogen pouch he had retrieved from the cabin, its looped extension string wound to his wrist. Then Jerry's head rolled onto his shoulder, forcing him to straighten the sleeping boy's leaning shoulders without waking him. He had bumped into Jerry, his clothes wet, on the cavern trail back to the cabin.

"If you're a vamp," said Jerry with his hands defensively in front of him, "tell me you've already eaten."

"Your guess is as good as mine," answered Joshua.

Jerry quickly fell lockstep in with Joshua back to his intended destination where they disposed of Rosa, Margot, and the neck-shredded Raúl, using a golf cart to transport them to a watering hole Jerry suggested. They left Roger covered beneath a bed sheet.

Afterward, with the key Milagros had left tossed on the floor, Joshua unlocked the door of the cabin's bathroom and freed the counselors, Dawn, and her mother.

"What happened to the other…bodies?" asked Ferguson after his release.

"What other bodies?" replied both Joshua and Jerry separately.

Horace and Otis made an appearance inside the wrecked cabin at that indecisive interim. "Man, oh man," said Otis, surveying the damage and holding a bottle of Mountain Dew. "It sure sounded like y'all were raising Cain."

Nodding to himself, Horace pulled out his tin of chewing tobacco, briefly scanning the sheet-covered body on the floor. Sticking a pinch into his lower lip, he asked in a flat, almost disinterested manner, "So what time are we leaving in the morning?"

During the silent pause that followed, Mrs. Landis inhaled deeply and locked arms with Dawn. Heading for the torn-away front of the cabin, she called, "Jerry," petitioning the teenager to join her.

"Mrs. Landis," said Jerry. "Can you… Do you mind if…?"

The woman understood Jerry's unstated request. Looking at Joshua, she offered no objection.

In the parking lot, with sunrise a couple of hours away, as the four prepared to climb into Mrs. Landis' car for the long ride home, Joshua paused to glance up at the moon, bright and hauntingly beautiful in the clear night sky.

In the front seat of the car, Dawn did not speak to him during the entire trip. The trip was made completely in silence. Not even when they arrived at Joshua's house did his former dream girl offer a good-bye or thank you.

"Keep fighting the good fight," said a wide-awake Jerry, sliding his palm over Joshua's, whose ripped flesh in both hands had healed from the previous pummeling in the cave.

Joshua thanked Dawn's mother and exited the vehicle which did not linger.

Outside the garage door, there conspicuously leaned Joshua's old bicycle with a note pinned to it and a small tote bag hanging from the handlebars. The bag contained Joshua's baseball glove and valued-team signed ball.

The note read in Thomas's handwriting: *Joshua, you can stay with the bike at St. Mary's. Your things will be packed by tomorrow for you to pick up.*

Joshua crumpled the note and threw it to the ground. He knew Thomas and Katherine were sleeping in like every Sunday morning.

Dejectedly, Joshua rolled his old bike to the sidewalk. He contemplated riding the outgrown bicycle but stingingly remembered the state of its deflated tire. He forlornly pushed the bike down the street and through several others. His head spun from exhaustion and his heart ached from a grievous sense of loss over not bonding more with his thought-to-be long-lost mother…and over Milagros…their heartwarming faces flickering over and over in his mind. Without thinking, he tapped the stickpin on his chest that had held firm throughout the night, pinned to his shirt.

Joshua did not know how long he had been walking when he heard a moving car honking its horn to gain his attention. He stopped, curiously observing the tall man stepping out from the halted vehicle's driver's seat. He heard the passenger door open and close but could not take his eyes away from the man, this man with blue eyes and steel-gray temples, this…splendid-looking man.

"Rodolfo," he called. "Rodolfo…Joshua Puig." Joshua remained riveted as the man came around the car. "I've had a hard time trying to find you. Finally tracked you to St. Mary's parish. They gave me your address. I just came from your house… I must have just missed you."

Joshua noticed the wrinkled paper the man held, Thomas' note. Joshua's mind flashed back with successively rapid snapshots of his younger self...of a plane...a charitable stewardess...and a dashing pilot.

"My name's Hickey," said the man. "I've relocated to Miami with my daughters, Sandra and Debbie."

Standing next to the car, teenage girls around his age, one blond, the other brunette, demurely smiled at Joshua.

"Can I give you a lift?" asked the pilot.

Grinning at the fetching sisters, Joshua squeezed the fibrinogen pouch in one hand, bringing the other over his mouth to hide what embarrassingly felt like sprouting canine teeth.

# Glossary
# Foreign Pronunciations and
# Translations

*Abuelas* [AH-BWEH-LAHS]: Grandmothers, plural

*Babalawo* [BAH-BAH-LAHW-O]: A chieftain of the Yorubá religion

Banes Bay [BAH-NEZ]

*Buenas noches* [BWEH-NAHZ * NO-CHEZ]: Good evening

*Café con leche* [KAH-FEH * COHN * LEH-CHE]: Coffee with heated milk

*Calle* [KAH-YEH]: Street, as in Aguilera Street

*Carnaval* [KARNA-BAL] carnival, as in festive, public revelry, incorporating music, dancing, and processions

*Décolletage* [DEH-KOLH-LEH-TAZH]: (French) Low-cut top of a woman's dress

*Derrière* [DAIR-REE-AIR]: (French) Rear-end, buttocks

*Desaparecidos* [DES-AH-PAH-REH-SEE-DOS]: Disappeared ones

*El joyero* [EL * HOI-YEH-ROH]: The jeweler

*Hermana* [ERH-MAH-NAH]: Sister

*Mariposa* [MAR-EE-POE-SAH]: Butterfly

*El Náutico* [EL * NOW-TEE-COH]: Restaurant in Antilla. Literally, 'the Nautical'

*El parque* [EL* PAR-KEH]: The park

*El Partido* [EL* PAR-TEE-DOH]: The party, a reference to the Communist party

*Guayabera* [GWHY-YAH-BER-AH]: Lightweight, short-sleeved shirt with multiple pockets worn untucked

*Júcaro* [HOO-KAH-ROH]: Name of indigenous wildlife forest

*Leche condensada* [LEH-CHE * COHN-DEN-SAH-DAH]: Condensed milk

*la playita* [LAH * PLAH-YEE-TAH]: The little beach

*Mijo* [MEE-HO]: Affectionate slang. My Son. Conjoined derivative of *mi* (my) and *hijo* (son)

*Mio* [MEE-OH]: Mine

Nicaro [NEE-KAH-ROH]: Cuban town

Nipe Bay [NEE-PEH]

*Nochebuena* [NO-CHE-BWEH-NAH]: Christmas Eve, literal translation: the good night

*Nos vamos?* [NOS * VAH-MOS]: Shall we go?

*Primo* [PREE-MOH]: Cousin

*Que encanto!* [KEH * EN-KAN-TOH]: How charming!

*Qué tal?* [KEH * TAHL]: How are you? Informal Spanish greeting

*Siesta* [SEE-ES-TAH]: Nap

Tacajó [TAH-KAH-HO]: Cuban town

*Tía* [TEE-AH]: Aunt

*Tío* [TEE-OH]: Uncle

# Expressions/Phrases/ Sentences

*Adónde vas, preciosa? [AH-DOAN-DEH * VAHS* PREH-SEE-OH-SAH]:* Where are you going, beautiful?

*Al fresco* [ALH * FRES-CO]: (Italian) In the open air

*Anda* [AHN-DAH]: Interjection. Run or come along

*Cojones* [KO-HO-NEZ]: Vulgar slang. Male testicles. Reference to having courage or 'balls'

*Está en la moda.* [ES-TAH * EN * LA * MO-DAH]: Fashion-conscious. Literal: He's in fashion.

*Fue amor a primera vista.* [FWEH * AH-MORE * AH * PREE-MEH-RAH * VEE-STAH]: It was love at first sight.

*Hoy y Mañana Se Presenta Dámaso Pérez Prado y Su Orquesta.* *[OY * EE * MAHN-YA-NAH * SEH * PREH-SEN-TAH * DAH-MAH-SO * PER-EZ * PRAH-DOH * EE * SUE * ORE-KEH-STAH]:* Appearing today and tomorrow Dámaso Pérez Prado and his Orquestra.

*Que elegante! [KEH * EH * LEH * GAN * TEH]:* How elegant!

*Raúl está aquí.* [RAH-OOL * ES-TAH * AH-KEE]: Raúl is here.

*Suéltame, demonio!* [SWELL-TAH-MEH * DEH-MOE-NEE-OH]: Let go of me, demon!

*Señora, lo siento mucho.* [SEN-YORE-AH * LOW * SEE-EN-TOW * MOO-CHO]: I am very sorry, madam.

*Yo soy la abuela de Raúl.* [YO * SOY * LA* AH-BWEH-LAH * DEH * RAH-OOL]: I am Raúl's grandmother.

*Vale* [VAH-LEH]: Colloquial, from Spain, meaning 'okay'

*Ven conmigo.* [VEN * KOHN-MEE-GO]: Come with me.

*Venga* [VEN-GAH]: Spanish interjection. Come on